BATTLETECH:

BLOOD WILL TELL

BY JASON SCHMETZER

BATTLETECH: BLOOD WILL TELL
By Jason Schmetzer
Cover art by Tan Ho Sim
Cover design by David Kerber

Printed in USA.

Published by Catalyst Game Labs,
an imprint of InMediaRes Productions, LLC
7108 S. Pheasant Ridge Drive • Spokane, WA 99224

I was never a soldier.

I try to do them justice, however I can.

While we remember, they endure.

Sergeant Harry James Austin, Seventh Battalion, Royal Sussex Regiment, KIA 9 April 1917, and Stoker First Class William Robert Austin, HMS Glasgow, KIA 22 March 1941.

Lest we forget.

CHAPTER 1

SASO
NEW SYRTIS
FEDERATED SUNS
30 AUGUST 3148

The snow began while Danai Liao-Centrella was inside the building. She stepped out onto the sidewalk and shrugged her shoulders, pulling the high collar of her overcoat even higher. The movement made pain shoot through her broken arm where the sling rubbed. She ground her teeth together, but made no other outward sign of discomfort.

"*Sang-shao...*"

Danai turned toward the speaker. The man was tall and pale, with close-cropped white hair and bags under his eyes. He wore the duty battledress of a MechWarrior of the Second McCarron's Armored Cavalry regiment. *Sang-wei*—the rank other realms called a captain—Noah Capshaw had served in her command lance for the last year and a half. He was a solid MechWarrior and a good strategist, but he was young, and sometimes didn't seem to realize he was a *janshi*—a warrior—of the Capellan Confederation.

Teaching him that he *was janshi* every moment was one of the duties she took seriously. Which was why he was in her command lance and not running a recon lance in the boondocks of Third Battalion.

"Pass the word to *Zhong-shao* Wu," she told him. "I want the regiment off this planet in twenty-four hours. Less, if he can manage it."

Capshaw frowned. "Of course, *Sang-shao*," he said, but didn't move.

Danai sighed. "What, Noah?"

"It's nothing, *Sang-shao*."

"Noah." The cool New Syrtis air slid down her collar, giving her a chill between her shoulder blades. It shook her whole body, which made her arm twinge in pain again. "Spit it out."

Capshaw's face worked for a few seconds, then he glanced down. "I wanted to ask how it went in there," he said. He looked up, met her eyes, and grinned shyly. "You met Julian Davion again, right?"

Danai controlled the eye roll she felt coming on. "I did," she told him. "He looked terrible."

"Terrible?"

"In a wheelchair," Danai replied. She looked down the street, where a platoon of Davion infantry was screening her APC through a checkpoint. Access to the building was tightly controlled; in addition to herself, most of the senior leadership of the Federated Suns military on New Syrtis was inside, including—as Capshaw had pointed out—First Prince Julian Davion.

The star nations of the Federated Suns and the Capellan Confederation had been enemies for centuries, going all the way back to before even the great Star League unified the Inner Sphere Great Houses into one homogenous realm. The destruction of that Star League had precipitated the centuries of warfare known as the Succession Wars, long decades of battle where Capellan and Suns soldiers and citizens alike learned to hate each other.

That hatred was in their blood. For many, it was all they knew.

As the APC lifted on its plenum chamber, its fans drove loose snow, dust, and street debris down the boulevard toward them. From long habit, both Capshaw and Danai turned their back and slitted their eyes until the gust of artificial wind passed, only then turning back. Danai used her good hand to pull her cap off and shield her face. The noise made it too loud to speak, which she was grateful for.

She didn't want to talk to Capshaw about Julian Davion, or anything else.

It all felt so useless.

This was not the first time she had negotiated a cease-fire with Julian Davion. Two years earlier, on Marlette, she had agreed with the Davion First Prince that the two realms would fight no more, only for Julian to abrogate the agreement and attack a swath of worlds on the way to this one, New Syrtis.

If she was honest with herself, Danai understood. New Syrtis was sacred to House Davion; for centuries it had been the capital of the Capellan March, the region of the Federated Suns that faced the Capellan Confederation. Thousands of attacks against Capellan people and property had been launched from this world. And just as many Capellan attacks had been launched toward this world.

Sniffing in the cold air, feeling her nostrils threaten to freeze shut, Danai wondered why.

She hated New Syrtis.

Inside the APC, she settled along one of the port side infantry benches and leaned back against the webbing. Her arm was throbbing, and now that there was no chance of an outsider seeing it, she let her facade slip and groaned.

Capshaw stepped inside the bay just as the hatch whined up to seal against the rear of the APC. A combat vehicle-helmeted head leaned back and raised a hand. Danai looked at the tanker and made a rally signal with her finger that meant "back to base." The tanker nodded and slid back into the driver's compartment. A moment later, the pitch of the vibrations running through the APC's frame changed as the driver lifted them off the ground. Loose bits of rock and metal danced across the floor, but the seat padding dampened most of it.

Capshaw sat down next to her, put on a headset, and handed her its twin. Danai looked at his outstretched hand for just a second longer than necessary, then put it on.

"Davion accepted your offer, then, *Sang-shao*?" Capshaw's voice was flatter across the intercom, but it really was too loud in the APC bay to talk without it.

"Yes," she told him. "Though he was the one who actually made it."

Capshaw snorted. "Of course he did, ma'am. He made it because we've pounded his regiments into the snowbank, and knew if he didn't sue for peace, he'd be taking your terms from the inside of a prison cell."

Danai closed her eyes. She wanted so badly to lean her head back against the hull, but she knew that would feel like putting her brains in a blender. In a limo she could have stared out the window, but she hadn't chosen a limo, despite what people expected.

A limo would have been appropriate. She was the third-ranking Liao in the entire Confederation. She could have come in the finest car on New Syrtis, with shining BattleMechs for escorts and Fa Shih battlesuits for bodyguards, and no one would have blinked an eye. In fact, that was what most of the people in whose orbit she was moving would have expected.

Instead, she had come in battledress, in a common infantry hover APC, and alone except for *Sang-wei* Capshaw.

Well, not quite alone. Some of the rest of her staff had come, a couple of the other regimental commanders, and of course two Death Commando "bodyguards," but she'd ordered them to wait in the lobby until she was away.

She wanted the APC. She wanted the clear, unmodified statement that she was coming and going as a soldier. She wanted Julian Davion and all of his officers and nobles to know that *she*, a common soldier and *not* the third-ranking Liao, had forced them to sue for peace.

Never mind that the peace would be better for the Confederation than Davion's realm.

"Ma'am, are you all right?"

Danai opened her eyes. Capshaw was leaning toward her, earnest young face twisted in concern. She smiled faintly and nodded. "Davion gave me everything I wanted," she told Capshaw. *Except for his death*, she didn't say.

It had been a near thing, two weeks earlier at Cilitren, where she'd come so close to killing the Davion ruler. She had caught the First Prince on the battlefield in his BattleMech, and had crushed him in an ambush of artillery and aerospace fighters. Davion's *Templar III* had been on the ground, broken and lame, beneath her hatchet.

Danai clenched the fist of her broken arm, this time savoring the pain.

Until that damned *Flamberge* had intercepted her, just in time to save the Davion prince. It was a lucky missile strike against her 'Mech's cockpit armor that had broken her arm.

"I wish we could have carried it through to outright victory," Capshaw said wistfully.

Danai glanced at him. The young MechWarrior was looking at the APC's dirty floor, but his expression showed his attention was somewhere else...probably remembering his own taste of combat. Probably imagining what his life would be like if he could go home and say he had been there, on the field, when his regiment had killed or captured the First Prince of the Federated Suns.

He was right. It would have been glorious.

And unnecessary.

Because for all that historical enmity, the Federated Suns wasn't the enemy that mattered.

That particular honor fell to the Republic of the Sphere.

The APC swayed as it negotiated the roadblock at the end of the street. Danai let her head sway with it. Once past, the fans rose in pitch again as the driver accelerated past the obstruction.

"What do we do next?" Capshaw asked.

"We pack up and board ship," Danai said.

"Yes ma'am."

Danai could hear the hesitation in his voice. She looked at him until he looked back, then raised her eyebrows in question.

"Where are we going, ma'am?"

Danai met his stare, then shrugged.

"Toward the fight that matters," she told him.

By the time the APC rattled to a halt back at the Second's cantonment, Danai's head throbbed from the fans' vibration. The cut on her forehead was already mostly healed, but she would have sworn the edges were starting to pull apart again as her skull exploded with pain. When Capshaw stood and slapped the knob that dropped the APC's hatch to the ground with a clang, she glared at him.

"*Sang-shao?*"

"You should be mindful of your colonel's headache, Noah," she told him. Danai pulled the headset off and hung it back on its hooks, then stood. Her back and legs were stiff from holding her in place against the APC's turns, and the wash of cold air that had filled the compartment as soon as Capshaw slammed the ramp down didn't help.

Capshaw looked like she'd killed his favorite kitten. "*Sang-shao*, I'm—" he gulped, but she cut him off.

"It's nothing, Noah." She gestured outside. "Let's go."

Outside, the sun was shining and reflecting off the fresh snow. Danai pulled sunglasses from the hip pocket of her battledress and put them on as a pair of officers stepped closer from where they'd retreated from the APC's fan blast.

"*Sang-shao*," said the senior of them, ducking his chin as he stepped closer. "I got your message. We can be off-world within twenty-four hours, but it means abandoning a great deal of matériel."

Zhong-shao—lieutenant colonel—Wu Feng was short, about 1.7 meters, and thickly built. Though he was a MechWarrior, he was routinely found in the infantry's gym, challenging the ground-pounders to weightlifting competitions. As her executive officer, it was his job to know everything about the regiment.

"Anything we need to worry about?" Danai asked.

"No," Wu said. He grinned. "It's mostly foodstuffs and basic maintenance materials for the armor regiment. We can replace it almost anywhere if we need to." He raised an eyebrow. "That being said, if we can delay three days, we can get it all aboard ship."

Danai rolled the idea around in her head, then shook it. "No; time is precious. I want you all in space and outbound at the earliest possible moment."

Wu ducked his chin in again. "Then we go. We can be in orbit in twenty hours, barring something unforeseen."

Danai nodded. She looked at the other officer, a tall woman of Slavic descent who'd waited patiently. "*Sao-shao* Maranov. How can I help you?"

Anya Maranov commanded the Second 'Mech Battalion. She braced, and then frowned. "I'm afraid I've got new orders, *Sang-shao.*"

"From whom?" Danai asked, icily. There was not another officer on New Syrtis, aside from *Zhong-shao* Wu, who could give the *sao-shao*—major—orders. If one of the other regimental commanders was stepping out of line…

"From Menke, ma'am."

"Oh."

"Yes, ma'am. Came in on the last supply DropShip. From McCarron himself."

Danai ground her teeth. "And where did the *sang-shao* send you, Anya?"

"I'm the new XO of the Fifth Regiment," Maranov replied.

Danai held her tongue while her mind raced. *Sang-shao* Xavier McCarron was the commander of all McCarron's Armored Cavalry units. Though the Armored Cavalry had given up its mercenary status a century ago to become regular units of the Capellan Confederation Armed Forces, the Strategios—the Capellan High Command—still gave the brigade significant latitude. One of those areas of latitude was personnel assignments.

She looked at Wu. "Did you know about this?"

"I got a copy of the orders when Anya did," Wu told her.

"Did I?"

"When was the last time you checked your queue?"

"It's been a couple days," Danai admitted.

"The orders came yesterday. It's probably in your mail."

Danai shook her head. "Well, as much as I hate to lose you, Anya, you deserve it." She looked at the two of them, then at Capshaw. "Can we go inside now?"

"Of course," Wu said, and gestured her to precede them.

A few minutes later, they were in what passed for a common room inside the heated building. Capshaw helped Danai get her coat off, being careful of the sling, and then sat down just outside the circle of senior officers.

"You're going to Liao," she told them.

Liao was the birth world of the Liao dynasty, former capital of a commonality in the Confederation, and the headquarters for military operations against the Republic of the Sphere. It had been a Republic world for decades, ever since it was stolen from the Confederation at the Republic's founding in the 3080s.

Wu slid a noteputer from his thigh pocket, touched the screen, and tapped a query. "Looks like about four months' journey."

Danai nodded. "That's what I figured. You should get there in early December."

"Forgive me," *Sao-shao* Maranov said, "but you said 'you're' going to Liao. Not 'we'?"

"I'm going to Sian." She sat back in her plush seat and grimaced. "Noah, can you send for Doctor Mitchell? I think it's time to get a new cast on." She gently waved her broken arm in its sling.

"Right away, *Sang-shao*," Capshaw said. He leaped to his feet like an eager puppy and strode out of the room.

"Sian?" Wu prompted.

"I need to explain to the Chancellor why we're letting Julian Davion keep New Syrtis."

"Then the rumors are true," Wu said. "It's just our regiment leaving."

"No," Danai told them. "Everyone is leaving. This is a sideshow. We're going toward the real battle."

"Against the Republic," Maranov said. Her blue eyes glared at Danai from beneath furrowed brows. "Now?"

Danai breathed deep as the bones in her arm moved and ached.

"It's past time," she told them.

CHAPTER 2

LUNG WANG-CLASS DROPSHIP *GLADIATOR*
NADIR JUMP POINT, IMALDA
CAPELLAN CONFEDERATION
2 OCTOBER 3148

The woman staring at Danai Liao-Centrella in the mirror was a stranger.

She stood in the small head attached to her DropShip quarters, hair still wet from the shower, and tried to imagine how she'd become this woman.

The face was familiar enough. She saw the same strong cheekbones, the same almond shape to her eyes, the same lips that always chapped too quickly. Her skin was still soft. The cut on her forehead was almost totally healed; just a small pink scar the surgeons assured her would be almost unnoticeable.

Danai frowned, looking at the lines around her mouth when she did that.

She knew what that said.

In her youth, she'd been a 'Mech fighter on Solaris VII, the game world. She'd followed in her illustrious cousins' examples and fought for the title of champion in the gladiatorial games still fought there. No one rose to any sense of prominence in that environment without the attentions of publicists, make-up artists, agents, and all the other grease that made the holovid-bound world of the games work.

She'd listened to what those people had taught her about being in front of the camera: That it was often less about what you said than how you said it and what you looked like when you said it.

So she stared into the small, steam-lined mirror, frowning, and tried to remember who she was. And why she was so afraid of what this face in the mirror said to people.

She'd passed her fortieth birthday, measured in Terran standard years, on the journey to New Syrtis. It was barely a third of what she could expect to live, but it still felt like a milestone.

Danai sucked on her lower lip for a second, then sighed and wiped her hand across the mirror, smearing the condensation. She turned and walked back into her cabin, pulling her long black hair into a ponytail. Water dripped on the deck as she squeezed the strands together. The cast on her forearm made it difficult, but she was used to it by now, and it made a handy sleeve for the chopstick she used to both scratch inside the cast and to stick into the bun of her ponytail to hold it in place.

If this was forty, so be it.

Gladiator, the DropShip she traveled on, was usually attached like a lamprey to the spine of the *Invader*-class JumpShip *Taihan Shan*. DropShips—intrasystem vessels that carried people and cargo from a planetary surface to the distant nadir or zenith jump points of star systems—couldn't travel faster than light. JumpShips did that, jumping instantaneously from star to star, jump point to jump point, up to thirty light-years at a time.

A DropShip like *Gladiator*, a *Lung Wang*-class assault ship, could be a warship, designed to fight its way in-system, but JumpShips were far too fragile. They were spindly constructions, needle-shaped, and sometimes nearly a kilometer long. They almost never left a jump point and were almost always unarmed. During the centuries of the Succession Wars, most of the knowledge needed to manufacture JumpShips had been lost. They were precious, every one. And while the knowledge had since been recovered, and new JumpShips were constructed every year, they were still exceedingly valuable. Many nations still considered it a war crime to attack them.

DropShips, on the other hand, were instruments of war.

A DropShip attached to a JumpShip in transit almost never detached, except to depart and go in-system. *Gladiator*, however, had routinely detached and tooled around the space near the jump point at standard 1-gravity acceleration and deceleration to give the appearance of gravity. This was cost- and fuel-intensive, but Danai could afford it, and the pseudo-gravity ensured the bones of her arm knitted correctly and spared her the embarrassment of floating in zero-G.

Though a JumpShip traveled from star to star almost instantaneously, interstellar travel still took weeks or months due to the need to recharge the JumpShip's capacitors. Every JumpShip carried a giant, flimsy solar sail that trailed behind the ship, soaking up every photon of energy it could from the distant star. JumpShips like *Taihan Shan* that carried enormous lithium-fusion batteries could jump twice, but they still needed to be recharged.

Taihan Shan and *Gladiator* had only arrived a couple hours prior. *Gladiator*'s captain had detached and began his circuit, but Danai had retreated to her cabin. She'd been dreading this moment, but she couldn't put it off any longer.

Imalda was an average Confederation world, but it boasted something rare beyond measure in 3148: a working hyperpulse generator.

Just like JumpShips traveled between stars, this same technology allowed for the FTL transmission of data packets at an even longer range. For centuries, the mystic order of ComStar had administered the HPG network for the entire Inner Sphere—until Gray Monday in 3132, when eighty percent of the HPGs succumbed to sabotage, viruses, or outright attack. Almost none had been brought back, which had drastically reduced the speed of interstellar communication.

Two options remained: carry the physical message on a JumpShip all the way to its destination system, or set up a Pony Express-style "command circuit," a series of JumpShips waiting to carry the message.

But where HPGs still worked, the messages could be sent on ahead.

Imalda was in transmission range of Sian, the Capellan capital. And even though Sian's HPG could no longer send messages, it could still receive them.

Danai was still eighteen days away from Sian, based on what *Taihan Shan*'s captain had told her. She could wait and deliver the message herself. Danai sighed, wiping wet hands on her soft slacks, and collapsed into the small chair of her desk.

She could wait, but she shouldn't.

The Chancellor needed time to deliberate. He needed all the time possible, given the sorry state of interstellar communications, to get the next steps moving. She had sent her regiment on ahead; the bureaucracy of the Capellan Confederation Armed Forces would need time to catch up with where they were.

The small desk had a mini HV recorder built into it. She called up a new message, set the priority for eyes-only to the Chancellor and Strategios, and pressed the key that started a countdown timer while the HV lenses came up out of the desk.

Danai drew a deep breath, centering herself. When the system chimed ready to record, she opened her eyes and stared at the lens.

"Brother," she began, and it took every ounce of her control to contain her revulsion.

Daoshen Liao, Chancellor of the Capellan Confederation was, to every outside observer, her brother, the eldest child of the acclaimed Sun-Tzu Liao. What almost no one knew, however, was that Daoshen wasn't Danai's brother.

He was her father.

And her mother was her "sister," Ilsa Centrella.

It was disgusting, but she had accepted it. It didn't make her like her "brother" any more than she had to, which wasn't very much.

"I must tell you that Capellan forces have withdrawn from New Syrtis," she continued. "I have concluded peace— another peace—with Julian Davion, who was nearly killed in the fighting."

She paused, still glaring at the pickup, then continued.

"You will think this a mistake," she told her *brother*, "but it is not."

Then she launched into the prepared remarks she'd spent the long weeks of transit from New Syrtis perfecting.

ZI-JING CHENG, FORBIDDEN CITY
SIAN
CAPELLAN CONFEDERATION
3 OCTOBER 3148

Tianzhu Liu feared nothing. As commander of the Death Commandos, the elite of the Capellan military, he was not permitted fear. It had been trained out of him.

But this day, in the small room where the Chancellor shared his sister's message with a select few military leaders and members of the civilian Prefectorate, he felt the first stirrings of that long-dead emotion beneath his immaculate black uniform.

The recording was running down toward the end. This was the second time they'd viewed it.

"*Davion is not the enemy that matters,*" the holo image of Danai Liao-Centrella said as it floated above the polished teak table. "*He will either salvage his realm from the Kuritas or he will die trying, and we can mop up the remnants at our will.*" The image paused, and it felt like Danai was staring into Tianzhu's soul.

"*The Republic is our enemy, and we must be ready. That is why I have sent our regiments to Liao. And why I will join them, after my visit to Sian.*"

The image nodded, then disappeared into static. After that, most of the light in the room came from decorative candleholders along the walls, where LED candles shined and flickered.

"She is not wrong," *Sang-jiang-jun* Isabelle Fisk said, finally.

Tianzhu looked at the general. She was, after the Chancellor, the supreme commander of the nation's armies. Only the Death Commandos and the Chancellor's warrior house orders were exempt from her direct control. He would have expected Fisk to back any attack on the Republic. Her family had been deeply wounded by them when she was a child, and she'd made her reputation in the recent victories after the Republic Wall went up.

The Republic of the Sphere occupied the very center of the Inner Sphere. It was a manufactured state, built out of the worlds of all the Successor States to serve as a buffer after the horrors of the Word of Blake Jihad a century ago. The Capellans had never agreed to it, but their worlds had been stolen from them anyway. More than a decade ago the Republic, pressured in the fighting that overtook the Inner Sphere after Gray Monday, retreated inside its so-called Fortress Republic and went dark, sealing its borders. And it still hadn't come out.

In those years, the Capellans had reclaimed many of their ancestral worlds, including Liao and Chesterton. But the Republic was still there, still hiding inside that impenetrable Wall.

And increasing evidence said it was starting to poke its head out. Whether or not everyone in this room had seen it, Tianzhu had. He was commander of the most elite, most feared military unit in the Inner Sphere. He saw anything he wanted.

"It is not a question of wrong," said Ki-linn Liao, the lady of Highspire. "She has abandoned a world that belongs to the Confederation. Worse, she has given Davion—" she spat the word like it held venom "—a victory over us they can crow about for a generation." The duchess' fine features twisted into a snarl. "'Little Danai has run away,' they will say. 'From a cripple. In a wheelchair!'"

"Who will say that, your Grace?" asked Lord Gregor Volkov. Volkov was director of the Ministry of Information Standards, who oversaw the Capellan Broadcast Service, the state-run news and entertainment conglomerate.

Tianzhu stifled a snort. *Say what it is, old man*, he chided himself. CBS was the state propaganda organ.

"I can assure you that CBS would never let such lies pass," Volkov went on, "and we make great efforts to remind our citizens that the media of other realms that might reach them is filled with lies and exaggerations."

Ki-linn looked at Volkov as if he were an insect. "Did not the Chancellor's sainted father once say 'the moral is to the physical as three to one'? We have given Davion and his people a moral victory. Or rather, Danai has!"

Napoleon Bonaparte said that, Tianzhu thought, *but perhaps Sun-Tzu Liao once said it too.*

Ki-linn waited, but no one else spoke. Finally, she twisted in her seat to look toward her royal cousin.

Daoshen Liao, Chancellor of the Confederation, sat mutely. His seat was raised on a dais, and he sat with his hand steepled in front of his face. His long hair fell forward, obscuring one of his eyes. The one Tianzhu could see burned with intense emotion as it stared at the point where his sister's holorecording had been speaking.

"Well, cousin," Ki-linn demanded. "What say you?"

Without knowing he was going to do it beforehand, Tianzhu cleared his throat. All eyes—except the Chancellor's—turned toward him.

"No matter the propaganda," he said, inclining his head toward Ki-linn Liao, "*Sang-shao* Liao-Centrella has given us an opportunity."

He looked next to Lord Volkov. "The people will believe what we tell them," he said, and Volkov nodded firmly back.

Finally, Tianzhu looked toward the head of the table. He traded glances with Isabelle Fisk, and then looked toward the Chancellor. "The Republic is coming."

"The Republic—" Ki-linn started, but Daoshen held up a long-fingered hand. The extra-long, carbon reinforced fingernails on the hand glittered in the light.

"We will make no decision now," the Chancellor said.

Tianzhu and the others bowed their heads in acquiescence. The others, that is, except Ki-linn Liao.

"No decision," she ground out.

"We will wait, and hear the *sang-shao* out when she arrives," Daoshen said.

"Wait," she spat.

"She is already gone from New Syrtis," *Sang-jiang-jun* Fisk put in, desperately trying to head off the confrontation the whole room saw coming. "Whatever your objections, the thing is done. The thing to do next is decide—"

Ki-linn jerked to her feet. Her ornate robes, flecked with gold and jade, swirled around her.

"There is nothing to *decide*!" she shouted at Fisk, who sat back in her tall-backed chair in shock. "Any *decision* on this matter was made over and over again, across centuries, as our ancestors were attacked and humiliated by the Davions!" She glared at each person at the table in turn, except her cousin. Tianzhu met her stare evenly.

Tianzhu Liu did not feel fear.

It had been trained out of him.

And the thing, as Fisk had said, had already happened.

Months ago, on New Syrtis.

Moments ago, in this room.

"You *cowards*," Ki-linn said. Her hands dipped quickly, rolling the long sleeves of her dress over her forearms to clear her feet and let her walk. "You sit here, in this dark room, fearing that the ghost of Devlin Stone and his Republic will ride through the walls and skewer you. You fear a nation of craven fools who hide behind a wall in space."

She stepped back from the table.

Then she finally glared at her cousin.

"How *dare* you," she hissed. "The very blood in our veins cries out for vengeance. For centuries of slights and murders and misdeeds committed against us." She sniffed. "Your father would be *ashamed*."

Someone at the table inhaled.

"Ashamed," Ki-linn said again. "Your grandmother would not have *waited*. Your grandmother knew the thing to do with a Davion when you had your heel on his neck was to grind down. Your grandmother—" She stopped.

A moment of only breath.

Tianzhu Liu waited, blood tingling. No one dared bring up Romano Liao, Sun-Tzu's mother, the tyrant who had murdered whoever necessary to save the Capellan state after the Fourth Succession War.

Not ever.

"She was my great-grandmother," Ki-linn Liao said. "Her blood flows in me." She swept around and stalked toward the door.

"I hear her voice now," she called over her shoulder.

CHAPTER 3

LUNG WANG-CLASS DROPSHIP *GLADIATOR*
ZENITH JUMP POINT, SIAN
CAPELLAN CONFEDERATION
9 OCTOBER 3148

Danai Liao-Centrella flexed her hand as the DropShip's doctor slid the broken cast down off her arm. She felt weakness, but there was no pain. She opened her palm and closed it.

"Rotate," Doctor Hewson said, and she did. "Anything?" Hewson was pale, with dark hair and a permanent stubble. He had wet eyes but an easy smile, and Danai liked him. He'd taken very careful care of her arm during the trip from New Syrtis.

Danai shook her head. "It feels okay."

"Make a fist again," Hewson said.

Danai did, then pulled her arm out of his grip and shook the fist under his nose. "It's fine," she told him. Then she used her other hand to scrape at the newly-exposed skin on her arm, giving it a good scratching for all the itches she'd been forced to endure.

"*Sang-shao*," Hewson said, "you still need to work on rebuilding your muscles. It has only been a few weeks, but you will have atrophied more than you know, especially with our time in zero-G."

"We've spent hardly any time in zero-G," she protested.

"It is enough." Hewson turned to a tray beside him, mouth open to say something, but the hatch opened and one of the DropShip's junior officers stepped inside.

"*Sang-shao*—" he blurted. He stopped, looking between Danai and Doctor Hewson, as if he was unsure whether to proceed.

"Yes?" she prompted.

"Ma'am...you have a transmission. From the Chancellor. Ma'am."

Danai sighed. She should have known Daoshen wouldn't wait until she landed. Sian's jump points were ten days from the planet. It was more than a week before *Gladiator* would deposit her on the capital's soil. But what would take a DropShip days and weeks would only take a message minutes and hours. She held out her hand—her good hand—for the noteputer he carried.

"Let's have a look, then."

The junior officer drew back his hand. "I'm sorry, *Sang-shao*, but it's for your eyes only."

"Then I'll watch it later," she told him. "Hand it over."

He did, and quickly braced to attention and left. Danai looked at the quiet device, then set it on the table and looked at Doctor Hewson. "Are we done?"

Hewson nodded. "I'll send you a physical therapy schedule. You should be back to normal in a couple weeks, but be careful. The break is healed, but the bone is still somewhat fragile. If you overstress it too soon..." his voice trailed off even as his eyebrows rose.

Danai grinned at him and stood. "Thank you, Doctor," she told him, and swept out of the compartment.

The HV was short, at least.

The image of her *brother* appeared over her table. He looked tired. *"Daughter,"* he said. *"Look what your actions have wrought."* Danai bristled at the tone, but there was no use in arguing with a recording.

The scene changed. Danai recognized the steps of the Summer Palace in the Forbidden City. Passersby went up and down the stairs, garish-dressed members of the directorship and the intelligentsia castes. Danai rolled her eyes and waited. There was clearly something here the Chancellor—her father—wanted her to see.

The view suddenly panned. A clutch of people in brilliant, billowing white robes were striding up the stairs. It looked like six or eight people. They climbed halfway up, pushing people out of their way, and then fanned out into a circle. The HV recorder was high enough that it could see over the ring of people, and the operator zoomed in.

"Ki-linn," Danai breathed.

Now her pulse quickened. Ki-linn Liao hated House Davion and everything about it. If Daoshen had told her about the withdrawal, she would be fuming. And she liked to act out. Doing so in public would be just like her, too. Her grandmother, Kali Liao, sister to Sun-Tzu and daughter to Romano, had been the same way, all too eager to put her emotions behind her reason.

She'll have one of her Thuggees act something out, Danai guessed.

The Thuggee cult had a long and shameful relationship with the Capellan Confederation, and the Liao family specifically. Going all the way back to ancient Terra, Thuggee fanatics worshiped the Hindu goddess Kali. The branch that resisted all efforts to burn it out on the Capellan world Highspire was especially militant. It viewed the Liao family, and primarily its daughters, as avatars of Kali reborn, and there was no act so heinous, so disgusting, they would not undertake to please their goddess' avatar.

A hundred years ago, the Thuggees had used nerve gas on Capellan worlds, just as they had months ago on New Syrtis. The Thuggees were an abomination.

"There are some who want peace," Ki-linn shouted. *"Peace with Davion!"*

On the stairs people stopped, one foot on a step higher than the other, turning to look. Couples and trios leaned closer to whisper as they recognized her. Danai frowned, absently scratching the pale skin where her cast had been.

"So you told her," she said, talking to her *brother*, still ten days away.

The duchess of Highspire looked around, up and down the stairs.

"There are some," Ki-linn shouted, *"who lack the resolve to do what must be done to bring the Davion curs to their knees! To keep them there!"*

The white-clad group with her spread out. Several of them bent down, toying with something hidden by their robes.

"The dynasty of the Celestial Wisdom does not lack resolve!" Ki-linn shouted.

One her followers stepped closer, carrying a white-painted can, and poured something over Ki-linn's head. The white robes stopped billowing immediately as the fabric drank in the liquid.

Danai's hand stopped scratching. *She wouldn't...*

Ki-linn raised her hand. She clutched something slender and red.

"Death to the Federated Suns!"

Danai's hand clenched. She recognized the red object.

That's a flare—

Ki-linn turned and looked directly into the HV camera's lenses.

How—

The flare's flame, bright and chemical, burst to life—but only for an instant before bright yellow, oily flames engulfed Ki-linn from head to toe.

"Death to Davion!" The scream from inside the inferno was fast and clear, but then the sound dropped away to nothing.

The images kept coming.

One by one the others in white doused themselves and lit themselves on fire.

No one stopped them.

As the camera zoomed back out, she saw the crowds recoiling in horror from the pyres. Clinically, her mind took in the billows of thick black smoke and told her it was probably kerosene. Within seconds the scene was nothing more than a pillar of twisting, oily black smoke with a glow at the bottom.

Finally soldiers appeared, infantrymen from the Red Guard's regiments, sprinting down the steps carrying fire extinguishers ripped from inside the building, but by then it was far too late. The HV flickered into darkness, then Daoshen reappeared.

"Your cousin is dead," he said unnecessarily. *"This recording was recovered from a raid on a Thuggee nest outside the Forbidden City."* Daoshen's mouth worked, as if he tasted something awful. *"She intended us to find it.* This *copy."*

Danai's stomach clenched as she understood.

The cameraman had been a Thuggee. Ki-linn had known the Capellan Broadcast Service would never allow the death of a Liao to be broadcast, not unless it was done in a heroic light and was approved by the Chancellor. That was why and how she'd known to look directly at the camera. CBS was a lot of things, but free and honest it was not. Danai swallowed bile, terrified that Daoshen had consented to release this to the public. It would make peace with Davion impossible.

Because there was no way Daoshen could let this come to light without twisting the story into one of heroism and using it to support state policy. A policy she had just done her damnedest to halt and turn toward the Republic of the Sphere.

"Maskirovka—" the Capellan intelligence service *"—informs us this has almost certainly gotten off-world already,"* Daoshen went on. *"It will soon be impossible to keep it from spreading, and we will have to get in front of it."*

Danai didn't breathe.

"We will discuss this when you arrive," the Chancellor said. *"This, and much else."*

The HV flickered off.

Danai gasped. Pain made her look down, to where she'd been squeezing her freshly-healed arm tight enough to leave marks. She let go, flexing her fingers. They were on the edge of cramping.

Her eyes went back to the empty space where the HV recording had been.

We will discuss this when you arrive, Daoshen had said.

That meant there was a chance he hadn't decided yet.

Danai blinked and looked away from the HV. Instead, she touched another control.

"Bridge," a voice answered. "How can I help you, *Sang-shao*?"

"I just received a message from Sian," she said.

"Yes, ma'am. We received it from the recharge station and forwarded it on."

"Send an acknowledgment," Danai ordered. "Just that. No reply, not yet. Just 'message received.'"

"At once, *Sang-shao*."

"Thank you." Danai keyed the intercom closed.

She needed time to think. To plan.

To mourn her cousin.

Because *Gladiator* was a BattleMech-carrying DropShip, its facilities included 'Mech simulators. Danai stood outside one of them in her MechWarrior combat suit, holding the integral helmet under her good arm. The combat suit was a form-fitting bulky black body stocking, shot through with tiny tubes to carry cooling liquid. The interior temperature of a 'Mech cockpit during combat could easily reach that of an oven; combat suits, and common cooling vests, kept a MechWarrior's internal temperature under control.

Danai wore it even in the simulator, because her famous ancestor Kai Allard-Liao had once spoken about doing so in an interview. Kai had been a champion Solaris VII 'Mech-games fighter, just like his father, Justin Allard, and like Danai herself. Both Justin and Kai had piloted the 'Mech she now piloted.

"*It's common sense,*" Kai had said in the old HV clip. "*You train like you fight. If you wear a combat suit in combat, you wear it in the simulator. There's a story going around that Phelan Kell wears his sidearm into the simulator.*"

So Danai wore it.

And her sidearm, a compact laser pistol.

Plus the two Ceres Arms Slasher knives in her boots.

With her free hand, Danai flexed her weaker arm. The movement was unconscious, automatic. She was deep in her own mind, trying to play out the mental chess game of politics against her father and her dead cousin.

A chime broke her concentration as the simulator pod irised open. She blinked, then lifted the heavy helmet over her head and climbed inside.

This was her personal simulator, built to match exactly the cockpit of *Yen-lo-Wang*, the 50-ton *Centurion* she piloted. She settled into the command couch and began connecting the various cables built into the couch to her combat suit.

After a moment, the 'Mech's—or in this case, the simulator's—security protocols came up. A synthesized voice demanded attention in Danai's neurohelmet.

"Who wakes the king of the nine hells from his slumber?"

"No revenge is more honorable than the one not taken," she replied.

The simulator came to life around her.

Since its invention centuries ago, the BattleMech had become the preeminent vehicle of ground warfare. Normally massing between 20 and 100 tons and standing ten to twelve meters tall, 'Mechs were fusion-powered humanoid walking tanks. They carried the toughest armors humanity had ever developed, and the suite of weapons available to them ranged from a simple hatchet to high-powered lasers, missiles of all ranges, automatic cannons, and particle projection cannons.

Common wisdom held that the only foe a BattleMech need respect was another BattleMech. 'Mechs, and the individuals who piloted and fought them—the MechWarriors—had become an aristocracy all their own in every realm of the Inner Sphere.

The voice security code was just one of the ways they were kept safe. The bulky neurohelmet did more than keep cool air flowing to the MechWarriors. It also passed electronic signals from the MechWarrior's nervous system—specifically, his or her sense of balance—into the machine's powerful diagnostic interpretation computer. That computer controlled everything about the 'Mech, including the massive gyro that kept the machine on its feet.

Only children believed the neurohelmet let the pilot's balance do that work.

If a 'Mech started up and the pilot gave the wrong code phase, the connection was strong enough that a feedback surge could be sent back through the helmet, incapacitating the pilot.

As with her suit and her weapons, the code phrase was a part of using the 'Mech. Danai had to say it in the field; she would say it here.

That requirement of compliance was a core part of who she was. And it was what made the conversations she knew would loom on Sian all the more daunting.

She knew she'd made the right decision on New Syrtis. Not only was the whole conflict with Davion a sideshow, the Capellans were on the verge of *losing*. She had made great strides by wounding Julian Davion, but Davion regiments were drawing closer, whereas the CCAF supply lines and reinforcement queue were drying up.

Continuing to fight would have cost the CCAF whole regiments.

Why couldn't Ki-linn see that?

Because she didn't care, Danai's mind filled in. *Because she didn't make decisions based on facts.* She decided things based on emotions.

The simulator's HUD came up. A digitized voice spoke to her through her helmet.

"Scenario?" The simulator's computer asked.

"One-on-one," she said.

"Setting?"

"Snowscape"

"Opponent 'Mech?"

Danai thought about her cousin. She thought about making decisions from emotions. She thought about things she couldn't change.

"*Templar III*," she told the simulator.

"Skill level?"

Danai thought about Julian Davion, the Julian Davion she'd met on Marlette three years ago.

"Expert," she told the machine.

Then she gripped the simulator's controls as the HUD came up with a snowy landscape and tried to forget about everything else for just a few minutes.

CHAPTER 4

Captain Tom Jordan throttled his *Kheper* down as he entered the maintenance bay. His HUD had highlighted the 'Mech technician with light paddles, giving him a ground guide into his assigned bay, and Tom followed the directions exactly until the 55-ton 'Mech backed into its cradle and the umbilicals attached.

It took him a few minutes to unhook the connections between his cooling suit and the 'Mech's cockpit. In that time, the technicians had adjusted the 'Mech cradle to support the 'Mech. A *clang* announced the arrival of the egress gantry against the hatch in the rear of the *Kheper*'s head. Tom toggled the control that unlocked the hatch as he climbed up and pulled a battledress jumpsuit from beneath his seat.

The *Kheper*'s hatch slid up into a recess in the armor, and a young man with green hair and thick, athletic-style glasses poked his head and shoulders through. "How'd she do, Cap'n?"

Tom got the shoulders of the suit up and slid his arms down. "She did great, Logan."

The technician, properly Staff Sergeant Logan Bean, grinned. "Course she did. Toldja, didn't I?"

Tom grinned back. Logan Bean was an Elgin native, from a small village barely twenty klicks outside Sochalladan, the planetary capital. His family still spoke the thick patois of Chisholian, the dialect that had evolved on Elgin's islands across the centuries. Tom still stumbled across the odd word or turn of phrase, but he got most. He should.

He was from Elgin, too.

The difference was Tom Jordan had been off-world for four years when he was training at the Sandhurst Royal Military Academy, on Terra herself. After that, he had another two years as a lance commander in the Tenth Hastati Sentinels before being transferred back home to take a company of Owen Boyle's Fourteenth Principes Guards.

He'd heard a lot of accents on Terra.

But Bean's enunciation still sounded like home to him.

Now Bean stepped back to let Jordan step past him onto the cut-metal gantry. The air was cool and crisp after the heat of the *Kheper*'s cockpit, and Jordan breathed it in, deep.

Elgin was a wet world, largely ocean, with scattered islands ranging from the subcontinental Jolo to average masses like Tom's home on New Ceram and down to little one-family steads of a couple square kilometers or so. The humidity was omnipresent, and locals barely noticed it.

Tom noticed it. He'd spent time on Terra in deserts and mountains and land that spanned not only for as far as he could see, but for as far as he could *go*. He'd been to landscapes that didn't sweat the water out of you every hour of the day.

Bean slapped him on the shoulder. "The M-7, yeah?"

Tom grinned back. "The M-7, yeah, is right. You got it calibrated just right." He mimed pulling a trigger with his hand. "Right through the bullseye."

The *Kheper*'s main weapon was a gigantic M-7 Gauss rifle, a magnetic weapon that accelerated 125-kilogram weights of ferrous metal to hypersonic speed in the blink of an eye. The slug did all of its damage from kinetic energy, but the recoil of accelerating that much mass that quickly rocked the medium 'Mech with every shot. That recoil had shaken some of the Gauss rifle's targeting systems loose until Bean and his team of astechs—assistant technicians—had recalibrated it.

It took a MechWarrior to fight and drive a BattleMech, but it took an army of techs and astechs to keep it running.

"Told you," Bean repeated. He reached out and touched the 'Mech's armor. "This baby, she easy to keep going."

Tom agreed. He took the moment while Bean was distracted to look around the bay. This provisional operations center was one of six built to house the 'Mech companies of the Fourteenth Principes Guards 'Mech battalions. The other twelve 'Mechs of his company, the Flankers, were all getting settled into their own maintenance cradles, and Tom allowed himself a bit of pride.

He'd led the whole company—properly F Company, Second BattleMech Battalion, Fourteenth Principes Guards—out to the proving grounds for unsimulated, live-fire training. They'd spent the day emptying their ammunition bins and destroyed notional targets like rusted-out old tanks from the days of the Jihad and derelict power-cable towers their computers pretended were 'Mechs. On the whole, the company had done well.

Not up to the standards of the Tenth Hastati, but coming up to it.

"Get it reloaded," Tom told Bean. "More practice rounds, if you can get them. I'd like to challenge D Company to an all-up fight if they can get the time free."

Bean spread his hands. "No can do, Captain," he said. "Orders say prep these machines for transport. DropShips be at Sochalladan day after tomorrow."

"Transport?" Tom looked around. "To where?"

"Orders don't say," Bean told him.

"Who signed the orders?"

"Looked like the colonel," Bean said. He pulled out a noteputer, swiped it open, and punched a few commands. "Just sent you the message, yeah?"

Tom's pocket comm chirped receipt. He nodded to Bean, told him to follow his orders, and started down the stairs at the edge of the gantry. None of this made any sense.

Elgin was one of the worlds inside the boundaries of Fortress Republic. In 3134, Exarch Jonah Levin had enacted the Fortress plan, cutting off Prefecture X of the Republic from outside contact with the rest of the Inner Sphere. Tom wasn't cleared to know how it worked; he only knew it *did* work. No outside JumpShip had reached a world behind the Wall in more than fifteen years. Tom had been a teenager when the Wall went up, but he was old enough to remember the high points of before and after.

Before, when the Republic was the shining beacon of peaceful cooperation in a galaxy torn by centuries of war.

After, when the Republic Armed Forces' frantic rearmament program shifted to overdrive to prepare the RAF to sally out from behind the wall and reconquer the fallen worlds of the Republic.

The year before the Wall went up, Tom Jordan had never thought of becoming a soldier, much less a MechWarrior. But within two years of its raising, he'd signed his intent to enlist and begun taking the battery of tests that would best determine his place in the RAF. At the time, he'd felt like it was just the right thing to do.

Now, after a half-dozen years in uniform and schooling at Sandhurst, he recognized the propaganda that had hooked him for what it was. Though now, he didn't care.

He *loved* being a MechWarrior. Nothing else in his short life had compared to guiding a 55-ton war machine across the battlefield in service to his lancemates and his nation.

Nothing.

Once he reached the ground, Tom made a beeline for the skimmers racked near the POC entrance. He claimed the nearest one, unhooked its refueling line, and brought the small hovercraft's lift fans up. Soon the skimmer was skittering across the ground, on a plenum chamber full of air, like a drop of oil on a hot pan.

He pushed the throttle forward, grabbed the yoke, and held on as the lithe little craft rocketed up to more than two hundred kph in seconds.

In Sochalladan, the Fourteenth Principes Guards administrative headquarters was still at the spaceport. Colonel Boyle had established it there when he founded the regiment to better meet incoming recruits to his Guards, but it had never moved. Instead, the temporary buildings had become permanent.

Second Battalion's offices were in a giant ferrocrete Quonset almost the size of an ancient dirigible hangar. The transponder in the skimmer got Tom past most of the checkpoints, but he had to stop and physically show his ID and then get biometrically scanned—handprint and retinal— to get into the building. It was annoying, but Tom agreed with every impatient step.

Inside, the building was usually a quiet, reserved place where small clumps of officers worked diligently on the problems facing them. Sometimes those problems were piles of paperwork. Sometimes those problems were prickly subordinates.

Sometimes it was disciplinary, and there was shouting.

Today, it was bedlam.

Tom stood there, just inside the security door, staring as officers and clerks ran back and forth, shouting orders and questions. He watched a captain with First Battalion shoulder flashes crash into a clerk carrying a sheaf of papers. The papers went flying, as did the captain. The clerk was every centimeter of two meters tall, and looked like he could bench press a BattleMech.

Tom stepped into the maelstrom and headed toward the office of his commanding officer.

When he got there, the room was crowded.

Major Salesi Crowe was short, slender, and had an annoying, nasal voice. Most people who met him were dismissive, until they either saw him in the field inside his 'Mech or had the unpleasant experience of getting on his bad side. He commanded the Fourteenth's Second 'Mech battalion, including F Company. When Tom reached his door, Crowe was shouting at someone on the HV behind his desk.

"—don't care. I really don't. I don't care if you have to climb a ladder to orbit and reach out with God's own mighty hands and gather up the DropShips for us. My orders say we're lifting off on that date, and that's the date you're going to hit."

Tom looked at the bulky man leaning against the door jamb. He wore captain's insignia just like Tom's.

"Joe," Tom asked, nudging the other captain, "we going somewhere?"

Joe Turner, captain of E Company, grunted assent over his shoulder. "That's what it looks like."

"Where?"

"I think we're about to find out."

"Jordan!" Crowe's shout brought Tom's attention back inside the room. "Where the hell have you been?"

"In the field, Major," Tom said instantly.

"You missed the recall?"

"I got no recall, sir. We came back in at the end of the exercise."

"Well, get your people ready. We're going off-world."

"Yes, sir," Tom said. There was no other appropriate answer, but he was confused. He glanced inside the office, where two more captains sat: Manon Prideaux, D Company's CO, and Captain Rita Magnusson, the Second Battalion operations officer. Magnusson ignored him, but Prideaux met his eyes and nodded. None of the other captains were leaving, so Tom took a chance and stood his ground.

"I don't know where we're going," Crowe admitted to the room. His eyes were looking at his desktop. Tom didn't get the sense the major was afraid to meet their eyes. It felt more like confusion. "Word is the colonel will have a briefing for us later tonight."

"I'm sure he will, sir," Captain Magnusson put in.

"I can't believe there aren't even rumors," Major Crowe muttered.

"Oh, there are rumors," Joe Turner put in. "They're just crazy. I heard a good one coming over here: the Wall is down, and the whole of Clan Wolf is waiting to attack Terra."

A chuckle ran around the room. Tom didn't join in. He was the most junior company commander in the battalion. The Flankers were his first company. He was still somewhat afraid of putting his foot wrong.

"The colonel will tell us," Crowe said, as if convincing himself. Tom believed him.

The Fourteenth Principes Guards could reasonably be called Boyle's Regiment. Colonel Owen Boyle could claim distant relations to the Elgin for whom the planet was named. He had been entrusted with building the Fourteenth, and he had succeeded so far. He was both taskmaster and father figure to much of the regiment. Certainly to the MechWarriors.

Still, Tom was confused.

The Fourteenth had been raised, Boyle's ancestor or no, to defend Elgin. Principes—certainly the modern Principes behind the Fortress Wall—rarely traveled off-world. That was the province of the Hastati Sentinels or the Triarii Protectors or, if the gods were angry at the enemy, the heavy regiments of Stone's Brigade. That homeward mission had been one of the reasons Tom had been so eager to accept this assignment.

He was *from* here.

He didn't want to see it burn, if the Wall ever failed.

His Flankers and the rest of the Fourteenth had been training for years to fight on Elgin. They were prime defensive troops, outfitted and acclimatized to fighting across Elgin's seas and archipelagos. Every MechWarrior in the regiment, for example, knew what sand in the bay was safe to step on, sixty meters below the surface, and which would swallow a 'Mech to the hip.

A fight—*any* fight—here was *their* fight.

And now they were going off-world?

Major Crowe's console chimed. He swung around, reading the information in the air-formed holograms. It didn't look like much; Tom couldn't read the letters since the holo wasn't formed for his viewpoint, but he could see the scale.

"Note from the colonel," Crowe said. And stopped.

"And?" Captain Magnusson finally prodded.

"It says prepare the 'Mechs for Hall."

Tom blew air out between his teeth. Hall was a nearby world, ancient as Elgin was, as any world this close to Terra was. Also inside the Fortress Wall, so safe for the Fourteenth to travel there.

But as a destination...

Joe Turner started laughing.

"Captain Turner?" Captain Magnusson spoke as Major Crowe spun back around in his chair.

Turner didn't stop laughing. He just waved an arm back past Tom, toward the door and the outside world. He used the same arm to slap Tom on the shoulder as he gasped for breath.

Tom understood. But instead of laughing, he felt cold between his shoulders.

"Hall," he said.

"Captain Jordan?"

"We're trained for Elgin," Tom said. "Probably no other regiment in the RAF can fight better here." The other captains, save Turner, who had turned purple, all nodded.

"Hall is a desert planet."

Now the other battalion officers looked at each other, then back at Tom.

Joe Turner burst into fresh peals of laughter. "Don't you *see*," he forced out, wheezing, "how much *sense* that makes?" He bent down, hands on knees, and tried to get his breathing under control.

"There's no water at all, compared to here." He stood, bracing one arm on Tom, who supported his weight. "So *of course* they send us."

Major Crowe, when he spoke, sounded as though he'd died four minutes earlier and no one had told him. "Briefing with the colonel in thirty."

CHAPTER 5

ZI-JING CHENG, **FORBIDDEN CITY**
SIAN
CAPELLAN CONFEDERATION
21 OCTOBER 3148

The meeting Danai had hoped would be private was not.

Instead of just her father, the small room also held Tianzhu Liu, commander of the Death Commandos, and *Sang-jiang-jun* Isabelle Fisk, commander of all Capellan military forces *except* the Death Commandos and the Chancellor's warrior house orders.

It was a close to a war cabinet as the Confederation could have.

The Chancellor sat on his raised dais at the head of the table, while the two senior officers sat in the first seats of the long table nearest the Chancellor. Danai stood at the opposite end, arms behind her back at parade rest. She knew the distance was intentional; her aunt Erde Centrella had taught her to read the politics of a room decades ago back on Canopus.

Danai had visited the Summer Palace immediately after landing. She'd seen the charred steps, seen the flowers and candles left there even as an army of servitors carried them away and tried to scrub the black out of the marble. She'd felt the mental weight of Ki-linn's action as she stood there.

Almost like the ghost of my cousin, glaring down at me.

Standing here, in this small room, with the three most powerful military figures in the Confederation, Danai still felt that ghost. She felt the pressure of all that power. It pressed down on her, making her feel smaller. She wanted to sit down, fold her hands, and listen to what the powerful people said.

But she didn't.

She was Danai Liao-Centrella. She was a Solaris champion. She had fought Julian Davion to a draw. She was a MechWarrior. A *janshi* of the Confederation.

She didn't wait.

And she didn't feel small.

"The Davion sideshow is over," she said. She saw the slight widening of Fisk's eyes as she usurped the Chancellor's traditional role of opening any conversation. "We need to focus on the Republic."

Daoshen stirred. The Chancellor wore his usual attire, red and gold robes of state, and his hair was pulled back behind his ear so both his eyes stared at her. "That was not your decision to make."

"I was there," she countered.

"*I* decide policy for the Capellan state!" the Chancellor shouted.

Danai didn't blink, but inside she was shocked. This was one of the few times she'd ever heard the "divine" Chancellor Daoshen not speak in the royal we, much less lose his composure.

"Your cousin Ki-linn—"

"—is dead," Danai said.

Now Fisk's eyes were huge. One did *not* interrupt the celestial wisdom.

Daoshen's eyes smoldered, but he kept his face neutral.

"Is this becoming a habit of yours, then?" Daoshen's voice dripped sarcasm. "Fight Julian Davion until you are losing, then give him peace and beg him to let you run back here, telling us you have won a great victory?"

Danai ground her teeth. "That was *your* plan, *Celestial Wisdom*," she spat.

Daoshen was taunting her with Marlette. Two years earlier, on the Davion planet Marlette, Danai had extracted beaten Capellan troops from a Davion trap and sued for the peace Julian had broken by attacking toward New Syrtis. Intelligence had told the CCAF that the Armed Forces of the Federated Suns was amassing logistical supplies to feed, power, and rearm a thrust into Capellan space. Daoshen and the Strategios—*these three fools here, plus a few more*—had ordered Danai's regiment and several others to attack the planet.

It had been a trap, and a deadly one. It had claimed *Sang-shao* Shaiming Tao, her predecessor as CO of the Second McCarron's Armored Cavalry, and many other Capellan soldiers. Danai had been forced to take command, and her negotiations with Julian Davion that secured the CCAF extrication had been all that saved the survivors.

For Daoshen to try lay the blame for that on *her...*

Danai still had nightmares about Marlette.

"Whatever the faults, the thing is done," *Sang-jiang-jun* Fisk said placatingly. "Help us understand your thinking, *Sang-shao.*"

Danai nodded, grateful for the interruption. She breathed for a few moments, getting her temper under control. When she spoke, her voice was even. She set her eyes on a point above and behind Daoshen's head and ignored him.

"The Davion forces on New Syrtis were being reinforced faster than we could replace our own losses," she said. "When the first gambit to kill Davion failed—" she so wanted to look down at Daoshen, because that act of mercenary treachery had been his brainchild as well, "—we knew the pressure had just gotten ratcheted up. Wounding him later was a coup, but we failed to kill him."

"At Cilitren," Tianzhu Liu put in.

"Yes, *Jiang-jun.*"

"My own people tell me that was a thing well-done, *Sang-shao,*" Liu rumbled. He nodded politely. "It was only dumb luck that you failed to kill him."

"Thank you, *Jiang-jun,*" Danai said. Inside, she was confused.

Both Fisk and Liu had shown her support. She hadn't expected that. She'd expected Daoshen to stack the deck with people who'd already decided against her course of action. To make the crucifixion that much more damning. But instead, they almost appeared to be her partisans.

"You had failed to kill Julian Davion," Daoshen said. "Please continue."

"The Davion military is largely a cult of personality," Danai said. "The fact that the First Prince has spent so much time in the field, in a 'Mech, shows that he doesn't understand that his first duty is to his state at large."

"A mistake many Davion princes have made," Fisk said.

"Maskirovka—" the Capellan intelligence agency, "—told me more Davion regiments were inbound," Danai continued. "They couldn't tell me when additional Capellan regiments would arrive. And despite the lull in tempo that fell when the prince was injured, it was clear to me that the force imbalance would only get worse."

"So, you ran away," Daoshen said.

"Yes," Danai said, defiantly. "To preserve the vital assets of the state in the form of the surviving soldiers of *your* Confederation, *brother.*"

Daoshen grinned ghoulishly at her.

"The state," he said, his voice at once patronizing and arrogant, "is the steward of us all."

Danai let the barb go. It was familiar language. It didn't bear a response. Instead, she went on the offensive.

"The Federated Suns is a sideshow," she said, again. "It doesn't matter. The Kuritas will either complete their destruction of the state or else it will collapse from within. We have much larger threats to confront."

She had to mention the Kuritas, rulers of the distant Draconis Combine, and the Federated Suns' other eternal enemy. For the past five years the Combine had been prosecuting a lightning invasion of the Federated Suns. They had even claimed the realm's capital world, New Avalon, which made Julian Davion a ruler without a throne. Excepting the Word of Blake Jihad a century earlier, it had been centuries since the realm of the Dragon had set foot on New Avalon, and they didn't seem interested in leaving anytime soon.

"The Republic," Fisk put in. "As you said."

"Yes." Danai nodded.

"There is no evidence the Wall is coming down," Tianzhu Liu said. He was testing her. She could tell.

Danai looked at the Death Commando commander. "You know better than that, *Jiang-jun*." She glanced at Isabelle Fisk. "You have seen the same reports I have. More and more raids are appearing on our worlds along the border." She waved a hand dismissively. "Raids from sources we cannot identify, using equipment we have never seen, or else Republic equipment. We know Julian Davion went into the Fortress and came back out with a Republic regiment. So it's possible."

"Raids are not an invasion," Fisk said diffidently.

"An increase in raids is a prelude to one," Danai said. "They are firming their intelligence."

"How do you know this?"

"Because it's what I would do," she spat. She gestured with both hands toward the generals. "And what both of *you* would do, if you were the Republic and didn't fear retribution." She put her hands on the back of the chair in front of her.

"They are scouting us," she concluded. "We need to be ready."

"And you alone see this," Daoshen said. His voice was saccharine with challenge and contempt. "Not these generals here, not the Strategios, not the Maskirovka. Not any of the strategic planners at work across the Confederation. Just you."

Danai squeezed the chair back so hard her fingers hurt. "I see it," she replied. Daoshen smiled and opened his mouth, but she drove over him. "And these others see it, too, if they have the courage to look at the facts of the world around them and not just tell you whatever they think you want to know."

No one spoke.

Danai felt her pulse in her temples, in her palms, where her skin was slick against the soft leather of the chair.

Daoshen steepled his fingers in front of his face, regarding her, and said nothing.

"It is not enough to just see," *Sang-jiang-jun* Fisk said, finally. "One must also understand." She glanced at Danai, then shifted in her seat to look at the Chancellor.

"The *sang-shao* is correct about the raids, Chancellor," she said. "They are intelligence operations. The Republic is coming."

Danai blinked. She couldn't believe—

"But," Fisk said, turning back to Danai. "There is little reason to believe the *sang-shao*'s claim of *now.*" She leaned back in her seat. "RAF intelligence raids have been going on for years. Longer, if we attribute some small mercenary actions to their sponsorship."

"They cannot do that forever," Danai put in.

"They have done it this long," Fisk said. She tilted her head. "Still..." she turned back to the Chancellor. "Celestial Wisdom, there may be an opportunity here."

Daoshen didn't look away from Danai. His gaze was like a target-lock. "Go on."

"Détente with Julian Davion would allow us to marshal our forces. We could stage into the Liao Commonality, and better prepare our logistical push for our eventual invasion when the Wall comes down."

Tianzhu Liu rumbled assent. "And if we need to attack into Davion space, we can do so via Tikonov." He shifted in his seat, turning slightly toward the Chancellor as well. "The Kuritas have already weakened the Davion border there. And if our other plans there—" he stopped, glancing at Danai.

Danai knew better than to react, but she wondered. *What other plans?* It was inconceivable that a man such as Tianzhu Liu, who moved at the very center of the halls of Capellan power, would allow anything to slip without meaning to. But then why the charade?

What was he trying to tell her?

"Enough," Daoshen said. "Leave us."

Fisk and Liu stood immediately. Each bowed to the Chancellor and then stepped back to depart. Liu came near Danai as he left, and his eyes met hers, but they revealed nothing.

When the guards outside in the corridors shut the heavy doors again, Danai exhaled.

"You had no right," Daoshen said.

"I was there," Danai said again.

"Your cousin—"

"Was an idiot, apparently, and is dead," Danai said firmly. She had already made her mind up about this aspect of the situation. "You cannot allow her ghost to lead you by the hand."

Daoshen's jaw clenched. "No one leads us by the hand," he said. "But reality is reality." He stood abruptly, robes swirling, dipping his hands to scoop his long sleeves over his forearms. The long nails on his small fingers flickered in the light.

"The footage of Ki-linn is everywhere," he said flatly.

Danai nodded. She knew CBS and even the Maskirovka would be ruthlessly suppressing the footage wherever they could find it, but the untold billions of servitors had their own networks. Evidence of that was clear in the displays at Ki-linn's death site; even as one servitor cleared away the signs, others replaced it.

"What is CBS saying?"

"That they have it under control," Daoshen said. He stepped down off the dais and began shuffling toward her. He wasn't old or slow, but he didn't move quickly. He almost seemed as if his mind were somewhere else.

"Do they?"

"Of course not," her father replied.

For a moment Danai wished they were somewhere else, somewhen else, talking about anything else. She had grown up without a father, believing her grandfather was her father, while her actual parent ignored her.

For a moment, she wished she'd known her real father as a child.

But that moment passed, and her iron control clamped back down. Indulging in those fantasies opened doors she'd held locked and closed for years.

"I made the correct decision on New Syrtis," she said. "Davion is a broken man. I hurt him badly. He will leave us alone while he battles the Dragon." She crossed her arms across her chest. "You know the Republic is coming."

"The Republic has been coming almost every day of my life," Daoshen admitted. "But you are missing the larger picture."

"What picture?"

Daoshen reached her. He stood there a moment, not speaking, just regarding her. His eyes held hers, as if it were a contest of wills.

Danai refused to back down. He may have been the Chancellor, may have been her father, but the wounds he'd inflicted on her were far too deep for her to allow him to see them.

No matter how intense the pain.

"You think of the realm," he told her. "Which is proper for a Liao and one of my line." Danai repressed the shudder of revulsion she felt. "But you lack insight into what makes the realm what it is."

"The Confederation is its people," she said. It was the primary school answer, but she knew it was what was expected.

"Exactly," Daoshen said. "But you know nothing of those people."

"Nothing," Danai repeated. "Are you saying I'm not Capellan enough?"

Daoshen smiled. Gone now was the malice of their earlier conversation. "Not at all. I'm saying you're too Danai."

His right arm made a movement, barely more than a twitch, but Danai saw it. She flinched back, out of his reach, before she could think of stopping herself.

The smile faltered, but didn't go away.

"It may have been a mistake sending you to Erde," Daoshen admitted. "You didn't learn about our people while being one of them. You learned about them from afar, from tutors."

"I learned everything I needed," Danai said. She bit back the anger Daoshen's claim made burn inside her. Her great-aunt Erde Centrella had raised her during her childhood, yes. She'd learned more from Erde than she had from anyone else—certainly more than she had from her *parents*.

Daoshen turned away from her.

"What don't I know?" she demanded.

"The people," was all Daoshen said.

CHAPTER 6

Tom Jordan made sure he was first to the hatch after the shaking subsided. The DropShip's landing had felt like a mountain falling down on them, but they always felt that way. He'd slapped his restraints clear and climbed to his feet even while the other battalion officers in the wardroom were exchanging grins and making jokes about rough landings.

He wanted to be there when the hatch opened.

Not for himself. He'd been off-world before.

But many of the Principes officers in Second Battalion had never been off Elgin.

He wanted to see their reaction to Hall.

As he came around the last bulkhead into the 'Mech bay, he met Joe Turner coming from the other direction. Turner looked a little worse for wear; the trip to Hall had been his first venture off Elgin. A lot of the Second Battalion troopers had the same look: a little caged-in and pale, even though it had only been a couple of weeks since they'd left Sochalladan.

"Jordan," Turner said.

Tom grinned. "Joe. How you holding up?"

"They're going to open the door now, right?"

"It's a hatch," Jordan said, ribbing the other officer, "but yes, any minute."

"Good. I need a breath of fresh air."

Tom gestured Turner to precede him through the 'Mech bay hatch and then followed. He turned and dogged the corridor hatch closed behind him. It was habit. Someone would almost certainly come along in a few minutes or even seconds and open it up again, but Tom didn't care.

He didn't do the things he did because other people might undo them.

"I don't know how you do this more than once," Turner muttered as Tom took a couple long steps to catch up.

"It's not so bad," Tom countered. "You get used to it. I only really notice it at turnover anymore." He carefully didn't look at his fellow captain. Turner was one of the many landsmen in the Guards who'd not taken well to zero-G.

"I notice it then, too," Turner said flatly.

A crowd had already gathered in front of the massive door across the 'Mech bay. Most of them wore Fourteenth Principes battledress with technical branch shoulder flashes—they were the support staff who kept the 'Mechs and tanks running—but there was a mix of infantrymen, ship's crew and even a couple of MechWarriors from Captain Prideaux's D Company. All of them were clustered near the door, looking up at it or joking with each other.

"What's the holdup?" Turner asked.

"Heat," Tom told him.

"Heat. Like in a 'Mech?"

Tom laughed. "No, the ground."

"The ground?"

"We just landed a rocket ship, Joe," Tom said. "Huge plasma motors. The ferrocrete beneath us is still radiating heat, I guarantee it. It'll take a bit for it to cool enough for us to open the hatch and not fry ourselves."

"Huh." Turned looked side eye at him, then shrugged. "If you say so."

"Patience," Tom said.

He took Turner's moment of distraction to look around again. The mood in the 'Mech bay was relaxed. The RAF servicemen and women were mixing without regard for rank, and there was little of the tension he'd expected. It looked as though the colonel's speech had worked.

The lift-off from Elgin had been a whirlwind. Barely an hour after Major Crowe had read them the colonel's note, the man himself had appeared to address the entire battalion. He'd told them they were being sent to defend another Republic world—Hall—and that it was just as important as defending their home.

"It's home to people just like you and me," Boyle had declared. "And those people need protecting." He'd looked across the assembled Principes, shook his head, and spoke again. "Those people *deserve* protecting," he'd said. And that had sealed it.

The Fourteenth Principes Guards was largely the cult of Owen Boyle. He said go, so they went.

All of the Second 'Mech Battalion, along with a regiment each of armor and infantry from the Fourteenth's support echelons, went. DropShips had appeared, the units had marched aboard, and the DropShips had lifted off. It was less than two weeks to arrive: ten days or so getting from Elgin to the jump point, the instantaneous jump to Hall's nadir jump point, and about three days' in-system flight.

A horn sounded, echoing loudly in the bay. Yellow warning lights began to flash along the edges of the hatch. It was a big hatch; it had to be to allow twelve-meter-tall BattleMechs to exit during combat.

"Here we go," Turner said.

Tom just grinned.

The hatch seals released with a burst of dust and burnt-oil smell. The massive hatch began grinding upward. A rumble beneath his feet told Tom the hugely-reinforced ramp was scrolling out from beneath them as well.

The level of anticipatory noise rose to a crescendo.

Tom braced himself.

The inrushing wash of hot air, almost superheated, pushed everyone back a step. The sounds of anticipation switched quickly to betrayal.

"Stone's balls, that's hot," Turner muttered. He tugged at the collar of his battledress.

Tom grinned harder.

"Is that from the motors?" Turner asked. He tried to edge forward, but the crowd was huddled like a wall, blocking the way.

"Only a little."

"A little?" Turner worked his mouth, trying to wet his lips. "It's so dry!"

"Hall is mostly desert," Tom replied. "Mostly sand, no trees, no water..."

"Yeah..." Turner said as he turned toward him. "Oh wait. No humidity, right?"

Tom just shook his head. "Only what we sweat out."

Turned swallowed. With difficulty.

"You were the one who was laughing about it back on Elgin," Tom reminded him.

"I knew it, but I didn't *know* it, you know?"

Tom slapped him on the shoulder, then pulled him forward. "I know. Now let's get out front, shall we? We're supposed to be leaders."

Joe Turner followed him. "You think the major is coming down?"

"Don't know."

"Maybe he'll bring water," Turner grumbled.

Tom just chuckled and kept moving forward.

Harney's spaceport makes Sochalladan's look like a backwater.

That was Tom's first thought as he stood in formation with the rest of the battalion, arrayed on the clear ground around the DropShip pit. Republic battledress made provision for an integral backpack water supply, accessible through a drinking tube over the left shoulder. Tom stood with his tube in the corner of his mouth, an old habit from his desert acclimatization in the Sahara back on Terra.

Hall was a planet of 2.5 billion people, give or take a few hundred million, as the last census had been a while ago. It showed in the size and majesty of the capital's spaceport, which sprawled across almost fifty square kilometers. While Elgin could claim the same lifetime in centuries, the distributed nature of island life kept the population of Elgin smaller. People mostly came to visit Elgin, not to stay, across the centuries.

Tom Jordan loved his homeworld. But Hall was something else, at least the parts of it he could see.

"Battalion, atten-SHUN!" came the shout from Master Sergeant Kira Wu. Tom and the rest of the Guards snapped to attention. The drinking tube fell to lay on his shoulder as Major Crowe and his staff strode out in front of the assembly. They all wore the same desert-pattern camouflage battledress as the rest of the battalion. A clutch of armor and infantry officers followed at a short distance.

"It's hot as hell here!" Crowe yelled. "Stand easy." There were a few chuckles. Tom allowed himself a grin as he relaxed to parade rest. For all his small size and annoying voice, Crowe was a good leader. He cared about his troops and he did all the things they'd taught Tom an officer should do.

"Welcome to Hall," he continued. "Now, first order: everyone drink!"

More chuckles, but they were overridden by the rustling noise of a few hundred soldiers adjusting their drinking tubes.

"I am not joking about this," Crowe went on. "If you don't have to piss, you should be drinking. None of us are used to this heat, or the lack of humidity. The first one of you who passes out from heatstroke because you were too dumb to drink your water gets busted a rank, and I am not kidding."

He paused, adjusted his own drinking tube, and took a sip.

"First order?" Crowe shouted.

"Drink!" the whole battalion shouted back.

"Very good." He stalked down the line, past the captains standing at the heads of their companies. Captain Magnusson and the rest of his staff followed along. Tom, still at rest but with a drink tube in his mouth, ignored them.

"I'm not going to make a lot of speeches. The colonel already told us all we need to know." Crowe paused and— for dramatic effect, Tom was sure—pulled his own drinking tube up and sipped. "We are here to do a job. I don't know for how long."

Tom listened, but he didn't hear any grumbles about that. It was all still too new, he figured.

Soldiers knew they could be deployed, across a continent or a star empire. It was part of the job. That didn't make it any easier to bear or any more fair, but they were all volunteers. They'd known—or should have known—what they were getting into.

"The people on this planet are just as much Republic citizens as you and me," Crowe went on. "We're now their main line of defense." He stalked back to the center of the line of troops, just in front of Captain Turner's E Company.

"Colonel Boyle assured me before we left that relief would follow as soon as he could arrange it." Crowe grinned conspiratorially. "Between you and me, that probably means those slackers in First Batt." Laugher rippled through the ranks. The rivalry between the First and Second BattleMech battalions was good-natured for all its ferocity.

"But that's the future," Crowe said. "For now, let's all get under cover, and your officers will bring the news. Orders will go out tonight or sooner." He paused. "What's the first order?"

"Drink!" The battalion chorus was strong. Tom joined in without hesitation.

"We're going to do the colonel proud," Crowe declared. Then he turned and stalked off, drawing the staff and other officers with him.

"Battalion!" Master Sergeant Wu screamed. "Atten-HUT!" Thirty-six pairs of bootheels snapped together. "Dis-MISSED!"

No one ran for the hangars. The movement was orderly.

But everyone was drinking.

The battalion staff had already set up a temporary tactical operations center in a nearby hangar. Tom followed Captains Prideaux and Turner into the cavernous building, drinking tube still trailing from his mouth. The air inside the building was still and stifling; the space was far too large for the expense of an air conditioner.

They found Major Crowe and the battalion staff, along with the supporting regimental staff, standing around a portable holotank. It was a lot of faces to take in, but Tom had met most of them in the officer's clubs back on Elgin.

"Here's the plan," Crowe said with no preamble. "We're splitting up."

"Okay," Joe Turner breathed.

Tom agreed. That tactic had led to defeat in detail for thousands of years. Concentration of force had been a principle of warfare since the weapons were swords and spears.

"I know what you're thinking," Crowe said with a knowing grin. "But it's our best shot. We can expect any Capellan aggressor to arrive in overwhelming strength. Our job isn't going to be to stand on the line and throw them back." He paused. "We're not Hastati, after all."

If the major had been trying for levity, it didn't work. Tom wiped sweat from his forehead and glanced around the room.

"We're going to break into three combat commands," Crowe went on. "One company of 'Mechs, with a battalion each from our brothers and sisters." He gestured to the armor and infantry officers. "Captain Magnusson has prepared your plans. They're on the server."

"Major?" Captain Prideaux raised her hand.

"Captain?"

"Who do we expect to fight?"

Crowe looked to Lieutenant Salinger, his staff intelligence officer. She was a young woman, barely halfway through her twenties, but Tom knew she was good. She was only a middling MechWarrior, but she plowed through intel reports like a tank.

"The Louies are marshaling on Liao," Salinger told the room. "We have indications of at least eight regiments of 'Mechs, with their attendant supports." She paused. "Xavier McCarron himself is on Liao right now."

Tom felt his eyebrows raise involuntarily. Xavier McCarron was the grand old man of the CCAF, the commander of the five-regiment brigade called McCarron's Armored Cavalry. Formerly mercenaries, the MAC, as it was called, had "gone legit" a century earlier and entered regular Capellan service. Despite a century of Capellan effort, many of the MAC's traditions and tactics remained, largely because of Xavier

McCarron. If he was there, the Louies—slang for Liaos— were serious.

"So, the MAC," Prideaux said.

Salinger nodded. "That's a good guess, ma'am."

"Any other surprises?"

Salinger looked to Major Crowe, who nodded. "Unknown, Captain. RAF has stopped the intel-gathering raids for the next little while."

Tom shared a glance with Captain Turner.

The Fortress Wall kept anyone from jumping into the Republic, but it also could be more of a door—if you had the right key. Intelligence raids, small military and clandestine forces, had been scouring the nearby worlds for information for the better part of a decade. Most of them were unnoticed, posing as traders and tourists from around the Inner Sphere. A few were discovered and destroyed, but that was the price of doing business.

Those raiders were the Republic's only eyes and ears outside the wall. If they'd been stood down...then the information by which RAF High Command made its decisions only got more and more stale with each passing day.

"Is this it, then?" Captain Prideaux asked. She was looking at Major Crowe. "Is the Wall coming down?"

Tom stared at Major Crowe, along with everyone else in the building. Everyone knew the Wall wouldn't stay up forever. It was what they had trained for, to go back out and recover the Republic. Hell, their presence on Hall as a for-real garrison force made it feel pretty damn likely. No one, Louie or anyone else, could get through the Wall, so why did they need to be here, unless the Wall was on its way down?

Major Crowe looked around the room, meeting as many pairs of eyes as he could.

"I have received no word," he said, carefully and clearly. But then he spread his arms.

"But we're here."

CHAPTER 7

Danai had no idea what to expect when the Capellan noblewoman was ushered into the sitting room of her small suite of rooms in the palace. She'd merely accepted the appointment out of boredom. She'd heard nothing from her father for two weeks, and her repeated requests to see him had been ignored.

She'd tried everything. She'd stood outside the throne room, near Red Lancer infantrymen who wouldn't let her in. Despite their exquisite courtesy, despite her status as a Liao of the ruling line, they wouldn't budge. Danai had tried messages, and she'd tried messengers. She'd even met twice with Tianzhu Liu.

None of it had worked. Daoshen had sent no word.

And today, this.

The woman who entered was an exemplar of the directorship caste. She was lithe without being tall, dressed in robes that were edged in crimson and gold, the colors of court. Her eyes had the almond shape so prized by the Capellan high caste, and her black hair was straight and shone with a high sheen.

Danai tried not to roll her eyes as she stood to greet her guest.

"Your Grace," the woman said, "I am Wilhelmina Liao."

Danai stopped, still a pace away, her hand half-raised to offer. "Your family..." she let her question trail off.

"My grandfather was Duke Hurtong Liao of Capella," the noblewoman replied.

"Oh," Danai said. Then "*oh*," as she understood.

In her grandfather's time, Hurtong Liao had been chairman of the Capella Commonality Bank and duke of Capella. Capella was, obviously, one of the most ancient and revered worlds in the Confederation. Hurtong's branch of the Liao family was a cadet branch from the ruling line, but they had almost never failed to produce Liaos wholly dedicated to the Capellan state. Hurtong had been instrumental in the reforms Danai's grandfather, Sun-Tzu Liao, had put in place. Those reforms had caused *xin sheng*, the rebirth of the Capellan state after the horrible drubbing it had suffered in Hanse Davion's Fourth Succession War.

Almost never... Danai stepped closer and finished raising her hand. "Your father—"

"My father is dead," Wilhelmina said simply. "He was Jun Liao." She took Danai's offered hand.

"Ah," Danai said. Jun Liao had been famous in the early 3130s, just as the HPGs were going dark. He had used his family name to defraud local branches of the Capella Commonality Bank of billions of *yuan*. He had traveled, world by world, to branch locations and demanded cash for the central commonality reserves. Almost no one had challenged him; his father was Hurtong Liao. By the time his crimes had caught up with him, he had almost set a record for consecutive months of debauchery on his personal DropShip.

Daoshen had made watching his execution a mandatory act for every Capellan citizen, so that they might know that not even the Liao family was exempt from putting the state before themselves.

Are you the lesson, I wonder? Danai thought as she shook Wilhelmina's hand. The other woman had a dry grip, firm without trying for power. It was the grip of woman comfortable with who and what she was. Danai hoped her own grip was like that.

"Yes," the other woman responded. "Him."

"Please, sit," Danai said, indicating a chair. "Tell me how I can help you."

When the two women were settled, a servitor scurried in to pour tea. Danai waited, then smiled at the small man. "Thank you, Lao-ting."

"Of course," the servitor said. He was a punctilious man, proud of his role and his place in Capellan society. He was deferential, as a servitor should be to two members of the directorship, but within his caste he was proud. He worked in the Forbidden City. In *Zi-jing Cheng* itself. Lao-ting bowed and withdrew.

"You are very polite," Wilhelmina observed. "To me, of course, but also to your staff."

"A servitor is no less a man," Danai replied. "He deserves no less than every courtesy." She hadn't grown up in the caste system, but she'd come to understand its function. She'd grown up in the Canopian court in Crimson. There, anyone who was rude to a servant got no service and was shunned at the court. Canopus, like every realm of the Inner Sphere, was a place of class structure, but it was not an unequal structure. Or at least uncourteous.

"I meant no offense, Your Grace."

"I took none," Danai said, frowning. "It is merely the truth."

"So it is."

"And the 'your grace' is not necessary, my lady," Danai said. "I am no duchess. I am merely Danai." She made a little brushing-away gesture with her weak hand. The bone had set, and she was doing her therapies, but rebuilding muscle weakened both by disuse and zero gravity took time. "Or *sang-shao*, if you prefer titles."

"I prefer Mina," Mina Liao said. "But..." She reached into her robes and pulled a small folio out. "You *are* a duchess. Your brother has seen fit to enfeoff you duchess of Castrovia."

Danai blinked, taking the folio in one hand. Castrovia was a one-world demesne near Sian, traditionally the personal landhold of the heir to the Chancellory. Her grandfather had been duke of Castrovia, in addition to being grand duke of

Sian. Her father—her brother, as Mina knew him—was duke of Castrovia. The title had always passed from parent to child.

She opened the folio and saw the verigraph inside. It was the patent of nobility acclaiming her duchess of Castrovia, for herself and her heirs. Danai blinked, eyes unfocused, trying to process. This was not something she had ever wanted.

"I don't know how to be a duchess," Danai said. It was honest, despite being blurted out.

"That is why I am here," Mina replied. "To teach you."

"Explain."

"I am a graduate of Sian University," Mina continued. "I studied sociology and political theory for six years. I am one of the foremost experts in Capellan political theory." She shifted in her seat but didn't look away from Danai. "I clerked for the Prefectorate and served a term in the House of Scions until last year."

"So you're a politician," Danai said. The Prefectorate and the House of Scions were what passed for legislature in the Confederation. The Scions were the assembled body of the Capellan *Sheng* nobility—the landholders—while the Prefectorate was a *de facto* executive council advising the Chancellor.

In practice, a Chancellor like Daoshen Liao had essentially unlimited power and authority, but by law he or she was required to consult with the Prefectorate and the House of Scions on many matters. It was the Chancellor's unquestioned and unbreachable control of the military and many of the mechanisms of Capellan bureaucracy that made his or her power complete.

"I am a Capellan patriot," Mina Liao clarified, simply and honestly, "and I seek to understand the state to better help it reach its best possible form."

"I see," Danai said, but she didn't.

"Your Grace—"

"Please," Danai interrupted, "in private at least, Danai. I've been a *Sheng* for about forty seconds. That's not me." She frowned. It still didn't feel real.

"It *is* you," Mina countered, smiling faintly, "but I take your meaning. Danai, then." She sat back, hands folded primly in her lap.

Danai sat and regarded her distant cousin for several long moments while her mind raced, trying to take all this in at once. She put being a duchess out of her mind for the time being. What was most important was parsing exactly why Daoshen had sent this woman to her.

When last they spoke, Daoshen had accused her of not understanding the Capellan people. Of not being Capellan enough to be a true Liao, in not-so-many words. And today this woman—Mina—was here. With a title to a whole planet of Capellan citizens Danai was now responsible for.

So much for putting it out of her mind.

"I can't be duchess of a planet," Danai said. "I am a serving military officer. I am already responsible for people. And I'm almost always deployed to the front." She clenched and unclenched her fingers. The tension inside her warred with her court training. She was supposed to sit here as cool and collected as Mina seemed, but she wanted to be on her feet, pacing, squeezing her fists and touching the wall. She felt suddenly and completely unmoored.

"It helps to touch your robe," Mina said, almost too quietly to be heard.

"What?"

"When you feel uncertain. Feel the fabric of your robe. It is as real as the wall or the door or that urn in the corner you keep looking at."

Danai stared. "What?" she repeated.

"I can see your tension," Mina answered. "It radiates from you." She glanced around the room, quickly, and then nodded. "I used to do it, too, when I felt tense. I would need to touch something. Often something not near me, so I could move."

"Are you reading my mind?" Danai demanded.

"Of course not," Mina replied with another damnable small grin. "But I was not always the woman I am today."

Danai said nothing. Instead, she concentrated on the feeling of the silk between her fingertips. She concentrated on her breathing. In a moment she felt better. Not okay.

But better.

"You're a witch," she muttered.

"A teacher," Mina said. "If you'll let me."

"As if I could refuse my brother."

"You could," Mina said. She hadn't moved. Her face was still calm, her hands still folded in her lap. Danai expected more emotion when someone casually mentioned was amounted to treason, which was what ignoring one of Daoshen's edicts meant.

"If I sent you away—"

"You could not," Mina said, cutting her off. "Of course not. But you could not listen to my lessons." She waited, but Danai didn't speak. "Good," she said. Another small grin.

"You spoke of being a duchess," Mina continued. "Of not being able to because of your military duties."

"Yes."

"A fallacy."

"A what?"

"You are responsible for these soldiers?" When Danai nodded Mina continued. "Yet you are not with them. Who is responsible for them now?"

"Ultimately, me."

"Ultimately, yes. You are a Liao. But who is responsible for them right now, this instant, wherever they are?"

"Wu Feng," Danai said. "My executive officer."

"So, you are not with them, but they are protected, with someone who is responsible for them?"

Danai glared at her. "I hated these lessons as a child." She made a fist and released it, then rubbed her knuckles against her knee. "You're saying I need an XO on Castrovia."

"A castellan, they are traditionally called, yes." Mina smiled, but this time it was the indulgent smile of a headmistress whose recalcitrant student had at last just made progress. "But yes. A deputy, whom you trust, who can oversee your people and your needs while you serve the state." Now she spread her hands and bowed her head slightly. "As you unquestionably do through your military leadership."

"What if I gave *you* the job," Danai asked diffidently.

"I would refuse," Mina responded. "My place is here with you."

"Because my brother sent you."

"Because I asked him to, yes."

That rocked Danai back in her chair. Now she did stand up, quickly, and swirled around to lean forward over the back of her chair. "Explain."

"My family was consulted on your appointment. It had been expected to go to a cousin, but," and now Mina made the same brushing-off gesture Danai had made, "the Chancellor will do as he wills. But in the course of the conversation, I saw my chance and struck."

"To teach me to be more Capellan," Danai spat.

"To teach you about *being* Capellan," Mina corrected her. "There is no such thing as 'enough' Capellan. Or too little. There is only the extent that we each choose, as individuals, to devote ourselves to the state." Danai understood the words; they were an interpretation of the Korvin Doctrine, one of the foundational theories of the Capellan state. But...

"I don't understand."

Now Mina stood. "I know. That is what I will teach you." The imp's grin returned. "Your Grace."

Danai grinned back. "We're going to be great friends," she pronounced. "Or else murder each other."

"Why not both?" They both laughed.

Danai sensed the end of the conversation approaching. "Well," she said. "You must let me know your schedule. I don't know how long I'll be on Sian, but I'll free up as much time as I can while I'm on-world."

"I will travel with you," Mina said simply.

"It could be years," Danai said.

"It will be as it will be."

"And I don't know when I leave."

The imp's grin. "But I do."

Danai shook her head. "It's going to be murder."

Mina reached into her robe and pulled another small folio out. She handed it over without a word. Danai opened and scanned the message summary; the memory built into the folio would have her detailed orders. "We lift in three days," she murmured, still reading.

"To rejoin your regiment," Mina confirmed.

"Then Daoshen agrees," Danai breathed. "The Republic is the greater threat."

"He does."

"And the armistice with Davion will stand." The words flowed out of Danai as her brain caught up with itself. All her stress had been for nothing. She wanted to sit now, to sink to the floor in relief. Her mind had painted so many dire predictions.

Mina cleared her throat. When Danai looked up, the other woman looked down. "Not exactly. He will condemn Davion aggression in a CBS broadcast tomorrow. His rhetoric will keep public opinion against the Davions at its current high point. He will not mention the Republic."

Danai stepped around the chair and sat down. She raised the folio half-heartedly. "But this…" She trailed off. She finally looked up at Mina. "I don't understand."

"You can ask him," Mina said. She raised her eyes and met Danai's stare. "We have an audience with him tomorrow, just before his address." She frowned. "You are directed to appear in full dress uniform."

"Full dress…"

"You will stand with the Chancellor during his condemnation of Davion."

Danai's rage returned in a flash. "I will not."

"You will," Mina said. She stepped back from her chair. "I will return for you in the morning."

"There is nothing you can say that will make me support this," Danai said.

"We shall see."

And with that, she was gone.

CHAPTER 8

ZI-JING CHENG, **FORBIDDEN CITY**
SIAN
CAPELLAN CONFEDERATION
5 NOVEMBER 3148

When Mina Liao returned the next morning, she did not come alone. *Jiang-jun* Tianzhu Liu came with her. The Death Commando commander was resplendent in his Liao-green dress uniform. Like Danai, he was entitled to wear a *dao* sword on his hip, but he eschewed it. Liu relied on his skill for security, not weapons. He followed Mina Liao in, like a tank escorting a diplomat, and bowed when he saw Danai.

"Your Grace," he said. When he sat, the flight flickered off the edges of the carbon-reinforced fingernails on his hands. Maybe he did not eschew *all* weapons, then.

Danai looked at Mina. "It is public, then?"

"I told him," Mina answered.

"It was only a matter of time," Liu interjected. "Just as you couldn't stay a *sang-wei* forever, you couldn't stay out of the *Sheng*." He ducked his chin. "And if you'll permit me, I think you will make a fine duchess for Castrovia."

"Responsibility for a world is a little more daunting than responsibility for a company," Danai told him.

Liu shrugged. "Responsibility is responsibility. Scale only changes the stakes."

Danai regarded him for a moment longer, then shook her head and stepped aside so the three of them could sit. Once they were settled, she speared Mina with a glare. "Let's hear it."

"It?"

"Your case for my standing next to Daoshen when he abrogates the agreement I made with Julian Davion live and on HV."

Tianzhu Liu shifted in his seat. "The Chancellor—"

Danai held up a hand. "Your pardon, *Jiang-jun*, but Mistress Liao has told me she will convince me. I would like to give her that chance." She waited until Liu ducked his chin in acquiescence before looking to Mina.

"Thank you," Mina responded. She folded her hands in her lap, paused, and then met Danai's stare.

"Put most simply, because it is the right thing to do," she said. "You will not agree with me, at first. But once we apply logic and responsibility to the idea, you will understand."

"Go on," Danai said. She found the whole idea preposterous, but she had to admit, even if it was just to herself, that she was curious. She'd spent a lot of time the previous evening thinking about Mina Liao, and she'd done some research of her own.

Lady Wilhelmina Liao, third daughter of the late Duke Jun Liao, was indeed a graduate of Sian University. Her instructors had noted her as a brilliant student, especially as it came to interpreting Capellan doctrine into the modern world. Every Capellan child learned about the Korvin Doctrine and the Sarna Mandate. Most could quote the Lorix Order word for word.

Mina Liao had tried to *apply* them in her studies. What's more, according to the notes of her instructors, she had succeeded. In fact, her thesis had been a scathing attack of Chancellor Romano Liao's pogroms of the 3040s, contrasted against the gains her son Sun-Tzu had made with the opposite tactics in the 3060s. It took something to be willing to criticize the Liao family in the Confederation, even if the target that criticism was a century dead and you yourself were a Liao.

"You gave your word to Julian Davion that Capellan attacks into the Federated Suns would halt," Mina began.

"I did."

"And he agreed to halt further attacks into the Confederation, correct?"

"Correct."

Mina smiled her imp's smile. "Then it is all *maskirovka.*"

Danai knew from her intonation she meant the original root of the word, military deception, and not the Capellan intelligence agency of the same name. The concept was baked into Capellan military training, thanks to the early and centuries-old influence of Tikonov and its Russian-inspired history. "Explain."

Mina looked to Tianzhu Liu. "*Jiang-jun?*"

"The Chancellor will condemn the Davion aggression and call for the renewed support of the people against the Federated Suns. He will announce the Davion treachery that forced you and your forces off of New Syrtis."

"Treachery," Danai said.

"Peace with Davion is impossible," Liu said simply. "Ki-linn saw to that."

Ki-linn again. Danai scowled. "The recording has spread, then."

Liu nodded. "The servitors have it, of course, but reports from Harloc and New Westin tell us it has spread into the ranks of the commonality there." He frowned. "There will be no controlling it, now. I expect CBS will switch from suppression to propaganda very soon."

The castes that made up the Capellan Confederation got larger the farther away from real power they were. The servitors were the largest, with untold billions of unskilled or semi-skilled laborers overpowering the relative handful, proportionally, of long-service servants like Lao-ting. The next-highest caste, the commonality, were the laborers who kept the industrial and agricultural engine of the Confederation running. They were just as numerous and, in many places, as organized and powerful as a small nation-state in their own right.

"So my word is nothing," Danai said after a moment.

"There will be no peace," Liu said. "But there will also be no war."

"I don't understand."

"The Chancellor cannot let up the pressure on Davion in the media," Mina said. "It would weaken his position with the people."

"The people," Danai countered, "will believe what CBS tells them to believe. What we—you, actually, in the directorship—tell them to believe." She shook her head. "That's what the Sarna Mandate is all about, isn't it?"

The Sarna Mandate was one of the bedrock theorems of the Capellan caste system. Paraphrased, it said that the elite of any realm—in the Confederation, the directorship, the entitled, the intelligentsia, the *janshi*—were the only people capable of realizing, challenging and solving the problems of a nation-state. The lesser—the servitors, the commonality—were too involved in the day-to-day mundanity of their common lives to recognize the necessary steps. According to the Mandate, the Capellan leadership were the only ones who could lead, because the mass of the commonality and the servitors lacked the education and power.

And it was true, especially after centuries of Liao rule erasing any social structure that would enable those castes to amass that power.

"Somewhat," Mina allowed. "But you're oversimplifying."

"I'm what?"

"You're oversimplifying. Yes, the people will listen to us, but only so long as what we say matches the reality they see." Mina glanced at Tianzhu Liu before she spoke. "No Capellan, be they servitor or Chancellor, is a drone to be ordered without regard for their own wants. The people will believe that we continue to hate Davion, because we do. The people will believe we continue to prosecute the war against Davion, because they expect us to. There are literally centuries of enmity between our two realms. The people—in this case, the commonality and the servitors—*do* hate Davion. There are still those few ancients who remember the 3057 war, and still wonder why we stopped. We must treat the people with respect."

"We have mutual ancestors who would disagree with you," Danai said. She was thinking of her great-grandmother Romano Liao, whom Mina had studied, widely regarded as one of the most psychopathic chancellors the Confederation had ever suffered. Her "reforms" had saved the Confederation, but only by all but destroying the citizenry and nearly polluting their opinion of the ruling Liao family beyond repair. If her son had been anyone else than Sun-Tzu Liao...but he had been the one to oversee the alliance with Marik, and the offensive in 3057 that recaptured many of the Capellan worlds lost in the Fourth Succession War, while the Federated Commonwealth was distracted by the Clan threat.

"Then consider the military implications," *Jiang-jun* Liu put in. "We cannot just *have peace* with the Davions." He clenched his jaw and sat forward, as if daring her to contradict him.

Danai leaned forward, too. She had never been one to back down from a fight.

"We can have peace if we're fighting the Republic," she insisted. "We can have peace when there is a Clan eating its way through the Free Worlds League. We can have peace—"

"We cannot," Mina interrupted. Her voice, for all its softness, carried a firm tone of finality.

"I gave Julian Davion my word!"

"Then that was foolish," Mina said simply. "The needs of the state are larger than your word of honor."

Danai stared at her, bristling, but she said nothing else. Liu, next to her, looked uncomfortable, but also said nothing. Finally, he cleared his throat.

"Your word will be good to Davion," he stated. "I understand a *janshi*'s word." He looked at Mina. "I even understand a Liao's word, whether I agree or not."

"Explain." Danai struggled to keep her temper under control.

"The Chancellor will condemn Davion," Mina said. "He will use their betrayal of your agreement as a pretext to keep the people inflamed. He will promise the Capellan Confederation Armed Forces will do all in their power to keep the people safe from Davion aggression."

"Breaking my word," Danai interjected.

"I ask you, *Sang-shao*," Mina said. Danai frowned at the title. "With the Republic pressing our borders and the Clans so near, how many resources can the military devote to punishing House Davion?"

"None," Danai replied flatly. She looked at Liu, baiting him to contradict her.

Instead, he met her stare. "I agree."

"Then that is what the Chancellor will send," Mina said.

"I don't—" Danai stopped. She looked at Liu. "*Maskirovka*," she whispered.

Liu only grinned his tiger's grin at her.

Danai rose to pace. She didn't care if Liu and Mina watched her. Her mind was too engrossed in parsing out the plan. She understood it, of course. It was so simple, so *Daoshen*, that she should have grasped it immediately. In the Confederation, reality was what the Chancellor said it was. So, if he said they would continue the war against Davion, the people would believe it. They would believe periodic "updates" about intelligence raids and the like. CBS would deliver whatever propaganda necessary to support the position.

But Davion would not attack if the Confederation didn't attack him.

And Davion would not attack. He couldn't, not with the prince's attention firmly on House Kurita. If there was another sinew the realm of House Davion could strain, it would be spent against the Dragon.

Her word would still be good. Technically.

Technically. She rolled the word around in her mouth like a tart fruit. To the public, she would be a liar. To the unthinking, she would be a liar. To the people of the Federated Suns, when these broadcasts reached them, she would be a liar.

Danai sighed. She sat back down. Her fingers rubbed fiercely at the fabric of her dress uniform trousers.

"I had hoped that by a certain point I'd get beyond this kind of thing," she told Liu and Mina. "Beyond having to keep track of what lie I was living." She stopped rubbing her pants and tried to fold her hands, emulating Mina. "I did that on Solaris. I did that for years here." She chewed the inside of her cheek. "I'd hoped, by now, as a colonel of the CCAF, I'd just get to be Danai."

"You should have had better tutors," Mina said. "At this level of politics, everything is the lie."

Danai thought back to her time in Crimson, the capital city of the Magistracy of Canopus, the realm her *sister*—her mother—ruled. Politics in the Magistracy court was just as Byzantine as any other aristocratic institution, but she hadn't found there the same presumptive dependence on the Big Lie that she had inside the Confederation. Her aunt, Erde Centrella, Ilsa Centrella-Liao's regent there, had raised her as if she were her own child.

"I had the best tutors," Danai said softly.

"Life is a lesson every day," Tianzhu Liu said. It was a proverb Danai had heard a thousand times, and even agreed with, but there was quiet sincerity in the Death Commando general's tone.

Danai exhaled. "Do I have lines in this farce?"

Mina smiled her imp's grin. "Of course," she said. She pulled another damnable folio out of her sleeve. "I brought them so we could practice."

Afterward, Danai stepped alongside Mina Liao for the procession to end the Chancellor's address. She leaned close enough to whisper. "How'd I do?"

"Very well," Mina replied. "You appeared to the casual observer as if you believed it."

Danai grunted.

"I'm curious as to which of your tutors in the Canopian court taught you that?" Mina asked. "To fall so deeply into a role?"

"That wasn't Erde," Danai told her. "That was Solaris."

"Ah."

Walking away from the Chancellor's address, Danai felt conflicting emotions. She felt anxious, knowing her departure date was so close. In a few short months she'd be back in the bosom of her regiment, getting ready to face down the Republic when the Wall finally collapsed. She felt none of the uncertainty there that she felt here. Here she felt anything but certain, even with Mina by her side.

She glanced at Mina, stepping silently along with her. *What does she get out of this?* Danai wondered. Danai had lived with Daoshen's caprices her entire life. Nothing her father ever did really surprised her, not anymore. Trying to discern Daoshen's mind was like trying to discern a tornado's intent. You thought you could see where the path of destruction was headed, but then for no other reason than whim, the tornado would leap off on a tangent.

The procession came to a halt, as these things always did, bunched up as they tried to get through the wide doors. Danai took the opportunity to look around. She was looking for a sense of the room, now that they were all out from under Daoshen's eye. The people around her were the movers and shakers of the Capellan capital; it was their mood that would get transmitted or carried back to their own wards and demesnes.

They appeared in good spirits, she was amazed to see. Daoshen had just spent most of thirty minutes railing about the horrors of war against Davion, calling on all Capellan citizens for renewed sacrifices for the war effort, warning them against the casualties that could come from Federated Suns aggression. They should be scared, or at least worried.

"Do they know?" She whispered to Mina. "That it's a lie?"

"Perhaps," Mina said, after taking her own surreptitious look around.

"Why are they happy?"

"Because this is what they wanted."

"War against the Federated Suns?"

Mina chuckled. "Only as a side effect."

"A side effect of what?"

"A continuation of the familiar," Mina said. "All of these people—all the leaders along the Suns border, for centuries—have built their entire power bases around that conflict. The Davion bogeyman is the fear they use to keep the commonality and the servitors in line. It is the yardstick against which the directorship measure requests from the entitled or intelligentsia." She made a small gesture with her hand, so small that no one except Danai would have recognized it. "I have already begun working on your first address to the people of Castrovia, warning them against Andurien predations while your military duties occupy you."

Danai stopped. "My what?"

"Every hero needs a monster to battle," Mina replied. Then she smiled that imp's grin and slipped away into the crowd, which had begun to open up as pressure eased through the doorway. Danai followed, but her mind was elsewhere.

The Duchy of Andurien nestled along the opposite Capellan border as the Federated Suns. It was a component state of the Free Worlds League, ruled by Ari Humphreys and his wife, Ilsa Centrella-Liao, Danai's mother. Conflict between the two had been endemic for all the centuries of the Succession Wars, but quiet for the last several decades. It was ludicrous to any serious strategist that the Anduriens would attack into the Confederation.

Never mind that the warden-general of the Free Worlds League, who controlled its vast military, was Danai's good friend Nikol Marik.

Danai moved to catch up with Mina. She caught her at the doorway, as they queued to go through. "Andurien?"

Mina nodded. "Not as overt as the Davions, perhaps, but a bogeyman nonetheless. Something for your people to assign their fears to, to help them focus on their tasks."

Danai shook her head. She was Capellan enough—Liao enough—to know the power of fear, but she was soldier enough to know the power of pride. Her regiment didn't fight because they were afraid of her. They fought not to let her down.

Danai had no interest in making those she was responsible for feel more afraid.

Life was challenge enough.

CHAPTER 9

FRANCO LIAO WILDERNESS PRESERVE
SIAN
CAPELLAN CONFEDERATION
5 NOVEMBER 3148

For most of the hourlong VTOL flight Danai ignored Mina Liao. Instead, she let her eyes stare blankly out the clear window while her mind turned over the prior day's events. She had slept little the night before. Her mind had kept working, turning over Byzantine machination after Byzantine machination, trying to understand.

On the face of it, it was simple: the lie would preserve the status quo. And the Confederation would prepare to face the Republic. That much of her goal was served.

But the rest...rankled.

Danai Centrella-Liao was not a woman accustomed to things rankling. "We really don't have time for this," she muttered, still looking out the window.

"You fear the DropShip will depart without you?" Mina's voice was even, a touch loud to be heard over the ever-present pounding of the rotors that no practical amount of insulation could fully keep out.

Danai gave Mina her best glare. It flowed off the noblewoman like sand through an hourglass. "Where are we going?"

"I believe we are here..." Mina leaned over, looking past Danai at the landscape that had only been a blur to her unfocused eyes.

They had flown south of the Forbidden City for several hours, into the wilderness of the Franco Liao State Forest Preserve. Danai looked where Mina was looking, and saw a broad floodplain filled with water, but the water stopped at the kilometers-long gray-and-red line of a hydroelectric dam. She frowned as she recognized it.

"The Great Dam?"

"Yes."

"I've seen it."

"In person?"

Danai shook her head. "In HV, any number of times. It was a hero project before the Blackout."

Mina nodded, as she might to an attentive student. "And have you ever visited in person?"

"No..." Danai looked away from the sprawling structure and back at Mina. "Is that why we're here? For a tour?"

Mina only offered a Gallic shrug.

A few minutes later, the VTOL landed at the marked helipad near the cavernous building at the center of the dam. It was mounted on pylons sunk into the wide lake before the dam. A small walkway connected it to the dam headquarters. The mountain of ferrocrete towered above the landscape. It reminded Danai of a squat fortress nestled against the forest, fighting to hold back nature itself.

It was a welcome change to be on solid ground, away from the ever-present buzzing vibration of the VTOL. Danai drew in several deep breaths, finding the cool, wet air beneath the hot tang of exhaust. When Mina stepped out to join her, she smiled.

"I like the cool air," Danai said. She started walking toward the thick hatch across the field, but Mina made no move to follow. "You coming?"

Mina shook her head. "It is important to see the whole picture."

Danai looked one way, then the other. The gray and red line of the dam extended as far as the eye could see in both directions. "I think I'm seeing it."

"Look again."

Danai walked back to stand next to Mina. The other woman ignored the landscape, instead watching her. "We arrived comfortably," Mina said, gesturing toward the VTOL. "In a few short hours." She grinned. "And because of our name, the hordes of servitors and the commonality inside will treat us with every courtesy while we are here."

"Fawningly, yes," Danai said guardedly.

"Did people like us build this dam?"

"Of course not."

"How did those people arrive?" She gestured again. "By air, do you think?"

Danai snorted. "Any way they could, I'd bet," she said. "I recall some of the stories. One of the reasons it was a hero project was because of the huge unemployment at the time." A hero project was a massive endeavor enacted for the good of the state, employing thousands or even millions of people.

"So with somewhat less privilege," Mina said.

"I'd think," Dana said.

"Stand here," Mina said. She stepped around Danai so she blocked the view of the dam entrance. "Imagine you were here forty years ago."

"I was barely born forty years ago."

"Today it is water," Mina continued. "What was it then?"

Danai frowned, thinking. "Swamp? I think I remember that was one of the reasons it was built? The water table was high and widespread already?"

"So these servitors," Mina said. "They came however they could. To a swamp." She stepped aside. "And they built this."

Danai looked past her. Then at Mina.

"I don't get it. Of course they did. It's right there."

Mina clucked her tongue, spun, and began striding toward the entrance. She didn't look back to see if Danai followed.

Rolling her eyes, Danai followed.

The small group was quiet as they stood in the small lift cage. Danai stood near the back wall because all the dam staff had insisted she precede them into the lift. Mina Liao stood next to her.

The reception had been all she expected, fawning over a visit by the blood royal. But it had been short. Mina must have called ahead, because Lady Bethany Fong, the dam's director, had clapped her hands, introduced a pair of grizzled commonality members, and excused herself.

"These two have lived a life with this dam, your Grace," Fong had said. "They will show you all you have come to see."

Danai still didn't know what she had come to see.

The lift rattled to a stop, but the doors didn't open. The small, wizened old man in a clean but worn foreman's outfit held his thumb on the door-closed control, waiting. His companion, a plump, matronly woman named Wen Liaoning, held a set of blocky ear protection up.

"Your pardon, your Grace," she said to Danai, "but the noise on the generator floor is quite loud. We must protect your hearing." She held a second pair up to Mina, who took them and placed them over her ears without a word.

Danai did likewise, and then waited until the others had pulled similar headgear out and put it on. The man, Peng Dai, grinned, ducked his chin, and released the button. Two of his upper teeth were missing.

The wall of sound that hit them when the doors opened lacked the crash and instantaneousness of 'Mech combat, but it surrendered not a decibel in raw power. Danai followed the others out of the car onto a small platform set above the main floor, her eyes wide.

The room they entered was massive, perhaps the largest enclosed space Danai had ever been inside in her life. Massive turbine generators sprawled across the floor, in quadrants coded by color. Men and women moved like ants among them.

"We generate the household electricity for much of the hemisphere," Peng said. He stood at the railing, hands above but not touching the rail, and even with the noise Danai heard the pride in his voice.

"How many people are employed here?" Mina asked.

"It depends on the season," replied Wen. "After the rainy season, when the water is highest and the damage worst, perhaps as many as 70,000." She shrugged. "About a third of that permanently." She glanced at Peng. "We are lucky," she said. Then her eyes widened. "Your Grace," she added.

Danai smiled, to show she didn't mind. She stepped to the railing beside Peng, looking. The sense of awe was unmistakable. You could fit a Solaris arena inside this structure, and she was only seeing part of it.

Mina stepped beside her. "Do not try to explain it now, but please take note of how you feel right now, in this space. I will ask later, and you will see why."

Danai raised an eyebrow. "Will there be a test?"

"Perhaps..." Mina grinned and turned to their guides. "Peng Dai. Tell the duchess how long you have worked here?"

"Since I was young, your Grace," he answered, proudly. He opened his mouth, then closed it, looking at Mina. When she nodded, he licked his lips, swallowed, and went on.

"I helped build this dam," he continued. He gestured toward a stairway down to the main floor, and they followed. He talked the whole way. "I came as a young man, after the factories in Hunan closed down after the peace. There weren't any other jobs nearby, you see, but the state provides."

As they descended, Peng patted the cool, damp ferrocrete affectionately. "There were days—*months*, your Grace!— when I thought my life would consist of nothing but running a ferrocrete machine or bending rebar. When I wondered if I would ever be dry again, or whether the mosquitos would drink me dry."

"I came with the first wave of administrators," Wen put in, from behind them. "By then there were barracks for us, but the offices were open to the air. They had cast the walls and floors, but the roof..." When they looked back at her pause, she pointed overhead. "No ceilings yet."

Peng led them around, beneath the stairwell. He leaned in close to the wall. "Here, look here." He held his hand up.

In the concrete wall was a handprint the size of his hand. Peng grinned his gap tooth grin at her when she looked from his hand to the handprint. "My hand," he said proudly. "Put here the day we took Mold 31 down an hour too early."

Danai grinned with him. She understood pride, and the permanence of mementos. There was a scuff in *Yen-Lo-Wang*'s head armor, where a shard of LB-X autocannon submunition had skipped off the armor. She refused to let the techs buff it out. It reminded her of her first Solaris match, where it had been earned, and the lessons she still took from that fight.

Foremost among them, the immediacy of life. It happened right then, every moment. Good moments and bad.

"You built an amazing thing," Mina said, into the silence.

"I was but one," Peng said. He looked past them, past the blanket of years. Danai knew he was seeing those days. "One, but each of us knew then we were working on something special." He blinked, and sniffed, then grinned at them. "As the administrator said: the hemisphere. I think on that a lot. Families eat, read, watch HV, and laugh because of what I built. We built. They are warm, or cool. Their food stays fresh. Their children learn." He patted the wall. "I know what we did," he said. Then he looked down, then up at Danai, guiltily. "What the state let me do."

"We all serve the state," Danai said, patting him on the shoulder. "Because we are the state."

Peng nodded, smiling. Danai took her hand off his shoulder and put it on the wall next to his. The wall trembled like a 'Mech under fusion power, the motion being transmitted into all the countless megatons of ferrocrete by the water and the turbines.

Mina smiled, both at Peng and then at Wen. "Perhaps we can show the duchess the distribution office?" She inclined her head. "So she can see how the power this dam creates is spread to the people?"

Wen bowed and led the way.

Peng came along, but he was a moment slow pulling his hand away from the wall. Danai saw he stood a bit straighter. His shoulders were back a little more than they had been. He looked forty years younger, for an instant.

In another hour, they were done and back inside the VTOL. Mina ordered the pilot to circle the dam until told otherwise, then settled into her seat, folded her hands in her lap, and regarded Danai.

"So."

Danai met her stare. "An impressive structure."

"Yes." She waited.

"The whole hemisphere," Danai added.

"Yes."

Danai waited. Finally, "What?"

"When we entered the building, what did you feel?"

"The reception, you mean?" Mina nodded. "I hate those things. I was counting the seconds until we could get back here."

"Fair." She lifted her fingernails, looked at them, then refolded her hands. "And the tour?"

"Impressive, as I said."

"Yes."

"This is going to take a while if all you say is 'yes.'"

Mina said nothing, clearly waiting.

"Peng Dai was proud." Danai frowned. "Everyone we met was proud." It wasn't the same quiet pride the palace servants showed, because of their position. "They are proud of what they built, of what the dam provides." Her brow furrowed. "They are proud of what their service provides to the state and its people."

"A very politic answer," Mina said. "Look outside. See how massive the dam is." She waited until Danai looked. "Now think about being inside. Think of the generator room. Put the size you see and the space you felt together."

"It's as if they built a mountain," Danai said softly.

"Now," Mina said, her voice changing tone. "Put on your *sang-shao* hat again. You and a lance of your BattleMechs. How long would it take you to destroy this dam?"

Danai chuckled. "Beyond function? Minutes. To rubble? Hours, maybe days. Depends on the number of 'Mechs." She looked at Mina. "Is that what you're trying to show me? How strong 'Mechs are? Because I already knew that."

"Of course not," Mina said. "I wouldn't presume to teach you anything about warfare. Rather the opposite." She gestured toward the window, and the dam and lake beyond. "How many years did it take to build this dam?"

"Something like four, I think?"

"Men and women like Peng and Wen have spent their lives building a thing that supports the people of the hemisphere. It gives them the pride you saw. What I want you to consider— not know, because you need to come to the realization in your own way, but *consider*—is that the contributions of the people to the state are just as important as the regiments of 'Mechs you lead."

Danai pursed her lips, but said nothing.

"Your work, the military, is necessary. The actions you took and will take on behalf of all of us are literally life and death. But so is what we just saw. You say you don't know how to be a duchess." Mina leaned forward. "What use does Peng Dai have for the duke of Sian?" She sat back. "We are all servants of the state, and the state is mother to us all. But each of us, from the *sang-shao* of a 'Mech regiment to the foreman of a construction crew on a dam in the jungle, finds pride in our contribution."

"You're saying I need to help the people," Danai said. "I need to give them jobs, projects."

Mina looked out the window. "That way leads to the socialist state the rest of the Inner Sphere accuses us of being. The state that many of our cities and even worlds are dangerously close to becoming, because the *Sheng* and the directorship haven't learned the lesson I am trying to teach you."

She looked back at Danai. "Think on Peng Dai and his life. Think of the pride you heard and saw. And think of the opportunity the state gave him, all those years ago, and every year since, to *earn* that pride." She sniffed. Her eyes were lit with a quiet passion Danai rarely saw.

"*That* is what the state can provide. Opportunity. Not everyone can grasp it. Not everyone will find it. But we move closer to the ideals of our nation when we align the most of us with the work, the occupation, the *life* that makes us most productive. *That* is the Sarna Mandate in practice."

Mina must have signaled, because the VTOL leaned over and angled north, back toward the Forbidden City. She left Danai alone with her thoughts the entire flight.

CHAPTER 10

HUNG LI MILITARY BASE
LIAO
CAPELLAN CONFEDERATION
6 DECEMBER 3148

By the time *Gladiator*'s hull had stopped trembling, Danai had already undone her restraints and stood. She was anxious to be out of the DropShip after the month of transit from Sian. It wasn't until she reached the hatch that she realized Mina Liao hadn't moved. Danai turned back and grinned.

"Are you coming?"

Mina glared up at her. Her normally olive face was pale, with the just the slightest sheen of sweat on her upper lip. Her eyes flashed with annoyance. "I have never landed in a spheroid DropShip before," she grumbled. "I do not enjoy the experience."

DropShips, the heavy vessels that carried people and cargo between the spindly JumpShips at the jump points and planetary surfaces, came in two forms: spheroid and aerodyne. Aerodyne DropShips were like giant airplanes, designed to use lift-generating surfaces such as wings to help them maintain atmospheric flight. They most often operated out of prepared spaceports, with long, hardened runways.

Spheroid DropShips like *Gladiator* came and went vertically, thundering up and down on thrusters that let them take off and land without the need for prepared runways. Both styles of design had their advantages and disadvantages, but landing in one was decidedly unlike the other.

Aerodynes glided down to softer landings.

Spheroids hammered their way out of the sky as if they were on the edge of falling every moment.

Now it was Danai's turn to grin the imp's grin. "You wanted the soldier's life, lady," she told Mina. She stood in the small stateroom and watched Mina take her restraints off and stand up, tentatively, as if she were afraid the ship was going to fall out from beneath her at any moment.

After a moment, Mina stood up straight, folded her hands in front of her, and assumed the mien of the haughty, educated noblewoman she was.

"I do not like you," she said primly.

Danai laughed and keyed the hatch open. One of the DropShip's junior officers was already standing outside, waiting to escort her to the debarkation port, but Danai waved him away. "I know the way."

Mina followed her down the corridors to the docking arm that extended from the ground facility. Because the danger of crash was so great, it was impossible for spheroid DropShips to land at a terminal like an aerodyne could roll up to, but small docking arms with internal bays and space for transport equipment could be nestled near the landing pit.

Four officers in the uniform of the MAC waited for her in the transfer lounge. She only recognized two of them.

"*Zhong-shao*," she greeted her XO. "Have you been down long?"

"Barely a day, your Grace," Wu Feng replied. "We considered slowing and letting your DropShip overtake us, but..." Wu shrugged his massive shoulders. "It didn't seem right."

"*Lèse majesté*," Danai murmured with a grin. She turned to the other familiar face. "Noah?"

"Welcome to Liao, *Sang-shao*," Noah Capshaw said. He looked much more rested than when they'd parted ways on New Syrtis last year. The bags under his eyes were less pronounced, and he looked bigger. Bulkier. She bumped him on the shoulder.

"Has the *zhong-shao* been taking you to the gym with him, Noah?"

Noah dimpled and looked at the ground. "He has, in fact, *Sang-shao.*"

Danai grinned back at him, then looked expectantly at Wu. He, true to form, half-turned and indicated the two other officers.

"*Sang-shao* Danai Centrella-Liao, may I present *Sao-shao* Ned Baxter and *Sang-wei* Emory Koltsokov."

Danai did not offer to shake hands. She regarded each of them. Baxter looked like he was one of *those* Baxters, a descendent of the family of the Big MAC commander who'd led the Armored Cavalry into regular Capellan service. He wasn't short, but he wasn't tall either. His hair was light and trimmed short, and there was something in his eyes she wasn't sure about.

Koltsokov was nervous; she was a powerfully-built woman, tall, with heavy shoulders. Danai could tell by the way she stood that she was heavily muscled, but her body language broadcasted unease; she shifted on her feet. Her hands were clenched tightly in front of her. She returned Danai's nod quickly, jerkily.

"This is Lady Wilhelmina Liao," Danai said, gesturing Mina forward. "She is one of the Capella Liaos."

Wu half-bowed to her, and the others followed suit. Mina inclined her head with a half-tilt but said nothing. Danai knew her well enough by now to know Mina read the tension in the room just as well as she did.

"Mr. Baxter is our new Second Battalion commander," Wu said without inflection.

"Ah," Danai said. She frowned. "I thought we discussed promoting *Sang-wei* Bloch?" Jinfeng Bloch commanded one of Wu's companies in First Battalion. He was an aggressive officer Danai was sure would be a *sang-shao* in short order. She had approved his promotion to *sao-shao* herself.

It disturbed her that her choice for battalion commander hadn't been honored. The Second was her regiment.

"We had," Wu began, but Baxter cleared his throat.

"If I may?" His voice was calm, but Danai felt like it had an oily quality. When she nodded, he smiled placatingly. Danai hated it. "*Sao-shao* Bloch was requested by *Sang-shao* McCarron for his staff. He sent me to take his place."

"I see," Danai replied, and she did. Xavier McCarron was the only man who could have countermanded her orders, and he had done so. Why he did was a mystery she would save for another time. "Well, we're glad to have you." Danai was too skilled a liar to fear that he heard any doubt in her voice. Making her voice say exactly what she meant was a skill Erde had encouraged and Danai had mastered on Solaris. She looked to the other woman.

Who frowned.

"Ms. Koltsokov is your new operations officer," Wu Feng said, again, without inflection.

"My new ops officer," Danai repeated. "Did something happen to *Sang-wei* Sawyer?"

"He was given command of Second Battalion, Fifth Regiment," Wu said.

"An honor," Danai remarked, her mind now racing.

It couldn't be Daoshen. She had traveled here from Sian as fast as any message could have been transmitted, given the state of the HPG net. This was Xavier McCarron. It had to be. First he put one of his officers in charge of one of her battalions, and now also a spy in her command lance.

But why?

Blinking, Danai shook the question off. That was for another time. "Is this your first staff position, Ms. Koltsokov?"

"Ma'am," Koltsokov stammered. She seemed to realize what she was doing, glancing at both Baxter and Wu Feng. She breathed in deep, through her nose, exhaled, and then met Danai's eye.

"Ma'am," she repeated, "two days ago I had Hatchet Company in the Green Knights. Your man, Sawyer? He would have been my CO. I'd like nothing better than for you to send me back there." Her features hardened, now that she was talking, as if she knew she couldn't take the words back. "I've never done staff work, no, ma'am." She sniffed. "I expected to be staff in a battalion first, ma'am."

Danai smiled. She heard the honesty in the other woman's voice. "First, no more ma'ams, okay?" She waited until Koltsokov smiled back and nodded. "Don't worry. We're going to do great things."

She looked around. "Any more surprises, *Zhong-shao* Wu? Am I actually commander of the Third Regiment now?"

"No, *Sang-shao*," Wu replied. "We can repair to the terminal. I have taken the liberty of assembling the regiment. I presumed you'd have something to say."

Danai smiled. "You presumed correctly." She glanced over her shoulder at Mina, who said nothing. Then she slapped Wu on the shoulder. "Let's go."

At the door of the transit lounge was a Blizzard hover APC waiting, fans idling. Danai grinned. After the limos of Sian, it was nice to feel like she was part of her regiment again. She led the group into the infantry compartment. Noah Capshaw, showing a bit more paleness than he first had, went forward to consult with the driver.

Mina sat down in the flip-down seat next to Danai. Her hands dipped to the side for the restraints without her having to look. Danai already had hers latched.

"Not the homecoming you expected?" Mina whispered.

"One learns to expect the unexpected," Danai remarked philosophically.

"Indeed," replied Mina. She opened her mouth to say more, but the driver spun up the fans, and quickly the noise and vibration were too much for unaided speech.

Danai watched the terminal building grow larger through a firing slit in the Blizzard's hull, her mind half going over the speech she'd practiced a dozen times, and half trying to parse the mystery of these new officers.

She didn't doubt they could do their job; deadbeats were cycled out of the MAC by these ranks. But they weren't the longtime Second Regiment officers she'd come to know and trust after so many campaigns.

And losing Kevin Sawyer...Danai shook her head. He deserved a battalion. But she'd been holding out for him to take over First Battalion when she pried it out of Wu Feng's clutches.

The Blizzard was already slowing. She put her hands on her restraint harness, feeling the tingles of anticipation she always got before she addressed her regiment. That was the Second's nickname inside the MAC: Danai's Regiment.

She grinned. She couldn't help it.

It was good to be home.

By the time Ned Baxter got back to his office, it was well after dark. Danai had insisted on an officer's call after her speech to the regiment, and that had turned into dinner. There was nothing he could do to get out of either of them. They were all part of the game of military leadership. Ned knew all about that game. He played it every day.

His desk was clean, and the display built into the desktop was turned off. He sat in the dark room, lit only by the light from the hallway outside, and let the day's events roll over him.

Wu had taken them out to the transit lounge to make sure Danai had time to process his and Koltsokov's presence before she saw the troops. He knew that. It was obvious. And the XO had been nothing except perfectly correct for the last 48 hours, after he'd presented his orders as soon as the Second debarked.

But he resented Baxter's presence. They both did, him and Danai Centrella-Liao herself. Ned had been in the MAC long enough to see the leeway regimental commanders were given. For the *sang-shao*—and in the Armored Cavalry, when you said "the *sang-shao*," that always meant Old Man McCarron—to put him here meant something.

He just had to figure out what.

Sitting there in his office, he was surprised by a tap on the doorframe. He was even more surprised by who it was. He leaped to his feet.

"*Sang-shao* Centrella-Liao!" He braced but didn't salute. The Second MAC didn't salute.

"Relax, *Sao-shao*," Danai said. Ned spread his feet and put his hands behind his back, at parade rest, because that was how he'd been trained. Danai saw this, and laughed. "I mean it. Sit down. It's your office."

Blinking, Ned sat. Danai didn't move, just stayed where she was, leaning against the doorjamb.

"We're taking the regiment into the field as soon as it can be arranged," his commander said. She wasn't looking at him, or at the wall she was staring at. "Tomorrow, if I can get it done."

There was nothing for him to say, so he said nothing.

"You ready to run a battalion, Ned?" She frowned. "Edward, right?" He nodded. "Ned? Ed? What do you prefer?"

"Ned, ma'am," he said.

"Ned. You up to this?"

"Yes, ma'am." He considered, then decided *so what.* "I've worked my whole career for this."

Danai smiled. "What was your last posting?"

"The Commandos, *Sang-shao,*" Ned said. He hoped he kept the smugness out of his voice. He thought he had, by the way Danai's head bobbed in appreciation.

Baxter's Commandos were the command unit for the whole Armored Cavalry. They traveled wherever Xavier McCarron went. Ned's distant cousin, Marcus Baxter, had led the Armored Cavalry into full Capellan service; his other cousin, Lindsey Baxter, commanded the Fourth Regiment.

"I see." Danai met his eyes now. Her gaze was electrifying. Ned Baxter was a confident man. He knew what he'd done. But here he stood with an heir of Capellan royal blood, who'd fought in the gladiatorial games on Solaris VII and then clawed her way to command of a MAC regiment. "Your predecessor, *Sao-shao* Maranov, ran a tight ship."

"So I have already seen, *Sang-shao.*"

"Come find me in the morning, Mr. Baxter. I need to get you up to speed on my little foibles before we lead a hundred 'Mechs into the mud and muck, don't you think?"

"Looking forward to it, ma'am."

She nodded and stepped back into the corridor. Then she reappeared. "You going to be here for a minute?"

Confused, Ned nodded.

Danai grinned and slapped the light switch, erasing the darkness.

Then she was gone.

Ned waited a moment to be sure, then leaned back in his chair and breathed out.

"What the hell?" he muttered, and flicked the desk console live.

Danai stood at the end of the hall, silent and listening. She heard Baxter's muttered oath, but she didn't hear him get up. Instead, she heard the low-frequency hum of his desk console starting up. She grinned, shook her head, and started walking.

A good commander should have some mysteries, she'd learned a long time ago. Shaiming Tao, who'd preceded her in command of the regiment, had confirmed it. He kept himself tight as a closed and sealed book to his officers.

That wasn't Danai's style, and besides...she needed to know how Baxter reacted to pressure.

His answers had been factually correct. All the right words said the right way to a commanding officer, but Danai had caught the note of tension again. And she was starting to believe he resented being put under her.

Which made her wonder if his presence in her regiment was less about her and more about him. Was that Xavier McCarron's plan? A trooper from the Commandos didn't need much instruction. You didn't get a slot with Cyrus McCarron, Xavier's son and heir, without earning it.

Or did McCarron put him here to annoy me?

Danai stepped into the cool air, toward the waiting vehicle, and grinned again.

At least this was a challenge she understood.

CHAPTER 11

LUNG WANG*-CLASS DROPSHIP *GLADIATOR
HALL
REPUBLIC OF THE SPHERE
3 FEBRUARY 3149

For a moment, alone in her cockpit, Danai reveled in just being a MechWarrior. The vibration of *Gladiator*'s drive as the DropShip moved into atmosphere, the glowing icons in her HUD, the smell of old sweat and fresh coolant in her cooling suit...Danai loved it all. That she was experiencing it just before an attack into the Republic made it even better. And...

The damned Fortress Wall was gone!

She had barely been on Liao a month, knocking the Second back into shape and testing her new officers, when the word came by courier JumpShip. A task force test had succeeded, and Daoshen and the Strategios had wasted no time: assault orders for four worlds inside Fortress Republic were sent immediately, including orders for Danai and the Second, along with the Second Liao Guards, to attack and capture Hall.

The jump series to get there had been tedious and full of doubt; the first jump beyond the Wall boundary had been nerve-wracking. She had spent the whole countdown afraid it was a trick, that the Republic had let Task Force *Chong Che* through as a ruse, and that the Wall would be back up.

She'd felt helpless, like she was leading her regiment to its death.

Danai hated feeling helpless. She always had, and she doubly-did after New Hessen. The jump succeeding had done little to calm her down. That sense of helplessness had been enough to trigger her post-traumatic stress syndrome. She recognized the signs.

She'd caught herself reorganizing her drawers in her small shipboard cabin for the ninth time. Making sure everything was just right. Making sure she felt the dopamine hit of making it *just right.*

It wasn't something she talked to the Second's doctors about. But she was plenty familiar with hypervigilance.

She knew how to cope. Since New Hessen.

"Two minutes to touchdown," *Gladiator's* captain said in her helmet.

"Roger," she replied. She toggled her command lance channel. "Emory, any updates from the pathfinders?"

"Negative, *Sang-shao,*" *Sang-wei* Koltsokov responded. "No changes. The LZ is still cold."

"Very well," she said. Upon making orbit unopposed, she'd sent down pathfinders—infantry scouts, VTOLs and light hovercraft—from the Gypsies, the conventional regiment attached to the Second to scout landing zones. She'd chosen two main zones, one for her Second and another for the Liao Guards. Both were near Harney, the planetary capital.

No RAF officers had challenged them since they entered the system. She'd chosen to come in at the nadir jump point, not the zenith, because the zenith had a recharge station for JumpShips and would assuredly be defended.

She hadn't known what to expect. Literally no one had seen into the Fortress worlds for more than fifteen years. There hadn't been time to organize scouting raids. The CCAF—and Danai—wanted to hit their target before the news of their arrival.

But Danai certainly hadn't expected nothing.

Not even once they arrived in orbit; none of the orbiting DropShips or reconnaissance flights from the Armored Mosquitos—her aerospace contingent—had spotted any defenders more serious than municipal militias.

She didn't know if they were hiding, or if they weren't there to hide.

Danai shook the thoughts off, worried her PTSD might be affecting her judgment. No commander ever had perfect intelligence. This was no different.

The tremble and noise of *Gladiator*'s drive changed as they neared the ground; first, the pitch increased as her pilot increased thrust to slow the descent, and then the mushing reflectance of her thruster pulses bouncing off the ground, but *Gladiator*'s crew was among the best.

A lurch—more sensed than felt—and they were down.

Immediately, the restraints holding Danai's 'Mech in its transport cradle withdrew. Across the bay, the massive bay door began cycling open. As soon as it was cracked hot air blasted into the bay. Hall was not a cool world, but this was even hotter than usual due to the air heated by the DropShip's thrusters and the superheating they had done to the ground as they landed.

Danai pushed her throttle forward, carefully guiding the 'Mech across the bay. It was too hot for a ground guide, but in a few steps she was down the ramp and on the soil of a world no Capellan had seen for more than a decade.

She licked her lips. She'd felt a thrill like this on Solaris, the first time she'd stepped out in front of the crowd. She brought *Yen-Lo-Wang*'s shield up into passive defense and let its sensors drink in the landscape even as the rest of her command lance debarked.

"No contact," Capshaw sent. His *Wraith* strode past Danai's 'Mech, insectoid head sensors swiveling to look for threats. His role on Danai's staff was intel work, but on the field he preferred to act as her bodyguard. The thought made her smile.

She was a Solaris-ranked MechWarrior in a BattleMech that had been famously dangerous for more than a century. She didn't need a bodyguard.

Around *Gladiator*'s far side more DropShips were thundering down from orbit: the rest of the Second Battalion, Second Regiment, and the attached civilian governmental transport. The members of the directorship caste aboard that vessel—*the bureaucrats,* Danai mentally amended—would work to establish the new Confederation civilian government on Hall once she declared the world secure.

"It's quiet," Emory Koltsokov remarked. "Too quiet."

Danai smiled thoughtfully. In the two months since she'd returned, Emory Koltsokov had turned out to be a valuable officer. Danai hadn't made it easy on her, but the pale woman had a flair for regimental operations. To be fair, the regimental ops shop did little more than set objectives for the battalions, but even in that Koltsokov found ways to excel.

Leading *Yen-Lo-Wang* around the DropShip, she saw the ovoid shape of Second Battalion's *Overlord*-class DropShip settling into a roaring cloud of smoke and steam. The final burst rose in a halo around the vessel as the pilot cut their thrusters.

Danai's smiled tightened.

She couldn't give the same praise to *Sao-shao* Ned Baxter. The man was always perfectly correct, and he was reasonably skilled. Most of his officers got along with him—no one, not even Danai, was universally liked—and he accomplished all the objectives she set for him.

But she just didn't *like* him.

"Let's get Two Batt unloaded," Danai said to her staff. "And then go find out whether we have a fight coming or not." She took a moment to look around her, taking in the landscape.

The DropShips had set down in a large bowl valley, with brown scrub and scattered patches of dry earth. The trees were small and stunted, with leaves that looked better suited to succulent plants than leafy plants. In the middle distance on all sides were low hills, and in the far distance a line of mountains was faintly visible.

A six-lane highway had run through the valley. Her DropShips had obliterated the center of the track, but civilian ground traffic had seen the DropShips coming and halted well back.

Danai suddenly felt very alone, which was strange on a planet of more than two billion people.

It felt very odd.

Tom Jordan huddled in the cave with Major Hernandez, who served as the staff operations officer for Colonel Rachel Tobin, commander of the 1461st Armored Cavalry Regiment. Colonel Tobin was the senior officer in Combat Command Gamma, the combined force Tom and his company had joined after arriving on Hall. He licked the edge of the drink tube in his mouth without thinking about it.

"Looks like they're all down," Hernandez said after a moment. He was too proud to turn his head and see if Tom agreed, but there was just a hint of question in his voice.

Tom stifled a grin and looked at the small screen on the noteputer. After a moment he grunted. "Looks that way."

Hernandez straightened up and stretched. His head almost reached the roof of the small cave, but they'd been down here long enough that they all knew not to get too high. "Then I think it looks about right for Baker-seven, don't you?"

Tom rocked back on his heels instead of standing. "I think so...unless they're slow unloading. Then Baker-four." He rubbed his hands together. His palms were dry, but there was grit from the cave floor between his fingers. "But Baker, either way, yes sir."

"Good. I'll inform the colonel."

As Hernandez stepped away Tom rolled back onto his backside, hands wrapped around his knees, and tried to imagine what was going to happen next.

It was pure luck that any portion of the Capellan invasion force had landed near where their combat command was hidden. The three commands had been placed near the three most likely landing zones, sure, but Tom hadn't had a great deal of confidence that what Major Crowe and his staff determined as "likely" would match the Capellan invaders' version of "likely." But the major had been right. And, miracle of miracles, the inevitable Capellan pathfinders had missed the hidden RAF units.

In the handful of months they'd had to work the three combat commands—Alpha, Beta, and Gamma, each a company of Principes 'Mechs plus a battalion each of armor and infantry—had come a long way. The officers had learned how each other thought, and the sub-units, Tom's 'Mech lances and the armor battalions, primarily, had found a good working cadence.

But that didn't mean they were ready to run screaming out of concealment, out of their carefully-constructed hidden laagers and bunkers, and overrun a Capellan landing zone. The few times they'd tried in exercise any of the Baker plans—the LZ assault plans—it was always costly.

But Tom understood. The first blow had to be a heavy one.

He leaned forward, grabbed the noteputer Hernandez had left behind, and began carefully zooming in on the images the infantry scouts had gotten. He saw an *Overlord*, which could carry a full battalion of 'Mechs, plus an *Excalibur*, which could put most of a whole additional regiment of conventional troops on the ground. And a couple smaller DropShips...he swiped to a different image.

The first was one of the Capellans' fancy *Lung Wang* raiders. He knew that from the recognition guides. But behind it was a cluster of three transports, what looked like an old *Danais* and two *Mule*-class freighters.

Tom tapped his finger against the image for a second, thinking.

Baker-seven called for an assault on a relatively undefended LZ, after the main ground force had moved out. If the Louies didn't leave too large a security detachment, they might have a chance.

Tom looked down at the cargo ships again. Then he stood.

"Major!" He strode through the narrow cave, careful to keep his head ducked. "Let me show you something, sir!"

The first Two Batt 'Mechs were striding down their DropShip's ramp when a ping announced a private call request. Danai pulled *Yen-Lo-Wang*'s throttle back to idle and accepted the call. Mina Liao's face appeared on her HUD.

"Danai," Mina said, "*Mandrinn* Chang is calling for you."

Danai frowned. Chang Baofeng was the leader of the directorship contingent, the civilian government. They had had several meetings during the journey from Liao to Hall, and she thought she had made clear the priorities of landing.

"Can you handle him?"

"He is most insistent," Mina said. "He seemed surprised to not find you aboard *Gladiator* when he called."

"Surprised," Danai repeated. She reached up and tapped the neurohelmet that sat on her shoulders, which would be visible to Mina in her display. "Did he forget what I do for a living?"

Mina frowned like a governess chiding a recalcitrant child. "Not everyone sees the world the way we do, your Grace."

The user of her title was a jab, and Danai felt its sting. Long conversations with Mina over the months were beginning show her what it might look like to embrace—really embrace—the true nature of what life in the Confederation could be. She had never really considered it, as an adult. Her upbringing, and her own nature, drove her to see the Confederation as an edifice of permanency in her life.

She was a Liao.

Her life was not hard, for she sat at the pinnacle of Confederation privilege.

Her life was not overcomplicated, because she was *janshi*, and a warrior's enemies are easily found across the field.

But she was also a noblewoman of the realm now. The people of Castrovia were hers to do with as she pleased, for all intents and purposes. Their successes were now her successes; their failures now hers as well.

Danai looked over at the *Danais*-class DropShip the bureaucrats traveled aboard. The cargo hauler, *Tianmu Shan*, had long ago been reconditioned as a transport, and had accommodations suited for the directorship.

Chang and his peers were the gears that kept the Confederation's engine running. The directorship, for all its supposed greed in the foreign press, was largely peopled by dedicated citizens who took the *noblesse oblige* of their position seriously. The difficult and painful work to reintegrate Hall's billions into the Capellan caste system needed to begin at the earliest possible moment, and that work was what Chang and the others were here to do.

She should talk to him.

She knew she should.

But her eyes went back to the 'Mechs debarking from the *Overlord*, marching to the assembly area to meet up with the conventional components from the *Excalibur*. They swept across the open plain and its wrecked highway.

The earliest possible moment was not yet here.

"Tell him I will call on him as soon as I can," Danai told her.

"Danai—"

"No." She brought *Yen-Lo-Wang*'s throttle up as she talked. "This has to come first. There can't be a government until the old one capitulates. Until then, Chang and his ilk can wait."

Mina looked like she wanted to argue, but instead she just nodded and cut the channel.

Danai frowned as she guided her 'Mech closer to the others. The three other 'Mechs of her command lance kept pace, and the two Yellow Jacket VTOLs that augmented her lance were already hovering overhead, rotors thumping the air.

She didn't know if she made the right decision. She didn't know if there *was* a right decision.

But she knew where her duty lay.

CHAPTER 12

GAMMA COMBAT COMMAND LAAGER CHARLIE FOUR
HALL
REPUBLIC OF THE SPHERE
3 FEBRUARY 3149

"Sir!"

Tom Jordan looked up from the map board he was going over with his lieutenants. The technician had been calling her superior, but Tom handed the board to Lieutenant Agarkar and stepped over to listen.

"What do you got, Hammond?" If the duty officer cared that the 'Mech commander was standing next him, he didn't show it.

"They're moving out," Hammond answered, putting a finger near the flat panel display she was monitoring. That display was wired by a hair-fine fiber optic cable to a recon camera mounted where it could see the whole valley. It was actually wired into an abandoned vehicle on the M5 highway.

Serried ranks of 'Mechs and tanks were indeed marching away from the camera, toward Harney.

"Do we have a breakdown yet?"

"No, sir," Hammond replied. "I need more time to see who moves. The column is just getting started."

The duty officer looked at Tom, then past him. Tom turned to see Major Hernandez and Colonel Tobin hurrying along the cave. "Sir, they're moving out," the duty officer reported to Major Hernandez.

"How many?" Tobin demanded. She was a short woman, built like a fireplug, with graying auburn hair and a fierce set of wrinkles. She'd spent a lot of her life on dawn cruises in Elgin's seas. Tom recognized the type. She was an old salt, like his father had been, now trapped in the endless deserts of Hall.

"Too soon to say," Tom put in.

Tobin looked at him and blinked. "Your people ready, Captain?"

"We'll be there with bells on, Colonel."

Tobin grinned. She slapped the duty officer on the shoulder and looked at Hernandez. "Get the warning orders out." She eyed the display like a fisher eyes the strain on a line. "Baker-seven unless you hear otherwise."

Tom grinned back at her, nodded, and went back to his two lieutenants. Master Sergeant Cork stood nearby, glowering.

"Let's get 'em saddled," he told them. "It won't be long now."

San-ben-bing Jennifer Hong walked about ten meters behind her squad, making sure the recruits checked each car like they'd been ordered. She carried her Ceres Arms rifle in a tactical carry, half watching the abandoned cars around her and half watching the other MAC infantrymen.

Behind her, she no longer heard the noises of the rest of the Second Battalion heading out for Harney. The first units had departed an hour ago, and the stragglers were themselves thirty minutes gone.

"Because," had been the *sao-wei*'s answer when she'd asked why her platoon was being sent on perimeter security when the rest of the battalion was moving on the capital. "Because." As if she were a child asking her parents why she couldn't have another snack.

"Parton!" Hong called. The recruit in question turned back so fast his helmet rocked down, covering his eyes. Because it was unsecured. Because of course it was. "Did you check that bus?"

"Yes, *San-ben-bing*!"

"No, you didn't, Parton, because I was watching you." She gestured with her rifle, careful not to actually present the weapon and sweep her team. "Now get in there."

"Yes, *San-ben-bing*!"

The infantryman hustled back and shouldered his way aboard a two-decker hoverbus that had been abandoned. The rubber in the soft skirts squeaked as Parton changed the derelict's center of balance.

Hong sighed. All the Rep civilians had run when they saw the DropShips come down. There were tracks in the medians where large vehicles, busses most likely, had gathered them up and run them clear of the danger.

Seemed like that was all the Reps did on Hall.

Run.

Certainly no one had contested the landing.

And now the battalion was just marching free through the countryside. *So many years of preparation*, Hong thought. *Wasted on this nonsense.*

In front of her, a thick, rolling engine chuckled to life, but was quickly replaced by the moaning whine of lift fans spooling up.

"God damn it," Hong cursed. She pressed her helmet earpiece against her ear. "Parton! What the hell are you doing in there?"

Parton reappeared out of the bus's passenger compartment and stared at her. He shrugged. "Wasn't me, ma'am," he said. His voice came through her helmet. The noise of fans was too loud for her to hear his voice through the open air.

The tone shifted into the full scream of a blower up on its skirts.

The sound moved, coming closer.

"Contact!" Hong screamed. She dashed to a nearby car and knelt, presenting her rifle.

A moment later a low-slung, familiar shape burst past her, moving along the highway. Hong, wide-eyed, watched it go. All she caught of the markings was a giant 14. It was a Zibler fighting tank.

She slapped her hand against her helmet. The screams of more blowers was so loud she couldn't hear her own voice.

"Command!" She screamed, or tried to. "Contact this position!"

The pits dug for Gamma's 'Mechs—F Company's 'Mechs, since they were the only 'Mechs in the combat command— were deep enough for the 'Mechs to stand up in, but getting out would be rough. Coming down the 2:1 graded steps had been rough, but Tom Jordan didn't think any less of the engineers. The pits had done their job.

His Flankers were less than two kilometers from the Capellan LZ.

On his HUD, remote views fed through hardwired connections showed him repeaters from the advancing hovertanks. The first wave was all Zibler Ds; their job was to piss the remaining security forces off, draw them out. Then the Flankers would hit them.

"Not quite yet," Tom warned. His voice travelled along the hardwired system to each of his 'Mechs.

His fingertips tingled, and he tasted metal in the back of his throat. Tom swallowed and concentrated on his breathing.

This was going to work, he knew.

But it was going to cost.

"Sir..." Preakness was starting to say, but *Si-ben-bing*—what other militaries called a sergeant—Travis Gardner had already seen the movement in the distance. He snapped his cigarette over the edge of the glacis and slid down into his Zhukov tank's turret. His hand slapped the hatch control without him thinking about it.

"Let's go!" he shouted even before he had his combat vehicle crewman's helmet on. "We've got incoming!"

"Incoming what?" asked Hertzel, the loader.

The tank jerked as Preakness got himself seated in the driver's compartment and started the tank moving.

"Blowers," Gardner snapped. "Get the guns up. Shotgun!" He jerked the chinstrap of his helmet tight and palmed the emergency channel. "Gypsy Six, Gypsy Six, Hotel Two-one. Inbound blowers, say again, inbound blowers." He read off the direction and estimated range and then ignored the rest.

"Danton, what do you see?"

Deep in the bowels of the 75-ton tank there was a commander's station, where he was supposed to sit. Gardner hated being that far from the guns, so he took the gunner's position. Danton took his spot and acted as sensor operator.

"At least a company," the small man said. Gardner knew he'd been leaning forward, squinting at the screens. "Maybe two. Look like Ziblers. Can't see what configuration."

"Raid like this, they'll be deltas," Gardner said. "Get in, hit with those big-ass PPCs, get back out."

"Where am I going?" Preakness yelled.

"Right at 'em," Gardner said. He ground his teeth, watching the reload indicator. The portside LB-10X autocannon came up green first, followed in less than a second by the starboard. Gardner gripped the gunnery controls and tapped his boot on the firing trip. "We got to keep them away from the DropShips."

"Loaded," Hertzel called from below. He didn't actually sling the rounds into the guns, but he controlled the routing from the magazines buried deep in the Zhukov's hull to the autoloaders.

"C'mon," Gardner urged the old tank. "Come *on*!"

At the first flash of blue-white PPC fire, Tom pushed the *Kheper*'s throttle forward. "Let's go!" he shouted before the fiber optic line parted as the 55-ton 'Mech moved out. It labored up the terraced steps to clear the pit even as the combination camouflage, IR masking, and ECM-proof roof fell away. His 'Mech was the first to clear its pit, but Master Sergeant Cork's *Warhammer* was next, leading the Three Lance machines into the fight.

"Best speed for the LZ," Tom ordered.

According to Baker-seven, once the blowers had the security force engaged, the 'Mechs were to move to within

800 meters of the nearest DropShip and engage targets of opportunity. It was expected the security element would follow the blowers back out of the nearer engagement zone—Tom's teeth lips skinned back from his teeth—where the 'Mechs could hit them.

"Baker-seven-beta," he sent. Alpha had been the hovertank assault.

Charlie would be quiet, he knew.

But delta… Delta would light up the valley.

At the end of the *Kheper*'s arm, the M-7 Gauss rifle hummed as it charged.

Travis Gardner settled the target ring on the bow of the Zibler screaming toward him and waited for the range to come down. The twin cannons were stabilized against the rumbling movement of the tank's tracks, but the vibration of so much metal caused panels inside the Zhukov's turret to rub against each other in a screech that annoyed him whenever he was aware of it.

He wasn't aware of it now. Gardner's whole existence was focused on his gunnery.

The Zibler's turret spun the huge barrel it mounted to the left a half-second before eye-searing blue-white lightning burst from it. He had called the Ziblers right—deltas with that big-ass heavy PPC. He felt sorry for whoever that was aimed at. Gardner and his crew had been hit with one of those on New Syrtis from a quick-firing Yasha VTOL. It had blown the port rear road wheel off. So of course they'd driven right off their own track.

The range fell as the Zibler's driver ignored him.

The target ring burned green.

Gardner's foot slammed the firing trip.

Both cannons boomed. The tank rocked with recoil. The turret was immediately inundated with the scorching, foul-tasting tang of burned propellant that leaked out of the breech.

Ahead, sparks flashed like fireworks across the Zibler's bow as the cluster rounds—the shotgun he'd called for—struck home.

Gardner's growl of approval was lost in the *ker-chunk* of the cannons reloading.

Private Sarah Jacoby grunted as she tried to lever her suit over onto its stomach. She'd skidded a good twenty meters across the ground as soon as she let go of the speeding tank, but one of the projectiles aimed at the Zibler had missed and gotten her Purifier battlesuit right in the chest. The adaptive mimetic armor corrected quickly for the damage, but she still lay still.

She'd been an idiot to volunteer for this.

The HUD inside a battlesuit helmet was much less capable than a BattleMech's, so she wasn't surprised when she couldn't find any of the other members of her squad. A Purifier battlesuit that wasn't moving was designed to look just like whatever it was sitting on.

The ground around her shook as the Liao Zhukov tracked closer, pursuing the Zibler who'd carried them inside the Capellan perimeter.

It'd be just her luck to get crushed like a rock while she was pretending to be one.

But she didn't move.

Instead she triggered a diagnostic in the weapon mounted at the end of her right arm. If that didn't work, all of this was for nothing.

"Baker-seven-charlie-down," Tom Jordan heard.

He shook his head. He'd met a lot of crazy people in his time in the RAF, but none who'd be crazy enough to volunteer for what those people had volunteered for.

"Eyes up," he told his company. "Hit whatever you can, but for God's sake don't step over that 800-meter boundary!"

On the command channel, Colonel Tobin herself was on the comm.

"Longarm, Longarm, unmask for the music."

The Zhukov tracked past without crushing her. Jacoby breathed out when the tank was past. It had come close enough that she'd rattled several centimeters across the ground like a loose stone from the ground shock of 75 tons moving fast, but it was past.

Slowly, she brought the Purifier's right arm around until it bore on her target. Then she squeezed the trigger, holding it down. A movement of her tongue opened the burst transmitter built into her helmet.

"Baker-seven-charlie-up," she whispered.

In the distance, down past the end of her arm, turrets moved on the high armored sides of the Liao *Excalibur*-class DropShip.

In the *Excalibur*'s CIC, electronic warfare rating Jirxi Venn frowned as a light lit on her board. She didn't recognize it immediately, but when she hovered her pointer over it a helpful tip popped up identifying the warning. Venn read the words, frowned even more, and then slammed her hand down on the alarm button.

"Sir!" She didn't even look around to see which officer was nearby. "We're being painted by target acquisition gear!"

A moment later Venn felt breath on her neck as the *kong-sao-wei* leaned over her shoulder to read the board. "What?!"

She pointed to the light. "TAG, sir, a spotting laser. From close aboard; computer says it's an infantry weapon."

The deck officer reached past her and slapped the open frequency live. "Spotters on the ground!" he screamed. "Find them!"

Gardner heard the call and closed his eyes for a long moment.

"Danton," he said, very calmly, "did we get the Guardian fixed?"

"Not yet," the sensor operator replied.

Gardner slapped his palm against the gunnery controls in frustration. Normal equipment on a Zhukov was a Guardian ECM suite, an active jammer that would block TAG emissions from working. It was a powerful device, and running it often made their tank the target of enemies across the field.

It was what had attracted the Yasha on New Syrtis; they'd been deep in the mix, disrupting Davion C3 networks.

It had been damaged. Repairing it was depot-level work. It wasn't like cracking track. No one on the crew could fix it. It just wasn't something they could do.

He opened his eyes, looking for the Zibler.

Killing that tank was something he could do.

If it ever came back.

"Keep your eyes peeled," Gardner told the crew.

"Say that again," Danai Centrella-Liao said in the cockpit of *Yen-Lo-Wang*.

"The LZ is under attack," *Sao-shao* Baxter repeated. His *Tian-zong* paced her command lance.

Danai pulled her throttle back and turned her 'Mech to face back the way they'd come. The column had already come to a stop.

"In what strength?"

"Unknown."

Danai squeezed her controls so hard her knuckles cracked. "Can they hold?"

"Unknown." To his credit, Ned Baxter sounded just as frustrated as she felt. "Reports said hovertanks and some 'Mechs."

"How many 'Mechs? What unit?" If there really were frontline RAF units on Hall, then she'd just stepped into the trap she'd feared on the journey in.

"The report didn't say." The *Tian-zong* twitched. "Wait one."

Danai waited, foot tapping against the steering pedals. It felt like forever, even though it was probably just a few seconds.

"*Sang-shao*: the DropShips are being painted for artillery."

Danai slammed her throttle to its gate. "Back to the LZ!" *Yen-Lo-Wang* leaned into a loping run, but she already knew it would be too slow. They were most of thirty minutes away. A corner of her mind reminded her Mina was still back there, but she ignored it.

By the time they got back, it would be over.
One way or another.

CHAPTER 13

LANDING ZONE BRAVO
HALL
REPUBLIC OF THE SPHERE
3 FEBRUARY 3149

RAF Sergeant Harry James Austin frowned at the screen until the squiggly line straightened, then stood and waved his helmet. "Good tone!" He turned the other way and shouted again. "Good tone! Let 'em fly!"

His job done, Austin slapped his helmet back down and ran for the APC. The rear ramp was lowered, but he could see the crew chief already taking up the slack in the mechanism.

Behind him, all six five-round box launchers of the Arrow IV battery swiveled to point up.

Austin wanted to be buttoned-up before those monsters tore a hole in sky.

Climbing aboard, he shouldered his way to the slender infantry trooper carrying the field radio and grabbed it from her. He jammed the earpiece under his helmet, clapped his other hand uselessly on the opposite side, and shouted, "Baker-seven-delta!"

The sky behind Tom Jordan's 'Mech erupted with fire and smoke as the Arrow IV missile artillery batteries went to rapid and continuous fire. He watched the streaks of light arrow overheard, scrolling quickly across his 360-degree vision strip. He drew the *Kheper*'s throttle back slowly, letting the 'Mech slow down. He'd controlled missile artillery batteries in sims and live-fire exercises, but this was the first time he'd seen them used in real combat.

He'd never seen this many before.

"As soon as the last round hits," he told his company.

"Anti-missile batteries released!" the *kong-sang-wei* shouted, but Jirxi Venn just rolled her eyes. *This tub doesn't have anti-missile systems*, she thought. But she knew as well as anyone that when you were afraid, you reached for anything to save you. Even things you don't have.

Blinking, Venn worked her controls, trying to count the number of discrete targeting beams hitting her receptors. It was at least three.

We're so screwed.

She hadn't joined the CCAF and come all these light years to get smashed by an Arrow IV missile. But all she could do was her job. She closed the EW receptor screen and opened the active sensor panel. If the groundpounders outside couldn't find the bastards, maybe she could. The radar, lidar and magnetic anomaly gear was built for deep space, but it was better than just sitting here.

Si-ben-bing Travis Gardner saw the incoming on his screens and ground his teeth. His eyes, practiced at picking out targets among the clutter, swept impotently across the ground in front of them, but he could find nothing.

"Preakness," he called to the driver, "get us away from the DropShips. There's nothing we can do now."

The Zhukov shuddered as one of the tracks slowed, turning the tank, but Gardner ignored it, just like he ignored the noise and the vibration and the feeling of his molars grinding together. His hands squeezed the turret controls so tightly his knuckles hurt, and he ached to bring his foot down on the firing trip, to shoot, to *do* something.

But there was nothing he *could* do.

And so he sat, in his turret, and drove away while he still could.

Sarah Jacoby held her arm steady, praying the sensors she knew were desperately searching for her aboard the DropShip would keep failing to locate her hidden suit. A Purifier battlesuit that wasn't moving wasn't *there*, is what they always insisted in training.

She studied the sides of the mountainous DropShip in her HUD. Her faceplate was looking at the ground, but the display adjusted. The sides were thickly armored, much more so than any BattleMech, and turrets and antenna sprouted from armored blisters. Several turrets were firing at the Zibler tanks, but having trouble tracking them because of their speed.

Her entire platoon had volunteered to be spread across the Liao landing zone, to paint the DropShips for attack. Her squad had been assigned to the military DropShips, and she knew if they were still alive, Harris and Bukato would be doing as she was, pretending to be a hole in the ground while lasing an *Overlord* or *Excalibur* with their target acquisition gear. But the other squads...

They were tasked for the supplies.

Jacoby wasn't willing to look away from her target, not this close to splash, to eyeball the *Mule* and *Danais* DropShips across the distance. Instead, she stared at the *Excalibur*, eyeing the thick armor, and tried to imagine what would happen to those more lightly armored DropShips when the Arrows hit.

She didn't have to wait long.

Tom Jordan's heads-up display caught it all.

At least thirty Arrow IV missiles has been fired at the LZ. That was enough firepower to humble a 'Mech company or decimate a smaller 'Mech lance. Against a handful of targets, even targets as tough as DropShips, it was devastating.

At least three impacted the fat-bodied *Excalibur* troop carrier.

"Splash," Tom whispered.

The techs would have to review the battleROMs later and tell him whether it was more than three. He counted three boils of light that, a second or two later, shook his *Kheper* with the sound of the explosion. He grinned a wolf's grin rictus at the images, urging the DropShips to collapse into pyres, but military DropShips were built tougher than that.

Three Arrows had struck the *Excalibur*. That was ten percent of the entire package. More arrowed down and struck the bell-shaped nose of the *Overlord*-class 'Mech carrier, he didn't see how many.

At least twenty missiles fell onto the cargo DropShips.

The cacophony of light and sound was too long, too constant and too stroboscopic for Tom to comprehend, but when the flashes ended and the shaking stopped, he swung the *Kheper*'s sensors around for a closer look, zooming in.

One *Mule* was heavily damaged; most of its hull was blackened and smoking, and he could actually see part of the rounded shape of the fat-bodied ship's hull had broken away. It was still basically intact, but it was wrecked as a DropShip.

The other, smaller vessel, the *Danais*... Tom bit his lip.

The *Danais* was a pyre, molten red and burning.

Anyone on that ship had died, and likely died screaming.

Travis Gardner stood up, triggering the turret hatch open. He didn't care that there were enemy 'Mechs on his sensors, didn't care that Ziblers were still zipping around. He had to see this with his own eyes.

The DropShips, all of them except the *sang-shao*'s little *Lung Wang*, were hit. The important ones, the troop carriers, were hit hard but still intact. Their heavy armor hadn't quite shrugged the damage off, but at least they were still in the fight. While Gardner watched, the *Overlord* triggered a PPC that pinned a Zibler to the ground, getting a moment's revenge for the attack.

"It's okay," he told his crew. "They only got the cargo ships."

"Unless there's more coming," Preakness muttered.

"*Si-ben-bing*?" Danton asked hesitantly.

"What?"

"The *Danais*, the little one..."

Gardner waited, but Danton didn't say more. "Spit it out."

"The little one was carrying the civvies, wasn't it?"

Gardner frowned, then jerked his head around to look at the wreckage of the *Danais*. One glance was all it took. No one was going to make it out of that.

"That can't be good," he muttered.

"Better button up," Preakness called. "Here come the 'Mechs."

The *kong-sao-wei* had fallen down when the first missile hit, but Jinxi Venn just gripped her restraints and rode it out. When the shaking stopped, she immediately leaned back toward her console and triggered a diagnostic.

"We're hit," she said unnecessarily, but it was still her job to say it. "Radar Two, Lidar Two are down. MAD gear degraded fourteen percent." She switched screens. "We're still being painted—" a light blinked off. "Correction. TAG emissions have stopped."

"Stopped," the officer repeated, still sitting on the desk, "or did we lose the sensors?"

"Stopped, sir," she replied. "EW gear comes back ninety-three percent up."

"So it's over," he said. Then he glanced around, saw no one looking, and climbed to his feet. Venn watched in the reflected glare off her screen.

New icons flickered on her electronic warfare screen. She dragged her cursor over them, reading the data, and bit back a curse.

"Not quite, sir," she responded. "New emissions. BattleMech targeting systems."

"Ours? Is the *sang-shao* back with the battalion?"

"No, sir," she said. "More Reps."

"Remember the plan," Tom Jordan told his MechWarriors. "Get in, tag some of the ships, and recover the Purifiers. They've done their job. Let's get them out of there so we can do it again another time."

A chorus of acknowledgments came back even as Tom pushed his throttle forward. He dialed a different frequency.

"Pointer Six, Flanker Six," he called. "Coming to pick up the children."

"Roger, Flanker." It wasn't the voice he was expecting. "Pointer One-three confirms. We'll start moving that way."

"One-three, status of Pointer Six?" Tom asked. If the Zibler company commander was disabled, maybe they could do a pickup.

"Ate a PPC," the Zibler tank commander said. "No one got out. One-three out."

Tom shook off the emotion he was feeling. Red highlights washed across his HUD as a nearby DropShip's targeting sensors swept his 'Mech, and he could already see carets for the defending armor company aligning to form a line against him. There was no real chance twelve tanks, already shook by the Zibler blitzkrieg, could stop his company from going where they wanted.

But they could make them pay for the real estate nonetheless. As Pointer Six had already proven.

"Stay tight and help each other," Tom ordered. "Hit targets of opportunity, but get in and get back out with the infantry."

He suited action to words, leveling the M-7 Gauss rifle at a charging Zhukov tank and squeezing the trigger. The hypersonic *crack* of the round leaving the barrel was almost as loud as the artillery had been.

Danai stood in the middle of her landing zone, *Yen-Lo-Wang* on standby behind her, while the other three 'Mechs of her Command Lance stood facing outward. *Sao-shao* Ned Baxter, his *Tian-zong* likewise quiescent behind him, stood clustered with two of his staff and a couple of crew from the DropShips. She stood alone, a few meters apart from the others, hands held behind her back while she desperately tried to radiate calm.

Inside, she was seething.

Barely three hours before she had left his place, securely held by the Second MAC. It had seemed the right decision at the time. But now...she turned, letting her eyes pass over the pyre that had been the *Tianmu Shan*. Oily, black smoke still boiled into the sky for kilometers, until it reached the level of the winds, where it spread like a disgusting blanket.

She had been wrong in her assessment of Hall's defenses. Civilians, Capellan *citizens*, had died as a result.

It was the violation of every oath she'd sworn as a *janshi*.

Breathing through her nose, Danai turned her back on the pyre. She was no Kuritan samurai, to give up after one defeat and slit her belly.

The Reps would pay for this.

"*Sang-shao?*"

She turned at Ned Baxter's voice. The MechWarrior stood apart from the others, back straight. He knew as well as she did that it had been his recommendation that had led her away from the LZ. A lot of other commanders—a lot of other Liaos—would take that as enough to crucify him and secure themselves against this defeat, but not Danai.

She'd given the order. She was responsible.

But if Baxter felt his own measure of it, so much the better. That would drive him on.

"*Changsha* and *Zibo*—" the *Overlord* and the *Excalibur*"— are both spaceworthy." Behind him, ship's crew and officers nodded in agreement. "The armor company I left on defense is decimated, but the survivors will be assigned to other companies."

"And the one who did this?"

"Fourteenth Principes," Baxter said immediately. "According to the insignia on the tanks we destroyed, including the bodies. If it's not the Fourteenth, then they went to a lot of trouble to make us believe it was them."

Danai stared at him. "And?"

"And they're gone."

"Gone." Behind her back, Danai clenched her fingers so tightly she worried she'd crack a bone, but nothing showed on her face.

"They were prepared to withdraw," Baxter said. "My infantry found their lair about ten minutes ago. They exited on the other side of that mountain—" he pointed, "—in good order and vanished into the desert."

"Vanished." She cocked an eyebrow. "It's been hours. They can't have gone more than thirty or forty kilometers, if that."

"No, *Sang-shao*." Baxter visibly gathered himself. "I have scouts out. We'll find them. But they were prepared to hit us here."

"And the 'Mechs? The tanks?" She brought one hand around to point at the burning pyre that had been the DropShip carrying the civilian government. "The ones who actually did this?"

Baxter swallowed. "Went with them, ma'am."

It was a significant effort of will for Danai not to scream. Instead, she lowered her arm, breathed calmly through her nose, and said, "Thank you, *Sao-shao*. See to your battalion."

Baxter braced and then turned away, back to his cluster of officers. Danai watched him, teeth gritted, then forced herself to look away. Another of the waiting Second MAC veterans caught her eye.

"*Si-ben-bing* Gardner?"

The tanker stepped forward and braced to attention, but didn't salute. The Second MAC didn't salute in the field on an enemy planet. "*Sang-shao* Liao-Centrella," he barked.

"Your tank?"

"It's a write-off, ma'am."

"That's too bad. Your crew?"

"All but one got out, ma'am. Thank you for asking, ma'am."

Danai grinned. "Stand easy, *Si-ben-bing*. I want to ask you something, and I need you to be honest. I don't want to hear what you think I want to hear. I want to hear what you think, got it?"

"You'd have gotten that anyway, ma'am," Gardner replied.

"Tell me about the Reps."

"Ma'am?"

"You fought them. That's more than I've done. Tell me how they fight."

"Damned good, *Sang-shao*, if you'll permit the language. They were ready for us. I know there's no way they could have known we were coming—landing here, I mean—but they were ready. They had a plan, and they followed it. And they kept to it—the 'Mechs, at the end, they could have stayed around and shot up every tank in my company. But they didn't. They made pickup on their groundpounders and took to the hills." He paused. "That takes discipline, ma'am, as you know."

"I do know," she responded. "It's hard."

"To run away when you're winning, ma'am, yes." Gardner looked worried, but he drove on, as she'd ordered him to. "Couple times we pushed too far, back on New Syrtis, when we were winning, ma'am, as I'm sure you recall. Cost us. They didn't make that mistake."

Danai grinned. "Why are you a *si-ben-bing*, Gardner? When you talk like an officer?"

Gardner grinned back. "Oh, they tried once, ma'am. But I couldn't keep from saying what's on my mind."

Danai chuckled. "See to your crew, *Si-ben-bing*. And send me the name of the one you lost. I'll want to add my own letter to the one I know you're writing."

"Thank you, ma'am," Gardner replied, bracing again and turning away.

Danai turned and stared at the pyre of the DropShip. She didn't have any idea yet how many people had died on that ship. How many more letters home she'd have to record. Her hands fell to her sides and curled into fists of their own volition.

It was too many.

Any was too many.

"Too many," she whispered.

CHAPTER 14

The Rep *Kheper* slammed a Gauss round into *Yen-Lo-Wang*'s shield. The impact would have pushed her 50-ton BattleMech back a step if she'd been standing still, but instead Danai leaned into the strike. The 125kg slug ripped the top corner of her scutum-style shield off and then *pranged* off the *Centurion*'s shoulder, doing some damage, but not nearly as much as it would have if she hadn't gotten the shield there in time.

That shield had gotten quite a workout over the last few weeks as the Second MAC hounded the Fourteenth Principes down. The Republic defenders had fragmented their forces after that first clash at the landing zone, using smaller units like lances and platoons to strike at targets of opportunity. Their strategy was clearly one of delay, buying time for something. Danai and her officers hadn't been interested in allowing them to make that purchase; they'd ridden down almost every probe, destroying the defenders piecemeal.

Danai licked her lips. It was possible this was the last Republic 'Mech force-in-being left on Hall. Noah Capshaw thought so, at least. And it was his job to know. Doing it across the last weeks had really brought the young man along; he was starting to show the real sense of backbone he'd need if he was going to become a true leader of soldiers.

The realization made Danai smile. That shepherding was one of the most rewarding parts of being an officer. It gave her a sense of pride little else matched, a sense that she was giving back to the state. Mina had taught her to recognize the feeling.

Raising her laser, she stalked toward the *Kheper.*

That made her smile, too.

Tom Jordan didn't know exactly what he'd expected the campaign to defend Hall to go like, but he knew it wasn't like this. It hadn't gone like the sims at all.

He jerked the *Kheper* back around a bend in the great stone canyons that gave Hall its name. The stone walls had become familiar across the last months, but now he hated them. They were too steep to climb, too thick to see through, and they were set in their eons-old paths that left him only so many ways to go. He felt trapped by them.

Be honest, Tom told himself, *you just feel trapped.*

The corridor he was traversing twisted back and forth every sixty meters or so, which was good. It let him break line of sight of the damnable *Centurion* and see if he could scurry away again. Over these past weeks he always had, even if others hadn't.

That thought sent a bolt of dread through his gut. Most of his Flankers were Dispossessed or dead now. At least three had been captured by the Capellans, and it was only himself and Master Sergeant Cork out here today. Looking through his HUD at the thinning, high clouds, Tom realized it might just be him. Aerial recon would have a clear view soon.

He hadn't heard from Cork in hours.

Biting back bile, Tom twisted the *Kheper* around another bend and tried to shake the thoughts from his head.

No. It wasn't over.

No one in Combat Command Gamma had heard from the other two combat commands in two weeks. They hadn't planned to coordinate their activities. Major Crowe had expected to lose Harney and most of Hall's communication infrastructure more or less immediately. His Combat

Command Alpha had based itself on the opposite side of Harney from Gamma; according to the public news reports, a whole second Capellan regiment had landed on that side of the city. Beta, the third segment of the divided Principes, had fallen off the radar almost immediately.

The first day's attack had been the high point of the entire campaign for Tom and the rest of Gamma. Their early success had given them a sense of invulnerability that lasted just a few days, until a Capellan DropShip had put a company each of armor and 'Mechs in the path of Lieutenant Penrose's Battle Lance and two platoons of armor and infantry in movement. A handful of troopers and fast, light hovercraft had escaped back to Gamma.

A quarter of Tom's 'Mechs had disappeared, just like that.

Three days later, partisans in Harney snuck word out that Ansley Penrose had died in the ambush. That was three weeks ago, and Tom still didn't quite believe it. He woke up every morning expecting to hear Penrose's high, pealing laugh in the mess, as he had a thousand times before.

Sniffing, Tom blinked his burning eyes and concentrated on the path in front of him. Master Sergeant Cork usually fought with Penrose's Battle Lance; he'd been absent that day because Tom needed his *Warhammer*'s firepower elsewhere. But every day since, he'd seen the pain in Cork's wet eyes. And felt the weight of the senior noncom's stare.

The *Kheper*'s shoulder caught a rock outcropping because he wasn't paying attention again. Tom squeezed his eyes shut until they ached, then opened them and adjusted his throttle.

Danai slowed as she approached the jigsaw-shaped path in front of her. The *Kheper*'s tracks—and *Yen-Lo-Wang*'s sensors, when they could paint the Rep 'Mech—told her it'd gone in there, but she didn't know what else was in there. She throttled back to an idle for a moment and called up a wider map.

"Zero Three, this is Six," she sent.

"Three," came back Noah Capshaw's voice.

"How goes the hunt, Noah?"

"*Sang-shao*..." Danai heard the chagrin in Capshaw's voice. "Are you by yourself again?"

"I do my best work alone," she told him.

"*Sang-shao*..."

"The hunt, Noah?"

"The hunt goes well, *Sang-shao*," Capshaw said. Behind his voice she heard the gentle tones of the *Wraith*'s first-stage heat alarm. Wherever he was, he was in the thick of it. Danai grinned, alone in her cockpit. She approved.

"Can you spare Horst or Bethany?"

"Five is down," Capshaw said. "She and her gunner are fine; the bird took a nick in the rotor, and she put it down before the blade could spin apart." He paused. "Zero Four," he said, and she heard the emphasis on the callsign, chiding her for using names, "is with Zero Two."

Zero Four and Five, Bethany Chang and Horst Ruhl, piloted a pair of PPC-armed Yellow Jacket gunships that augmented her command lance. The pair worked well with her warriors, and their height and speed advantage had come in handy more than once. Unfortunately, they were damned flimsy, as proved by Chang setting down when she had damage. It was the smart move, but it denied Danai of tactical aerial recon.

"Is the Mosquito high-altitude recon up yet?" Air-breathing spotter planes had been supplementing her recon lances for two weeks, ever since the Capellan aerospace coordinators had declared air supremacy. If the Republic had sent aerospace or air-breathing fighters to Hall, they were well hidden. The municipal militias in each city had some, but she'd already told those cities what would happen if they interfered. Thus far the planet's Republic governor and legate had ordered them to stand down; that may change when she came for the cities.

"Not yet," Capshaw told her. "Cloud clover is clearing, but we've also caught some rumors about hostile air, so we're holding them back. It's probably nothing, but I don't want to risk the pilots if we don't have to."

"Fair enough." She hid her pleasure that he'd just made the decision about the pilots without asking her. He was coming along *nicely*. "What about Two Batt?"

"*Sao-shao* Baxter says the engagement at the canal went as expected. At least two Republic BattleMechs destroyed, though he's not sure they accounted for all the blowers." There was no judgment in Capshaw's tone as he relayed the information; it was a familiar litany.

The fast little hovercraft were damn near uncatchable in the sandy wastes of Hall. With no obstacles, they just accelerated to their top speed and sprinted away, turrets spun around and firing all the time. And the Capellans' own tanks and VTOLs couldn't be everywhere.

"Very well," Danai said. "I think I've got mine cornered, but I don't know what's in there with him."

"Wait for support," Capshaw replied immediately. Then, after she waited, he chuckled and added, "with all due respect, ma'am."

"Your concern is touching," Danai said, letting some of her grin into her voice. Capshaw was just finding his confidence; she didn't want to shatter it. "But if I wait too long, he's likely to sneak away, and then we're doing this again tomorrow."

"*Sang-shao*—" Capshaw began, but she cut him off.

"Send support here," she interrupted, and read off her coordinates. "Tell them to follow me in, and watch their target ID." She nudged *Yen-Lo-Wang*'s throttle forward. "I'm going in."

"*Sang-shao*—"

"See you soon, Noah," Danai said, and toggled the channel closed. She swiped the map back down normal size, tapped her booted foot on the 50-ton 'Mech's steering controls, and squeezed her gunnery yokes.

"See you soon," she whispered.

Tom Jordan had picked his spot well; the hall had opened out into a straightaway, about 200 meters long. He'd sprinted the *Kheper* to the opposite end and spun around, weapons trained. The end of the switchbacks had surprised him; maybe it would surprise the *Centurion*'s pilot.

He knew who she was, of course. There was no mistaking *Yen-Lo-Wang*. But he found if he kept thinking of it as a *Centurion*, then he didn't automatically think about how he was fighting a deadly Solaris gladiator whose last name just happened to be Liao.

The pressure was enough as it was.

The M-7 was down to just three rounds of Gauss ammunition; the last communique from Master Sergeant Bean was that more rounds had been scrounged up, but they were all the back at the hidden log point, and he was here.

Too many of those logistic points had been found and destroyed or captured by the Capellan invaders. Some had been detected, and some had been revealed when retreating RAF units had led the Capellans pursuing them right in the front door. The plan had relied on the gigantic mass of the Helmand to shield the log points; in practice, it turned out it's a lot easier to comb the desert when you have a map. Or a guide.

Tom pressed the load queue for the multi-missile launcher, toggling in long-range missiles. Two hundred meters was just about their sweet spot, and he was just about out of SRMs anyway. He was only going to get one, maybe two, good shots off before the *Centurion* got clear of the switchback and charged. He needed to make them count.

Static blipped in his helmet as the *Kheper*'s computer struggled to isolate a transmission meant for him. Jordan blinked sweat from the corner of his eyes.

"—er Six," he heard, a man's voice, scratchy but recognizable. "Come in."

"Cork?" Tom asked.

"—ome in," the voice said again. Tom adjusted his radio.

"Cork! Is that you?"

"—aptain?"

"I'm here!" The channel broke into a screaming wail that drilled an instant's pain into Tom's eardrum, then flattened out as the computers searched for the best frequency.

"Captain?" Master Sergeant Cork's voice was much clearer. "Cork!"

"Sir, abort. I don't know where you are, but the mission is a bust. They were waiting for us."

Tom grinned. He couldn't help it. "I figured that out, Myron." He pressed a control, sending his coordinates. "I managed to get clear for a minute." There was a pause; Tom assumed Cork was looking at the map.

"Sir, you need to bug out."

"Where are you?"

"You need to get clear and back to the rest of Gamma, sir."

"Master Sergeant: tell me where you are."

"I'm facedown in the canal, sir."

Tom frowned. "The canal..." His mind clicked the words together with the map reference. "Stone's frozen balls, Cork, that's inside the Louie perimeter!"

"Yes, sir. I managed to break through, but they got my gyro. I splashed into the water, but it's only a matter of time before they pull me out of here."

"Cork—"

"Sir. You need to get clear."

Tom ground his teeth together so hard he felt something chip. Or he would have, if his consciousness was aware of what physical pain he was feeling. Right then it was subsumed in the raw emotional agony of losing the last link to his company.

If Cork was down, there, that meant there was no chance Veerasamy's *Shadow Hawk* was still upright. Still... "Sergeant Veerasamy?"

"She's dead, sir," Cork said, without hesitation. "I saw it happen. Cockpit hit."

"Goddamn it."

"Yes, sir." Cork's voice was amazingly calm. "That's why you have to get clear, Captain." His voice slipped, getting a little raw. "You're the last of us."

Tom touched the throttle control, but before he could move it, his HUD painted a red caret at the mouth of the switchbacks. Lips drew back from his teeth in a snarl as the *Centurion* appeared, crouched like a coward behind its shield.

"Do your best, Master Sergeant," Tom said. He panted, hyperventilating. He didn't care. "Get clear if you can, E and E out."

"Captain—"

"Gotta go," Tom said, and slapped the channel closed.

The crosshairs in his HUD flashed gold from the ready-green.

The M-7's crashing report shook dust and small stones free from the hall walls in a cloud as it fired. The reverberations of the hypersonic *crack* of the round's passage slapped the medium 'Mech like a wave, rebounding from the walls.

The slug took the *Centurion* square in the center of its shield; the heavy round went right through, staggering the Louie 'Mech.

Tom slammed the throttle forward, loosing his LRMs as he did.

The *Kheper* charged the Liao invasion commander's 'Mech. Just then, Tom didn't care where else she'd fought.

He just wanted the fair measure of blood for his people.

CHAPTER 15

The Gauss slug ripped through *Yen-Lo-Wang*'s shield and crushed a serious percentage of the shield arm's armor along with it. Danai rode the impact out, using her foot pedals and her own sense of balance to keep the 'Mech upright. Her HUD, shaking as her hands brought the gunnery controls back to battery, steadied down. She dragged the heavy laser around, listening, heard the tone, and fired.

All while she was still off-balance.

The horrific beam stabbed deep into the *Kheper*'s thigh, but the 'Mech didn't fall. Instead, it kept charging at her. LRMs soared overhead; rushing must have spoiled the Rep MechWarrior's aim. Danai ignored them. She hunched down behind her shield and stalked forward at a calm, measured pace.

She'd go to meet her enemy, but she'd do it on her own terms.

The *Kheper* staggered left and then right; she couldn't tell if it was intentional or not, but it had the same effect. It shook her target lock. Danai struggled to reacquire the same aiming point while the laser capacitors whined through a recharge cycle. The heat in her cockpit was stifling but not quite enough to activate her triple-strength myomers. One more shot from her laser would be enough, though.

Normal, everyday myomers were the gray pseudo-muscles that drove BattleMechs. Just like human muscles were attached to ligaments and bones, 'Mech muscles were stretched between actuators and alloy bones. For hundreds of years the formula was a fixed, known quantity: gather this much myomer, input this much electricity, get this much contraction. A little more than a century ago, though, scientists had discovered a formula that contracted at three times the normal strength, so long as they were hot enough. For a time, it threatened to revolutionize 'Mech warfare. Heat was a MechWarrior's *bête noire*, a by-product that reduced the efficiency of their war machines. Now it made them stronger?

Unfortunately, while it did make a 'Mech stronger, it did nothing to mitigate any of heat's other dangers: it didn't keep targeting systems and weapon actuators from frizzing out, nor did it keep stored ammunition from cooking off. It quickly became a specialty weapon that took a lot of skill and practice to manage.

Danai had that skill and practice from her time on Solaris.

When activated, *Yen-Lo-Wang*'s hatchet struck as if a *Berserker* was swinging it.

That hatchet strike could be in just a few seconds...

Tom Jordan saw red.

He told himself it was the HUD caret. He told himself it was tunnel vision from his adrenaline; he'd learned all about the physiological response to fight-or-flight at Sandhurst, how blood vessels constricted to narrow his focus. He told himself that's all it was.

That's all it is.

It wasn't, couldn't be, the frothing incandescent rage he felt. It wasn't the chasm of loss he felt in the center of who he was, wasn't the fact that his entire company was gone, for what sure felt like *nothing*.

He told himself it wasn't that, either.

The Gauss rifle's recharge indicator pinged ready. He squeezed the trigger immediately. He hadn't let the targeting reticle slide off the *Centurion* yet. The *crack* of the round smashing through the sound barrier rolled off of him. The slug took the *Centurion* in its shield—just like the last three had.

Tom screamed in frustration. He triggered another salvo of long-range missiles, but he'd let the range fall too far; only a pair of missiles hit, doing paltry damage to the *Centurion*'s right shin. He triggered his lasers: the extended-range medium laser burned ineffectually at the shield and the medium x-pulse laser spent its bolts wastefully against the hall wall.

The last Gauss round fell into the rifle's breech; Tom held his fire.

He was going to get around that damn shield if it killed him.

And he didn't really care if it did.

Ahead, the *Centurion* let its shield fall.

Danai hissed a snarl as the Gauss round hit her, but the shield did its job, as it had so many times before. She rode the impact, ignored the laser pulse and the missiles, and then let the shield fall to the low guard to unmask her LRM 20.

Smoke and heat wreathed her 'Mech as the slim rockets arrowed out; guided by her Artemis IV fire control system, almost all of the warheads exploded against the *Kheper*'s armor. The 55-ton 'Mech staggered but kept its course; Danai snapped the shield back up and angled the heavy laser opposite. She knew from her days on Solaris that right now her 'Mech looked like an ancient legionnaire, huddled behind his shield with just his helmet and sword showing. That shot had done most of her promotional work on the Game World.

"Come on," she whispered.

The LRMs hadn't quite added enough heat to trigger her triple-strength myomers; nonetheless, she unlocked the hatchet controls. Her fights always came down to physical range.

Danai licked her lips in anticipation.

At that range, she was unbeatable.

Tom triggered his lasers again as she closed inside sixty meters. Both burned hard at the shield. He'd triggered the MML feed queue to replace his LRMs with SRMs, but that would take precious seconds.

And he was holding the last round in his Gauss rifle.

Breathing ragged, eyes burning, Tom Jordan set himself for the last charge.

"—Six! Flanker Six, come in!"

Tom blinked. "F-Flanker six," he said, swallowing.

"Sir, Hotel Seven-Four; we're about a half-klick away in a parallel channel. Draw her this way, sir, and we'll give you a hand."

Tom coughed, his entire breathing pattern changed. Hotel was a Gamma callsign, an armored cavalry company. His eyes flicked to his HUD, searching, but the *Kheper's* computer hadn't found the friendlies yet.

The *Centurion's* right arm shook out, brandishing its hatchet, thirty meters away.

"Not gonna happen," Tom radioed. "Get clear. Tell the colonel all the Flankers are down."

"Sir—"

"That's an order," Tom sent. He toggled his radio off before the last step.

The last step before the two 'Mechs struck, Tom spun the *Kheper's* torso right, trying to get his left elbow behind the edge of the shield. *Khepers* lacked hand actuators so he couldn't grab it; he needed the leverage of the elbow to try and claw the shield out of the way so he could bury the last Gauss round into the *Centurion's* chest.

The elbow skittered across the shield as the *Centurion's* pilot anticipated him.

Danai snarled. "Not a chance," she muttered, drawing the shield back flush against the LRM launch tubes in *Yen-Lo-Wang's* chest. She triggered the heavy large laser, and hellish light blossomed between the two 'Mechs at a handful of meters' range.

Heat suffused her cockpit; alarms screamed to life, warning her about the DI computer's efforts to get it back under control. Her HUD flickered as heat interfered with the circuits.

A small, innocuous telltale on her movement console burned green.

Danai gripped the hatchet controls.

"Now—" she began, but the *Centurion* lurched.

The *Kheper*'s elbow caught in one of the sharp-edged holes Tom's Gauss rifle had blasted in the shield. The *Kheper*'s myomers and actuators screamed as if it were trying to lift the world, but the shield moved aside.

"Got you," Tom ground, controls jammed to the stops, still urging the *Kheper* around. The right-arm Gauss rifle slid across the *Centurion*'s chest, scraping the green paint, sparking where it met hardened metal, but not stopping. He held his shot...held it...

There.

He fired.

The world exploded.

Danai clutched at her controls, but even with myomers at triple-strength, she couldn't change the angle of *Yen-Lo-Wang*'s arm to get leverage and hold the *Kheper* back. The laser had done some damage, but now the right-arm Gauss rifle was pointed dead at *Yen-Lo-Wang*'s heart. She stomped her pedals, jerked her controls, tried to do something to throw the Rep MechWarrior's aim off—

—the barrel slid past her centerline and nudged into *Yen-Lo-Wang*'s armpit—

The world went loud and white.

Tom blinked and tried to make the world stop spinning. His HUD was flickering and mostly red with damage warnings, and it took him a moment realize he was lying on his back.

He reached up for the controls and started rolling the *Kheper* to its feet.

It was made harder by the 'Mech's missing right arm.

Ordinarily the capacitors for the M-7 were wrapped in blowout panels in case they exploded. It took a lot of energy, released in a very sudden and specific order, to accelerate 125 kilograms of mass to hypersonic speeds. If that energy released in a non-specific order, bad things happened.

But when you fire the weapon in contact with another 'Mech, there's not really space for the blowout panels to, well, blow out. Especially not when the magnetic flux from the barrel itself is already warping things around them. It was a miracle his neurohelmet hadn't fried half his brain from feedback.

*Kheper*s' knees bent the wrong way, but he had the 'Mech back up in a moment. Blinking, opening and closing his mouth to try and pop his years, Tom looked for the *Centurion* in his half-rasterized HUD.

An impact was his answer.

Danai licked blood from her lip and swallowed it, unwilling to take her hands off her controls long enough to open her neurohelmet's faceplate to spit it out. She worked *Yen-Lo-Wang* to one knee and took stock.

The explosion had knocked both 'Mechs down, but the *Kheper* had gotten the worst of it. Or at least its pilot had. Danai struggled *Yen-Lo-Wang* upright, gritting her teeth through a wave of nausea and dizziness. The 'Mech immediately lurched right. Danai didn't understand why until *Yen-Lo-Wang*'s foot came down on something that lurched, throwing her off-balance again. She looked down.

It was her 'Mech's whole left arm, shield included.

The *Kheper* had blown it off.

"Well," was all she said.

A short distance away, the *Kheper* stirred. Danai's mouth flattened to a hard, straight line as she pushed her throttle forward. *Yen-Lo-Wang* limped, but the heavy large laser swung into line. And the right arm still swung.

She triggered the laser.

Tom struggled to keep the *Kheper* upright. Half his HUD was razzed out; the half he *could* see showed the one-armed *Centurion* coming for him, and he didn't have much to meet her with.

A tone sounded; the *Kheper*'s computer painted a green friendly caret on his map. No ID came up, but it had to be the Hotel unit that had called earlier. It was speeding up the hall to his right.

Tom triggered his x-pulse laser without aiming, hoping to knock the *Centurion*'s aim off. But she was too good. She trusted her armor, even without the shield, to take to the blow.

The Gauss rifle's explosion had knocked the rage out of him; now he just felt cold, even in his stifling cockpit, and an irresistible urge to not let Danai Liao-Centrella finish the destruction of Flanker Company. He started the *Kheper* stepping backward, trying to hold the distance open, to stay away from that hatchet.

But it was no use.

The *Centurion*—*Yen-Lo-Wang*—was too fast. She was on him in seconds. He watched her wind up for a full-arm swing, then reached between his knees, grabbed the yellow handles and pulled. His feet twitched the 'Mech into a lean to the right.

Another impact slammed the consciousness out of him.

Danai saw the *Kheper*'s head come apart even as her hatchet cut into the stump of the 'Mech's right arm. The hard-alloy edge bit deep into the side torso, crushing the protective containment fields for the *Kheper*'s extralight fusion engine. It collapsed into a hot, sparking and smoking heap even as the MechWarrior's ejection seat roared into the sky on rocket meters. Its parafoil deployed, she saw, but the seat came down in the next canyon over.

Danai slumped against her restraints, gasping in the heat.

It was over.

Finally, it was over.

Well, almost.

Turning *Yen-Lo-Wang*, she trudged toward the wall of the hall where the Rep MechWarrior had disappeared. It was higher than *Yen-Lo-Wang* was tall, and quite steep, covered in loose scree. It took her a minute or more to reach the top and look down into the hall for the ejected MechWarrior.

They were gone.

In the distance, *Yen-Lo-Wang*'s sensors painted a dust cloud as a retreating Rep hovercraft; they must have picked the Rep MechWarrior up. Danai frowned, but declined to pursue.

Instead, she put her 'Mech into standby, unlatched her neurohelmet, and cracked her cockpit. The smells of battle flooded in immediately: dirty smoke, the sweet tang of leaking coolant, the savory scent of overheated lubricants, even ozone from the exploded Gauss rifle. The air was hot and stifling, but cool compared to the interior of her cockpit.

After a few long moments, she sat back down and opened her comm.

"Zero Six to Zero," she sent. "Coordinates to follow; someone come get me."

The vibration woke Tom Jordan up. He came awake slowly, bathed in unfamiliar pains. He was on his back again, but this time a loose metal panel was buzzing against the back of his skull. He cracked his eyes, blinked, and tried to look around. He couldn't; his head was restrained.

He was in a neck collar. His blood turned to ice.

"Don't worry, Cap'n!" a voice shouted. A scrawny, brown-haired man wearing big ear protection appeared over him. That made Tom aware of the screaming sound of fans; he was in a hover APC. He blinked and tried to swallow, to work up the saliva to ask a question, but it was too much.

"The brace is just in case!" The trooper grinned and showed him a thumb's up. "We'll get you back to the medics and they'll check you out!"

"Who are you," Tom asked, or tried to. He couldn't hear his own voice, but the trooper must have read his lips.

"Sergeant Harry James Austin, sir!" he shouted in reply. Austin waved his hand at his forehead in a ragged salute and then disappeared as he sat back down.

Tom closed his eyes. He was so tired. He wanted to do so much, to ask where they were going. To ask about Cork and the others. To curl up in a ball and cry until it all made sense.

Instead, he squeezed his eyes shut and tried to ignore the pain.

By the time Danai got *Yen-Lo-Wang* back to the landing zone, night had fallen. Mina Liao was waiting for her when she climbed awkwardly down the chain-link ladder to the ground. Danai looked at her friend, then up at *Yen-Lo-Wang*, then back at her friend.

"You lost a piece of your BattleMech," Mina said.

Danai barked a laugh. "Yeah," she replied. "I did."

Mina regarded her. "Are you done playing your soldier games, then?"

Danai stopped laughing. "Games—"

"Are you ready to get to the real work?"

"What real work?"

Mina's expression didn't change, but Danai knew her well enough to know she desperately wanted to roll her eyes. "You have won the battles, *Sang-shao*," she told Danai, "but now, your Grace, it is time to win the people."

Danai shook her head. "Lead on, *sifu*," she said, pointing.

Now Mina did roll her eyes.

CHAPTER 16

This time, they traveled by limousine.

With the Fourteenth Principes Guards' BattleMechs defeated, Danai felt it was time to call on the Republic government to surrender. She and Mina Liao, along with an honor guard from both the Second McCarron's Armored Cavalry and the Second Liao Guards, had notified the Republic governor and his legate that they would parlay—the outcome of which would be the formal surrender of Hall to the Capellan Confederation.

There had been no reply, but Danai put that down to spiteful pride. They were going anyway.

"We should have done this a month ago," Danai grumbled.

"The issue was in question a month ago," Mina reminded her.

Now Danai pinned Mina with her stare. "The 'issue,' as you put it, was never in question. I had six battalions to their one; it was only a matter of how long they prolonged the inevitable."

Outside the limo's windows, the towers and buildings of Harney slid past. The footsteps of the company of 'Mechs following along were transmitted up through the limo's wheels, but Danai could not see them unless she craned her neck around. Which she could not do, given the formal robes she wore.

Mina had insisted.

"When is it easier to surrender?" Mina probed. "When you have hope? Or when you have none?"

Danai looked away from the city to glare at her. "Hope has nothing to do with 'Mechs. They probably feel like they made a good fight of it. It took me a month to run them down, and Noah thinks there are still a lot of the Principes conventional troops out there." She shrugged. "If they have expectations of reinforcements or a counterattack, they could just be playing for time." She shook her head. "What else have they been doing all these years, then, if not preparing for attacks like this one?"

Mina smiled wryly. "Perhaps you should remember all that, then, when you meet with the governor."

Danai ground her teeth. "I really do hate you," she told Mina. "I know."

A few minutes later the limo stopped in front of the governor's mansion in the heart of Harney. It was a low building, just a few stories tall, built out of native rock and modeled as if it were a natural formation. As Danai climbed out of the limo, careful to lift her robes a few centimeters off the ground, her experienced eye picked out the subtle defenses.

The ground was laid to funnel people toward the main entrance, with enough "rocks" placed strategically to disrupt a vehicle attack. The buildings around the ground were all taller than the mansion; they had the thick corners that suggested reinforcement. No doubt antipersonnel installations were hidden behind the featureless transpex walls.

No one waited for them.

"I expected at least an escort," Danai murmured as Mina climbed out of the car.

"Do they seem in a surrendering mood?" Mina turned and pointed to the front fender of the limo, where a small white flag with a red S fluttered. "Or should we take the flag with us?"

Danai chuckled.

Out of the APC that had followed the limo, a squad of unarmored infantry in Liao-green battledress appeared.

The six troopers and a *sao-wei* carried weapons with no magazines in the well.

"*Sang-shao*," the *sao-wei* said. "Shall we retire? This could be a trap."

"A trap?"

"There is no escort, ma'am," the *sao-wei* said. Her name tape read *Nuthall*.

"Then you're our escort, *Sao-wei*." She gestured ahead. "Let's go."

Sao-wei Nuthall braced to attention and then waved to her squad. Danai let them get a little ahead, then beckoned Mina to follow. The two women gave the infantry some space to do their job, waiting while the troopers entered the building.

A few moments later *Sao-wei* Nuthall stepped back outside, alone. Her face was distorted with worry. Danai saw her swallow as she stepped closer.

"*Sang-shao*, the building appears deserted."

"Deserted?"

"There is no one inside," Nuthall reported. The young woman's pale skin flushed red, and she refused to look anywhere other than over Danai's right shoulder. "The doors are all open. But no people."

Danai looked at Mina. "I don't understand."

"It c-could be a trap," the *sao-wei*—what other realms called a lieutenant—stammered. "The building could be wired to explode."

Danai looked past the infantry officer and then back at the street where the limo and her escort waited. It couldn't be called crowded, but there were people on the streets. Many stared, but she expected that. She looked at Mina.

"In a way, it is a surrender," Mina said. "If they refuse to remain and control the city, then no one will oppose us."

Danai considered. Then she asked for Nuthall's comm. When she handed it over, Danai turned and looked at the 'Mechs behind her. "Wu."

"*Sang-shao*," came the instant reply from her XO's *Prefect*.

"Get me a battalion of the Gypsies in here to secure this building. Small chance it's wired, so let's get EOD in here. As soon as it's safe we're moving our HQ in there, got it?"

"Yes, *Sang-shao*."

Danai handed the comm back to Nuthall and then looked around. After a moment she pointed across the street. "That looks like a coffee shop, doesn't it?" Mina looked where she was pointing, then nodded. "Shall we see if they have tea?"

Mina dimpled. Danai grinned back.

"Let's go, *Sao-wei*. The Lady Liao is thirsty."

THE HOLE
DUNSBOROUGH
HALL
REPUBLIC OF THE SPHERE

Tom Jordan still felt unsteady on his feet, but he had on clean battledress. Sergeant Austin led him through the dark, barely lit tunnels. They passed RAF troopers wearing a mix of patches: Fourteenth Principes, old Hall Standing Guard, Dunsborough Urban Battalion...it was too many.

After a while Austin stopped. "In there, Captain," he said, beckoning to a hatch set in a stone wall.

"Who's in there?"

Sergeant Austin just grinned. "Not cleared to know that, Cap'n. But I'll be here when you get out. I'll lead you to our billet."

Tom gripped Austin's shoulder. It had been a long series of overnight blower rides to get here, and he barely knew where "here" was. He'd caught sight of the Grimsbay as they exited the vehicle, so he knew he was somewhere south of Harney, but that was about it. He wanted to shake his head, to say something, but instead he just opened the hatch and stepped through.

The room inside was clearly a command center; a low holotable dominated the room, but there were flatpanel workstations around the periphery with uniformed RAF troopers manning them.

A cluster of four people stood around the tank; he recognized one of them. "Colonel Tobin," he said, stepping closer and bracing.

The armor regiment commander turned away from the tank, regarded him, then beamed. "Captain Jordan. Good to see you, son." She twisted back, touching the arm of one of the men with her. "Sir?"

When the older man turned, Tom nearly saluted. "Legate Fernandez," he said. "I didn't recognize you, sir."

"No reason you should have," the legate replied. Fernandez was a big man, getting soft around the middle and shoulders like most men did as they climbed into middle age. In the prewar Republic, a legate was the highest military authority on a planet, answerable only to the governor or the lord governor of the prefecture. Since the Fortress, the legates' power had diminished. Tom couldn't remember Colonel Boyle ever talking about Legate Reed on Elgin, for example. "I'm sorry for the loss of your company, Captain. Trust me—they weren't spent in vain."

Tom felt his face flush at the words. He shook the legate's hand, and met his stare, but he wasn't ready to think about whether or not his people had fought and died for a reason. He was still stuck on "fighting and dying." He let go of the legate's hand and mumbled, "Thank you, sir."

"He's not lying," an older woman interjected. She stepped around the other side of the holotank. "Every citizen of Hall thanks you and your people, Captain."

"Captain Tom Jordan, meet Governor Yvette Hakima," Colonel Tobin said, grinning slightly.

"Governor," Tom said, bowing. This was too much—too much brass, much too fast. He felt like he was dreaming. "Why aren't you in Harney, ma'am?" he blurted. He knew he should have been horrified, but he felt almost like he was watching himself right now.

Luckily, the governor chuckled. "Because then I'd be obliged to surrender," she replied. She smiled—not unkindly, but still, a politician's smile—and gestured with her chin for the legate to return to the holotank.

Colonel Tobin stepped closer, still grinning. "That's a lot at once."

"Yes, ma'am," Tom said. "Ma'am. Any word on the rest of my battalion?"

Tobin's smile fell away, and she looked past his shoulder. "There are a handful of 'Mechs unaccounted for, Tom. But otherwise, you're it."

"Me?"

"It looks that way."

"From all three companies?"

Tobin nodded. "We have confirmation that Major Crowe and his staff were captured about a week ago. Captain Magnusson is dead. Captain Prideaux's 'Mech went into the water and never came back up, and Captain Turner was killed during the first skirmish Combat Command Beta fought with the Second Liao Guards."

Tom looked around for a chair, afraid he was going to collapse.

Tobin must have seen it. She stepped closer, grasping his elbow. "Are you okay?"

"Yeah—" Tom closed his eyes, breathed deeply, and then straightened. "Where are we?"

"The Hole."

"The Hole."

"I know, not very original. But it's what we've got." She gestured around. "From here we can do our best to coordinate the resistance." When Tom frowned, she squeezed his elbow. "The fight's not over, Captain."

"But—"

"We did our job. We bought a month. And now the Louies will relax. Let their guard down. We can strike at targets of opportunity, keep them from getting comfortable, and generally stay a nuisance until the colonel and the rest of the RAF come to kick them off Hall."

Tom must have looked skeptical. Tobin chuckled, then let go of his arm and pointed to the door. "Get some rest, Captain. Sergeant Austin will show you your hole. He has your first set of orders, but not until tomorrow, okay? Rest first."

"Orders?"

"Tomorrow, Captain. That's an order."

"Yes, ma'am."

HARNEY
HALL
REPUBLIC OF THE SPHERE

Danai sat at the governor's desk, looking around the opulent room. Night had fallen, and the Gypsy EOD teams hadn't found any bombs or booby-traps. She and Mina had taken this office and waited for the last teams to finish sweeping, which had taken the majority of the day. Now Mina sat across from her, hands folded in her lap, staring out the window at the courtyard where they'd waited earlier in the day. Two MAC BattleMechs stood sentry.

"What are you thinking?" Danai asked.

"About generations," Mina replied. When Danai raised an eyebrow in question, she went on. "It has been 125 years since this planet was Capellan. Enough time for five generations to have been born, if not lived. There are probably not more than a thousand people on this planet who were alive the last time the Capellan flag flew here, and they were children then."

"A long time," Danai agreed.

"Daughters, mothers and grandmothers have lived entire lives here, absent from the Confederation."

Danai recalled what a defeated MechWarrior had once told her, a couple weeks ago. "A planet is its people."

"Exactly." Mina blinked and met Danai's stare. "And here we are."

"You're thinking of what comes next," Danai said.

"Are you not?"

"I was trying not to," Danai replied. "I'm not looking forward to it."

Mina frowned, something she rarely did. "Why not?"

"You said it yourself: five generations, these people have been 'free.' Free to do whatever they want, sacrifice their gifts, malinger, fail to contribute to the state. They're going to be loath to give that freedom up." Danai sat forward, picking at the edge of the inset noteputer in the governor's desk with her thumbnail. "It's going to be hard. Probably violent."

"Not if we do it well." Mina's voice was firm.

"And what does 'well' mean?"

"I do not know yet," Mina responded. "But I will figure it out."

Danai looked at her friend and tried to see the world through her eyes. A brilliant woman, unquestionably, but this was the first time she'd ever been on a conquered planet. She could convince a *tree* of the brilliance of the Sarna Mandate or the Korvin Doctrine, because she'd devoted her life to it. But she hadn't been out on these worlds to see that put to the test.

From a certain point of view, the resistance only reinforced the Sarna Mandate and the Capellan castes. The noisiest resistance would come from the hundreds of millions of soon-to-be members of the commonality—what passed for middle class families in the Confederation. People comfortable enough to ignore the staple influence of the state in their lives, who could spend time and treasure crowing about "freedom" without paying attention to where that freedom came from.

But, by and large, they were unwilling to make the hard decisions of the directorship.

Which was why there was a directorship caste.

But getting Hall's billions to agree to that meant getting most of them to agree that they were wrong in their deeply-held beliefs.

Danai sighed. "I have faith you will," she told her friend.

But her mind was already turning back to the military situation.

CHAPTER 17

**FORT LEXINGTON
HALL
REPUBLIC OF THE SPHERE
28 MARCH 3149**

Sao-wei Heather Teng of the Second Liao Guards regiment was zoned out. Her *Gravedigger* stood sentry at the highway exit for civilian traffic into Fort Lexington, with the other three 'Mechs of her lance scattered in a diamond formation around the four points of the interchange. The two platoons of infantry from the First Liao Foot Guards—the leg infantry regiment assigned to support the Second Liao Guards—that were augmenting her lance manned a checkpoint for traffic stops. The lance had been out here for six hours.

Four vehicles had gotten off the highway. Three of them had turned around and gotten back on.

The fourth had a long-haul trucker asleep in the driver's cab.

"Is it time to go home yet?" asked MechWarrior Enid Ruskaya. Her *Roadrunner* had spent the last few hours scraping holes in the sand with its right foot. The Liao-green paint was now washed with brown dust and scrapes where she'd ground all fifteen tons of her 'Mech into a rock.

"No," Heather snapped. "Stop asking."

"How about now?"

"No."

"You're just encouraging her, *Sao-wei*," interjected MechWarrior Stan Beatrice. "Girl needs to be taught a lesson." Beatrice's *Roadrunner* had stood still the entire day.

"Children..." Heather warned. She put a tone in her voice, but this was an old game.

"I hate it when mommy and daddy fight," said the fourth MechWarrior in the lance, *Si-ben-bing* Pasha Voltikov. Voltikov's *Anubis* was well back from the others. Armed with long-range missiles and light PPCs, swathed head to toe-claw in stealth armor, the 30-ton 'Mech was the lance's backstop.

Not that they'd needed a backstop out here.

Heather checked her long-range sensors again. The only inputs were the big tracking systems behind her at Fort Lexington and the scrolling icons of civilian ground traffic along the highway. Nothing was going on.

Just like the last couple weeks.

Since the Second MAC had taken care of the Principes 'Mechs, the Rep defenders had gone to ground. The Capellan liberation force—Heather was smart enough to snort at the euphemism—had moved immediately to occupy Harney and other important strategic sites on the Wass continent. The local Rep government had fled, and they'd all seen the pirate HV and net broadcasts of the Hall Republican government-in-exile.

"Right out of the playbook," *Sang-shao* Liao-Centrella had declared when she spoke to the officers of Heather's battalion two weeks earlier. The Chancellor's sister had gone on to tell them that the fight for Hall was just getting started; the Reps still had a fair amount of conventional forces unaccounted for, true, but the real battle was theirs to fight every day: the battle for the hearts and minds of the new Capellan civilians on Hall.

"These people are our people now," Liao-Centrella had said. "They're learning their way back into the bosom of the state. It is a huge change for them, and change is difficult. It causes pain, and pain make people lash out." She'd stopped then, looking each of the young officers in the eye. "These people are now as much a part of the state as the people of Sian. It is now your job to protect them. Even from themselves."

Heather had listened attentively to the *sang-shao*'s words. Danai Liao-Centrella, for all her closeness to the Celestial Wisdom, felt more *real* to people like Heather Teng. She was out here, with them, fighting to make the Confederation stronger. And not just figuratively. Heather had friends in the tech staff, and the technician teams of the Second Liao Guards were friendly with their counterparts in the 2/MAC. She'd seen the raw HV of the *sang-shao*'s battered 'Mech coming back in from the field.

She *fought.*

Heather was not a person who really thought in terms of role models, but Danai Liao-Centrella was someone she wanted to be when she grew up.

"Guess nap time is over," Beatrice commented.

Heather checked her HUD; movement was careted. The sleeping truck driver had awoken and was walking toward the refueling station a couple hundred meters away from the highway, off the interchange.

"Maybe he has to pee," MechWarrior Ruskaya said. "I sure do."

"Use the relief tube," Beatrice snorted.

"Easy for you to say," Ruskaya shot back. "You're a guy. It's easier for you to hit a target."

"Children," Heather muttered. She watched the truck driver out of the boredom of nothing else to do. He got to the parking lot, stepped over the curb, and started over toward the small restaurant.

"Little after-nap snack, I guess," Ruskaya said.

Heather shifted her attention to the small number of vehicles, both ground and air-cushion skimmers in the parking lot. Most of them were cold; they were belonged to the station's staff. One or two were hot; new arrivals from the boonies around them.

As she watched, a hover truck spun up its fans, bellied backward from the recharging post, and scuttled around. It pointed it nose north, away from the interchange and the 'Mechs, and accelerated away.

Two more vehicles, both three-person skimmers, followed almost immediately.

All three went north.

"Is it time to go home yet?" Ruskaya asked.

"No," Heather told her. "You and Beatrice, switch positions." Beatrice's *Roadrunner* lurched into motion immediately, adjusting its course so that it wouldn't crash through the parked truck.

"Are you putting me in the corner?" Ruskaya pouted. "Is this time-out?"

"Just move your ass," Heather growled. She was grinning, alone in her cockpit. But she didn't let any of that into her voice.

Ruskaya's *Roadrunner* kicked one more puff of dirt and dust into the air, like a petulant five-year-old, and then stepped off toward Beatrice's position. Where the quieter MechWarrior was passing in front of the truck, Ruskaya angled to go around the rear.

Heather expected the young woman to blow Beatrice a raspberry over comms as they passed. She waited, channel opening, listening to Ruskaya breathe, waiting for it.

"Hey Beatrice—" Ruskaya called as she neared the truck's trailer.

The trailer exploded.

HARNEY
HALL
REPUBLIC OF THE SPHERE

Mina leaned close as the servitor moved to open the door. "Keep your temper," she warned Danai, who rolled her eyes and refused to deign to respond. Instead, she focused on folding her hands in her lap and getting her shoulders placed comfortably in the governor's palatial chair behind her desk. She'd seen holos of Governor Hakima; she wasn't a giant. Why she had a giant's chair was just one of the questions Danai was looking forward to asking her once she was finally captured.

The last few weeks had been quiet; the remaining RAF regular forces had vanished into the wilderness. Danai fully expected them to begin an insurgency as soon as they could, but she'd still taken advantage of the precious time they'd given her.

Detachments from the Second Liao Guards had been spread around the Wass continent to disarm and register the various municipal militias and begin the process of converting the planet's defense systems to a Capellan system. She'd given them very specific orders regarding the treatment of Hall's people, and so far, aside from a few minor incidents, it had gone well.

The absence of Hakima and her government meant a formal surrender under the Ares Conventions, the centuries-old agreement that governed how warfare was conducted, was impossible. It was more tradition than law—most Successor States, including the Confederation, had put the Conventions aside at the fall of the Star League—but it was still a tradition that held weight.

It was the other thing that made Danai sure there would be an insurgency. Hakima had kept herself out there as a rallying cry, she was sure of it.

But the woman had been oddly silent. And it's hard to rally behind nothing.

The door to the office opened and the servitor ushered in a man in late middle age; his skin was dark, but his hair was going ashy, and Danai could see the losing battle he was fighting with his waistline. Still, he carried himself with a military bearing. His suit was civilian, but cut with military lines. He nodded to the servitor, marched to a measured distance from her desk, and bowed.

Danai resisted an urge to smirk. Everything about this man screamed "soldier."

"Your Grace," he said. "I am Themba Olatunde." He glanced at Mina, then met Danai's gaze. "I was told you wished to speak with me."

Danai smiled politely. "I did." She gestured him to a chair. "I was told it was Sir Themba," she said as he sat down.

Olatunde settled himself with a smile. His voice was strong and precise, and if he was uncomfortable, he didn't show it. He folded his hands across his stomach. "It was. But I have been mayor of Harney longer than I was a soldier." He glanced past her, out the palatial windows. "There was some early noise about recalling me, but I quashed it. I can do more good as administrator of this city than I could in a tank."

"It is a difficult thing to give up," Danai said, watching him carefully. "The life of a soldier."

Olatunde shrugged. "Not for me."

Danai grunted agreement to fill the time while her mind raced. Her intelligence shop, including Noah Capshaw, believed this man had to be involved in the coming insurgency. He was a former Knight of the Republic, a leader who commanded respect across Hall. His position as senior civilian official of the planet's capital city gave him access to immense resources and contacts.

Her official Maskirovka contingent had died in the landing zone attack, so the resources of the regiments were all she had for now. And she was unused to it.

All the worlds she'd fought on during the actions against the Federated Suns were swarming with hidden Maskirovka assets, from quiet little intelligence gatherers to covert teams of assassins from *Zang shu jian*, the Chancellor's Sword. All she'd had to do was have Noah put a recognition signal in a specific place in his files, and sooner or later a Mask operative would show up. Even in wartime there is commerce, and the Mask had centuries of institutional knowledge on how to insert operatives.

But the Wall had changed all that. No one had set foot on Hall for most of two decades from the outside. And certainly no signals had come out. The recognition signals Noah had were years out of date, and though he'd done his best, none of the old Mask deep-cover operatives had shown up to act as a local intelligence resource. Whether the signals were too old, the agents dead or captured, or just gone native, she didn't know. And she didn't have time to care.

She was forced to make up it as she went. Which led to meetings like this one.

Which, she was reasonably certain after having met the man, was a waste of time. Olatunde may have once been a soldier and still carried the veneer of that life, but he was not one now.

"I was impressed by your bow," Danai commented. If the *non sequitur* affected the mayor, he did not show it. He merely grinned and inclined his head. "Not many non-Capellans manage to do it without seeming condescending."

"Courtesy costs nothing," Olatunde replied. "And the ways of Capellan life are not unknown here. We have not been a Capellan world for centuries, but many of our communities retain their ancient heritage. Here in Harney, the population of, shall we say, ethnic Capellans, is quite large."

"Ethnic Capellans..."

"Asian-influenced." The mayor glanced again at Mina, who had said nothing and not been introduced, but said nothing more.

"I see," Danai said.

"Your Grace," Olatunde continued, to fill the awkward pause, "I hope you did not ask me to come here to surrender the planet." He frowned and brushed at the knee of his suit. "I do not have that authority."

"Hall is mine," Danai said simply. She said it without rancor or pride, in the way she might claim a drink in the mess when someone set down a stack of bulbs. "Governor Hakima abdicated when she fled the city and its people. In the Confederation—" she paused, waiting until Olatunde met her eyes, "—we know that duty to the people entrusted to us is the greatest service we can provide the state."

"We believe that here also, your Grace," Olatunde said. Danai was pleased to hear a little steel in the man's tone.

"Good." Danai paused. She wanted to chew the inside of her cheek, lick her lips, do something to give herself a sensory input while her mind raced. But she knew Olatunde would see that, and she knew now he was too canny a man to not notice it. Instead, she slid her fingertips, beneath the level of the desktop, back and forth across the fabric of her robes.

Mina might have made a sound. Danai might have imagined it.

"We have not yet begun the civilian side of the hard and necessary work of bringing Hall back into the bosom of the Confederation," Danai said. "The military situation has been in flux, and the governor's abandonment of her people makes it more difficult."

"I have appreciated the reprieve," Olatunde said. His posture visibly stiffened. "I presume you have summoned me here to relieve me of my post as the city's leader?" He stayed seated, apparently aware how much of a sense of defiance standing would add to his words.

Danai said nothing.

"We of the Republic do not assign our people into castes," the mayor continued, "though we do we ask them for proof of service before offering them citizenship. I am no director, and I have not served." He offered a thin grin. "I can read, however, and our understanding of Capellan social custom is quite complete. We know, for example, that common Confederation procedure is to assign conquered peoples to your servitor caste."

Danai opened her mouth to respond, but a knock sounded an instant before the office door opened. Danai frowned and watched as *Sao-shao* Ned Baxter and Emory Koltsokov strode quickly into the room. Baxter stopped in front of her desk and braced; Koltsokov did the same, but glanced down at Olatunde quickly.

"*Sang-shao*," Baxter said. "I apologize for the interruption, but I need a few moments of your time."

Danai glared at him, composed her face, and looked to Olatunde. "My apologies," she said to the man. She stood, and he did also. "Now, what is it, Ned?"

Baxter glanced at the mayor. "Ma'am..."

"Out with it," Danai spat.

"There's been an incident."

"An incident."

"A bomb. Near Fort Lexington. One of the Second Guards' 'Mechs is down."

Danai ground her teeth. She looked at Olatunde, questioning her prior conviction that he had nothing to do with it. It would take real chutzpah to time an attack for when he was in her office, but it would also be a dramatic way to suggest his own innocence.

"Your Grace," he interjected before she could speak, "by your leave, I can liaise with emergency services in Fort Lexington." His voice was flat, devoid of fear or judgment. "I know the coordinator up there."

"We have our own resources," Baxter spat.

"*Sang-shao*, if this is the beginning of a general attack..." Koltsokov's face was flushed. Her eyes flicked to the side, but she didn't turn her head. "It could be a demonstration to draw out more of our forces. Or even attack the rescuers. It is a common tactic in terrorist insurgencies."

Olatunde's voice had steel in it. Danai had heard it from the first syllable, but the words, when they came, were not what she expected. "Be that as it may, your Grace, that doesn't absolve us of our duty to the wounded." He turned his head and looked at Baxter like the Capellan officer was a snake. "No matter what uniform they wear."

Danai bit her lower lip, glanced at Mina, and then shook her head. "We'll all go," she said. "You can use the comm in the chopper," she told Olatunde.

CHAPTER 18

FORT LEXINGTON
HALL
REPUBLIC OF THE SPHERE
28 MARCH 3149

"Ruskaya!" Heather Teng shouted. Her *Gravedigger* was too goddamn slow! She had the throttle to its stop, but the balky 'Mech just lumbered along as its top range.

"No contacts," Voltikov reported. His voice was cool, but he was clipping his consonants. That was how he demonstrated stress. Both his *Anubis* and Heather's *Gravedigger* had been far enough back from the blast that it had only rocked them with blast wave. The two *Roadrunner*s...

"Ruskaya," Heather repeated.

"*Sao-wei...*" croaked MechWarrior Beatrice.

"Stan!" Heather looked for his 'Mech.

The two ultralight 'Mechs had been nearest the truck when it exploded. She didn't know if that had been the assailant's plan or if they just gotten lucky. But whether chance or design, the blast had been ruinous to the 15-ton machines.

*Roadrunner*s had barely any armor; they were high-speed, surgical units designed to move and not get hit. Being in the blast zone of an improvised explosive device was not in their design document.

"I'm okay," Beatrice groaned. His 'Mech was on its side, an arm and a leg missing. Sparks shot from its actuators, and huge gaps were visible in its remaining armor. "I'm okay," he repeated, slurring his words a little.

"Just hang on," she ordered. "Voltikov, get on the radio and get us medics!"

"On it," the taciturn MechWarrior replied.

"Ruskaya," Heather said. Her 'Mech had finally reached the blast zone. The crater where the truck exploded was still black and smoking, sending a column of black smoke into the sky. She swept the wreckage with her sensors, but the *Gravedigger* didn't see anything it thought was a threat.

There was no reply from her fourth MechWarrior.

Cold, icy hands gripped the strings to her heart.

She'd never lost a MechWarrior before.

Swallowing, Heather turned the *Gravedigger* in place, giving her sensors a chance to look carefully in every direction.

"Enid," Beatrice mumbled.

"I said stay there!" Heather shouted. "That's an order, MechWarrior!"

"S-rest," he slurred.

"Voltikov?"

"I got the duty desk at Fort Lexington," the *Anubis* pilot said. "They're scrambling the reaction force and sending medics."

"How long?"

"They didn't say."

"Then goddamn call back and ask!" she screamed.

"They want a threat assessment, *Sao-wei*."

Heather cut her mic, cursed, and then glanced at her threat board. It was clear. She toggled the channel open again. "No threats."

"What about the driver?"

"What about him?"

"He could still be in that building, waiting to trigger a second strike."

Heather twisted the *Gravedigger* around. The fuel point looked empty and the hover vehicles that had pulled out earlier were already gone over the horizon. She dragged her targeting reticle down, aimed, and squeezed the trigger for her autocannon. The gun burped a sleet of submunitions. The fuel point was far out of what would be normal range for targeting another 'Mech or any other moving target, but buildings don't dodge.

The quintet of tungsten-alloy penetrators slashed into the thin-skinned building. One of them struck sparks hot enough to ignite the hydrogen reservoirs used to refuel fuel cell vehicles. The fuel point vanished in a blue-orange fireball.

"No threats," Heather repeated.

Ned Baxter wanted to be in his 'Mech's cockpit.

Or in his office back on Liao.

He wanted to be anywhere except where he was, clutching the hail-Mary handle of an infantry-variant Ferret light scout VTOL the *sang-shao* had commandeered from the Gypsies. A trio of Aeron thrust-vector jump jets screamed along behind them at max throttle to keep up with the handy little Ferret. Ned knew there was next to no chance they'd be intercepted, but next to nothing was not zero.

He didn't want to die in the fiery crash of a toy helicopter.

"Any update?" he heard in his earmuff headset.

"No, *Sang-shao*," was Koltsokov's reply.

Ned twisted his head to look out the small porthole, rather than glare at his CO and the others in the infantry bay. He didn't even need to be here. He should be back in Harney, getting his battalion ready in case this was a prelude to a general attack.

"No other incidents reported?" Danai asked.

"None."

As if we would be hiding them from you, Ned thought.

"Your Grace," came the quiet voice of the other lady, Mina Liao.

"Not now," the *sang-shao* said.

"This is a mistake," Mina said.

Ned wanted to turn his head back in to see how that landed, but he was afraid any movement would betray that he could hear the exchange. They all could—the chopper's intercom circuit only had one channel—but whatever Mina disagreed with, Ned wanted to hear.

"Taking the 'Mechs would have taken too long," Danai said.

"That is not what I mean."

"Then say what you mean," Danai snapped. Ned stifled a snort.

"Any of your officers could see to this response."

"I am responsible for these soldiers!"

"Yes. And every other human on Hall. Will you next be visiting every traffic accident, every domestic dispute, every person sent to the hospitals?"

"This is different."

"Only because you are making it so," Mina insisted. She never raised her voice, never changed her tone. If she was at all bothered by the rough ride in the military helicopter, she hadn't shown it.

Now Ned did turn his head and look, but at Mina Liao, not Danai.

The noblewoman met his eyes as if she'd been expecting it. He ducked his chin once, quickly, in acknowledgment of the eye contact, then looked down at the deck. He was curious, but he didn't need to be part of this argument. The dirty floor of the cabin had already marked the hems of Mina's robes with dirt and grease.

"You are, at present, the governor-general of Hall in the Chancellor's name," Mina went on, looking back at Danai. "Until a replacement *diem* arrives, you are responsible for a great deal more than the military situation."

Danai looked daggers at her friend. Enough of the anger in her stare leaked out that Ned looked away as soon as he glanced at her face.

"Your Grace," the local put in, carefully.

"What."

"I'm told your military forces are responding from Fort Lexington," the Harney mayor said. "Civilian fire and rescue are following, though, in case they are needed."

They won't be, Ned wanted to sneer, but he held his tongue.

Emory Koltsokov was doing her best impression of a bulkhead.

After a longer pause than she probably liked, Danai exhaled loud enough to trigger her microphone. "Thank you."

"Your concern does you credit," Mina continued. "But you have larger concerns, especially if this really is the beginning of the insurgency you fear."

Of course it is, Ned thought, but told himself he couldn't expect a civilian to understand that.

"A MechWarrior is down, maybe dead," Danai insisted. "And I led them here."

"I am not saying you are wrong to care," Mina continued. "I am saying this is not how you should react."

"No one will follow me if they don't know I care about their lives," Danai insisted, but even Ned could hear the defeat in her voice. And, if he was being honest, he understood the logic on both sides. If it had been one of his 'Mechs that had gone down out there, he'd be exactly where she sat.

He hadn't expected to think that.

"That's a fallacy, and you know it," Mina chided. "Billions of Capellans follow the Chancellor's will without ever meeting him. He does not attend their weddings or the birth of their children. He does not comfort them when their parents die, or grieve in their home with them when disaster strikes. And yet they serve his will through their devotion to the state."

"It's not the same," Danai pouted.

"It is," the Harney mayor said. What amazed Ned was the same words left his mouth at the same time. He and Olatunde shared a glance, then the local nodded for Ned to go first.

"*Sang-shao*," he said, and waited until she nodded for him to go on. "I would be right where you sit if this had been my battalion," he explained. When she opened her mouth to respond, he raised his hand. "But I would also be wrong. Because my responsibility would be to my entire battalion. I have officers for this. Just as you do. As Lady Liao has been telling you."

"You don't want to be here?" Danai asked.

Ned shook his head. "I go where I'm ordered," he said. "But right now every officer in that MechWarrior's chain of command feels the same way you do, from *Sang-shao* Krishnamurthy to the lance commander we're going to meet. That MechWarrior was each of those officers' responsibility, too." He looked at the local.

"Your officer already said it, your Grace." Olatunde offered a small smile.

"So we should turn around."

"We are nearly there," the local countered, with a shake of his head. "But we shouldn't stay long." He looked around and touched the cabin wall with what looked like affection. "It's been a lot of years since I was in an infantry compartment, and this feels more like home than I want to admit," he said. "But if this is about to erupt in Harney, I need to be there. To stop it if I can, or deal with the aftermath if I can't."

"You were trying to quit when all this started," Danai reminded him.

Ned glanced between them. It was clear the two had managed to find some small connection before he and Koltsokov had interrupted them, but she was shockingly informal with a local she'd just met. *Not that she is all that formal a person generally, but still...*

"And if you demand it, I will," Olatunde said. "But until then, those people are my responsibility." Ned didn't like to admit how much he admired the quiet dignity in the old man's voice.

"Apparently I'm the one shirking my duties," she said, glancing around the group with a tight grin. "We'll see how the day plays out."

The Ferret banked to the left. The pilot's voice crackled into their headsets. "Coming into view."

Danai and Ned twisted as one to look out the small portholes. There were only three; the local, who'd been sitting on the right side of the bay, unbuckled quickly with old muscle memory and stood. He stepped across the pitching deck with admirable ease and leaned over the last port.

"Jesus," Ned whispered. The crater was already visible.

"That's no IED," Olatunde said. "That's high explosive."

Ned believed it. He touched the control on his earpiece. "Get us down there," he ordered the pilot.

THE HOLE
DUNSBOROUGH
HALL
REPUBLIC OF THE SPHERE

"It worked!"

Tom Jordan looked up from the report he was skimming on his noteputer when Sergeant Austin stepped through the hatch. The gangly sergeant held out his own noteputer. Tom set his reading aside and took it. There was a message on the screen, and an attached flat video. He skimmed the text and played the video, fifteen seconds of shaky footage the culminated in a huge fireball.

"Did we get anything?" Tom asked as he handed the noteputer back.

"Word is, timing was perfect. Right as two 'Mechs were nearby. Both reported down, but we won't know how bad until they get back to the Fort."

Tom grunted and let his eyes unfocus, thinking. Fort Lexington was a sprawling RAF reserve base that had been an infantry training center for several years after the Wall went up. They chose not to defend it against the Capellan invasion because their plan hadn't been to mount any static defenses, but that didn't mean they didn't have a network of informants seeded into the support staff still there. The Capellans had occupied the fort, but invaders rarely bring their own cooks and janitors.

But those information sources wouldn't last forever.

Neither would the remaining RAF insurgents, if the colonel didn't come soon.

"Feels good to *do* something, don't you think, sir?" Austin asked.

"After doing nothing these last couple weeks, you mean?"

"Yes, sir."

"I guess it does, Harry. But I just hope it was the right thing."

"Two 'Mechs down, sir," Sergeant Austin remarked. "That's got to count for something, don't it?"

"It's something, no question." What he didn't say was *two down, two hundred more to go.* But he thought it. Instead, he waved the sergeant out of the room and picked up his noteputer again. He looked at the dates in the file, then at the date displayed in the top corner of the noteputer screen, and chewed his lip.

RAF strategic planning had small mercenary units coming to help them. It was all part of the larger plan that Tom hadn't been cleared for until after the first phase of the defense. With the Wall down, fast couriers had taken recruiters to Galatea—the Mercenary's Star—to do some quick hiring.

If the first phase failed—Tom snorted—*when* the first phase failed, the follow-on troops were meant to give the insurgency some teeth. They wouldn't be enough to drive two regiments off Hall, but they would drastically slow down the pace of assimilation and extend the time the insurgency could hold out. All of that meant more time for Colonel Boyle to get a relief force assembled and over to them.

And it meant, when the mercenaries arrived, that Tom would have a new command: liaison to the 'Mech forces. It fell to him, a senior MechWarrior left uncaptured.

Tom set the noteputer down and closed his eyes. The incipient headache he'd felt coming on hit him suddenly beneath both temples, and kneading his knuckles only changed the shape of the pain. It didn't make it go away.

Eyes still closed, Tom chuckled. That was a nice metaphor for the campaign he envisioned coming. The mercenaries, if and when they came, would let him cause the Capellans pain. But they'd only change the shape of the fall of Hall if the colonel didn't come too, and soon.

Tom opened his eyes, looked down at the noteputer, and began a new file called Operation Headache. If he was going to have more 'Mechs to direct soon, he needed to get a head start on the staff work now.

In the back of his mind, he wondered if they should have waited for the mercenaries to start the active phase of the insurgency. It would have certainly given it more teeth.

And the Capellans wouldn't be looking for them so hard.

Surely it was easier to land 'Mechs undetected when the whole invasion force wasn't combing the desert. Tom shook his head. That was Colonel Tobin's problem, and the legate's.

His was to have plans ready for the mercenary 'Mechs when they got there.

When.

Not if.

When.

Hall wouldn't survive an *if.*

CHAPTER 19

**HARNEY
HALL
REPUBLIC OF THE SPHERE
4 MAY 3149**

Danai closed her eyes and counted to five as the door to her office closed. When she opened them, Mina Liao had moved to stand in front of her desk and was looking at her with that damn smirk.

"What?" Danai asked.

"I sometimes think you would prefer to be out there in your 'Mech with people shooting at you," Mina said.

"Let me clear up any doubts: I would. Unquestioningly."

Mina offered a Gallic shrug and nodded. "The proverb is true, then?"

"The proverb?"

"It is more difficult to build than destroy?"

Danai groaned. "Don't start that again. I don't need another Great Dam story. Not today. I'm not in the mood." She spread her fingers on the desktop and stretched her palms flat, enjoying the sensation of stretching the tendons in her hands and fingers. Too many hours of clenching them into invisible fists in her lap had left her stiff and achy.

In the month since the bomb at Fort Lexington, there had been two more attacks, both bombs that struck her military supply convoys between cities. Three more Capellan soldiers were killed, including two from her own regiment. She'd already written the letters. But she hadn't gone to the site. She was trying to take what Mina and the others had told her to heart, hard as it was.

Intellectually, it made perfect sense. She had the military education to know her duty, and she'd risen through the ranks enough to understand that all her officers felt that same sense of failure she did. Danai completely understood the arguments: that it wasn't her job, that it undercut the appearance of her trust in her subordinate officers. She could practically recite the war college lectures on the subject.

But none of that changed how she *felt*.

"What's next?" Danai inquired. "A military briefing, perhaps? Haven't I been a good student so far today? Smiled at all the right people, said all the right things? Don't I deserve a cookie?" Mina wanted to roll her eyes; Danai could see it. It made her grin. "Please, headmistress?"

"Perhaps you do," Mina responded. "And perhaps this will be it." She smiled angelically. "Mr. Bancroft is next."

Danai's grin died immediately. "Bancroft."

"Yes."

"How did Bancroft get on my schedule?"

"Mr. Olatunde thought it best that you speak with him," Mina said.

Danai clenched her jaw and gave Mina her best glare. As always, it was wasted like water on a duck's back.

Ilya Bancroft owned the holding company that owned a double-digit percentage of the consumer goods industry on Hall. He was in the Top Ten richest people on the planet list. He'd been one of the loudest voices in the planetary media decrying the Capellan invasion and Danai, in particular, as vicious, bloodthirsty, and hellbent on destroying everything the fine people of Hall cared for, starting with the Republic and ending with every child's favorite doll. According to Olatunde, he wasn't nearly as stupid as his bombastic pronouncements made him seem.

Danai reserved the right to make her own judgment.

"What do I say?" Danai asked.

"I suggest you begin by listening," Mina answered. "As I will."

"When does he get here?" Someone knocked on the door. Danai glared daggers at Mina. "I *really* hate you."

Mina smirked, bowed, and came around to stand at Danai's shoulder.

Bancroft, when he entered, ignored the servitor who opened the door for him. That immediately put him on Danai's bad side, but she tried to counsel herself not to make too many prejudgments. He was tall, just climbing out of middle age, with a face that had obviously seen all the best plastic surgeons in the Republic. His hairline was razor-sharp. His suit was conservatively cut, but Danai had grown up at court, and knew that you could buy a reasonable set of 'Mech parts for what that suit cost.

Bancroft stalked forward and planted himself in front of her desk. He waited, but when she didn't speak he rolled his eyes and sat down, crossing one leg over the other angrily.

Still, Danai said nothing. She didn't think Mina had meant for her to be this rude, but everything about Bancroft pushed her buttons. She was Danai Liao-Centrella, gladiator of Solaris and duchess of Castrovia. She would put her patience against this fool's any day.

He gave in before she did. "Lady Liao—"

"*Duchess*," Mina interrupted.

Bancroft glared at Mina for a moment. "Fine. Duchess Liao—"

"Duchess Liao-*Centrella*," Mina corrected.

"Duchess Liao-Centrella," Bancroft repeated, jaw clenching, "I'm here to come to an understanding." He stopped. Danai just returned his stare. She wasn't surprised that he didn't bother to introduce himself; he probably hadn't failed to be recognized since he was a child.

"About?" Mina asked. Danai wanted to smirk. Apparently only Danai was to listen.

Bancroft looked back and forth between them. "Listen, which one of you am I talking to?"

"To me," Danai said. She was getting impatient with the game.

"Fine. I'm here to make a deal."

"I believe Lady Liao asked you, a deal about what?"

"The future."

"Ah."

"I know how this usually works. I've kept up with the news. I know what you Capellans do when you take over a world." He shrugged. "That's your affair. I just want to look after me and mine."

"I see."

"I want into the *Sheng*, I think you call it," Bancroft continued. "Me and my whole family. And I want to keep my holdings. None of this nationalization crap." He clapped his hand on his knee. And stopped talking.

Danai raised one eyebrow. "And what would the Capellan state receive for granting these wishes?"

"My support."

Danai laughed. She couldn't help it. The sheer hubris of this man. Bancroft frowned and crossed his arms. Good. Danai knew body language. She was a master of it. *Go ahead*, she thought at him. *Go ahead and broadcast your defensiveness.*

"And why, pray tell, would the Confederation need your support?"

"Because I'm an important man on Hall," Bancroft replied. "I own more of the economy than anyone else besides the government. If I don't give out a holiday bonus one year, there's a depression in the spring. What I do matters to you. I can make this whole takeover a lot easier."

"Your Grace," Mina said.

"What?"

"'This whole takeover a lot easier, *your Grace*,'" Mina responded. "Courtesy is a form we treasure in the Confederation of which you are now a part, Mr. Bancroft."

Bancroft's mouth worked for a moment. He stared daggers at Mina, and Danai desperately wanted to turn her head and see if his glare bounced off just like all of hers did, but she refrained.

"Your Grace," Bancroft struggled out.

"What form would this help take?" Danai asked.

"If I bring my whole portfolio over, it makes it a lot easier for everyone else to say yes, don't you see?" He leaned forward, elbows on knees, hands outstretched. "This is a good deal. We don't have to do business with anyone that resists—that's something you Capellans do right—and everyone *has* to do business with me. Once the mob knows their jobs are safe, they'll come over like flies." He grinned and spread his hands. "It'll be a coup." He stopped talking, waiting.

Mina cleared her throat.

"Your Grace," Bancroft added.

"I see," Danai said. "So in return for securing your fortune and privileges, you'll help me blackmail the people of Hall into joining something of which they are already a part?"

Bancroft sat back. "Already a part…"

"I have taken Hall, Mr. Bancroft. The governor fled. Her claim to authority is over. The Republic Armed Forces have fled. Their claim to authority is over. The Exarch, the paladins, your precious knights—they are all gone." Danai let her tone harden. "Under the Ares Conventions, the more ancient laws of war, and *common goddamn sense*, I already own this world."

"B-but—"

"But nothing," Danai cut him off. "The Confederation wants nothing other than for every civilian to have the chance for citizenship, for every civilian to have the chance to earn their way into the caste that best suits them." She didn't move. Settled back into her chair with her hands folded, she didn't need to change her posture to convey her intentions.

She was the mountain that stood before the wind. The rock upon which the ocean broke. She wasn't going to be moved by this despicable *stain* of a man.

"Citizenship… what the hell do you mean? I've lived on Hall my whole life!" Bancroft argued. "I earned my way out of the residency *decades* ago!"

"This is not the Republic," Mina Liao put in, before Danai could speak. "The Confederation does not confer upon anyone that which they do not earn. Our citizens earn their citizenship, Mr. Bancroft, as Republic citizens do, but their service enriches the state that succors them. In the Confederation, we know the State is our best path to the enlightenment of Greater Humanity. We know this because each of us, every citizen, chooses to sacrifice something in service to it. Our time. Our effort." She gestured at Danai with one hand. "Our service in the military."

"Sacrifice! I offered you my whole damn company! My *life*!"

"No, Mr. Bancroft," Danai corrected him. "You offered to extort your company to us." She smiled, trying for the angelic innocence that Mina captured so easily. "It was amusing for you to think it was still your company, though." She touched a stud on the underside of the desk edge nearest her.

"Extort—why you—of course it's my company!"

"No, Mr. Bancroft," Danai said, as the doors behind Bancroft opened to admit two infantry from the Gypsies. "It belongs to the people now. Those same people whom you threatened with hardship, starvation, and death."

Bancroft looked over his shoulder, saw the soldiers, and twisted back to face her. "Listen—we got off on the wrong foot."

"Your Grace," Mina prompted.

"You-your Grace," Bancroft stammered. "Look, you can't arrest me. My people will make these last few bombings look like a graduation party to get me back."

Now Danai stood. She leaned forward, knuckles on the desktop. "I sincerely hope not," she told him. Then she looked past him. "*Sao-wei* Nuthall: Mr. Bancroft is under arrest for extortion, bribery, and threatening the well-being of the State."

"Yes, *Sang-shao*," Nuthall said. "Mr. Bancroft. Please come with us, sir."

Pleading having failed, Bancroft turned to bluster. "Listen, you—"

Behind him, the infantry *si-ben-bing* with Nuthall racked the charging handle of her Ceres Arms Crowdbuster. The full-size stunner was way too much weapon for a room this small, but the angry building whine as its capacitors charged filled the space with menace.

"Mr. Bancroft," the *sao-wei* repeated. She put her hand on her sidearm, a sonic stunner more suited to the space.

"You can't do this," Bancroft growled. He didn't move.

Danai stepped out from behind the desk, pulling Mina along with her. She moved to the side of the room. Bancroft turned to follow her with his eyes, fists balled.

"I'm going to fight this—"

"That's enough," Danai ordered. She jerked her chin at Nuthall, who drew her stunner, raised it, and fired in one smooth motion. Danai grimaced as the side scatter assaulted her ears, but Bancroft fell, twitching. Two more infantry troopers entered the office from the antechamber, sidearms drawn.

"Lady Liao will be in touch to arrange his trial," Danai told Nuthall. "I'll have the room's HV recordings sent down tomorrow."

"Very good, *Sang-shao*," Nuthall said, bracing. She holstered her stunner and nodded to her troops. "Grab him and let's go."

When they were gone, Danai twisted around to grin at Mina. "*Just listen*, you said."

"I apologize," Mina said meekly. "I perhaps could have handled that better."

"Perhaps," Danai said mockingly. She walked over and sat down on a low couch in a corner. "That felt good," she said. "Did it feel good for you?"

"I don't like to admit it," Mina replied. She sat down on the matching low sofa across from Danai. "Why will I be in touch?"

"What?" Danai was replaying Bancroft's expression when the stunner hit him in her mind.

"You told the *sao-wei* that I would be in touch. Why will I be in touch, and not you?"

Danai smiled. "That was a nice speech you gave Bancroft."

"Perhaps," Mina agreed. "You're not answering my question."

"I'm appointing you *diem* of Hall," Danai told her.

"You're *what*?" For the first time since they'd met, Danai thought she'd finally caught the other woman off guard.

"You're about to become the civilian head of Hall," Danai said. "I will remain governor-general, officially. But you're taking over the day-to-day of the integration."

"I'm what?"

"The insurgency is going to heat up. Bancroft as much as admitted it. I need to be free to deal with that. So I'm turning this crap—" she held up her hands, "—I mean, this very important work, over to you."

"You have not listened to any of my lessons."

"I have," Danai responded, suddenly earnest. "Mina, I have. And I have taken them to heart. But I am a soldier. I am learning to be a duchess. But we no longer have time to let me make a mistake, ask you what I should have done first and then correct my mistakes. The people of Hall demand more from us."

"I cannot do this alone," Mina said.

"Am I alone?"

"You have me." She glared. "Who will I have?"

Now Danai finally got to smile the imp's grin. "You'll never guess."

Now Mina rolled her eyes. She sat back, letting her back hit the plush cushion of the sofa. She closed her eyes for a long moment. Danai waited. She knew it was coming.

Finally, Mina sat up. She adjusted her seat, crossed her legs at the ankle, and folded her hands in her lap. When she looked up, her face was impassive.

"I do not like you," she said.

Danai howled. It felt good to laugh, to *really* laugh. And so right that she couldn't remember when the last time was that she'd felt this way.

CHAPTER 20

**HARNEY
HALL
REPUBLIC OF THE SPHERE
5 MAY 3149**

"This is never going to work," Mina declared.

"Trust me," Danai told her.

The two of them sat in the palatial courtyard outside the governor's mansion, taking in the dry, cool morning air. The people in Harney gave the downtown atmosphere a more humid air than much of the rest of the continent, but it was barely noticeable. In an hour or two the heat would be oppressive, the air tainted with the scent of warm lubricant and hot wheels from the commuter traffic. But for now...it was peaceful.

A Gypsy infantryman appeared, leading a fit man toward them.

"Here he comes," Danai said.

"This is never going to work," Mina repeated.

"It'll work." She stood, off the bench she'd been sitting on, to greet the new arrival. "Mr. Olatunde. Thank you for agreeing to see us so early."

"I am at your Grace's service," Olatunde replied. He ducked his chin at Mina, respectfully. "How can I help you this fine morning?"

"I hope you'll forgive me if I am blunt?"

Olatunde grinned. "I may not be a soldier any longer, but I remember how, *Sang-shao*," he said.

"Where do your loyalties lie, Themba?"

"With the people of Harney," he said immediately.

Danai glanced a triumphant grin at Mina, who ignored her. "Not with the Republic? As you said, you were once a soldier. You swore an oath." She schooled her expression and looked him in the eye. "I know what my oaths to the Confederation mean to me. I do not expect yours mean any less to you."

"Indeed," Olatunde said. He breathed in, and then out, clearly marshaling his thoughts. "I served the Republic for many years. I fought for it, sacrificed for it, *bled* for it." His right hand rose to massage his left biceps. Danai had never seen him favor it, but she knew well the phantom pain that old wounds carried forever.

Knew it *well*.

"I was proud to be a Knight of the Republic." He was looking past her, at the mansion, but his eyes were unfocused. "But that is behind me now." Olatunde looked at Danai, and then Mina, and then back at Danai. "I have served Harney and its people for longer than I wore a uniform. They have put their trust in me, and I have never betrayed it." He steeled himself. "I won't betray it now."

Danai smiled. She reached out, slowly, to pat the hand he still gripped his arm with. Olatunde started, surprised at the contact. "I would never dream of asking you to." She regarded the older man for a moment, then decided she'd been right. "I want to name you provisional refrector of Hall."

"Refrector..."

Mina spoke. "In the Confederation, a refrector is the people's representative to the planetary ruler," she said. "A tribune of the plebs, you might say."

"You want—" Olatunde took a step back. "I thought you wanted my resignation."

"The opposite," Danai said. "I want you to serve the people of Hall as you have been. I want you to work with Lady Liao," she beckoned to Mina, "to oversee the integration of Hall into the Confederation. I want you to continue to serve the people you have served for so long." She smiled up at him. "I want your help."

"I am a Republic official," Olatunde protested. "I don't care what you say, your manuals have to say the same thing as ours used to. There's no way you can trust me. I could be lying to you. I could take this position and use it to engineer a revolution." He frowned at her. "You can't be serious."

"I am."

"But—"

"Everything thing you just said is true," Danai told him. "Except that I do trust you. Or rather, I trust your sense of duty." She gestured around them, at the city. "Every time we have met, your concern for these people has been radiantly evident. You have fought for nothing else in every conversation. I need you to keep fighting for them."

She lowered her arm. "This integration will be hard. It will feel as though we're destroying everything that makes Hall feel like Hall. People will shout at you. Threaten you. They will call you traitor. They will threaten your family. They will curse your name and hate you forever." She smiled. "Just like they do me."

"I am not afraid of doing my duty," Olatunde said.

"This is now a world of the Confederation," Danai said. "Many of its people don't understand that yet. Many of them will never accept it. But it is a fact."

"The Republic could return," Olatunde countered.

"It could try," Danai agreed. "But where is it?"

Olatunde had no response to that.

"You said 'provisional,'" he finally said.

"I did." Danai gestured to Mina again. "Lady Liao has been named planetary *diem*—noble ruler, for all intents and purposes. My brother, the Chancellor, will no doubt replace her with someone he prefers. He may replace you as well. I cannot stop that, in the fullness of time." She looked around, breathing in the warm Hall air. "What I can do, here and now, is make the best decisions I can. You know this world and its people. You can help us make the integration as painless as possible."

"There will certainly be pain, as you already said."

"Less, I also said."

Olatunde breathed deeply. "It is hard," he said. "I see now why you asked about oaths."

"If it helps, I will name you a Capellan citizen for your past service to the people of Harney. I will enroll you in the directorship caste, because that is where you clearly belong. These things are not bribes. By any definition in the Confederation, you have earned them. Part of your job will be helping Mina and her government make those kinds of decisions for the rest of Hall."

Danai looked back to meet Olatunde's eye. "We do not live our lives like the people of the Republic, that is true. But neither are we monsters. We venerate family, as do all people. We want each of our people to yearn for citizenship, and to find the place and caste where they best contribute to society. On their own terms."

"Your Grace—" Olatunde objected, but Danai held up her hand.

"I know what your Republic media says about us. That it is all forced labor and socialism, that the *Sheng* are no different from any other oligarchy anywhere in the Inner Sphere. That we will rip people from their homes and send them to work gulags on other worlds." She spread her hands. "I cannot claim those things have not happened. They often have, in our history."

She brought her hands together. "But no realm's history is pristine. All I can promise you is that those days are behind us, by a century or more. The Republic calls Capellan servitors slaves, but slavery has been outlawed for a century. It is possible for every citizen to move between castes, and every citizen's child will enter the caste they are best suited to."

"A servitor may become a director, is what you'd have me believe?"

Danai shrugged. "Yesterday I arrested the richest man on this planet. Millions of people living in poverty believe they can become just as rich as he was. Is that dream any less likely?" She didn't wait for an answer. "Lady Liao will tell you. In the Confederation, we want each citizen to strive for their best potential. For billions, that potential is a safe, quiet job in the commonality or even in service, yes, as a servitor. You have homeless people here, in this city. I have seen them. Did you deny those people opportunity, or did they just fail to grasp it?"

"It is not that simple…"

"In many cases it is not, you are correct. But in many cases, it is exactly that simple." She put her hands behind her back. "Are you going to help me give those people—these people, all around us—the best chance they can have for success?"

As they walked back into Danai's office—soon to be *Mina's* office, Danai thought with relish—Mina cleared her throat. "That was well done."

"Thank you."

"That does not mean it will work."

Danai groaned as she collapsed into the chair behind the desk. "You're going to be great at this. You've been preparing for it your entire life."

Mina sat in one of the chairs across the desk.

"I'm only doing what you told me to do," Danai said slyly.

"I never told you to do this!"

"You did. You keep reminding me of my duties, of not overstepping when I have a competent subordinate to handle them. That's what I am doing here." She spread her hands, taking in the whole office. "You're so much better at this than I am."

"I am not one of your soldiers," Mina corrected.

"No; you are a daughter of the Confederation."

Mina glared at her. "That was low."

Danai laughed. "What are you afraid of?"

"It is one thing to make decisions and statements in an academic situation. Or abstractly, as part of politics. Or even to advise *you* while *you* do it. The ultimate responsibility is yours. It is an entirely different thing when it is just me making decisions for literally billions of other people."

"That responsibility comes with the name, sister," Danai said. "My brother, my aunt—*both* my aunts—they all beat that into my head from the moment I learned how to spell 'Liao.' It's what being in the directorship means."

Mina sighed. "Yes, I suppose you're right."

"Of course I am. I had a good teacher."

"I suppose."

"It comes down to this," Danai continued, tiring of the argument. "I have spent time being *governor*-general. I didn't seek it, but I did the necessary work. And it has been difficult, painful, frustrating, *fulfilling* work."

"As your brother hoped you would learn."

"And I have." Danai stood, turned, and looked out the window. "But as you keep reminding me, I don't have to do everything myself when there are competent people to handle it. I've done good work here, work you and Themba will continue."

She turned back around to face her friend. "But now it's time I spend a little more time with the 'general' part of governor-general."

"If you say so." Mina looked up at her. "But I think you're retreating back to play with your 'Mech toys."

Danai laughed. "Maybe a little." She sat back down. "Now. Tell me your plans."

"I have had the job for half an hour."

"Don't be coy. You knew what we were going to do here before we left Liao. Don't think I haven't felt your puppet-master fingers pulling my strings this whole time."

Mina smirked. "We will continue along your lead." She straightened a little in her chair. "Tomorrow I will issue blanket provisional caste assignments that confirm everyone on Hall in their current positions. Remind them that the still have jobs, livelihoods, incomes. That their children will have food and education. That the lights will stay on."

"Olatunde writ large," Danai said, nodding. "Makes sense. What else?"

"We have had no word about a replacement directorship delegation?"

Danai shook her head. "I had expected word by now; it's only three weeks, dirt to dirt, between here and Liao. And it's not like they're short of bureaucrats there. Perhaps they sent back to Sian for guidance. That would slow things down."

"Without word, I must proceed as if they are never coming. We both know they will, but I cannot make promises to these people only to have to keep moving the deadlines back because the JumpShip has not appeared."

Mina looked down, clearly thinking. Danai waited.

"Unless your Mr. Capshaw gives me a reason not to, I will confirm all the local government fixtures as well. Provisionally. There is provision for that in the traditions of warfare, is there not?"

"There is," Danai answered. "It's not in the Ares Convention itself, but it was common practice during the Succession Wars. How the bureaucrats of Hall will take to it after a century in the Republic and all these years behind the Wall, we will have to see."

"That will buy me time, then," Mina said.

"Me, as well."

"And how will you be spending your time?" Mina asked.

Danai just grinned.

EXCALIBUR-CLASS DROPSHIP ZIBO
HARNEY INTERPLANETARY SPACEPORT
HALL

The DropShips had long since relocated into the Harney port since the initial landing battle. Since then, the crew had worked on repairing what damage they could and backing up the native Hall deep-space network. They were linked into all the civilian jump point satellites, for example, which means someone had to sit watch in CIC and monitor the feed. It was dull, mind-numbing work, sitting there waiting for a light to change color when a satellite detected the electromagnetic or infrared signature that announced a JumpShip's arrival at the jump point.

The light changed color.

"Signal from the jump point," Jirxi Venn called out. "New arrival. Makes the fourth one this week." She blinked her eyes and tried to remember how to do her job. She felt like she'd been staring at this screen for half her life.

"Which one?" the officer of the watch asked. He sounded bored.

"Zenith," Venn told him. "IFF coming through now." She checked the codes. "Another merchant from the Confederation," she said. "Reads as *Jane's Escape*, in from Hsien." A new window popped open on Venn's screen. "Confirmed; codes are good."

"Pass it up the chain, then, Venn," the OOW said. "Good work."

Venn did as she was told. They wouldn't know for another little while whether the JumpShip had released any DropShips into the system. Two of the prior three had. The first group was two cargo hulls and an escort *Leopard* under contract to the CCAF, carrying parts and munitions for the Liao regiments on Hall. They'd be down in another thirty hours or so.

The other was a trio of old *Danais*-class merchants coming out of the Free Worlds League, looking for trade now that the Wall was down. They were a few hours behind the Confederation ships.

Venn closed the window and went back into the dull state of watching the light panel not change color again. *It's getting positively crowded over here*, she thought. And that didn't even include the flotilla at the nadir point, occupying the recharge station there.

She still had nightmares about seeing that TAG emission light go on; that had been enough getting shot at for the rest of her life, if she had anything to say about it.

But *Lord Liao's ass*, it'd be nice to see a change of pace.

CHAPTER 21

ROCKFALL MAZE
HALL
CAPELLAN CONFEDERATION
6 JUNE 3149

Tom Jordan held his hand over his eyes as the DropShip clawed its way down from orbit. At its current height it looked like a pinprick balanced on a flat-bottomed pillar of fire, but he knew it would grow quickly.

"Strange how something shaped like that can fly," Sergeant Harry James Austin observed from beside him.

Tom looked down, and then looked over at the sergeant. He didn't want to chance turning his eyes toward the DropShip's drive plume. "We came on one shaped like that."

"Yes, sir, I remember. Felt damn strange then too."

Tom was struck suddenly by Austin's accent. He sounded like pure old-salt south Jolo; Chisholian accent not quite so thick as to be impossible to understand, but close. "Harry, what the hell are you doing here?"

Austin frowned and turned away from the descending DropShip. "Sir?"

"You sound like you should be on an inshore boat sixteen hours a day," Tom told him. "Back home, I mean. No boats to speak of here."

"Some," Austin said. He glanced behind them. "Not hereabouts, no, sir. But back Dunsborough way, that was a coastal town. Nighttime you could just about smell the salt marsh, if the wind was right. Not off the desert, you know I mean, sir."

Tom laughed. "That's exactly what I mean."

Austin grinned awkwardly. "Seemed time to do my part, sir," was all he said.

"People need fed," Tom told him. "Your part could have been running a boat, bringing home the catch every night."

Austin shook his head sadly. "That's my brother, sir. William Robert Austin. Billy Rob, my older brother, sir. Favorite of our ma's. And rightly so."

"Where's he?"

Austin turned his head as if he were going to look at the DropShip. It was close enough they could hear it coming; a constant, though far-off, rumble of thunder. The gangly NCO didn't look up, though. This close there'd be danger to their retinas.

"Don't rightly know, sir. He joined the Navy, the real Navy, you know? Up in space? Last I heard he's in the *Auspicium* at Terra." Austin chuckled. "Leave it to Billy Rob to pick the biggest damn target there is." He scratched at the skin under his eye for a second, then shrugged. "Anyway, sir, it seemed like if Billy Rob was going to do all that, it just seemed fair I do this. Except I lucked out and got hooked up with the colonel. Got to stay home." He rolled his eyes. "'Cept for now, of course, yes, sir."

"'Cept for now," Tom repeated. Then he shook his head. "I'm glad you're here, Sergeant." He turned back to face the DropShip but kept his eyes down. Then he laughed.

"Sir?"

"Billy Rob. That mean I should be calling you Harry Jim?"

"Oh, no, sir, please don't. My ma tried to call me that once, but it never stuck."

Tom laughed the rest of the way the DropShip came down.

By the time Sergeant Austin drove their skimmer toward the DropShip, water buffaloes—big tanker trucks with sprayers to cover about thirty meters on a side—had already backed up and drenched the area. Steam rose in billowing clouds, but it would make the blasted ferrocrete pad cool enough to drive across and move equipment.

It wasn't pleasant, by any stretch, but it beat having their lungs seared to ash by air superheated by the heat radiating off the ground. H2O was a fantastic heat sink.

All the hatches on the DropShip ground open as they approached. Tom pointed, and Austin steered their skimmer toward a smaller personnel hatch that slid open. The open bays were black holes; no interior lights were strong enough to overcome Hall's harsh sunlight. Tom took a chance and slid over the skimmer's side and headed for the open personnel hatch. He hoped he wasn't about to walk up on a DropShip crewman bound and determined to be the first to piss on a new planet, but he'd deal with that if he had to.

It turned out his instincts were correct.

A short woman waited, in shorts and cooling vest over a sports bra. She wore an enormous slug-throwing pistol on her thigh. The sides of her head were shaved MechWarrior fashion, and she stood arms crossed, one foot tapping.

"Captain Gruner?"

"You my contact?"

"Tom Jordan," he replied. "You want the countersign?"

Gruner snorted. "Buddy, if you aren't my contact, we're dead already. Let's just get this show on the road before— shit, too late. Here comes the ship's captain."

Behind her, an internal hatch squealed open and a man with no hair and the round, sagging features common in people spent a lot of time in low or no gravity stalked out.

"This the guy?" he asked Gruner. She rolled her eyes at Tom and nodded.

"Tom Jordan," he said, holding out his hand. "Captain, Republic Armed Forces. You want the countersign to verify my identity?"

"Den Rabchev," the spacer replied. "And no, keep your spy shit. We don't have time." He turned to Captain Gruner. "Why aren't your 'Mechs moving?"

"This guy hasn't told me where to go yet."

Tom grinned. It was such a pleasure dealing with professionals, even when you were the one holding them up. He held out a datacard to the MechWarrior. "Navs are on here. You'll be met at the end of the sequence. It's all rock and desert, so use your navs. You'll get lost if you eyeball it."

Captain Gruner took the map and rolled her eyes again. "We'll be off the ship in ten minutes."

"Good!" Rabchev called after her. Then he chuckled and looked back at Tom. "I like that girl. She don't take no shit." He shook his head, breathed in and out, then slapped his thighs. "Okay. What's the plan then, Captain, Republic Armed Forces?"

"Far as we can tell, your cover story held," Tom told him.

"'Course it did," the DropShip captain said. Then he coughed. Then he coughed again, great wracking heaves. "Sorry," he gasped finally. He pointed at the open hatch. "Ozone from the drives. Plays hells with my lungs." He finally straightened up, still breathing hard. "How long do we have?"

"Records tell us inspectors from Harney usually take a couple hours to get here when there's a need," Tom said. He was repeating what he'd been told, but he had no reason to disbelieve it. "By then, we'll have the 'Mechs gone and their traces covered."

"Radar was clear when we came down," Rabchev said. "I was afraid they'd scramble some fighters to escort us down."

"They didn't."

Rabchev chuckled. "You'd have known if they had, boy; we'd have impacted at terminal velocity in a flaming ball of rubble. This here's a hundred-year-old *Danais* tramp freighter, not a fancy assault DropShip. She usually carries the IndustrialMechs we're here to pick up."

Tom nodded. The general brief had been in the strategic notes.

Rabchev stared at him. "You need to use the head?"

Tom blinked. "What?"

"You hungry? You need something else?"

"No..."

"Then get the hell off my ship, Republic Armed Forces. I got inspectors coming, and I need to make this old bitch look like she really does have the engine trouble I told them she had when we diverted out of the drop toward Harney."

Tom grinned, slapped the DropShip captain on the shoulder, and spun around. "You should have plenty of time," he called over his shoulder. "We planned a diversion."

HARNEY
HALL
CAPELLAN CONFEDERATION

Si-ben-bing Travis Gardner hated his new tank. He hated that it was a 60-year-old Manticore tank they'd claimed from the Harney municipal militia to replace his lost Zhukov. He hated that it smelled weird.

Mostly he hated that it only crewed four, instead of five, which made it feel like Orsino had never been needed at all. Never mind that they couldn't scrape enough of Orsino out of the old turret to send back to his family.

"Turn coming up," Preakness reported.

"Roger," he confirmed.

As they came up on the turn, the heavy rubber road coat on the treads squealed like a gutted pig as Preakness twisted them to the side. Gardner put his hand on the traverse controls; even the damn vibration felt wrong!

"Two klicks on this course," Preakness added.

"Roger," Gardner growled.

The rest of his crew had adapted to the replacement vehicle well, he knew. They knew their jobs, and they'd thrown themselves into familiarization training. The Zhukov had been a tanker's tank, built to put its bow toward the enemy and charge in, both cannons belching fire. This Manticore was more a sniper; the heavy PPC hit almost as hard as both the old Zhukov's autocannons had, and the paired multi-missile launchers let them shoot at any range.

But the gap where Orsino would have been glared in every conversation.

"No contacts," Danton called from the sensor operator's station deep in the Manticore's hull.

"Roger," Gardner replied. There hadn't been contacts in weeks.

There wouldn't be today, either. They were on escort duty, bringing the limo bearing the *diem* and refrector back into the city center. He'd heard they were out toward Deal, meeting with the local government there to explain what the next step of the Capellan integration would look like. Their 'Mech and VTOL escort peeled off as soon as they got in among the buildings and people; now it was Gardner's short platoon of three tanks' job.

"Tail reports no contacts," Danton added.

"Roger," Gardner replied again.

"Look, I don't know who Roger is, but I don't think he wants to talk to you," called Hertzel, from the missile loading compartment. The loader forced a chuckle, but the attempt at humor fell flat in the extended silence.

"Coming up on the turn," Preakness said.

Gardner opened his mouth, considered, and closed it. He waited.

"Roger?" Hertzel prompted.

Sarah Jacoby flinched when her personal comm vibrated on the tabletop. She shook down the shiver of cold it prompted as adrenaline flooded her bloodstream; instead, she picked it up and looked at it. *There's nothing strange about getting a message on vibrate*, she told herself. *Happens a million times a day all across the planet.* She swiped the notification clear and set her comm back down; then she picked up her coffee and looked across the square.

A blue-painted Manticore snuffled around the corner, rubber squealing, and proceeded into traffic.

Jacoby sipped her coffee, picked up her comm, and sent a short message. Anyone watching would think she was replying to the previous message. Because she was.

But instead of words, she sent an arming code.

Then, setting her comm in her lap, Jacoby picked up her coffee and waited.

ROCKFALL MAZE
HALL
CAPELLAN CONFEDERATION

Tom Jordan had his skimmer waiting when Captain Gruner climbed down from her *Gunsmith*. He kept the fans idling, the skimmer sitting solidly on its skirts. The dust in this cavern was still swirling through the air. When Tom looked at the *Fennec* in the next makeshift 'Mech bay, he saw the same dust being driven into whorls by the output of the machine's heat sinks.

Gruner climbed into the passenger seat and slid the earmuff intercom on over her head. "What's the plan?"

"The plan is we get out of here and back to base, then bring you up to speed."

"Rabchev said something about a distraction?"

Tom spun the fans up; the skimmer rose on its air cushion, sliding like butter on a hot pan. He dragged the nose around and headed toward the mouth of the cave at a walking pace. Once he was on course, he dragged his comm out of his battledress thigh pocket and looked at the time.

Then he grinned at Gruner.

"Should be going off right about now."

HARNEY
HALL
CAPELLAN CONFEDERATION

Sarah Jacoby sipped her coffee as the limo came into view, following the Manticore. She tapped her finger on the case of her comm, presenting to the world the facade of a woman trying to figure out how to answer a message. Her eyes seemed unfocused.

They weren't.

Jacoby had chosen her seat carefully. The marker—a housing where the underground power and telecommunication lines came above ground to be threaded into the open market down the side street—was in a direct line with the sewer housing inset in the pavement. She'd already watched the Manticore trundle across her line of sight.

She set her coffee down. In her peripheral vision she saw the nose of the limo.

She opened the message app. She typed just one character: a period.

The limo bumper edged into her sightline.

She pressed send.

This part had been briefed into her, and she desperately wished she was back inside her Purifier battlesuit. She had a second to put her phone down, and reach for her coffee, but it was critical that she not watch the limo or even look interested. In the fullness of time, forensics would track down the detonation signal. They'd find her in HV recordings or flat security cam feeds.

But for right now, she just had to sit and take it.

Period.

She never saw the flash, but the shockwave blew her out of her chair, along with everyone else in the open-air cafe.

The Manticore lurched forward as if a 'Mech had kicked it hard in the rear armor. Gardner jostled against his restraints, but his hand hit the panic bar and dropped the Manticore into battle mode even as his brain registered the pain.

"What was that?!" Preakness yelled.

"No contacts!" Danton called. "What's going on? Did we hit something?"

"Guns up!" Hertzel yelled.

"I don't know!" Gardner shouted. His display was covered in smoke and debris; something had exploded, that much was clear. He dragged the turret controls left, looking for the limo. "Where's the limo?!" he demanded.

"Checking," Danton said.

"C'mon," Gardner urged the turret traverse. The Zhukov would have been around by now. The Manticore's sensors were grayed out with smoke. He toggled IR, but there were fires everywhere; he switched back to visual light and prayed a breeze would come up. "Preakness, get us spun around!"

"On it!"

"I can't find it," Danton said, almost too soft to hear. He was talking to himself. "I can't *find* it! The limo—I think it's gone!"

Gardner made sure the internal hatches were closed, so he wouldn't clog the whole tank with smoke, then hit the control that undogged the turret top hatch and raised his seat so his head and shoulders were outside.

The air was thick with smoke and dust. All around him he heard yelling and screams. A siren started up in the far distance, attenuated by the tall buildings all around him. He coughed, wiping a gloved hand across his face. It came away gray with soot and dust.

The turret stopped at 180 degrees. At his knees, the primary sensor screens just painted a mess of fires, craters and smoke.

Of the limo, Lady Mina Liao, or Refrector Themba Olatunde, there was no sign.

Gardner was still staring when the first emergency vehicles arrived.

CHAPTER 22

**HARNEY
HALL
CAPELLAN CONFEDERATION
8 JUNE 3149**

Danai's hand never stopped moving against the fabric of the thigh of her battledress. She sat in a terminal chair at the holotable and stared into the display. In it, a tiny black limo glided down a busy city street, and then it exploded. Then the HV looped back around.

She'd maybe slept four hours of the last forty-eight. Most of the time she'd spent right here, listening to the susurrus of people moving around her. The part of her brain she'd carefully trained to be an officer across the last decade was screaming at her, telling her she was setting a terrible example, telling her she was showing weakness, telling her all sorts of things that she knew were true but that she could do nothing about.

She just didn't care.

Mina was gone.

It wasn't the first time she'd lost people around her. But it was the first time the person she'd lost was a noncombatant. An innocent. A kind and brilliant woman just trying to do the best for the maximum number of people.

"*Sang-shao*," someone said. She ignored them.

The holotable flickered into darkness as someone turned it off.

Danai blinked and looked up. Wu Feng stood there, with her staff flanking him. Noah Capshaw looked grim and angry; Emory Koltsokov was blank-faced. And Fan Bing, quiet little Bing, stood glaring at the space where the HV had been.

"*Sang-shao*," Wu Feng repeated. When she focused on him, he smiled tightly. "We are prepared to tell you what happened, as best as we can discover."

"Tell me," she commanded. She tried to stand, but her legs wouldn't support her. They were numb. She lurched against the edge of the tank. Noah Capshaw took a long step forward and caught her shoulder.

"Just stay there, *Sang-shao*," he said. Leaning in close, he asked, "How long has it been since you ate or drank anything?"

Danai frowned. "What day is it?"

Noah nodded once and straightened up. "Tea for the *sang-shao*!" he shouted. "And some food!"

"We can do this here," Wu Feng said. He slid a new datacard into the holotable and a new holo formed. It showed a heavy steel or iron hatch, corroded over with thick flakes of old, orange-topped, white-bottom paint chipping off it.

"This is where they entered the sewer," he said. An inset window popped up, with a caret blinking on a 2D map. "They waited until our sweep teams went through, then followed. We had the route on a daily scan schedule. They knew the schedule."

"Someone told them?" Danai demanded.

Wu shrugged. "Or they just watched. The patrol had gotten complacent." He made a sound, deep in his broad chest. "We all had."

"The platoon's *sao-wei* has already offered to resign," Emory Koltsokov put in. Her face was pale as always, but she had bags under her eyes and her battledress was rumpled.

Danai's fingers clutched at the fabric between them, feeling the crease there. She felt the ridges of the rough cloth on her fingertips; she'd tried counting the strands of thread from feeling alone but failed. That failure had made her angry in a hollow, painful way.

"Gypsy forensic analysts insist the bomb was triggered manually; we don't know if it was mechanical or electronic. If it was mechanical, if someone was down there with it, then that person is dead. If not..." Wu spread his hands. "We have not found them yet."

"We may never," Noah added. "I sat with the analysts, *Sang-shao*. They convinced me it's like trying to count the sands in the Helmand."

"They're giving up?" she asked hoarsely.

"They are not," Noah replied. "But the odds are the odds."

At that moment, a private appeared bearing a tea tray. Danai sat up a little straighter; she didn't know the private's name, but Erde's voice in her head was sharp. "Thank you," Danai made herself say when the private set the tray down and poured her a small glass of tea. The private braced, backed out of the room, and disappeared.

The tea was ginseng, already steeped. Danai let the steam rise to her nostrils, blowing softly on the top of the glass. "Continue," she said, without putting the tea down. Heat was flowing through the glass, burning her fingertips. She relished the new sensation.

And, if she was being honest, the quiet sense of punishment the pain engendered.

"The charge itself was military," Wu continued. "Examination of the residue confirms it. Republic military, if there was any doubt. C8, manufactured here on Hall."

"There wasn't any doubt," Noah muttered.

"So it was the Reps," Danai said. "The insurgency."

"Yes," Wu said.

"Yes," Noah confirmed.

Danai sipped her tea. It burned the tip of her tongue. She set the glass down on the edge of the holotank. She let go of her pants with her other hand, flexing her hand several times to stretch the tendons. From her pocket she drew a new datacard and slid it into the tank; the limo disappeared, and a view of the Hall star system appeared. A trio of green dots blinked in between Hall itself and the nadir jump point.

"The DropShip *Culai Shan* will be on the ground tomorrow. It carries Lord Pyotr Zheng aboard; he is the new *diem* of Hall, sent here by the Chancellor to take over from me." Danai was almost whispering. She didn't care. "With it are two more ships of the directorship, as well as the new Maskirovka resident."

"That is welcome news," Wu Feng said.

"It is," Danai agreed. She stood, swayed, but caught herself. "I'm going to sleep. You five are going to build me a plan for putting an end to the insurgency on Hall. Assume that my time will be free once Lord Zheng arrives." She looked down at her hand, where her fingertips still rested on the holotank. "We are going to end this before anyone else we're supposed to be protecting gets hurt."

She walked out before anyone else could speak.

Or before she could no longer control the sobs within her.

THE HOLE
DUNSBOROUGH
HALL
CAPELLAN CONFEDERATION

"And that's our plan, Captain Gruner."

Tom Jordan stood next to Gruner, both of them facing the legate and Colonel Tobin across a 2D map table. They'd just spent the last thirty minutes listening to a dull repetition of the plan Tom had already passed on to the mercenary leader.

"Thank you, sir," Gruner said.

"Any questions?" the legate asked.

"No, sir. I need to spend some time with Captain Jordan here on the tactics, and then get with you, colonel—" she nodded at Tobin, "—on integration, but the strategy is understood: we're buying time for an eventual RAF counterattack." She paused. "Any idea how long that will be, sir?"

"None."

Gruner nodded. "We'll just have to do our best, then."

"Just so," Legate Fernandez said. He glanced at Tobin, who shook her head, then looked back at the pair of MechWarriors. "Thank you, then, captains."

After they were out of the room and on the way to Tom's, Gruner let out a sigh. "You guys put up a hell of fight," she observed. "And you haven't been able to free any of your people?" He knew she was talking about his Flankers, the MechWarriors from his company.

"No. We know seven are still alive and in captivity," he admitted. "There are nine of the other companies' MechWarriors in our hospitals, but they're not coming out anytime soon.

"Maybe that's a mission for us, then? Get your people out?" Gruner grinned. "A good old-fashioned prison break."

"We'll see," was all Tom said.

Gruner looked at him. "Captain Jordan—"

"Tom."

"Tom, then. I need you to understand something. I signed the papers on Galatea in good faith, and my people will do our duty. We'll do the best we can. But we're only a company against two regiments of Louie regulars. You've already fought them. You know what I mean. Orders or no, I'm not leading them out there in some grand charge for freedom." She watched his face as she spoke. "You're my CO, but you need to know the score."

Tom nodded. "I appreciate that. Our positions reversed, I'd probably give you a speech just like that." Then he shrugged. "Besides, I've got more companies coming in, if my schedule holds true."

Gruner chuckled. "The money your people were throwing around in Galaport holds out, you're going to have every merc between here and Black Earth beating down your door."

Before Tom could reply, someone shouted. He looked past Gruner to see Sergeant Austin striding down the corridor at them. "Harry?" he asked when Austin got close enough.

"Have you heard, sir?" Austin looked angry. "Did she tell you?" He glanced at Gruner with enough venom that if she'd been regular RAF, he'd have dressed Austin down for conduct unbecoming a senior non-commissioned officer.

"Tell me what, Sergeant?" He put some steel in his voice. He'd never spoken that way to Harry Austin, but he needed to make the point without having to overtly made the point.

"Elgin's fallen, sir!"

Tom forgot whatever else he was going to say. "*What?*"

"I got it from a guy who was talking to this lady's people," Austin said. He turned his head toward Gruner. "Begging your pardon, Captain, you'll be forgiving me this just now," he said. "The Louies hit home, too!"

Tom blinked. It made sense, but surely someone would have said something before now...he turned to Captain Gruner. "Is that true?"

"You didn't know?"

That means it's true. Tom tried to make sense of the questions jumbled in his head. "Tell me—us!—Tell us what happened. Right now."

Gruner frowned and held up her hands. "Okay, cool, damp the heat, all right? We got a download during recharge; the Louies hit here and Elgin and couple other worlds, all at the same time. Scan I read said Elgin was a walkover—RAF didn't leave anything there except militia."

"Where was the colonel?" Austin asked.

"The colonel?"

"Colonel Boyle," Tom put in. "We're only half the Fourteenth Principes. A whole other 'Mech battalion, another bunch of armor and infantry regiments. They stayed behind on Elgin when we came here last year."

He felt like he'd been punched in the gut. Major Crowe had never, not once, in all the planning and wargaming, ever hinted that the colonel and the Fourteenth might get pulled off Elgin.

"I don't know. They weren't on Elgin, apparently."

"Why would the colonel leave home defenseless with the Wall coming down?" Austin demanded. "Sir? It don't make no sense." His face was set in angry rictus. "Why the hell did we come die for this dustball when we could have fought at home?"

Tom didn't have an answer. All he had was questions. Foremost among them...

"Then who's coming to relieve us?" he whispered.

HARNEY
HALL
CAPELLAN CONFEDERATION

Danai didn't go to her room to sleep. Not immediately. First, she went to the detention centers beneath the city administration building. The doors were manned by infantry squads from the Gypsies; they passed her without question. When the *sao-wei* in charge asked her how she could be of help, Danai gave her the prisoner's name she wanted. Then she waited.

A few minutes later, a small man in an orange prison jumpsuit was escorted into the room.

"Would you like an interview room, *Sang-shao*?" the *sao-wei* asked.

"This will be fine," Danai said.

"Going to shoot me in front of all these witnesses?" Major Salesi Crowe asked. The commander of Hall's RAF defenders had an annoyingly nasal voice that grated on Danai's nerves, especially now.

"Have they told you what happened two days ago?" Danai asked quietly.

"They said a couple of your high officials were assassinated," Crowe said.

"They tell you who?"

"I don't know if you've been a prisoner before, lady, but we don't get regular news downloads in here."

"The Lady Mina Liao, *diem* of this planet, and Themba Olatunde, former mayor of Harney and current refrector, were killed. Along with 57 other people, six children among them."

"So, one of your relations and a traitor?"

"They were noncombatants," Danai ground out. "They were civilians, working to protect the best interests of the people of Hall." She reached out and jabbed Crowe in the shoulder. "And your *people* blew them up like trash."

"The 'best interests of the people of Hall' are not working with you, lady," Crowe said. "*You* invaded *us*, remember? The RAF defends the people under—"

"*Children*!" Danai shouted.

Crowe blinked, but didn't move. "If you hadn't occupied the city, they would never have been at risk."

Danai squeezed her eyes shut. She counted to four. "I'm going to root out every last one of your people," she said, quietly, but with sincere conviction. "I'm going to capture as many as I can. And I'm going to ensure they're tried, in a court of law here on Hall, for war crimes under the Ares Conventions." She opened her eyes. "For murder."

Crowe shook his head. "The Exarch will be here before you get to that," he retorted. "Every day you waste chasing ghosts in the Helmand is another day closer the RAF counterattack gets. Depend on it." He lifted his chin, daring her. For all his annoying qualities, Danai had to admit the little man had a spine.

"Take him back to his cell," Danai ordered the Gypsies. She turned and walked back outside without another word. The sun had set, and the air was cooling rapidly. Above, the sky was clear, and she saw a handful of stars that weren't hidden by the city's light pollution. She pulled out her comm.

"Yes, *Sang-shao*," Noah Capshaw answered.

"Noah. The RAF major thinks he's holding out for an RAF counterattack. When Zheng's flotilla gets here, I want you to get with the Mask team and figure out whether there's any danger of that."

"Of course, *Sang-shao*!"

"And I don't mean a hemmed and hawed 'well, anything is possible, and we can't know everything' kind of answer, okay? I want odds. I want to know, if someone were to come, who is coming. By now we've hit four or more Republic worlds that were behind the Wall. Maskirovka should know some things beyond guesses. Find out."

"I'll contact the DropShips now."

"Good," Danai said. She closed the connection and pocketed her comm. A boot scraped pavement behind her, and she turned to see a pair of Gypsy infantry troopers. "*Sao-wei* said to make sure you get in your vehicle, *Sang-shao*," the young woman said. "We'll make sure no one bothers you."

"Thank you," Danai replied.

She looked up at the stars again, wondering if Mina was somewhere, looking down on her. Probably disapprovingly, Danai knew.

"I know I killed you," she muttered to the sky. "And you wouldn't like vengeance. But I've had my fill of pain I just have to swallow."

Danai squeezed her burning eyes closed. They were wet. Tears leaked out onto her cheeks. "No more," she told the stars.

CHAPTER 23

**HARNEY
HALL
CAPELLAN CONFEDERATION
17 JUNE 3149**

The siren—the long, whining Hall RAF-style siren that was so different from the klaxon she was used to—was still winding down when Danai rounded the corner at a run, headed for the 'Mech bays. The report was close enough, barely off the edge of the Helmand, that she had a real chance of reaching the action in her 'Mech. And even more: the report said enemy BattleMechs! They'd been sure they'd accounted for all of the Principes Guards' 'Mechs. If the sighting was correct, that meant either more RAF forces had snuck on-world, or they'd been hidden here the entire time.

Danai burst through the final set of doors and nearly ran into Noah Capshaw. The MechWarrior stood there, in his cooling suit, hands loose at his sides, but with a set expression and posture. "Noah, what are you doing? Get to your 'Mech!"

"In a moment, *Sang-shao*," he said. He had a touch of his old stammer, but the last few months had really finished burning the boy out of the young man. "With all due respect, you need to leave this one to us and stay here. Or better yet, trust *Sao-shao* Baxter and his troops to deal with it."

Danai's blood got very cold. "Get out of the way, Noah."

"Ma'am...please. Don't go out there."

"Are you telling me what to do, *Sang-wei*?"

"No, ma'am. Just...respectfully requesting."

"You're way out of line here, Noah."

"I know, ma'am."

Danai looked past him. The other two 'Mechs of the lance, Fan Bing's *Dola* and Emory Koltsokov's *Vindicator*, were already active. Both MechWarriors were in their cockpits, but the 'Mechs hadn't disengaged their umbilicals yet. No matter what Noah thought, the other two members of her Command Lance expected to fight.

"Let's go, Noah."

"Ma'am, *please.*" Capshaw looked on the edge of trying to physically restrain her. "Don't go out there. They're targeting our leadership. That's what the bomb was. If you go out there and expose yourself, then you take the chance they can get you, too."

"I'll be safe. I'll be in my 'Mech."

"You remember our last conversation in the desert about that, ma'am?" Capshaw's mouth was a thin line as he sucked on his lips. "You remember what I said then? Everyone knows that 'Mech. *Everyone* knows *Yen-Lo-Wang.*" He clenched his fist at his side. "I'm your intelligence officer, ma'am. It's my *job* to know what they're planning. And I'm telling you, they're gunning for you."

Danai pushed past him. "Let them." She strode across the bay floor toward *Yen-Lo-Wang*. Over her shoulder, she called, "Get in your 'Mech and let's get going, *Sang-wei.*"

"Yes, *Sang-shao,*" Capshaw barked in his best parade ground voice.

She knew he meant well. She knew he was probably even right. There hadn't been another attack since the bomb that killed Mina. If this sighting was even real, then it was the first time the RAF insurgency had come out from whatever hole they were hiding in.

Danai would miss that over her dead body.

She reached the bottom of the gantry and began climbing, three steps at a time. The cut-steel stairs rang with her boots' impacts. The sound echoed across the bay, but was smothered beneath the whine-*clomp* of Koltsokov's *Vindicator* taking its first step clear of its gantry.

Danai kept climbing.

"I need confirmations!" *Sao-shao* Ned Baxter yelled into his microphone. "I don't want to hear indications. I want vectors and sightings, or else you can figure on finding a new battalion to serve in tomorrow, got it?"

"Yes, *Sao-shao!*" the recon lance commander said.

Ned closed the comm, breathed out slowly, and checked his screens. His *Tian-zong* stood at the edge of the city proper, where it turned from high-rise buildings to low industrial and residential districts where the buildings were rarely taller than his 'Mech. The other three 'Mechs of his command lance were around him, but he'd sent all three 'Mech companies and their augments off into the Helmand after the reported 'Mechs.

He desperately wanted to kill something. And nothing else appearing, it might be the career of the company commander who'd let that lance CO report with so little information.

Ned had only met Mina Liao once or twice, but her death had still hurt. He was used to combat and war, where the other side's military was busy trying to kill you before you could kill them. And he was a scion of one of the powerful houses of the Capellan nobility; he knew death was as often a political tool as a military one. But blowing up a kind, brilliant woman whose only sin had been to be born a Liao...that rankled.

A supply convoy coming back from Deal had reported a column of BattleMechs along the edge of the Helmand. The duty officers had noted the call and logged it, but they hadn't gone to the trouble of checking to see whether there was supposed to be 'Mechs out there. It wasn't until a Third Battalion *sao-wei* came through the ops center, saw the note, and checked the duty rosters that the alarm was raised.

The mystery 'Mechs had received a forty-minute grace period to go wherever the hell they wanted. Ned had scrambled his battalion and sent recon lances sprinting out, but that had taken too long.

"Did we hear back from air about an overflight?" Ned asked.

"Negative," an unexpected voice sent. Ned looked up into his 360-degree vision strip and saw a quartet of 'Mechs approaching from behind him. A squat *Centurion* with a big shield led the lance

"*Sang-shao*," he said, greeting Danai. "*Zhong-shao* Wu didn't tell me you were coming, ma'am. I would have left escorts."

"I didn't tell him," Danai said. Her 'Mech came abreast of his. "What's the situation?"

Quickly, Ned filled her in on what he knew. And what he suspected. Unfortunately, the latter was a longer list than the former. "Good plan, Ned. Smart." She sounded distracted, but he couldn't detect any tone of mocking in her voice.

"We'll find them, ma'am," he told her.

"You asked about air. I endorsed your request for aerospace fighter overflights, but they're all tasked on orbital missions right now. Our new Maskirovka office thinks there are more Rep reinforcements coming. Regular or mercenary or both."

"More?" Ned asked. He hadn't heard about any reinforcements.

"A DropShip came down in Rockfall Maze on the day," Danai said. He didn't have to ask which day. "Engine trouble, it sent. We sent inspectors, and it came up clean, but again, our esteemed comrades in the Maskirovka question that report. The ship was an old IndustrialMech carrier."

"So maybe we're looking for MODs, you mean, *Sang-shao*?" If so, that meant his patrol routes were too far apart. He'd planned on the speed an average BattleMech could maintain. 'MechMODs—IndustrialMechs converted to carry rudimentary armor and weapons—were slower.

"Could be, but the bays for MODs are the same as for BattleMechs."

"I see..." Ned said, but that was just to fill the space. "Is the ship still there?"

"Lifted off the day before the *Culai Shan* hit atmo."

"Convenient."

Yen-Lo-Wang swung its ax back and forth. "That's just what the Mask said." There was a brief squelch of static as Danai brought more people into the conversation. "Emory, you have Ned's deployments?"

"I do, *Sang-shao*," Koltsokov said.

"Find us a gap. Let's go have a look around."

"*Sang-shao—*" Ned said, but she cut him off.

"Inform me the instant you get new information, *Sao-shao*," he heard. "If these really are 'Mechs, I want them taken down. Fast."

"Yes, ma'am," he replied. It was all he could say. He didn't quite know what else he wanted to say, but he felt something nagging at him. That surprised Ned. He wasn't a man prone to unfamiliar feelings.

Yen-Lo-Wang led the other three 'Mechs of its lance down the street toward an open-ended cul-de-sac. At the end it paused, and half-turned to look back at him. "Ned?"

"*Sang-shao?*"

"All the fighters were busy, I told you. But I forgot to mention: I told them to put a DropShip up instead. So listen for aerial recon reports, would you? Make sure they retrans to me?"

"Yes, *Sang-shao!*"

Being back inside her Purifier felt like home to Sarah Jacoby. She lay behind the military crest of a sand dune, with a clear line of sight all the way to the edge of Harney. None of the lances or companies that had come out earlier had come anywhere near her.

Jacoby had spent a lot of time looking at the towers of Harney. She couldn't go back there until the invasion was over, she knew. Maybe not even then, depending on who eventually won. By now the Louies would have her face from security cams around the explosion. Even if they didn't know her name, they knew she was one of the people close enough to have triggered the bomb.

They had to know that, unless they were incompetent. And the colonel hadn't trained her to give free points to the other side.

Movement along the edge of the city caught her eye; it was another lance of four blue 'Mechs. Jacoby dialed up the zoom on her optics and sucked in a fast breath; the lead 'Mech was a *Centurion* with a heavy shield!

Jacoby used her chin to toggle her comm open, then caught a still image from her display. She attached it to a quick message, whispered, "she's coming out," and filled in the coordinates. Another chin bump sent the message to be processed, compressed, and squirted out in a high-speed burst that was almost impossible to trace even if it was detected.

Tingling in her fingertips tried to convince her it was time to leave, but she ignored it. That was only adrenalin. Laying still, half-covered with blowing sand, her Purifier was a hole in the desert. That 'Mech lance could step over her and she'd be almost undetectable.

This part had been her job.

The next part was someone else's.

Sarah Jacoby went back to staring at the distant buildings, wondering if she'd ever be allowed to walk inside them as a free woman again.

**THE HOLE
DUNSBOROUGH
HALL
CAPELLAN CONFEDERATION**

Tom Jordan was waiting by the map table when the call came in. He watched Sergeant Austin plot the red icons' positions and paint them into the holo, then looked at the long tails of blue writhing like a snake in the Helmand. He zoomed in the view, watching the terrain. The computer projected red and blue bands in the direction of each force, with estimated travel times inset.

"New report!" a rating called.

Tom straightened up and turned to look. Colonel Tobin was closer. "Read it out," she ordered.

"DropShips, at least one, in pre-heat at Harney spaceport." Tobin, frowning, looked over at Tom. He turned back to the map table. Plans and scenarios ran through his head. Aerial recon just meant they needed to speed the timetable up.

"Hotel-baker-seven," he said, then stabbed a finger into the map display. "Right here."

"Hotel-baker-seven," Sergeant Austin confirmed. "Sending the plots."

Tom looked at Colonel Tobin, nodded once, and turned back to the table. He reached down, grabbed a handset, and held it to his ear. He typed a code by memory. "Gamma Six."

"Six," a scratchy voice came back.

"You're going to need to lead her in, Lieutenant," he said. He looked at Austin, who nodded. The data was sent. "You should have the navs."

"That's affirm," came the laconic reply. "Six out."

Tom set the handset down and looked at Colonel Tobin. "Ma'am, do you want to get the legate and governor? They might like to watch."

Tobin's eyes narrowed, old sailor's eyes looking for ripples along the horizon. She stepped down into the pit where the map table was and stood close to him, shoulder to shoulder. To anyone watching, it would look like they were regarding the map, but they were close enough that they could speak in low tones and not be overheard.

"Harry, take a break, would you?" Tom said. Austin nodded and stepped away.

"Let's make sure it's going to work before we bring higher in, Captain," the colonel said.

"As the colonel says, but ma'am," he paused. "It's going to work."

"I hope so. It's going to cost, that's for sure."

Tom didn't answer. On the map table, the blue lines of RAF armor and mercenary 'Mechs shifted their paths, aligning toward the point Tom had designated. If Gamma Six did his job, that's where Danai Liao-Centrella's lance would be just as the largest contingent of RAF strength arrived. There was opportunity for a short, sharp battle before the RAF units withdrew.

He knew it would work. He'd done the staff work to make sure that it would. There hadn't been a great deal else to do across the last few weeks.

The news that the Fourteenth had abandoned Elgin had hit the remaining RAF troopers like a thunderbolt. All the officers had their work cut out for them to maintain discipline. A lot of the fortitude the Principes had shown was due to the certainty that Colonel Boyle was coming for them. That home was safe. That the duty they were doing here was worth something, because someone else was doing that same duty on Elgin.

Except they weren't. Gruner's sources were impeccable.

There was no Elgin to go back to.

Tom had thrown himself into his work, planning a surgical strike to decapitate the Louie command structure. They'd waited until Capellan troop rotations left just a battalion of the Second McCarron's Armored Cavalry in Harney. The increased aerospace tempo across the last week had been a godsend. Tomorrow he needed to get to work on new plans for getting the next wave of mercenary reinforcements through that blockade, but that was tomorrow.

"It's going to work," he repeated. "And yes, it may cost. But those are good soldiers out there. The colonel made us that way. They'll get the job done and get away."

"I just hope it's worth it," Tobin breathed.

Tom chuckled. "To kill or capture the sister of the Louie Chancellor? I think it's worth it."

Tobin patted him on the shoulder and stepped away. Tom leaned forward, hands on the edge of the map table, thinking about the last time he'd faced *Yen-Lo-Wang*. Gruner would have her work cut out for her, taking down Danai Liao-Centrella.

His hand curled into fists.

It would be worth it.

Reaching down, he toggled a new channel. "Obsidian: here's your nav." He sent the coordinates.

"That's a rog," Captain Gruner replied. "We'll be there."

CHAPTER 24

HELMAND DESERT
HALL
CAPELLAN CONFEDERATION
17 JUNE 3149

Danai felt almost giddy when the first red icon appeared on her HUD. She jammed *Yen-Lo-Wang*'s throttle forward, lurching into a run. The incredible sense of release she felt washed through her like a cold shower. She'd spent enough time in her own head to know that the emotion wasn't healthy, that she wasn't reacting to the stimuli in the correct way, but she didn't care.

These were the people who'd killed Mina. For at least a little while, she could let her vengeance out and be justified.

Lips skinned back from her teeth, snarling inside her neurohelmet, Danai ignored the shouts of her lancemates. She only had eyes for the red icon. Her finger took up the slack on the heavy large laser trigger, despite not having a target; if she got the 'Mech hot, *Yen-Lo-Wang*'s triple-strength myomers would get her there even faster.

"Get Baxter in here," she ordered her people. "I don't want a single one of these bastards to escape. And I want prisoners!"

She'd get something back for Mina. But she was still enough Danai Liao-Centrella to know she had to put a stake through the heart of this insurgency, too.

RAF Lieutenant Tan Underhill jerked the yoke and swung his APC around; fans screaming, the JI2A1 flew backward for a few hellish seconds as the fans overcame the blower's inertia. On his screen, the four red icons of the Liao lance he'd been sent out to poke on the nose were accelerating toward him. Over the intercom he heard his gunner, Private Koh, swear as he was thrown around in the turret.

If the cargo made any noise, Underhill ignored it.

"Command, Gamma Six," he sent. "Contact made. Out." The APC's computer zipped the message and burst it out without his input; he wasn't interested in having a conversation. The two surviving blowers of his platoon swung around behind him, though they angled around instead of skidding.

"Make for the final nav," he told them. "Drop your ticks when you get there."

Double-clicks on the frequency were the only acknowledgment.

Underhill eyed the map, did some math in his head, and toggled the intercom.

"Ten minutes," he told them.

There was no reply.

Underhill steered left, down into one of the random hallways marked on the nav board. It was a chase now.

And a stern chase was a long chase, as they said back on Elgin.

"*Sang-shao, please*, wait for support," Emory Koltsokov pleaded. "Two Batt will be here in fifteen minutes. We don't know what's down there." Her *Vindicator* was pounding along at its maximum speed, trying to keep up with the faster machines.

Danai had held her lance to the *Vindicator*'s maximum, sixty-five kph, but every time the red caret wobbled into an estimated contact, she glared at the machine's image in her HUD.

"I am not letting them get away." She throttled *Yen-Lo-Wang* up and guided the 'Mech down into the hallway. "Send

Baxter the nav. Tell him to follow as quickly as he can." Danai closed the channel. Then opened it again.

"And someone find out where that damn DropShip is!"

Underhill blew past the nav at almost max speed and looked around. If any of the other RAF forces had beaten them here, they were well hidden. He couldn't even spot the mercenary 'Mechs that were supposed to be there. Maybe they were late. He didn't care. Gamma had done its part.

Underhill toggled the intercom. "It's going to be a rolling dismount."

"Thanks for the lift," a woman's voice said.

"Any time," he told her. Then he dumped air from the plenum chamber, drew the blades back to generate minimum lift, and held on. All 25 tons of blower APC came down on the skirts; steel struck stone and sparked. The blower lurched left, banged into something, and lurched right. As it slowed he punched the button that dropped open the infantry compartment ramp and angled the blades for lift again.

When the APC scuttled back up on its air cushion, it felt significantly lighter. Underhill spun around, looking.

The sandy bottom of the hallway stared back at him.

"Damn," he said, "that's some good camo."

"Ticks down," Two and Three sent.

"Then let's *didi-mao*," Underhill ordered.

Koh chuckled on the intercom. "You don't even know what that means, do you?"

"No, but I heard you say it once."

"At least you used it right." The turret swung around to cover the rear quadrant. There was almost no chance the Louies would be close enough behind to be in range of Koh's missiles, but the gunner wasn't taking any chances.

Underhill approved.

Danai slowed as she led her lance down the corridor, shield held at the high guard. For all her burning need to get payback for Mina, now that she was down in the deep with the high stone walls on both sides of her, all she could think about was the sight of that *Kheper*'s Gauss rifle pointing at her as she rounded a corner.

"No word on the DropShip," Koltsokov sent. "I've asked for an update twice."

"Very well," Danai said. She inched the *Centurion* around a corner, sensors at maximum, but there was nothing there. The canyon opened out into a straightaway, about 300 meters long and half that across. Boulders, long-since broken off the walls, were strewn across the ground. None of them were larger than two meters across.

Danai kept her shield up and stepped out. With this much open space, if the blowers they'd been chasing were in here, *Yen-Lo-Wang* would have detected them.

Which meant they'd continued on.

Are you done playing soldier? the ghost of Mina asked. Danai blinked, sniffed, tried to shake her head. She didn't remember when exactly Mina had asked that—she'd asked it a lot—but it wasn't a thought she needed or wanted to hear just then.

Yen-Lo-Wang walked on while Danai was distracted, DI computer dutifully clenching and releasing the muscles that drove the machine. Danai's feet steered the machine around the boulders without her mind being conscious of it.

A spot of red flashed and then disappeared on the left corner of her HUD. Danai's eyes snapped back into focus and she twisted the 'Mech's torso that way, toward the threat. If it was a threat.

"*Sang-shao*?" Noah Capshaw asked. He must have seen the movement.

"Possible contact," Danai said.

"Ambush?" Fan Bing asked.

"If it is, we're already in it," Capshaw snapped. "*Sang-shao*, we need to withdraw."

"No—" Danai started to say, but a red caret appeared behind her. "Maybe it's nothing..."

This caret didn't disappear.

"Target lock!" Fan yelled. Her *Dola* ripped itself free of gravity on snarling jump jets. Static growled on the comms as her *Dola*'s Angel ECM suite spun up. The lance's comms would adjust in seconds; the computers all knew the Angel's patterns.

Something exploded against the rear armor of Emory Koltsokov's *Vindicator*.

"Contact!" Danai screamed. She stamped the pedals to bring the 'Mech around.

Something punched *Yen-Lo-Wang* in the back.

Ned Baxter heard the *sang-shao* call contact and swore. He jammed his *Tian-zong*'s throttle to its stops and pressed the alert panel. "Rally on the *sang-shao*!" he sent on the all-battalion channel. Then he toggled a different channel. "*Changsha, Changsha*, Idol Six, report status, over!"

"Idol Six, *Changsha*. Lifting in five, over."

"Lift now," Ned ordered. "The *sang-shao* is under attack!"

"We'll be up as fast as we can, Idol," the DropShip's captain said. "But it's not going to be much less than five minutes. These drives take time."

Ned swore again and slapped the channel closed.

He was too far away.

The DropShip was too far away.

Damn *the woman. Why couldn't she have waited*?

Danai searched her HUD as red carets appeared and disappeared all around them. She lowered her heavy large laser's point of aim, settled it on one of the boulders, and fired. The hideously overpowered beam shattered the rock into shrapnel; it exploded like a grenade. A flickering form revealed itself as it rolled across the sandy ground; it was man-shaped, with a gigantic gun.

"Battlesuits!" she called. She adjusted her aim, but the suit vanished before the laser capacitors recharged.

The straightaway was a haze of smoke, exhaust, and kicked up sand and dust. The sun was low enough in the sky that the shadows were deep and difficult to penetrate. Danai twisted the *Centurion* around; about thirty meters in front of her there was a sudden swirl of smoke, a streak, and an impact against *Yen-Lo-Wang*'s chest.

"Recoilless rifles," Noah Capshaw confirmed. His *Wraith* pointed down with both arms and scattered pulse laser fire across the dirt at its feet. If he hit anything, Danai couldn't see.

"Okay, everyone calm down," Danai ordered. "Our armor will hold for a minute. Let's get back to the mouth of the corridor, where we can bottle them up. Watch for jumpers." She suited action to words, reversing her throttle. The laser chimed ready.

"I hate battlesuits," Fan Bing grumbled. Her *Dola* had both arms out in front of it. From the shimmer, she'd activated the giant vibroblade the 'Mech carried. Danai couldn't help but grin; the *Dola* was four times taller and many times heavier than any battlesuit.

Danai had barely taken four steps backward when a new caret appeared on her HUD, at the far end of the corridor.

It was a BattleMech. Her sensors painted it as a gunmetal-gray *Gunsmith*, a Federated Suns machine she knew well. The machine didn't carry any insignia aside from a flat white G.

"Well, it wasn't 'MechMODs,'" she muttered.

"Time to go, *Sang-shao*," Noah Capshaw said. His voice was clipped, tone grim.

The *Gunsmith* stepped into the long canyon. More 'Mechs crowded in behind it.

"Right now, *Sang-shao*," Capshaw insisted.

Danai halted *Yen-Lo-Wang*. She could have sworn she heard Capshaw sigh resignedly.

She smirked.

The count of mystery 'Mechs was up to six; so far the heaviest was a 60-ton *Argus*, but that was enough. Danai had fought enough of the Davion machines to recognize the five-delta: heavy PPC and a dozen Streak SRMs per salvo. In her mind, Danai felt something almost *click*.

Danai Liao-Centrella, duchess of Castrovia and *sang-shao* of the Second McCarron's Armored Cavalry, receded.

In her place came Danai Liao-Centrella, gladiator of Solaris VII; Danai, who cherished the incredible, if short-lived, friendship she'd had with Mina Liao; *Danai*, who still screamed at the universe in the darkest, most personal places of her mind that a cretin like Caleb Davion had ever been allowed to *exist*, much less lay a finger on her.

Yen-Lo-Wang's shield snapped up into guard; the heavy laser tracked a little to the right.

The *Gunsmith* lurched into a run.

Danai smiled.

"Idol Six, Zero One." Ned Baxter heard.

"Six," he replied.

"ETA, Six?" Emory Koltsokov asked.

Ned looked down at his board, calculating. "Twenty minutes for me. You should see a recon lance within ten. And *Changsha* is in the air."

Koltsokov opened her mic, but instead of words Ned heard the distinctive sound of a *Vindicator*'s PPC ripping ions out of the air as it fired. He knew that sound well; his first 'Mech at the academy had been a *Vindicator*.

"Hurry," was all Koltsokov said.

Ned Baxter had never felt so helpless.

Danai didn't wait for the *Gunsmith* to get in range of its pulse lasers. She let her shield drop to unmask her LRM battery, set her sights, and triggered a full barrage. A full score—twenty missiles—erupted from *Yen-Lo-Wang*'s chest and arrowed across the distance on a flat trajectory. A little more than half exploded against the *Gunsmith*'s armor; the remainder screamed past and angled; three more struck the *Fennec* trailing the *Gunsmith*. The entire group rippled with surprise.

Danai had known the next fight would come in a canyon. Fighting on Hall had always come down to the canyons, for centuries. So when she'd ordered the refitted 'Mech armed, she'd filled *Yen-Lo-Wang*'s LRM ammunition magazine with Swarm warheads, designed to take advantage of tightly-packed enemies.

She only had six salvos. But in this terrain, all six would count for the most.

"Concentrate your fire," she told her lance. "Keep the battlesuits off each other."

"*Sang-shao*," Noah Capshaw yelled. "*Sang-shao*...Danai!"

Danai ignored him. The shield came back up as the first LRMs from the gray 'Mechs began to fall around her. Several pranged off the shield; a handful chipped armor from her 'Mech's legs. She ignored that, too.

Crouched behind her shield, heavy laser leveled, Danai ordered the King of the Nine Hells forward.

RAF Private Theresa Siu crouched behind a rock in her Angerona scout battlesuit while the autoloader refilled her recoilless rifle. She trusted in her training and in her technology, but the environment around her had just become a lot more hostile.

The plan hadn't been for the armored infantry to start the ambush on their own, but Garcia had fobbed his movement and then fired, and the rest of the short platoon had opened up. She'd put her first round into the *Centurion*'s back.

"The *Centurion*!" the sergeant kept yelling. "Every shot you get, 'til your gun is dry, put it in the *Centurion*!"

The ground shook suddenly as a 'Mech got close; she looked up, around the rock. It was the *Centurion*. The recoilless rifle *clunked* the next rocket into the breech and chimed green.

The Liao *Centurion* strode past her.

She leaned around the rock, extended her arm, and triggered the gun. Like every time she fired it, she half-closed her eyes and braced for a stronger recoil than she got. She'd been trained on the physics of recoilless guns, but that didn't mean her animal brain accepted it at face value.

The round rocketed up like a slow laser and exploded against the *Centurion*'s back. If the pilot noticed, she didn't respond. She just kept stalking forward, crouched behind her shield.

"Nice shot, Siu!" the sergeant called. Then, "Look out!"

Theresa Siu twisted around to see a 30-ton *Dola* come down close enough to her that the wash from its jump jets warmed her suit. The Angerona's camo system flashed yellow with degraded systems warning. But Siu never saw that.

All she saw was the shimmering, vibrating edge of the vibroblade longer than her suit was tall coming down toward her.

And then she saw nothing at all.

CHAPTER 25

HELMAND DESERT
HALL
CAPELLAN CONFEDERATION
17 JUNE 3149

There were voices, but they were just noise. Danai ignored them. She brought the shield back up and banged the hatchet off it a few times, like she was some ancient berserker. The trio of gray 'Mechs in front of her didn't waver; the *Gunsmith* stuck its arms out and spat verdant pulse laser fire at her. Most of spattered across her shield, but some melted patches on her shoulders and legs.

Yen-Lo-Wang ignored the damage. He craved the heat.

Danai triggered her laser; the brilliant beam of hellfire hit the *Gunsmith* straight in the chest. Danai frowned; the hit pattern looked different, almost *attenuated*. Then an old bit of knowledge slid into place in her mind: *Gunsmith*s were wrapped in laser-reflective armor, designed to lessen the impact of laser weapons.

Her frown peeled back into a grin. Had they selected 'Mechs specifically to fight her?

The *Fennec* with the *Gunsmith* hit her with both PPCs; both hit her shield, but enough of the energy bled through to rip some armor off of *Yen-Lo-Wang*'s chest. The third 'Mech in the lead, a four-legged *Sarath*, slammed a heavy PPC shot past her; she didn't see where the round fell, but someone in her speakers grunted with an impact.

The range was down to less than a hundred meters. Despite the presence of more 'Mechs in the backfield, despite the unknown number of stealthy battlesuits crawling around in the dust, still firing at them, Danai was desperate to close the range. Heat crushed the atmosphere in her cockpit, but her cooling suit kept the worst of it at bay.

In close combat, *Yen-Lo-Wang* was unbeatable.

The hatchet clanged off the shield again.

The laser recharged. Danai triggered it again, this time taking the *Gunsmith* in the right thigh. Again the beam failed to penetrate, but the little green light on the motivator board lit; the triple-strength myomers were hot enough to fire.

Yen-Lo-Wang leaped forward, hatchet raised. The *Gunsmith* hadn't been expecting that burst of speed; it couldn't duck out of the way fast enough.

Danai's hatchet came down of the soft part of the *Gunsmith*'s right leg, where the laser had just hit. The hard alloy edge bit deep, lurched, and then went through the light 'Mech's leg, driven by the awesome power of the triple-strength pseudo muscles. The *Gunsmith*'s volley of pulse laser fire went wide as the 'Mech went down.

Danai snarled. The *Fennec* twisted on its birdlike waist toward her. *Yen-Lo-Wang* was too close for the PPCs to easily hit, but the *Fennec* pilot burned at her with both medium pulse lasers. One slipped past her shield to burn at the *Centurion*'s chest armor; the other missed entirely.

Fan Bing's *Dola* fell out of the sky behind the 'Mech. The *Dola* landed in a crouch, blasting dust and sand up from its jump jets, but stepped in close behind the *Fennec*. Her laser burned at the armor over the gray 'Mech's elbow, but that was just a sideshow.

The *Dola* spun its wrist, turning the vibroblade from a down-thrust weapon to an up-thrust one. The tip of the hyper-vibrating sword ground through the thin armor where the 'Mech's right kidney would have been. Fan stabbed once, like an assassin, and then jumped away before the rest of the gray 'Mechs could react.

All the gray 'Mechs in Danai's vision flinched, if a 'Mech could be said to flinch at all. Something happened. The machines were back into smooth motion almost immediately, but Danai had seen it.

"Bing?" she asked.

"Got the C3 computer," she gasped. That much jumping, combined with the laser, would have the heat in her cockpit oven-like. "Should keep them from coordinating so well."

"Well done!" Danai had forgotten that, too. *Fennec*s were lance command machines, with a huge master command, control, and communication computer buried in their right chest. With that active, all of its lancemates could coordinate their fire. Without it, the gray 'Mechs were fighting on their own.

"I can't be everywhere," Fan said. Danai chuckled. The *Dola*'s Angel ECM would have cut the *Fennec*'s links just as well, but only when it was close by. Danai twisted *Yen-Lo-Wang* to face the *Fennec*; she ignored the *Gunsmith* on the ground, clawing at the loose sand with its one remaining foot, trying to get turned around.

The medium-weight machine started backstepping.

Danai followed.

THE HOLE
DUNSBOROUGH
HALL
CAPELLAN CONFEDERATION

"Obsidian Six is down!" a rating called.

Tom Jordan swore and zoomed in on the map table. It didn't change the scene; he wasn't watching a live feed. But he didn't know the rest of the mercenary MechWarriors well enough to know how they'd react to their commander going down.

"Down or dead?" he demanded.

"Report says down," the rating said.

"What do we do, sir?" Sergeant Austin asked.

"Keep to the plan," was all Tom said. "Is Charlie ready?" At Austin's definitive nod, Tom chewed his lower lip for a moment, then nodded. "Send them in."

HELMAND DESERT
HALL
CAPELLAN CONFEDERATION

Sao-shao Ned Baxter heard the first report from his leading lance and drew his throttle back, slowing his 'Mech. "Say that again," he ordered.

"Ambush, sir," the captain reported. "My recon lance got hit as soon as they entered the corridor. Tanks and infantry, in good positions."

"Can you get past?"

"I can see a DI Morgan tank from where I am now, sir. I can get through, but it's going to cost and it's going to take time."

Muting his mic, Ned swore. "Wait for support," he ordered. Then he thought again. "On second thought, don't. All your jump-capable 'Mechs: send them down adjacent hallways. Anything that can't make it over the wall later on, pin down that armor. The rest of the battalion is right behind you."

"On it, *Sao-shao.*"

The RAF insurgents had planned this ambush quite well. The little war college instructor voice in his mind was reciting all the ways he'd failed to prepare for this. It was lecturing him on the strategic defensive, on the use of small units to tie down larger ones. Ned knew all of that.

He pushed the throttle up again. "Keep your eyes open," he told his command lance. "Bastards could be anywhere."

Combat, amazingly enough, settled enough of Danai's rage that she could see what was going on around her. Even as she put a full flight of missiles into the *Fennec*, she saw Emory Koltsokov's *Vindicator* in the backfield, putting very accurate PPC shots into any target that presented itself. Noah Capshaw's *Wraith* shook a pair of battlesuits off its left leg like a man shaking off a biting dog, then lowered its arm and blasted the space where they fell with pulse laser fire.

The *Fennec* hit her with one PPC, in the leg. The impact threatened to kick *Yen-Lo-Wang*'s leg out from under her, but Danai snatched the 50-ton 'Mech back into balance at the last moment. Her own laser replied almost immediately, eating deeply into the *Fennec*'s chest. Seeing her opportunity, Danai dashed closer, raised the ax and brought it down with all the force she could muster.

Right into the *Fennec*'s left chest, where her laser had just hit.

The hard alloy edge crushed what armor was left and buried itself in the reactor containment systems for the *Fennec*'s extralight engine; the 'Mech fell as if its strings were cut as the fusion reactor went into emergency shutdown.

The *Sarath* that had rounded out the leading group spun like a trapped beast. Its back-mounted turret spun back and forth. The MechWarrior inside couldn't decide who to target, and so wasn't shooting at anyone.

"The *Sarath*," she sent, raising her laser.

All four of her lance's machines fired on the quad 'Mech. It writhed in the fire, ducking and trying to twist away like an animal caught in a fire hose spray, but it couldn't. The MechWarrior broke, spinning around and sprinting back toward its confederates. The big *Argus* leading that group stepped aside to let it pass, then put a heavy PPC bolt into the sand at Danai's feet.

"They still outnumber us," Capshaw warned.

"Yeah, but we've taken down two of theirs," Danai said. "At least one of them was an officer, by the way they're acting. They look scared."

"We have a chance to break contact," Capshaw said. "Get back with the rest of the regiment, then come back and deal with them." The pause before the next part, to his credit, was just to catch his breath, not because he doubted himself. "We should do so, *Sang-shao*."

Danai licked her dry lips. Noah was right. She knew he was.

"No," she said instead. "If we let them get away, we'll never find them. More people will get hurt."

"I don't think—" Capshaw started, but Danai cut the channel.

Capshaw's *Wraith* put a burst of medium pulse laser darts into the ground near her 'Mech.

Danai stared, shocked. She toggled the channel back open. "Are you insane?" she shouted.

"*Changsha* is overhead, or shortly will be," Capshaw said evenly. "They're not going to get away."

"*Sang-shao*," Fan Bing interjected, but Danai ignored her.

"Noah. You just fired on your commanding officer."

"No, *Sang-shao*. Due respect. But I fired at a battlesuit attempting a leg attack on your *Centurion*." He stopped, then went on. "Their camo systems are very advanced. You may not have seen it."

Danai opened, then closed her mouth.

"*Sang-shao*!" Fan Bing shouted.

"What?" she said, but then she saw what Fan must have seen.

The *Argus* and the other 'Mechs had gotten tired of waiting.

The first PPC bolt flicked past her shoulder and struck Capshaw's *Wraith* full in the chest.

More of the smoking wrecks he passed belonged to the RAF than his own battalion, Ned Baxter was pleased to see. The leading company had shoved the ambushing armor company back into the hallway and pressed it deeper into the crags and turns.

It wasn't until he turned the corner and found a blasted *Yinghuochong* draped across the pitted hull of a burned out DI Morgan tank that he stopped. The dead 'Mech was missing its cockpit, but the rear-panel markings were for a *sang-wei*.

"You did good," he told the captain's ghost.

Then he stepped his *Tian-zong* past. His duty was to the living.

He hoped.

Danai blasted at the *Argus* with her laser, but it wasn't enough. She saw the flickers of motion as the protective shutters on the 60-ton machine's SRM launchers opened; flame burst from deep inside a dozen tubes. Danai cringed in the second or so she had before they struck. Streak missiles didn't miss.

The warheads blasted all across her 'Mech. One exploded against the *Centurion*'s head, ringing the armor like a bell and throwing her painfully against her restraints. The neurohelmet slipped, wrenching her neck. Hissing in pain, Danai tried to grasp her controls, but the explosions kept coming for what felt like forever.

When the thundering gongs faded, she took stock.

Yen-Lo-Wang was a wreck. The previous fighting had opened just enough gaps in her protection that the SRMs had done meaningful damage. Her knee actuator was shot, which was going to slow her down, but worse, one of the rockets had pranged the elbow actuator of her shield arm. The blocky mass of metal was still there, but she couldn't adjust it, and it was out of position.

Pushing down the pain in her neck, Danai pulled the *Centurion* back into line. Her LRM seeker tone switched to a lock, but she was too close: the Swarm warheads would attack her just as easily as the gray 'Mechs.

Noah Capshaw's *Wraith* sprinted past her like a striker on the pitch; it spat green pulse laser fire into the *Argus*' side and arms as it passed the gray 'Mech. He planted the *Wraith*'s foot, twisted around behind the heavy 'Mech, and lashed out at its birdlike leg with his own. The kick connected, knocking the *Argus* off balance. It crashed down like a train wreck.

Before Noah could move, the *Sarath* put a heavy PPC round into his *Wraith*'s back. Light bloomed on the secondary IR display as the ravenous bolt ate into the 'Mech's reactor shielding. Danai opened her mouth, but before she could speak the *Wraith*'s head came apart as the MechWarrior ejected on flaming rocket motors.

"Noah!" Danai yelled. She jammed her throttle forward just as the *Argus* was getting back to its feet over the sprawled corpse of Capshaw's 'Mech. She held her fire, instead swinging the hatchet underhand. It caught the *Argus*' stumpy gun-arm, mangling the armor there.

"Hit 'em!" she screamed.

The *Argus* started backing up.

"Yes!" Danai exulted.

"*Sang-shao, get down!*" a new voice shouted.

Danai dropped her 'Mech prone, accepting the new pains from her restraints. Already-screaming muscles took more of the neurohelmet's weight. Danai gritted her teeth and looked at her HUD for the newcomer.

Ned Baxter's blue *Tian-zong* stood behind Fan and Koltsokov. While she watched, the heavy Capellan 'Mech stomped down once with its foot, crushing a last hidden battlesuit. The big barrels on its shoulders adjusted their aim, and then with a double-*wham* that shook dust loose from the hall walls nearby, fired. The Mydron Concussor Gauss rifles lived up to their name; *Yen-Lo-Wang* shook.

The *Argus* ate both Gauss rounds; one of its arms blew completely off. The shots staggered the 'Mech, but it stayed on its feet and ran back the way it had come.

"Get after them," Baxter ordered, and more blue-painted Second MAC 'Mechs pounded past he and *Yen-Lo-Wang* both. Baxter stepped closer, then reached down with one giant hand.

"*Sang-shao*?"

Danai worked *Yen-Lo-Wang* to its feet, then laughed. "Perfect timing, Ned." She said. "Just perfect."

THE HOLE
DUNSBOROUGH
HALL
CAPELLAN CONFEDERATION

Tom slumped down into a chair. "It's confirmed?"

Harry James Austin nodded. "Yes, sir. Gruner's company is pulling back."

"Without Captain Gruner."

"Seems that way, sir, yes, sir."

Tom looked around at the ops center and the people working it. He was the senior officer present; Colonel Tobin had never come back. The legate and the governor had never appeared. "That's it, then."

He breathed in and out. "Harry, all of you. Listen to me. It's over. You should get out of here, go to ground, and wait for the RAF to come back."

"Sir?"

Tom waved to the table. "We failed. And the colonel isn't coming."

"What about you, sir? I can't just leave you here."

Tom shook his head. "Gruner knew about this place. She'll talk, if she's still alive."

"We're still in this fight, Captain Jordan," Austin said firmly. A couple of the ratings in Tom's sightline nodded. "We can fall back on one of the alternate hides. Keep the fight going until someone, the colonel or someone else, gets here."

Tom nodded. "Do that, then."

"What about you, sir?"

Tom smiled faintly. "I'm right behind you."

CHAPTER 26

**HARNEY
HALL
CAPELLAN CONFEDERATION
13 JULY 3149**

"It seems your work is done here, your Grace," Lord Pyotr Zheng said. He was seated at what had been her desk in the Harney governor's mansion. What had been Mina's desk, for a few too-short days.

Danai frowned. "I don't understand."

Zheng smiled in a grandfatherly way. He was an older man, with silver-white hair and fine wrinkles around his eyes and mouth. Danai would have liked to have believed they were laugh lines, but she knew her father's court too well; jovial men and women rarely did well in Daoshen's light, and Zheng was Daoshen's creature through and through. "I speak of your great victory, of course."

"The insurgency is still out there," Danai asserted, firmly. "We have taken the last of Captain Gruner's mercenary 'Mechs, that is true. And routed out the hidden nest in Dunsborough. But at least a regiment of Principes armor and infantry remain unaccounted for. As well as the governor."

Zheng wasn't entirely wrong; they had made great strides in the last month. The tempo had switched almost entirely into the Liao liberators' hands, as each captured group of insurgents gave up information about the next. Captain Gruner had made only token protests at being interrogated, and had given up the so-called Hole almost immediately. It was largely cleaned out by the time a battalion of the Second Liao Guard attacked it, but they'd managed to take a number of plans and, even better, the planetary legate, who'd been careless with his escape plan and wandered where Capellan recon overflights could see his vehicle. It had taken a little more time for the Maskirovka interrogators to break Fernandez, but he was singing whatever tune Zheng gave him now.

The bruises were almost invisible beneath the makeup, on HV. Capshaw had explained how that was intentional. "Too obvious and people get angry," he'd said. "But if you leave a hint, just enough that people who are looking for it will find it, then it scares them. They start to see themselves beneath that makeup. They start to imagine what must have been done to a person to make them say those things." He shrugged. "It only works on the weak-willed, but in a population of two billion, there will be enough of those to make a difference."

And he'd been right. More and more Capellan patriots— as the news now called them, not the collaborators they would have been two months prior—were passing the CCAF information about the RAF insurgency.

Danai had stared when Noah Capshaw had explained it so matter-of-factly. The boy from New Syrtis was gone. That boy would never have been able to speak so casually about fear as a weapon, but the man who'd been her intelligence officer for most of a year now saw the world around him with more clear eyes.

The officer in Danai was pleased; she was repaying the investment the Confederation had made in her forward. But the woman in Danai mourned, quietly where no one could see, the death of Noah Capshaw's innocent need to please.

"True," Zheng allowed. "But I remain confident *Sang-shao* Krishnamurthy and the Second Liao Guards can handle it." He touched one of the many message folios on his desktop. "These are orders that arrived only yesterday via JumpShip. You, your Grace, are to ready the Second McCarron's Armored Cavalry to move off-world when summoned, readiness to be assumed not later than the first week of August."

Danai blinked. "Orders, my lord? From who?" She expected to hear Xavier McCarron. In her quiet moments she'd been amazed he'd left her alone this long. The grand old man of the MAC positively reveled in stirring up trouble.

"From your brother, in fact."

"The Chancellor?"

"Indeed." Zheng smiled, a politician pleased that he had information a peer did not. Danai kept her face neutral, but she knew the expression for what it was. "He has relocated his headquarters to Liao, to be closer to our grand liberation of the Republic."

"To Liao," she repeated.

"Yes, your Grace. In secret, for now."

"I see."

If Daoshen was this close, then the other attacks that had lifted off from Liao near the same time they came to Hall must have succeeded. *He would never leave Sian to castigate defeated troops.* Danai licked her lips, thinking. "I imagine there is a strategic download in there?" she said, inclining her head at the folio.

Zheng's smile dripped insincerity. "I wouldn't dream of intruding in military matters, your Grace, so I'm sure I wouldn't know."

You read every word, you snake, she thought. Smiling, she leaned over and picked the folio up. "May we speak on another matter, my lord?" She straightened, holding the folio behind her back, and took two steps back.

"Of course, your Grace."

"I'm told you intend to rescind all the provisional caste assignments made here since the liberation. Is that true?"

"It is."

"May I ask why?" He opened his mouth, but she held up a hand. "Please understand, I and Lady Liao put a lot of effort into building a civilian infrastructure to shepherd this world back into the bosom of the Confederation. I suppose I still feel a sense of, if not ownership, at least motivated curiosity, if you will." Danai laid on her most simpering grin. "I have not been long a *Sheng*, but Lady Liao was an excellent teacher. She would not like it, were I not to ask."

"A tragedy," Zheng commented, professionally grave. "The Lady Liao was a light we will not see again, I fear."

"Indeed," Danai agreed. *Now answer the question.*

"As for the caste assignments, as I'm sure you're aware, your Grace, the policy of the State has always been to place all liberated civilians into the servitor caste for a period of not less than five years, to give the directorship time to make proper caste assignments at the end of that time."

Danai nodded gravely. "I am aware, my lord, yes." She frowned. "But I wonder..."

"Yes?"

"Lady Liao was a firm instructor," Danai continued. "Part of her education of me included a lengthy study of the practices—both successes and failures—of other liberations, both historically and in recent times when we took back worlds from the Federated Suns."

"I see," Zheng said, but his narrowed eyes told her he didn't see anything.

"The directorship must make any decision," Danai said. "That is, by their very nature, their duty and responsibility. But in the intervening time, is not the State strengthened by people who contribute all they can, rather than gutting the economy of a planet by making everyone on it servitors?"

"Your Grace..."

"Lady Liao cited many examples," Danai persisted. "Including the many—almost incalculable—times that recently-liberated members of the *Sheng* were able to reach their caste assignments much more swiftly." *Because the corrupt bastards buy their way in, just like that asshole Bancroft tried to,* she didn't say.

"Be that as it may, your Grace," Zhen responded, after a pregnant pause, "surely you can see how I am unqualified to alter the policy of the State, a policy your brother himself supports."

Danai nodded, as if agreeing, but then frowned. "It is a risk," she agreed. "But I suppose I could tell my brother that it was my fault. That you requested to apply the correct policy, but I declined to allow it." She smiled and shook her head, as if imparting a shared disappointment. "After all, *my lord,* you could hardly be faulted for following the wishes of a *duchess*, especially not a duchess who is the Chancellor's sister and, arguably, third in line for the Celestial throne itself."

Zheng opened his mouth, and then closed it.

Danai ducked her chin, a tiny bow for politeness' sake. "I have much to do," she said, brandishing the folio with her orders. "I'll stop intruding upon your time."

Zheng rose and bowed. "My time is yours, your Grace," he said, but Danai heard the flat hardness in his voice.

Good, she thought but didn't say. *You understand your place.*

Danai smiled politely, spun about, and strode out of the office. She slapped the folio against her thigh as she walked.

It's not a lot, Mina, she thought, waiting for the elevator, *but it's something I could do. For the people.*

GRIMSBAY FORWARD OPERATING BASE
HALL
CAPELLAN CONFEDERATION

Heather Teng knew something was up when she saw the *sang-wei* waiting for her when she racked her *Gravedigger* near the mobile field base. It was after dark, but the night fighting position was well lit with actinic floodlights.

The *sang-wei* stood waiting, arms clasped behind his back, while she climbed down the chain-link ladder to the field. Voltikov had already come down from his *Anubis* by the time she got there, but she waved him back.

She saluted. "Sir?"

"Stand easy, Heather," *Sang-wei* Sergej Kharpov replied. The red-haired MechWarrior was short, squat, and built like his *King Crab*. "Any problems tonight?"

"Nothing, sir," Teng answered. "We thought we had a contact, but it turned out to be a couple of kids out in dune buggies." She and Voltikov had paired up with a pair of infantry APCs from the Foot Guard and gone out looking for insurgents—the Mask thought they had a hidden fuel dump somewhere within sixty klicks of Dunsborough—but tonight's vector had been a bust.

"Let 'em go with a warning?"

"Couldn't even keep up with them," Heather responded. She didn't say, *that's a task I would have given to Beatrice or Ruskaya*, her *Roadrunner* pilots, because Ruskaya was dead and Beatrice still in the hospital. But she thought it.

"Good enough," Kharpov said. He glanced over at Voltikov, then waved him over. The MechWarrior stepped over quickly and braced, but didn't salute, since Heather already had.

"Easier to tell you both together," he said plainly. Teng stiffened, but Kharpov raised his hands. "It's not bad news. At least for you." He glanced between them. "You're being transferred to the Second MAC, effective immediately."

"We're w-what?" Teng stammered.

"Scuttlebutt is Danai's Regiment is going to get shifted off-world to a new assignment soon, so they're bringing it up to strength. You two are being assigned to Five Company, Second Battalion. *Sang-wei* Peterman." He pulled a noteputer out of his waistband, behind his back, and held it out. "Your orders. Apparently, you're getting two MAC boys who had their *sao-wei* shot up in the first month engagements. They've been working attached to the company CO's lance, but he wants an officer in charge of the lance again. You're it."

"Sir..." Voltikov started, but then stopped.

"Go ahead," Kharpov said. When Voltikov hesitated, he barked, "Fear is the enemy, the *only* enemy. Out with it."

"What about Beatrice, sir?"

Teng had wanted to ask the same question. "He'll stay with the regiment," Kharpov answered. "I'll make sure he gets a good lance when he comes back." The company CO looked at Teng. "Any other questions?"

"Why us, sir?"

Kharpov grinned. "You were requested, *Sao-wei*. By the *sang-shao* herself."

Teng gaped. "Requested...?" she mumbled.

Kharpov laughed and slapped her shoulder. "Some of us get it easy, eh? My family had to fight its way into the Confederation, fight for our citizenship. Almost broke my parents, scraping to get me ready for the academy. And the *sang-shao* asks for you!"

He smiled to show it was a joke. He needed a sense of humor. He piloted one of the few assault 'Mechs in a regiment made up of lights and mediums.

"C'mon. I've got the rest of the company waiting to give you a proper send-off!"

**HARNEY
HALL
CAPELLAN CONFEDERATION**

Danai found Noah Capshaw in the 'Mech bay, staring up at his new BattleMech. The *Wraith* had been a write-off after the battle in the hallway; the Second's techs had stripped it for parts, but more and more Capellan military resupply ships were reaching them now. A handful of replacement BattleMechs had arrived to supplement what they'd been able to salvage from the Principes.

"What do you think?" Danai asked, as she walked up behind him.

Glancing over his shoulder, Capshaw grinned. "*Sang-shao.* I know I should feel honored, but right now I don't know how to feel. I've never even simmed this machine."

Danai stopped next to him and looked up at the machine. She'd never seen one before. At 60 tons, the Clan-built *Sojourner* was a heavy 'Mech, but it had a supercharger and jump jets that made it more maneuverable than its mass might suggest. It was an OmniMech, but she knew the 'Mech had come without any refit kits to its other configurations. The Second's tech team could whip them up from parts and stock, if necessary, but Capshaw had never piloted an OmniMech before. He'd probably be satisfied with its current configuration.

She glanced at him. They'd never talked about the fight in the hallway where he'd lost his 'Mech. She'd chosen to accept his lie about shooting at the battlesuit and not her 'Mech to get her attention. In hindsight, he'd been right, and she'd been wrong. And she trusted that he'd matured enough that he recognized what was happening without needing it explained to her.

"The manual has a Clan Wolf-in-Exile logo on it," Capshaw commented with a chuckle. "I wonder how it got to us?"

Danai leaned close. "Never question the provenance of the Sea Foxes," she whispered, naming the mercantile Clan that traded from space across the Inner Sphere. "We have *yuan*. They have wares. It all works out in the end."

"I should get in the sim," Capshaw remarked. "Still no word on when we lift?"

"It's only been a couple hours, Noah."

"So that's a no, then, ma'am?"

"That's a no."

"So there's time."

Danai grinned. "Yes. But before you do that…I wanted you to be the first to know. The ship that brought this 'Mech for you lifted off this morning. It took *Yen-Lo-Wang* with it."

Capshaw turned to face her, surprised. "What?"

"You were right, Noah. He is the deadliest 'Mech in the Inner Sphere, but he isn't the right machine for me any longer. I sent him back to St. Ives." She glanced up at the *Sojourner*. "Gruner's 'Mechs were watching for him when we left the city that day. She confirmed it. They knew to look for the shield and the hatchet. I put all of you at risk."

"No, *Sang-shao*…"

Danai spread her hands, ending his objections. "Yes. It's only the truth. Next time we drop, I'll ride something more appropriate." She grinned slyly. "In fact, I just got the sim sets for my new machine, too."

"What did you choose?"

Danai laughed. "That would ruin the surprise, *Sang-wei*. I'll see you in the sims in thirty minutes. We'll see who learns their new 'Mech faster."

Capshaw's grin was easy and comfortable, she was pleased to see. "Apparently the *Sojourner* has extended-range pulse lasers. You don't see many of those. I may surprise you."

Danai's grin turned wolfish. "Oh, there will be surprises."

Together, they walked out of the 'Mech bay, headed for the simulators.

CHAPTER 27

Solid, flat ground was a premium commodity on Liberty. The planet was nine-tenths ocean, with the remaining ten percent spread across bands of islands. That the Second MAC had found enough space to put their DropShips down within striking distance of the Dronane, the capital city, was something of a miracle.

Danai really hoped it wouldn't be the only miracle her regiment would get.

The courier delivering Danai's orders had been late, which meant her regiment arrived two weeks after the other Capellan units had landed. Those two—the Fifth McCarron's Armored Cavalry and the Warrior House Imarra—had landed and attacked.

And been repulsed.

From the data she'd reviewed in the JumpShip downloads, most of the rest of the attacks in Operation Tiamat had gone about as well has Hall had. Tiamat itself had been the largest surprise: learning that Daoshen had crafted an alliance with the Draconis Combine to attack into the Republic from two sides had shocked her to the core. While the Confederation drove up from the bottom, the Dragon would drive a sword down from the top. The update she'd received was light on details, but she could read a map as good as any MechWarrior.

She hadn't believed her father was capable of trusting anyone enough to give up any semblance of control over the invasion of the Republic. CBS may be telling everyone the liberation was about retaking formerly-Capellan worlds, but she knew better. His ambition would force him to snap up every planet he could, even old Terra herself, if he could get away with it.

Giving some of those worlds to the Kuritas didn't fit that image. Danai didn't like to have her image of Daoshen challenged.

Danai had gone to *Changsha*, Second Battalion's *Overlord*-class DropShip, to use its better CIC for her initial planning. She was waiting for the other two Capellan commanders to arrive, and she tried to use the time to understand the situation. But the summaries she read didn't make a lot of sense.

Liberty, unlike most worlds, had an absurdly short transit distance from the jump point, barely two-and-a-half days. In total, the Second had been aboard ship for a few minutes less than eight days, and that hadn't given her a lot of time for planning.

"Did we get the intel download?" she called across the room.

"Literally just now," Noah Capshaw said. He was huddled around a small screen with Wu Feng. "Trying to get the high points, *Sang-shao*."

"Good," she said. Next, she looked at Emory Koltsokov. "Noah's busy. Tell me about this regiment."

The pale operations officer nodded, set her noteputer down, and stepped closer. "Stone's Fury, they're calling it."

Danai snorted. "Stone's Fury. Stone's Lament. Soon there will be Stone's Boredom. Stone's Snoring. They really need more original names."

"As you say, *Sang-shao*." Koltsokov grinned, but Danai saw her attempt at lightening the mood had fallen flat. "Stone's Brigade is the elite of the Republic Armed Forces, or were before the Wall went up. From the reports I've seen so far, the Fury is living up to that reputation." She indicated the holotank, and when Danai nodded, activated it.

"The Fifth advanced first but was stopped quickly by a heavy battalion in good cover," Koltsokov said. In the holotank a tactical map sprang up, battalion and company markers instead of battleROM footage; the modern equivalent of a sand table exercise.

Danai eyed the terrain. "Gwen went left?"

"She did," Koltsokov confirmed. In the tank, one Liao green block, a battalion of *Sang-shao* Gwendolyn Vaughan's Fifth MAC, moved left to try and enfilade the Republic position. "House Imarra moved up from the reserve as well, and attempted to hook around the Republic position and attack it from the right flank."

Danai nodded. Those were standard tactics for attacking an entrenched position, and had been since before humanity left Terra. Use an engaged force to pin the defender in place, then send flying columns around his flanks to attack from the side or rear. The frontal pressure makes it difficult-to-impossible to react to the other attacks.

"And?"

"And the Fury beat them all off and withdrew in good order," Koltsokov said.

Danai stared at her. "They did *what*?"

"Imarra managed to take a few prisoners. From what they've learned, the Fury is made up of many former Knights of the Republic and the usual mix of veterans you find in Stone's Brigade. They refused their lines, beat the flank attacks off, and withdrew behind a screen of fresh companies." Koltsokov frowned. "Losses in the Fifth were heavy; Imarra less so, but Imarra started with less."

Danai nodded. A modern warrior house order of monastic MechWarriors was two battalions of 'Mechs and two battalion of armored infantry integrated to fight augmented. She'd put any battalion of her regiment up against one of theirs, but knew in a fight her battalion might win, but it'd get mauled. For a battalion of this Fury regiment to hold back that much force...

"I want to see the ROMs," she said. Koltsokov nodded and called one up.

"I was watching this one when you asked, *Sang-shao*. Watch this *Lich*..."

Heather Teng stood when the *sao-shao* entered the small ready room off the 'Mech bays aboard *Changsha*.

"Sir," she said. "*Sang-wei* Peterman just left; I'm not sure if she's coming back." The company commander had been giving her a patrol route; Teng's first deployment as a member of McCarron's Armored Cavalry was a patrol circuit around the landing zone.

It was an easy mission, but it made sense. She and Voltikov hadn't had much time to get used to their new lance.

"Rest," *Sao-shao* Baxter ordered. "And that's okay, *Sao-wei*. I came to see you. I already spoke to *Sang-wei* Peterman."

Heather spread her feet and relaxed to parade rest, but she didn't relax much. She had met Ned Baxter on Hall, of course, but aside from that initial introduction they hadn't spoken until now. In the battalion, Baxter had the reputation of a hard taskmaster who expected the best from his *janshi*. From what Teng had seen from the Second McCarron's Armored Cavalry, that attitude was everywhere. It didn't bother her; that was the same standard she set for herself. "Sir?"

"I hadn't realized before we lifted and I had time to catch up on my paperwork that *Sang-shao* Liao-Centrella had personally requested you for my battalion." Baxter's eyes were intense; his light hair was cut short—freshly, it looked like. He hadn't asked a question, so Teng said nothing. "Do you know anything about that?"

"Only that it happened, sir," she replied. "I had only met the *sang-shao* once before."

"At Fort Lexington," Baxter filled in.

"Yes, sir."

"You lost two MechWarriors there, correct?"

"Yes, *Sao-shao*."

"To an insurgent bomb."

Teng swallowed. "Yes, sir."

"Tell me what happened."

"It was a truck bomb, sir. They blew it as my two lightest 'Mechs, a pair of *Roadrunners*, were crossing nearby. Killed one, wounded the other. The medics weren't confident he'd recover when I left the Guards, sir." She stopped.

"And what did you do?"

"Sir?"

"When the truck blew. What did you do?"

"I saw to my wounded, sir," Teng said, frowning. *Is there another answer?*

"What about the insurgents?"

"They were gone, sir. No one to fight. At that point, my mission was my MechWarriors."

Baxter regarded her. He breathed in one, a long breath, and then exhaled. Teng could see the calculus going on behind his eyes, but she had no idea what it was about.

Finally, he shook his head a little and held out his hand. "Welcome again to my battalion, *Sao-wei*." As she took his hand, he held it firmly, not letting go. "Care for your new troops as much as you obviously cared for your last ones, and we'll get along fine." He let go of her hand and turned around, headed for the door. He stopped at the hatch, one hand on the coaming, and looked back.

"By the way. Your papers for *sang-wei* will come through tonight. You're taking over for Peterman. She's getting kicked upstairs. We'll talk to the troops tomorrow. Five Company will be yours then. Now, get out on your patrol."

Then he was gone, leaving Teng blinking in shock.

Danai looked up as a crewman escorted two unfamiliar officers into the CIC. Unfamiliar, but not unknown. Danai grinned and stepped toward them, holding her hand out to the taller, heavier woman in with MAC shoulder patches.

"Gwen," she said. "Good to see you again."

"You Grace," Gwendolyn Vaughan replied, smiling back. She shook Danai's hand with the same dry, bone-crushing grip Danai remembered. The Fifth McCarron's Armored Cavalry regiment was the equal of any of the others, and much of that was due to Gwen Vaughan's unceasing drive for excellence.

That there was also an irreverent streak a mile wide beneath the tall woman's facade was something else that endeared her to Danai.

Danai turned to the other officer. This man was nondescript: average height, average features. It wasn't until you met his stare and saw the holy fire of devotion burning there that you realized there was more him. As *gang-shiao-zhang* of Warrior House Imarra, the senior warrior house among the Chancellors' warrior house orders, Jiang Hui had authority far exceeding that of a normal man. He shook Danai's hand stiffly, saying nothing. His nod of respect communicated all it needed to.

Hui is Daoshen's man as much as Zheng was, Danai reminded herself.

"Thank you both for coming," she said after they'd been introduced to her staff. Near the tail end of the introductions, Ned Baxter had slid through the hatch and positioned himself against the wall, where he could see the holotank. He leaned there, arms crossed, just observing.

"You've had a hard fight," she told them. "We've been looking at the data you sent over."

"These guys are no joke," Gwen Vaughan said. "That's a fact."

"Tell me your impressions," she said.

Vaughan glanced at the house master, but when he said nothing, she launched into a detailed and critical review of the past two weeks. Danai was impressed; she did not overly highlight her successes and try to hide her failures. She spoke with a sort of detached objectivity that surprised Danai. If their roles were reversed, she wasn't sure she could have described the Second's failure to make progress as evenly.

"There are two critical factors," Vaughan reiterated as she wrapped up. "They are damn good soldiers, and their technology is fantastic. I feel like I know what those oldsters thought a century ago, when the Clans first came. They have a couple gigantic three-legged 'Mechs unlike anything I've ever seen before." She glanced at Hui, who remained as taciturn as ever. "I know we've had rumors of tripod 'Mechs for a while now, but I'd never seen one before with my own eyes."

"Me either," Danai said. "They weren't present on Hall, but the ships that brought us here had reports of other Confederation regiments engaging them across the liberation." She glanced at Noah Capshaw. "Noah, do we have any idea how many of those things there are?"

Capshaw nodded to *Sang-shao* Vaughan and the house master before he spoke. "Our review of the data provided by House Imarra and the Fifth suggests most likely a lance of four. Perhaps as many as eight, if they are not OmniMechs." He waited half a heartbeat for either of the two Liberty veterans to contradict him; when they did not, he continued. "It is possible there are more in Dronane. There is at least one additional battalion of the Fury that has not yet taken the field."

Vaughan nodded. "My own people said the same thing, your Grace."

Danai looked at Hui. "*Gang-shiao-zhang*? Anything to add?"

The house master met her stare evenly. "No," he replied simply.

Danai worked her jaw but held her tongue. *He is used to being in charge*, she told herself. In almost any situation, a warrior house was the senior unit present when paired with a regular Confederation regiment. She was sure Gwen Vaughan had deferred to the house master thus far. The warrior houses were too favored by the Chancellor, their ultimate superior, to challenge for most CCAF officers.

But Danai was not most officers. And while Daoshen Liao might be Jiang Hui's liege lord, he was her *father*. Her brother, as far as the wider world knew, and that was close enough.

She had no intention of subordinating herself beneath this *asshole*.

The tension in the room was thick enough to cut; Danai knew it, recognized it, but couldn't quite get her temper in order to bring it to an end. She knew that if Mina Liao had been here, the deft woman would have found a way to break the deadlock.

"*Sang-shao*," a voice said from behind her. Danai couldn't believe it. Of all the people she'd expected to break the silence, Ned Baxter was not one of them. "Why don't you tell us your plan?"

He stepped away from the wall and stood beside *Sang-shao* Vaughan. Gwen was sharp enough, picking right up on it and standing a hair's breadth closer to the battalion commander to show her support.

Danai smiled. "Of course." She turned toward the holotank. "Emory, if you'd be so kind?"

As Koltsokov fired up the tank, Danai turned back. "If you'll all look here," she said, "I want to show you this." She caught Ned Baxter's eye, where he stood at the very back end of the pack.

He nodded, once, and grinned.

Not what she would have expected *at all*.

CHAPTER 28

Danai squirmed around, trying to get comfortable in her new 'Mech's cockpit couch. Her entire career she'd fought in *Yen-Lo-Wang*. That seat felt like home after so long; she'd always just sat down, and she was instantly comfortable. In her new *Black Knight*, the cushions were different, stiffer. They were shaped differently. She felt a seam beneath her right knee that was driving her mad.

Finally, she huffed, clenched her hands into fists, closed her eyes, and screamed silently in her mind. Change was hard. She knew this. But there were more important things in the grand scheme of things.

She opened her eyes, took her controls, and throttled up out of the temporary laager, followed by Koltsokov's *Vindicator*, Capshaw's *Sojourner* and Fan Bing's delicate *Dola*. The pair of Yellow Jacket gunships swooped out of the sky to hover overhead, pacing her. She half-listened to Koltsokov running through comm checks. Her attention was already on the strategic map painted over her HUD.

Dronane, Liberty's capital city, sat along the edge of a large bay on the western edge of Klieska. On many other worlds, Klieska would have been an island, but on Liberty it almost qualified as a small continent. The bay served as a storm harbor and shipping port for much of the on-world and off-world trade that came through Dronane. It was also the headquarters of the Liberty blue-water navy, a Republic militia force that had so far stayed out of the conflict.

The prior attacks had driven straight at Dronane from the east and hit a series of prepared positions manned by Stone's Fury. With more than a decade to prepare for the anticipated invasion, the RAF had built a truly fearsome belt of fixed fighting positions for 'Mechs and tanks, each with clear evacuation routes to the next ring. As the Fifth MAC or Warrior House Imarra had attacked, the defending Fury companies had fought and then fallen back, using cover and concealment, using companies to hold back battalions. Danai and her staff, together with *Sang-shao* Vaughan and House Master Hui, had pieced it together overnight.

Well, to be fair, Noah Capshaw had put it together. Danai and the others had just happened to be in the room.

The redundant positions made it hard for the usual tactic—a hooking flank attack—to work; the flankers just ran into another belt of defenses. And while the Confederation liberators could turn around and go attack any of the other thousands of tiny islands, there were just a handful that mattered. Klieska, and Dronane, mattered most of all. That was why the Fury was concentrated there, and not spread in penny-packets across the oceans.

That was why the Capellans had to deal with the Fury to take Liberty.

Now if the plan would only *work*.

There was no way the Fury could have missed the arrival of Danai's Regiment; the DropShips would have been visible coming down like rockets for hundreds of kilometers, so they'd know the Capellan liberators had been reinforced. She knew the Fury commander would think the Fifth MAC and House Imarra now felt new vigor.

Anyone would feel it, when a third-again their numbers landed to help them.

So, the Capellans repeating the same tactic, hoping their increased numbers would let them win the day, would be something the Fury CO would have to plan for. If that CO had a low opinion of the Capellans, they might even expect it. Danai intended to play into that persona. She'd sent the Fifth and the warrior house to attack the same positions again.

The Fury would see what they expected to see: Capellan companies and battalions advancing to contact, leaving a force engaged to hold the defenders in place and sending hooking attacks around to feel out the flanks. The RAF would get complacent, seeing their enemy doing exactly what they expected and achieving the same result.

They'd focus their attention there.

And never see the Second MAC making a knife thrust down from the north for the city itself.

Si-ben-bing Travis Gardner was pleased to see the shapes of the DropShips getting smaller in his display as the battalion headed out. He'd dreaded the idea of his tank getting left behind to guard the landing zone again like it had been on Hall. He wanted to be out in the fight, making a difference. His whole crew did. So as Preakness drove away from the DropShips, he knew he should be satisfied.

But he wasn't.

The regiment was marching north, to get into position. The compass on his console pointed south, toward the Fifth MAC lines.

Gardner worked his mouth. The plan left a bad taste in his mouth.

He understood the plan. Gardner was a veteran; he knew all too well that most soldiers fought the enemy in front of them, and if that enemy looked like they expected, then they didn't think too much about it. So when the *sao-shao* had explained they needed a Second MAC presence with the demonstration attack, Gardner had nodded and asked what time they were leaving.

But inside, he was seething.

"'Mechs coming up," Danton called.

Gardner spun the turret around until the gunsight bore on the new contacts; it was a lance of blue Second MAC machines. He didn't recognize the *Gravedigger* in the lead, but he knew they'd taken a lot of replacements from the Second Liao Guard before leaving Hall. This had to be one of them.

"Preakness," he called to the Manticore's driver, "echelon left with the 'Mechs in the lead, got it?"

"Got it."

"Make it sharp."

"Don't I always?"

Gardner rolled his eyes. Toggling his radio, he called out to the 'Mechs.

"Glad to have you with us," the *Gravedigger* replied. The MechWarrior sounded young, her voice a little high. "And before you ask, no, we're not allowed to turn around and rejoin the regiment. I already asked."

Gardner laughed. At least he wasn't alone. "*Si-ben-bing* Gardner," he sent.

"*Sang-wei* Heather Teng," the *Gravedigger* replied.

"Pardon me for saying, *Sang-wei*, but you seem a little short of your company," the tanker sent.

As he spoke, Teng and her lance overtook the platoon of tanks, who slid aside and then fell into echelon as cleanly as any parade unit she'd ever seen. Teng grinned and shook her head. She recognized showing off when she saw it.

"They're off with the *sao-shao*," she told this Gardner.

"Then I guess we're it. Ma'am."

"Yeah," she said. "But we'll do the regiment proud."

Teng closed the channel and checked her HUD. Voltikov had the rest of the lance, Pullman, in her ancient *Targe*, and Lao, in his *Snake*, were right where they were supposed to be. The new combined group was on the right heading and right schedule. Everything so far was going along with the plan.

Which gave Teng more than enough time to worry about the mission. And why she had it.

Why would the sang-shao *request me and then send me away?*

Danai led the bulk of the Second McCarron's Armored Cavalry to the designated step-off point and halted. Around her, the regiment spread out. Security lances and platoons broke off to put out observation and security points. Wu Feng saw to all of that without her attention; it was his job. Her job was to pay attention and send the strike in at the perfect time.

No pressure.

Noah Capshaw's *Sojourner* was nearby, as always. The 'Mech seemed canted back a little, as if it were looking up at the early dawn sky. Danai chuckled when she realized that's exactly what it was doing. She opened a discreet channel. "Noah."

"*Sang-shao?*"

"Relax. Air supremacy will hold. *Kong-zhong-shao* Sze Lung How knows his job."

"I know, ma'am. It's just if he's wrong…"

"Even if he is, it's out of our hands." Still, even as she said, Danai couldn't help looking up at the brightening sky. Much depended on the aerospace forces keeping the RAF from conducting recon overflights. With the wings of two MAC regiments available it should be a relatively easy task… but Danai knew as well as anyone if the RAF decided the information was worth the life of a handful of pilots, those fighters would be able to blast their way overhead and radio back the news, even if they died doing it.

The Fifth had, as a matter of course, sanitized the orbital lanes clear of recon satellites. But they couldn't halt every overflight by crazy civilians. If one of them happened to look down, and radioed the information…

Danai blinked the thought of her head. As she'd told Capshaw; it was out of her hands.

"The Armored Mosquitos have never failed us," she told him. "They'll do the job today, too."

They had to.

Heather Teng's first experience with the Fifth McCarron's Armored Cavalry was a massive *Pillager* BattleMech that stepped out in front of her ersatz column. The 'Mech had a gray torso with blue arms and legs and the rampant plumed knight of the MAC on its shoulder.

It waved one of its gun-barrel forearms. "Come on," the MechWarrior sent. "*Sao-shao* wants to see you."

"Lead on," Teng replied.

A few minutes later, her 'Mech came face-to-face with another Fifth Regiment BattleMech, a medium-weight *Men Shen* OmniMech. The 'Mech stood silent in standby while the man who had to be its MechWarrior stood at its feet, a small holoprojector playing from the ground. He looked up at Teng and waved her down. She waved the *Gravedigger*'s arm to confirm the order, told Gardner to join her, set her 'Mech into standby, and climbed down.

Si-ben-bing Gardner waited for her at the *Gravedigger*'s feet. He was an older man with thinning hair and a perpetual frown; he carried a Ceres Arms Striker carbine slung muzzle-down under his right arm. He nodded to her when she stepped down. "Ma'am."

"*Si-ben-bing*, let's go." She led him over toward the cluster of MechWarriors.

When they got close enough to see the *sao-shao*'s face, Gardner groaned. She looked at him.

"Oh, hell, ma'am, just get ready."

"*Sang-wei*!" The man's voice boomed through the group. Teng spun and braced, but held off saluting. The Second didn't salute in the field. She realized she didn't know if the Fifth did or not, but decided she didn't care. She was part of Danai's Regiment now; she'd follow that code.

"Sir."

"Welcome to the Renegades," he said. "Otherwise known as Second Battalion, Fifth McCarron's Armored Cavalry, affectionately known as Gwen Vaughan's Green Knights. I'm Kevin Sawyer." He held out his hand, and she shook it, but he looked past her as she did and his eyes widened. "Gardner! Who the hell let you near my battalion?"

"Wasn't my choice, sir," the laconic tanker replied. "I see you've met *Sang-wei* Teng?"

"Heather Teng," she amplified. "Pleasure, sir."

Sawyer let go of her hand and stepped past to wrap Gardner in a back-slapping hug. The tanker didn't reply. He just took it, careful to hold his rifle in place against the jostling. "God, it's been too long, Gardner!" Sawyer laughed at Gardner's discomfort, then looked back at Teng. He must have seen her confusion.

"I used to be Danai Liao-Centrella's ops officer," Sawyer explained. "I transferred out just before you all left for Hall."

"Oh—*Oh*, sir, I see, yes, sir." She didn't see, but she had to say something. Sawyer was like a force of nature.

"*Sang-wei* of..." Sawyer prompted.

"F-Five Company, sir," she said, blinking. "Two Batt, under *Sao-shao* Baxter."

"Five Company," he repeated. "Good troops. What happened to *Sang-wei* Peterman?"

"Promoted," Teng said.

"I see..." Sawyer regarded her for a moment longer, then seemed to make up his mind. "Pardon me for saying this, *Sang-wei*, but you don't seem like the normal company-grade officer for the Second."

"I just transferred from the Second Liao Guards, sir," she said. *What the hell did not-normal mean?*

"That explains it," Sawyer said with a grin.

"The *sang-shao* requested her, sir," *Si-ben-bing* Gardner put in. Teng and Sawyer both turned to stare at the taciturn tanker. *How the hell did you know that?* Teng wondered. Gardner, for his part, ignored Sawyer and shrugged at her.

"That explains it," Sawyer repeated. He flashed her a grin, then took her shoulder and turned her toward the group of Fifth MAC officers waiting. "Let me introduce you around. People! Come meet the best company commander in the Second. And some asshole tanker she brought along."

This time when Gardner groaned, Teng wanted to join him.

Danai jostled the gunnery controls in her cockpit, watching how the gunnery pip moved with each action. *Yen-Lo-Wang*'s weapons had been chest-mounted, with a smaller range of azimuth than the *Black Knight*'s arm-mounted extended-range PPC. It took some getting used to; the two chest-mounted ER large lasers moved in a way she was familiar with; having another quartet of ER mediums was something else to get used to.

"It should be any minute," Emory Koltsokov said.

"Be better to get it over with," Fan Bing chimed in.

"New planet, new 'Mechs," Noah Capshaw said, after a minute. "We're all just stretching our comfort zones."

"You name that beast yet, Noah?" Fan asked.

"Nothing has really stuck yet."

"What about you, *Sang-shao*?"

Danai chuckled. "I've got one or two in mind, but I want to get a fight under my belt first to see what fits."

"You MechWarriors and your names," put in Yellow Jacket pilot Bethany Chang.

Danai opened her mouth, but a new light burned on her comm console. Before she could say anything, Koltsokov's strong voice cut across the line. "House Imarra has reached the jump-off point, *Sang-shao*." There was two beats of silence. "*Sang-shao* Vaughan reports the Fifth is ready as well. *Zhong-shao* Wu reports we are ready. No sign that we have been detected. All signals say it's time to go."

Danai tugged her restraints tight then gripped her controls. "Then let's go, Emory."

The two Yellow Jackets dropped their noses and swung forward like predatory insects; Noah's *Sojourner* stepped off first, but the other 'Mechs were only a step or two behind. Danai brought up the rear.

"All units," Emory Koltsokov said on the general Confederation frequency, "this is Zero. The order is go."

There were no acknowledgments.

Just the sound of 'Mechs and tanks moving in earnest.

CHAPTER 29

Heather Teng had sweaty palms. It was pissing her off.

Her lance, with Gardner's platoon spread in two-vehicle elements on each side, was moving with Hatchet Company of *Sao-shao* Sawyer's Fifth MAC battalion. Teng's Second MAC unit was attached to the lead company, so they'd be easily observed by any scouts Stone's Fury had out. The 'Mechs should be easily distinguishable; Teng and her lance were a darker, more gunmetal blue with accent colors, whereas the Fifth's paint scheme used lighter blues and whole-gray torso or turrets. They should be able to do their job: convince the first Fury scouts that saw them that the Second MAC was in line with the rest of the Confederation units attacking from the east. That wasn't what made her palms sweat.

What had her gloves feeling slippery was the weight that had settled on her shoulders as they'd saddled back up after Sawyer's staff conference. She'd seen the way the Fifth's officers had looked at her and Gardner. It was a lot like the way Teng and her former Second Liao Guards troopers had looked at them back on Hall.

Danai's Regiment was the lead regiment of McCarron's Armored Cavalry. It might be numbered second, but the brigade command battalion—Baxter's Commando—spent more time attached to the Second than any other McCarron's regiment. Across the centuries of the Armored Cavalry's life, as regular CCAF troopers and before that—when they'd been a long-hired Capellan mercenary brigade—this tradition had held. Danai Liao-Centrella being a sister of the sitting Chancellor did little to hurt that perception.

The MechWarriors, tankers, and infantry of the Fifth were proud, skilled, and dedicated soldiers. But they looked to the Second for leadership.

Right now, they looked at Heather Teng.

The same Heather Teng who'd been a member of the Second for what felt like ten seconds.

I should be standing on your side, she wanted to yell at them every time she caught one of Sawyer's lance commanders looking at her with interested eyes. But she couldn't, because she was enough of a leader to know that doing so would undo any of the mystery that really did exist. If it wasn't all in her head.

It had been real in the Second Liao Guards. It was probably real here.

She was determined to live up to that reputation. Even though she hadn't asked for it. Her *Gravedigger* now wore the dark blue paint. It was her job.

As her lance got closer to the Rep lines, Heather Teng focused on making sure her 'Mech and lance moved in the most professional, most relaxed way possible. They were there to do a job. Young as she was, Teng knew enough of leadership was just making it look easy for those under you.

Alone in her cockpit, alone in a sea of Fifth McCarron's machines, Heather Teng sweated and tried to make it look like she wasn't.

Please, God, let someone start shooting soon, she prayed.

"Man, she's a stickler for spacing," Preakness muttered, as he nudged the Manticore back in line after the *sang-wei* had prodded Gardner about it.

Gardner didn't reply; he tracked the turret back and forth between zero and 90 degrees azimuth. His tank was lead tank on the right wing; the 'Mech lance would watch full-forward; he had forward-right, and behind them Nen's Po swept 90-to-180 degrees.

"Possible contact," Danton called. A red icon blinked on the left side of Gardner's screen. He jerked the turret controls left, swinging the big barrel of the heavy PPC back into line. A red enemy caret flickered in and out in the distance, about a klick off. Gardner thumbed his comm.

"*Sang-wei* Teng—"

"I see it," the MechWarrior said, cutting him off. "Passing to battalion." She closed the channel.

"You're welcome," he muttered.

Teng's voice came back on the comm. "Good eyes, Gardner."

Gardner looked down to make sure he hadn't accidentally transmitted his muttering. He hadn't. On the tank intercom, he heard Danton stifling a chuckle. If Preakness and Hertzel had heard, they were keeping quiet. Gardner decided he'd see it as funny, too.

"Any idea what it is, Danton?"

"I'm hoping the 'Mechs will tell us," the sensor operator said. "Their sensors are better. It looks like a 'Mech, but it could be a big tank or a mass of iron in a hill for all I can tell."

"Keep on it," Gardner said. He reached down and toggled the Manticore's supplemental targeting computer active. Heavy banks of circuitry deep in the Manticore's hull flickered to life, ready to supplement the Manticore's base TharHes tracking system. "Hertzel: LRMs in the tubes?"

"Hot and ready," Hertzel confirmed.

Gardner squeezed the turret controls and tapped his toes on the firing trip. He didn't like being this far away from the battalion, but he had to admit that if he had to go into battle with someone else's battalion, he could do a lot worse than one commanded by Kevin Sawyer.

The man was infuriating.

But he was a damn good officer and a better MechWarrior.

Red carets blinked to life and burned solid on Gardner's gunnery screen. The Manticore's computer began cycling through them, flashing unit descriptions across the bottom corner of the display: 'Mechs and tanks, with a few battle armor types thrown in for good measure.

"More contacts!" Danton called. He wasn't telling Gardner; Gardner could see them already. He was telling the rest of the crew. Surviving the next little while would require the four of them to work as a well-oiled team, and part of that was making sure that they all knew what was going on. That was Danton's real job.

Just like it was Preakness' job to steer and Hertzel's to make sure the right missiles were in the tubes when Gardner needed them. It was a dance they'd done on a dozen worlds in two different tanks.

The first LRM traces appeared from the Rep lines.

"Guess we're here," Preakness said.

The Manticore rumbled with the accumulated frequencies of the moving parts inside it. It trembled with restrained power. It hungered to let some of that power go.

Or maybe, with his leg tapping furiously, that was all Gardner.

It wasn't that fast, Teng knew, but it sure felt like one minute they were walking toward the Reps and the next the whole sky was falling on them in the form of LRMs. She accelerated the *Gravedigger*, trying to get past the inbound LRMs while searching for something to shoot at. Her *Gravedigger* carried Streak long-range missiles. Unlike the flights fired half-blind at the Capellans, her missiles would hit what they were aimed at. Or else they wouldn't launch.

Movement. She dragged her reticule to the right, settled it over the shape of a Republic *Avalanche*, and squeezed the trigger. A harsh, nulling tone burned in her ears. She'd rushed the shot and the Streaks hadn't fired. Comms off, she groaned in frustration.

Voltikov's *Anubis* fired from behind her, his standard LRMs not needing a Streak lock. Whether he hit anything or not she didn't see; more Rep 'Mechs and tanks were showing themselves every instant.

"Hit 'em!" she heard Kevin Sawyer call. The *sao-shao*'s *Men Shen* triggered both its PPCs; the blue-white lightning bolts flickered downrange faster than the eye could track. A Rep Kelswa assault tank bogged down as the ravening particle bolts ate at its thick frontal armor, but it shook the damage off and plowed forward.

Teng adjusted her aim to the same Kelswa. Her Kingston ER PPC compounded the damage Sawyer had done. The Kelswa's crew must have taken offense; the giant twin-barreled turret spun toward her, but before the Gauss rifles could fire, her follow-on autocannon shot hit. Only four of the five submunitions struck, but the tungsten alloy penetrators dug deep. One must have nicked the tank's engine shielding; it spiked hot on IR and then went dormant.

Teng snarled in satisfaction.

She was still smiling when a Rep *Sun Cobra* stepped across the Kelswa's corpse and blew her *Gravedigger* off its feet with its paired Gauss rifles.

Gardner triggered the LRMs again. Seven missiles swept up and then down, but if they hit anything he couldn't see. The confusion along the 'Mech line was too much. This wasn't what he'd been warned to expect. Based on the briefings, the Reps should have sat quiet in their hides and blasted away from hidden positions, making the Confederation units pay for each meter of ground as they moved up to clear the defenses.

But these Reps were charging them, leaving the prepared defenses behind.

A Rep *Berserker* sprinted toward the Confederation lines; the assault 'Mech was fast for its weight and had the armor to shrug off most of the Capellan fire. It was clear the MechWarrior wanted to get their gigantic hatchet into the fight.

Gardner swung the turret around, waited for a solid tone, and fired. The heavy PPC vomited a gout of ions that would have done any Clan-built ER PPC proud; the shot took the *Berserker* in the knee, guided by Gardner's skill as a gunner and the advanced targeting computer in the Manticore's belly. The 'Mech stumbled, but didn't fall. It slowed to a walk, looking for its attacker.

Gardner swallowed as the 'Mech's cockpit aligned with his tank. The *Berserker* stamped the ground with one foot; the hatchet swung back and forth, as if it were a twelve-meter-tall man loosening up. The MechWarrior, melodramatic as all their kind were, triggered the head-mounted flamer.

"Hertzel," Gardner said evenly, "SRMs."

"Reloading now," the loader confirmed.

The *Berserker* broke into a run. Right at them. And the heavy PPC was still recharging.

"Preakness, back us up!"

Teng struggled to work her *Gravedigger* back to its feet. Lao's *Snake* stood its ground in front of her, LB-X autocannon blazing away, trying to cover her. Pullman's *Targe* had already run forward, trying to close the range. Teng put one of her gun-barrel arms carefully against the ground, pushed, and shoved the 50-ton 'Mech upright. The *Gravedigger*'s gyros screamed in protest, but the 'Mech was back on its feet.

Teng looked for the *Sun Cobra*, but it was already gone. What she saw instead was a 100-ton *Berserker* headed in her general direction. She brought her 'Mech's weapons up, aimed, and triggered a whole spread. She hadn't started the 'Mech moving yet, so she had a relatively stable firing position. All of her weapons hit, but the assault 'Mech's thick armor just drank it in.

"Hit the *Berserker*," she ordered her lance.

The RAF 'Mech ignored her fire. Instead, it put a PPC bolt of its own into the nose of Gardner's Manticore. The 60-ton tank shook the damage off, but Teng knew from fighting them that the Manticore couldn't take too many more hits like that.

It looked like most of an RAF battalion had appeared in front of them; that wasn't what was supposed to have happened. In all the prior engagements the Confederation forces had been stymied by company-size units in prepared positions.

Now a battalion was charging across the field.

"Keep hitting them!" was all she could say.

Gardner kicked the foot trip and fired the PPC, this time with missiles going along with it, but still the *Berserker* kept coming. He snarled and pounded his fist on the console; the damned 'Mech was just too big, too heavily armored. The cocky MechWarrior kept coming, half-again as fast going forward as the Manticore was reversing. At this rate, even with *Sang-wei* Teng's lance helping, the *Berserker* would get them before they got it.

And his ears still rang from the PPC hit.

"Preakness," he said. "Spin us around. I'll shoot over the back."

"Armor's weaker," Preakness protested.

"Not at the moment," Gardner snarled. "Not after that last hit. Now spin us around."

"It'll look like we're running away."

"We *are* running away, god damn it!" He jammed the turret controls to the side, rotating as fast as he could, as Preakness jerked the tank's body around harshly.

Gardner toggled the platoon channel. "Everyone hit the *Berserker!*"

By the time the Manticore was turned and Preakness was accelerating, the turret had come around. Gardner settled the pip on the *Berserker*. He fired. And missed.

Just as he touched the trip, the *Berserker* stopped.

"New contacts!" someone screamed on the Fifth MAC channel. Teng looked at her HUD but didn't see anything. She saw the *Berserker* stop and grinned wolfishly. The *Gravedigger*'s autocannon and missiles scattered fire across the 'Mech, but it ignored her.

Then it turned and ran back toward its lines. The 100-ton machine passed seventy kilometers per hour, faster than anything that large had a right to move, as the MechWarrior engaged their myomer acceleration signal circuitry for an emergency boost of speed.

"Blake's black *bones*, what the hell are those?" the Fifth MAC speaker cried.

New 'Mech icons appeared on Gardner's display, but something was broken. Nothing on the ground moved that fast. "Danton, the sensors are busted!" Gardner spun the turret, holding the lock on the *Berserker*'s back, and triggered a flight of LRMs, but the missiles just chipped armor.

"Diagnostic's coming back okay," Danton said.

"Check again," Gardner insisted.

The new contacts were coming out of the backfield at something near *four hundred kilometers per hour*. They read as 'Mechs, but no 'Mech was that fast. A half-dozen of them were arrowing at the Capellan line as fast as an airplane.

"Green," Danton confirmed.

"So you're telling me the Reps have a 'Mech that can cross *twelve hundred* meters in *ten seconds*?"

"That's what the sensors say," Danton said.

Gardner rolled his eyes and opened his mouth to snarl again, but a flicker of moment on his display caught his eye. He looked, but it was already gone. He tracked the turret right, searching. He couldn't find it.

Then he saw another one. For a second.

"Screw this," he muttered. He palmed the bar that opened the overhead turret hatch and raised his seat up so his head and shoulders were clear of the turret.

"Gardner!" Danton screamed, "shut your hatch!"

If the Republic had magic 'Mechs, Travis Gardner was going to see them for himself.

"That's not real," Heather Teng whispered.

According to the *Gravedigger*'s computer, it was a half-dozen 15-ton ultralight quad-style BattleMechs, moving like a pack and faster than anything on the ground had a right to be. They'd slowed from their initial surge, staying around 240 kph, but it still wasn't right. She remembered Ruskaya and Beatrice's *Roadrunners* back on Hall, but these were faster.

"I see one!" Pullman yelled. The *Targe* pilot pointed with her 'Mech's arm.

That's a dog, Teng thought. And it looked like one, sort of. It was painted black, with oddly-mottled armor and spikes on its shoulders. It stopped atop a small rise, like a pet looking for its owner. The pause was less than a second, then it leaped down and charged at the Capellan line.

Teng looked at her sensors.

It was passing 350 kilometers per hours when it penetrated the Capellan lines.

CHAPTER 30

NORTH OF DRONANE
LIBERTY
REPUBLIC OF THE SPHERE
1 SEPTEMBER 3149

When the first enemy carets appeared on her screen, Danai felt her heart sink. Her recon lances were still fifteen kilometers outside the northern edge of the Dronane suburbs; she'd wanted to get closer before encountering any Rep defenders. Every centimeter they got closer to Dronane was a centimeter they wouldn't have to fight over to get into the city and then take the Stone's Fury defenses from behind.

"A scout platoon," Noah Capshaw reported. "Looks like Dronane militia, not regular RAF. The recon lance got them all."

"But they will have sent a contact report," Emory Koltsokov reminded everyone.

Danai toggled a different frequency, bringing her battalion commanders on the line. "We've been detected. Phase Two, right now." All three officers acknowledged. She didn't need to say anything to her Command Lance; they were all copied on the transmission.

Phase Two meant "plow the road." With secrecy lost, the Second's best chance was to get into the city fast, before the Fury had a chance to organize to fight them. With luck, they'd be able to take the city proper without having to fight a major battle through it. Danai didn't think Mina would have approved of a huge battle in the heart of a soon-to-be-Capellan capital city.

She'd found herself thinking a lot, during this march, of the visit she and Mina had made to the Great Dam on Sian. She kept replaying the conversation they'd had about how long it would take a lance of 'Mechs to make the dam nonfunctional. And how Mina hadn't tried to force the point that it was so much easier to destroy than create.

The Ares Conventions forbade combat in populated areas, and while the great nations of the Inner Sphere had formally abandoned those conventions centuries ago, as a practical matter most MechWarriors tried to follow them. The exemption to that prohibition was if a critical military target was inside the populated area, and that exemption had been claimed by every military force that had fought its way through peoples' homes since the ink had dried.

The RAF's main presence on Klieska was at the Dronane spaceport, and that spaceport abutted the natural blue-water port the city had built itself up around. It was the single most absolutely critical military target on Liberty, aside from the 'Mechs and tanks of the Fury itself. She *had* to take it.

Which meant she *had* to go through the city.

But she didn't have to like it.

And maybe, just *maybe*, if they were fast enough, they'd be able to get there before the Fury.

EAST OF DRONANE
LIBERTY
REPUBLIC OF THE SPHERE

The dog-'Mech sprinted straight through the Capellan lines, a dozen or more MAC 'Mechs firing at it. The retreating Rep BattleMechs were forgotten. None of the Capellan 'Mechs hit the dog as it loped into and through them. Teng watched it in her vision strip: it ran back, most of a kilometer behind them, as if it were looking for wherever the Capellans had come from.

"A scout?" Voltikov asked.

"I have no idea," Teng responded.

The dog-'Mech spun around and accelerated back toward the Capellan lines. Fewer Capellan 'Mechs fired on it this time, only those in the rear of the formation that weren't afraid to spin around and expose their weaker back armor to the Rep main lines. Teng watched, confused. If the fast 'Mechs had been a scout they should have continued moving away.

Part of her wondered how anyone managed to pilot a 'Mech moving that fast. Ruskaya used to complain about how beat up she got piloting a *Roadrunner* because the 'Mech's ride was so rough. These monsters were faster than that; the MechWarriors had to be getting beat to shit.

She expected the dog to slip right through the Confederation battalion and return to its own lines. It was pretty clear no one could hit it. Almost no MechWarriors were trained to hit a target moving across the ground at speeds they normally saw aerospace fighters move.

So when the charging dog-'Mech set its shoulder and, at over 380 kph, slammed into the back of a Capellan *Men Shen*, the OmniMech exploded as if a bomb had been planted in its chest, its arms and legs flying in all directions. If the MechWarrior had been able to eject, Teng hadn't seen it.

"What the hell just happened?" Voltikov demanded.

"That dog-'Mech just suicided," Teng said. She twisted around, looking for the others. They were so fast they could have swung around while she was distracted.

"Um, *Sang-wei*..." MechWarrior Lao started, but stopped.

"Spit it out!"

"I–it's not dead."

Teng looked back, jaw slack. The *Targe* pilot was right. The dog-'Mech was shaking itself to its feet. Amazingly, it looked relatively unscathed. A few armor plates looked loose, and a cluster of the spikes on its shoulder haunches were bent out of shape, but it was up and moving.

"That's impossible," she whispered.

No one could have survived that impact. She didn't care how advanced Republic technology was. Simple physics meant that a MechWarrior who'd decelerated as fast as that 'Mech had would have died.

It was impossible.

Impossibly, the dog-'Mech loped into a run back toward the Republic lines.

"Here come the others," Voltikov warned.

"Get us turned back with the lance," *Si-ben-bing* Gardner ordered.

"You sure about that?" Preakness asked. "You saw what those things did to the 'Mech." The tank was already turning.

"I know my duty," Gardner snapped. "And I know we have a better chance with more guns around us."

"I have six of those things on scope," Danton said. "I don't see any more."

"One was enough," Hertzel muttered.

"We just need to do our jobs," Gardner told his crew. "And trust the MechWarriors to do theirs." It was the right thing to say, but he didn't really believe it.

It was just all he had.

This time, all six of the freakishly fast 'Mechs came in at once.

"Take 'em down," Teng ordered. She didn't even bother trying for a target lock with her Streak LRMs. Instead, she put a sleet of autocannon submunitions into the air in front of the lead 'Mech. A pair of her alloy penetrators sparked off the 'Mech's odd armor, but her PPC shot fell forward. The 'Mech leaped like a hunting dog through the spray of dirt, dust and smoke her shot put up.

No one else had much luck, though they tore up a lot of terrain.

The pack split up as it closed. One of the charging machines missed when its target, a 55-ton *Wraith*, lit its jump jets and rocketed skyward, all the while shooting harmless pulse laser darts down with no effect.

A trio of Fifth MAC machines died as the dog-'Mechs, with their incredible kinetic energy, just crushed through their armor and destroyed vital systems. One of the charging 'Mechs, the one that had retired before, seized up and fell in the tetanic-like clutch of a myomer breakdown. It skidded to a stop across thirty meters.

The last one came right at Heather Teng's *Gravedigger.*

"Oh, damn," she whispered, as soon as it was apparent. She reversed her throttle and brought her weapons in line, but the cannon was still reloading and the PPC recharging. The *Gravedigger* began walking backward, but at a snail's pace compared to the rocket approaching her.

Clutching her controls, Teng readied herself. The *Gravedigger* lacked jump jets, so the *Wraith's* exit was closed to her. The best she could try and do is throw the 'Mech to one side at the last minute. The dog-'Mech came closer and closer. As it crossed 200 meters away from her Teng threw the *Gravedigger* to the left, not even trying to keep the 'Mech upright. She crashed down, ignoring the pop and snap of armor plates breaking loose, and screwed her eyes closed. If the Rep monster was going to hit her, she didn't want to see it.

"You got it!" Pullman shouted.

Teng opened her eyes, confused.

Gardner had been tracking the quad 'Mech with the PPC but it was almost faster than the turret traverse. He was dragging the pip along behind it in a losing race as it came abreast of the Manticore and then passed, headed for the *sang-wei's* BattleMech.

"Turn!" he screamed at Preakness.

And then suddenly the charging 'Mech fell, and the PPC pip tracked past it. Gardner jerked it back around.

"It's down!" Danton said. "Did it trip or something?"

"SRMs are up!" Hertzel added.

Gardner ignored both of them. He settled the pip over the dog-'Mech's inert form and took up half the slack on the foot trip. If it moved, he was going to blast it.

Teng frowned as she worked the *Gravedigger* back up on its feet. The dog-'Mech lay on its side, one leg canted back where it had fallen. "Who got it?" she asked. She guided the

Gravedigger toward the downed machine. "Pullman, Voltikov, keep an eye on the Reps."

"Yes, *Sang-wei*!"

"It just fell," *Si-ben-bing* Gardner put in. "I was tracking it, and it just collapsed."

Teng looked around. "No one shot it?"

"We all shot *at* it. No one hit it."

"That doesn't make sense." Teng checked the larger picture. The other dog-'Mech that had fallen was still down, but the other four had survived their run and sprinted back behind the battalion again. A few of the leading House Imarra 'Mechs, following in reserve to exploit any gains the Fifth MAC opened, fired long-range shots at them, but if any connected it wasn't obvious. She looked back at the fallen 'Mech. As she did, her gaze crossed her comm board where a scarlet light burned.

Son of a... "Everyone, weapons hold. I'm going to try something."

"*Sang-wei...*"

"That's an order." She gave it a couple seconds, then toggled the *Gravedigger*'s Angel ECM suite off.

The dog 'Mech climbed to its feet, shaking its limbs out.

"*Sang-wei*!" Teng turned the Angel back on.

The dog-'Mech collapsed.

"What—" Gardner began, but she cut him off by slapping the general Capellan frequency open.

"They're drones!" she shouted. "The dog-'Mechs, they're drones! Rally around your ECM suites!"

Sao-shao Sawyer came on the line. "*Sang-wei* Teng, you're sure?"

"I've got one at my feet, sir. Tested it with my ECM."

"Nice work, *Sang-wei*. I see why Danai asked for you."

Teng beamed.

NORTH OF DRONANE
LIBERTY
REPUBLIC OF THE SPHERE

"Contact!" Emory Koltsokov yelled.

Danai swiped away the map she'd been discussing with Noah Capshaw and took her controls in hand. A cluster of red carets appeared on her HUD, about a kilometer away and heading in fast. The *Black Knight*'s computer painted them as a quartet of Scapha hovertanks. The platoon bore in at maximum speed.

How they'd penetrated the Second MAC's lines was a discussion for tomorrow.

The Command Lance was laagered in at the end of a long, narrow valley with an old fishing trail at the bottom. It was about two kilometers long, and the sides had been logged back far enough that it was about a hundred meters wide. That meant the hovertanks would either turn tail and run, or they'd charge right through. Their fragile air skirts made it all but impossible for them to enter the wooded terrain; that would funnel them toward the lance.

"Get ready," Danai told her lance.

The first tank crested the small rise at the end of the valley at full speed; Danai settled her targeting, waited a half-second for the *Black Knight*'s targeting computer to sync, then let fly. The paired ER large lasers stabbed into the Scapha's bow. Both bolts attenuated against the Rep tank's reflective armor; the follow-on ER PPC blast stabbed directly into the cloud of vaporized armor and drove the hovertank's bow down hard enough that it drove the skirt into the packed gravel of the road. Dust bloomed out of the exhaust ports as the fans sucked gravel up.

Koltsokov's PPC flashed over the tank; she'd been aiming for where it would have been if Danai's fire hadn't hit home.

Noah Capshaw's new *Sojourner* put a pair of ER large pulse laser shots into the Scapha as well. One spent its verdant darts flickering off the reflective turret armor in dazzling flashes; the other hit where Danai's PPC had already eaten. It was enough to startle the driver, apparently. As the tank came out of the dust, the fans drove it off to the side into the tree line. There was almost no chance it would be able to claw itself out.

"One down," Noah crowed.

"Don't get cocky," Danai warned. "Three more coming."

As if summoned, three more sleek hovertanks crested the rise together at speed. They didn't fire, but they didn't slow down, either.

Fan Bing chuckled. "I don't think you scared them, Noah."

The speedy tanks had covered most of the distance by the time Danai's lasers recharged; she toggled the PPC out of the circuit and replaced it with the quartet of extended-range mediums. She dragged her reticule across the left-side tank's profile, but it fired before she could. The large barrel of the modular turret belched smoke.

The *Black Knight* rocked, but not in the way it would have if the Scapha had hit her with a Gauss rifle or a large-bore autocannon. Damage flashed across her display; something had hit the left side of her 'Mech. Two more impacts shook the earth around her.

"It's the Thumper version," Koltsokov declared, and Danai realized she was right.

Scaphas used modular omni technology like OmniMechs; this configuration carried a Thumper cannon, a cut-down Thumper artillery piece. Like all artillery weapons, they were area-affect weapons, not true rifled cannons. Perfect for when you wanted to shoot at everything in a sixty-meter radius.

Or when your targets were clumped at the far end of a narrow valley, hemmed in with trees on both sides.

"Into the trees," Danai ordered. The hovertanks wouldn't be able to follow them. She led the way in her *Black Knight*. She triggered an offhand blast from her PPC on the way, but the shot went wide. A few seconds later the tanks were out of sight behind the wide blue fronds of the trees.

"So, we just wait here then?" Capshaw asked. "Until they're gone?"

"No," Danai replied. "If you didn't catch the insignia on those tanks, those were Stone's Brigade machines. That means there could be more strength in the city than we expected, or else they're reacting faster than I'd hoped."

Explosions rocked the forest, shivering the trees around them. They seemed to get farther away as they proceeded.

A moment later, Fan Bing leaped her *Dola* out to check.

"Or we could wait until they're gone," she radioed. "'Cause they're gone."

CHAPTER 31

EAST OF DRONANE
LIBERTY
REPUBLIC OF THE SPHERE
1 SEPTEMBER 3149

Heather Teng kept her 'Mech and its ECM suite near the fallen dog-'Mech. With the Fury battalion withdrawn, the four remaining drones kept a rotating watch on the Fifth MAC. *Sao-shao* Sawyer asked for and received permission to pass Warrior House Imarra through his line and let them take the next stage of the attack while his companies consolidated and refit. Teng knew, because he'd copied her on the transmission, that he'd also wanted the time to secure the dog-'Mech drone she had isolated. The Confederation knew how to deploy drones. Everyone did. But they didn't have anything like a 15-ton machine that could charge its way through an entire 'Mech.

The warrior house companies were reconfiguring as they moved forward to defend against drone strikes. Instead of three clean echelons, they formed into clumps of four or five 'Mechs huddled around an ECM-equipped 'Mech. The groupings were unwieldy, to say the least, but they were less costly than getting hit by one of the charging dog-'Mechs.

"Glad to let them have a turn," *Si-ben-bing* Gardner sent. Heather looked through her vision strip; the tanker was seated half-out of his turret, butt on the coaming with his legs dangling inside. He still wore his combat vehicle crewman's helmet, so he could talk and hear reports from his tank crew. He looked away from her, toward where the warrior house 'Mechs moved forward.

Teng followed his gaze. The warrior houses were the elite of the Confederation, part of its military, and yet not part of its military. They answered to the Chancellor, and no one except the Chancellor. They trained every day of their lives, and this warrior house—Imarra—was paramount above all the others. Teng was rightly proud of her skills and her regiment, but she knew she'd never be as good a BattleMech pilot as those adepts.

"You and me both," she told Gardner.

The four remaining drones surged toward the warrior house clusters. Fire licked out at them, primarily lasers and PPCs. Just as last time, little-to-none of the warrior house fire landed. Teng didn't want to see any more Capellan lives or machines lost, but she found that a little comforting. Even House Imarra was not omnipotent.

But instead of striding in, each of the four drones broke off to do laps around one or more of the Imarra clumps. Teng frowned. It reminded her of a childhood memory, of sheepdogs corralling the herd of sheep.

That was when the first cruise missile flashed overhead, jets screaming, and dove into the center of the nearest Imarra clump to explode among the ivory-and-gold-painted BattleMechs.

NORTH OF DRONANE
LIBERTY
REPUBLIC OF THE SPHERE

"Cruise missile fire control!" cried Ned Baxter's intelligence officer.

Ned checked his *Tian-zong*'s threat board, but it didn't show any targeting locks on it. Not even any search or fire control radar painting him, which told him those monster missiles weren't targeted on him.

"Where away?"

"I got a couple seconds' track," the intel officer said. "Headed west."

Toward the demonstration assault, Ned realized.

"Counterbattery?" If they could tell where the cruise missiles were launched from, there was a chance they could take out the launchers.

"Toward the city, probably the port."

"Keep tracking," he told her. "Ops, turn the point of the assault toward those launchers." Both officers confirmed, but Ned was already changing channels.

"*Sang-shao...*"

"...we've detected three more waves," Baxter reported. "They have to be coming from the port, whether dedicated launchers or the ships there."

Danai was looking at her strategic map as they talked. "Agreed. And agreed on your plan. Get in there and silence those launchers. They have to be playing hell with the attack."

"On our way," Baxter said.

Danai stared at the map, thinking. First, that this may have been the first time she'd had an interaction with Baxter that didn't rub her the wrong way. He had proven himself a superb battalion commander. And in this case, he'd told her his plans to solve the problem instead of asking for *her* plan. Initiative like that in a subordinate was a rare and uncommon treasure. She didn't regret the way she'd felt about him when they'd first met, but she was quite pleased that he'd given her reason to reconsider her opinion.

Second, she thought about the plan. The Second had penetrated to the suburbs without encountering a single Fury BattleMech. The scattered armored ambushes were delaying them, but the hovertanks and armored infantry were making as much effort to preserve themselves and get away as they were delaying the Confederation companies. Every time Danai tried to put herself in her opponent's shoes, to try and understand the choices they were making, she came up with just one course of action that made sense: they were playing for time.

Not time in the strategic sense, as the Fourteenth Principes had tried to do on Hall. Time, in the tactical sense: hours, maybe even a day or two.

But why?

In the end it didn't matter. If the enemy wanted time, it was her duty to deny it to them.

"General signal," she told Koltsokov. "Attack."

EAST OF DRONANE
LIBERTY
REPUBLIC OF THE SPHERE

Travis Gardner took one look at the explosion that sent Imarra 'Mechs crashing to the ground and slid back into the warm, smelly embrace of the Manticore's turret. The hatch slid closed above him even as his hand cinched the restraints tight across his chest.

"Cruise missiles inbound," he barked. "Anti-missile systems free!"

On the back of the turret, a small radar-guided minigun spun its barrels in a test mode; the anti-missile system was designed to shoot down the swarms of short- and long-range missiles that filled a modern battlefield. Gardner didn't know if it was rated for a gigantic, skimmer-sized cruise missile, but he knew he wanted every bit of help he could get.

Another two missiles struck, each targeted on a different clump of Imarra 'Mechs. A stream of tracers whipped into the sky from an anti-missile system, but the big cruise missile bored right past them. The explosions felt like hammer blows, even through the Manticore's armor.

The Imarra 'Mechs were trapped. While Gardner watched, one of the gold-and-ivory machines broke away from its cluster to escape the cruise missiles. As soon as it was more than 200 meters away, the drones began a long, looping attack that struck at terminal velocity. The first one missed when the Imarra MechWarrior stepped aside at the last moment; but they never saw the other drone mirroring the first. It impacted low, ripping the *Lao Hu*'s leg off at the hip. The drone 'Mech bounced away, feet splayed, trying to maintain its balance.

"Time to go, boss?" Preakness asked.

Gardner looked around at the 'Mechs. *Sang-wei* Teng had her *Gravedigger* posted near the inert drone; she didn't look like she was moving. That made them a prime target for artillery like cruise missiles, when the best defense was to not be standing where you were when they were fired. He toggled his comm live. "*Sang-wei*? Time to go?"

"We're not leaving the drone," Teng said firmly.

Gardner frowned. "*Sang-wei*, I don't even know if my anti-missile system can shoot those things down. And even if it does, the way it goes through ammo it's only going to get a couple of them."

"We have orders," Teng replied. "And the Confederation needs examples of these things if we're going to figure out how to stop them."

"I think you got it pretty well stopped," Gardner protested. "Just takes an ECM suite. My old Zhukov could do that. Any of the stealth armor-equipped machines. But we can't report that if we're dead."

Another flight of three cruise missiles landed. Again, the Imarra clumps came apart and reformed. The ivory 'Mechs were taking a pounding, but Gardner had to admit the reputation of a warrior house MechWarrior was well earned. Those 'Mechs picked themselves up, took the damage, and stayed together.

And they continued advancing. It was inspiring to see.

But how long could it last?

Heather Teng heard the frustration in Travis Gardner's voice. She did. But she couldn't do anything about it. She meant every word she said to him. There was no way she was betraying the trust placed in her by *Sao-shao* Baxter and *Sang-shao* Liao-Centrella by running away.

Across the field, the Imarra 'Mechs fought their way forward. As she watched, one of the MechWarriors got in a lucky PPC shot that blasted one of the drones off its feet. That clump of 'Mechs immediately streamed forward, breaking for the edge of the forest the RAF occupied. No fire was coming at them from there yet, but it would come. The Stone's Fury battalion had retreated in too good order to not be ready for them.

The last three drones broke away from their encirclement and raced toward the sprinting Imarra BattleMechs. As if on cue, a dozen Imarra 'Mechs turned and faced them. All were assault 'Mechs, and each blazed away at the advancing drones.

Impossibly, another drone went down. But there was only time for one fusillade.

One of the remaining pair targeted a hulking *Yu Huang*; the 'Mech crouched, arms spread, looking for all the world like a Kuritan sumo wrestler welcoming its opponent's charge. The drone bore in, accepting the challenge, and the sound when the two struck was audible through the *Gravedigger*'s cockpit armor.

The drone hit like a missile, dead center. The *Yu Huang* MechWarrior wrapped the 'Mech's arms around it as he fell. Just like a wrestler, the pilot managed to squeeze the drone into an ungainly bear hug and then roll over on top of it.

The other drone blasted the leg off a rare *Atlas III*, rolled for sixty meters, then sprang up and sprinted back into the tree line.

No cruise missiles had fallen during that attack.

Teng released a breath she hadn't realized she'd been holding.

The first Imarra 'Mechs reached the RAF positions without being fired on. They burst through the trees, jumping down into fighting positions, weapons ready, but the hides were empty.

The Fury was gone.

DRONANE
LIBERTY
REPUBLIC OF THE SPHERE

"*Sang-shao!*"

Danai looked up at the shout, but by then it was immediately clear what Capshaw was shouting about. A rumble of low, unending thunder rolled across her; in the distance, a sizable spheroid DropShip clawed its way into the sky.

Danai and Emory Koltsokov had dismounted from their 'Mechs and climbed aboard a heavy hover APC converted to serve as a mobile command post. The blower lacked the full facilities of a dedicated mobile headquarters facility, but it had the speed to keep up with a mobile advance. Danai needed access to the better maps and comms. Her *Black Knight*, on standby, stood in a *cul-de-sac* of what must have been middle-class homes. Gypsy infantry security troopers had already escorted the homeowners and their families away.

Ned Baxter's *Tian-zong* and the rest of his command lance were standing in downtown Dronane, outside the governor's mansion. The governor had already tried to surrender to him, but he'd sent him by motorcade back to Danai. The motorcade was still on the way, escorted by a lance of Second Battalion 'Mechs, which was another reason Danai wanted to be on the ground.

Another DropShip ripped its way into the sky. Then another. A pair of fat-bodied aerodyne vessels struggled up, angling out over the bay and then the sea, but already banking back around. This close, only kilometers from the port, the ascending vessels shook the ground.

"Driver," Emory Koltsokov barked. "Be ready to move."

The APC's fans spun up, making everything in the compartment vibrate, but Danai waved the trooper away from closing the hatch. She glanced at her ops officer, who shrugged.

"Those things can strafe," Koltsokov said.

"You think that's their plan?"

"I think I don't want to be blamed for not anticipating it if it *is* their plan, but no, ma'am. I think they're leaving. We'll have vectors in a couple minutes to see if this is sub- or trans-orbital."

Danai grinned at her but continued to watch the DropShips. She thought they were leaving, too. What she didn't understand was *why*.

Her plan had only partially worked. The Second MAC had taken the city, sure. But the bulk of the Fury had stopped the Fifth and the warrior house cold. The drones she was just starting to hear about had been devastating. Using them to pin the Imarra 'Mechs in place to pound them with cruise missile artillery had been brilliant. If they'd only held to their plan, the Fury could have almost certainly decimated the Confederation units on that flank.

Another DropShip clawed its way toward space.

They clearly weren't short transport assets. In her opponent's place, Danai would have ground up as much of the Confederation liberation force as she could, then hopped islands and made the liberators do it again and again. Quantico was defensible, for sure.

But to just *leave*? That made no sense.

"They're gone," Koltsokov said a minute later. "First ships are already out of orbit. They didn't even slow down. Headed for the jump point." The operations officer grinned. "And the pickets just passed the governor's convoy. Do you want to change?"

Danai looked down; she wore the same MechWarrior cooling suit she always did in the cockpit. Her hair was pulled back, out of the way. Her pistol was in its thigh holster. "No, I think this is the right outfit."

"Congratulations, *Sang-shao*," Koltsokov said with a grin. "It sure looks like Liberty is yours." The few ratings in the compartment joined her in clapping.

Danai grinned, but quickly waved it off. "Thank you," she told them, "but let's wait until we're sure."

The APC driver set the blower back down on its skirts. As the noise died away, a cool breeze blew in through the open hatch. In the distance, the smoky pillars of exhaust from where the DropShips had lifted stood like cloudy pedestals. The strong winds from the ocean were already starting to distort them.

Danai was glad they were gone, but she desperately wanted to know where they were going.

And why.

CHAPTER 32

HUNG LI MILITARY BASE
LIAO
CAPELLAN CONFEDERATION
28 SEPTEMBER 3149

Danai stood when the elder *sang-shao* entered the small office granted her on the Hung Li grounds. The other man looked supremely fit for his eight decades of life; his hair was just beginning to thin, but his skin was bright and, aside from the faintest beginning of a crow's neck, it didn't hang. His uniform was immaculate, but bare—except for the *sang-shao*'s insignia and the plumed knight of the Armored Cavalry.

"*Sang-shao* McCarron," Danai said. "You honor me."

Xavier McCarron grinned at her. "It is I who am honored, your Grace," he replied. "May I sit?"

"Please."

Danai waited until the other man sat, then lowered herself into her chair. Xavier McCarron, ultimate commander of all five regiments of the Armored Cavalry, was a complicated man. In his youth he had been a powerful MechWarrior. As he'd aged, he'd transferred that tenacity into command of the Armored Cavalry and being its steward in the Capellan court, as well as becoming a brilliant strategist. He was, in the strictest military sense, her superior officer. Aside from the Chancellor, no one else had as much sway over the Armored Cavalry as he did.

But he'd greeted her with deference, and with her noble honors. Which meant he hadn't come to her office to speak with one of his subordinates. He'd come to speak with the Chancellor's sister, as he knew her. Danai swallowed the habitual scowl of revulsion as her mind filled in the truth. None of it showed on her face. It was old, familiar pain she carried everywhere.

"Your victories on Hall and Liberty are in the best traditions of the Armored Cavalry, your Grace," McCarron said, but held up a hand to forestall her reply. "I am sure we will talk of those at length in the coming days. But that is not why I have come."

"Thank you, *Sang-shao*." She had considered offering him a "my lord," but he was not, in truth, the lord of Menke demesne. That honor fell to a Baxter. Xavier's grandfather, Archibald, was the McCarron that had made much of the Armored Cavalry's reputation a century earlier, but his death had come before his son and daughter were of age to take over. Command of the Armored Cavalry had fallen to Marcus Baxter, and it had been Baxter who had shepherded the Armored Cavalry into permanent Capellan service.

It had been a Baxter, not a McCarron, who had received hereditary hegemony over the Armored Cavalry's traditional base world, Menke. Danai had often wondered if, as rumor suggested, that rankled the elder McCarron. She knew his son hated it; Cyrus McCarron was not a subtle man.

"I have come to speak to you about your brother," Xavier allowed.

Inside, Danai smiled. What other reason could there have been?

Barely a week after Stone's Fury jumped out of the Liberty system, orders had arrived from the Strategios ordering Danai's Regiment and Warrior House Imarra back to Liao with all possible haste. Danai had been confused, hesitant to leave Liberty's complicated reentry into Capellan society so quickly. But orders were orders, so she'd turned the defense over to Gwen Vaughan and her Fifth Regiment, and trundled everyone else back on the DropShips. It was three jumps here, to Liao. They'd landed yesterday.

She'd noticed the orders had come from the Capellan High Command, not from McCarron himself.

"He is here, on Liao," Xavier added.

Danai blinked. "I know, though he hasn't told me where yet?"

"In Chang-an. It is not widely known, obviously. But he felt it necessary to be closer to the front. He and the Strategios are ensconced there, where they can be close enough to direct the outcome of the war against the Republic." Xavier all but spat the last few words out. She could tell he'd already forgotten that he'd come here as a supplicant. His tone was that of a superior conveying information to a junior. "I'm told he will announce his presence when the Red Lancers arrive in force. They were delayed in transit."

"He is Chancellor," she said, testing the waters.

"And his will is the will of the State," Xavier said. "I do not challenge that. But he has rejected my counsel. I am hoping he will not ignore his sister." He met her stare evenly. "If I can convince you of the obvious course, your Grace."

Now we're back to what he needs, Danai thought.

"Your brother intends to attack Terra," Xavier said simply.

Danai blinked and sat back. She was not surprised, not really. Daoshen's ambition was limitless, and every victory only convinced him more of that belief. Failures were due to others; successes, his alone. She couldn't conceive of being that person, but she'd been exposed to it her entire life. Water was wet, the ground was cold, and Daoshen Liao was ambitious. These were truths of the universe.

"Is Terra exposed?" Danai asked. Obviously, the Fortress Wall at large was down, but she hadn't heard if any scouting forces had penetrated as far as humanity's birth world. If the planet was exposed, and the RAF as scattered as it had seemed, then perhaps there was an opportunity Daoshen had seen that McCarron had not.

"He believes so," Xavier said. "It is not confirmed. I'm told the Maskirovka is preparing a ruse to check in March or February of next year."

"I see," Danai remarked to gain time. Her mind raced, trying to assemble the pieces of a puzzle to which she didn't even know if she had all the pieces. *If Terra is exposed...if they could get there, could they do it?* "Do we have any intelligence on how well the system is defended?"

"We have nothing," McCarron replied.

"So, you wish my help in convincing him to turn away from this idea?"

"I do, your Grace."

"Why?"

Xavier frowned at her. "I would have thought it obvious." When she didn't reply, he nodded and grinned slyly. "Yes, I'd want to hear me out without giving anything away, as well." McCarron sat back in his chair; his posture changed as well, from supplicant to master lecturing an acolyte.

"At the end of the Star League, no other world took more force to subdue from the Usurper than Terra. The same was true at the end of the Word of Blake Jihad a century ago." McCarron's diction was precise; he was relaying facts, not seeking input. "Today, it has been the seat of the Republic since that last battle. Whatever Stone has been doing behind that Wall, it has been centered there." When Danai made no interruption, he continued.

"We have no idea how strong the remaining RAF is. Our attacks have taken almost every world we targeted, for far fewer losses than we anticipated. This has made the Chancellor cautious. And rightly so. We expected the Republic to be stronger than it has shown itself to be."

Danai thought of the fight on Liberty. Stone's Fury was every bit as strong as any regiment she had ever seen. The advanced technology they'd used—the drones, the cruise missiles—put them on par with even the Clans. And the Clans...

"But beyond that, we have only speculation," Xavier finished. "We have no idea where the Republic Navy is; we expect in Terra. We have no idea how many other new regiments the Republic raised behind the Wall. You yourself fought a Fourteenth Principes, which presupposes a Fourteenth Hastati and Fourteenth Triarii. And how many more sets could there be? Eighteen? Twenty? A hundred?" He spread his hands. "We have no idea."

"To contemplate a blind attack on Terra is nonsense," he went on. "I am not saying never. But we *must* know more before we attack."

"You're saying the Chancellor declines to offer you that time?"

"I'm saying he has already ordered the marshaling of JumpShip assets for the attack."

Danai said nothing. But that was a premature step, she agreed.

"We need time," Xavier insisted. "Time to complete our liberation of the rest of the worlds on the road to Terra. Time to bring additional units and logistics forward into this area. And most of all, time to figure out what could be waiting for us in the Terra system."

"You said all this to the Chancellor." Danai did not frame it as a question. She already knew the answer. His delivery had been too precise, too practiced.

"I did."

"And he demurred?"

Xavier barked a laugh. "He ignored me."

"And now you wish me to present your words."

Xavier sat forward. "No. I wish you to present reality." He pointed toward the empty wall. "All of known space converges on this point, at Terra. We are here. The Combine is here. The Davions are a jump or two behind, but they are here. And at least two Clans—the Wolves and the Jade Falcons—are baying at the door. All of us wish to reclaim the birth world. The Clans wish it because their entire culture is built on the premise. The rest of us...sure, we would prefer the cachet of owning Terra. But it is the riches to be found there, among the corpses of the Star League and the Word of Blake and the Republic, that are worth claiming."

"Say we invade and defeat the Republic at Terra. Let us be conservative and say Devlin Stone can summon only ten regiments in his defense. That means we need thirty regiments to ensure victory." He spread his hands. "That is more than half our military. What will Davion do if we strip our borders that much? Will the agreement you brokered with Julian Davion hold when the whole of Victoria is laid bare? Will your sister's presence in Andurien be enough to keep Humphreys in line, in the face of *naked* worlds?"

"And if we succeed in that, how damaged will those regiments be? How will we keep every other realm, whose leaders are this very moment asking the same question, from attacking us in our weakness? If we're lucky enough to take Terra, how will we *hold* it?"

"As you say," Danai said to buy time to think. Xavier McCarron was accounted one of the finest strategists in the Confederation, but any first-form academy student could articulate the basics that Xavier had just stated. They were obvious. And they should be obvious to Daoshen. He had many flaws, but he'd had a solid grounding in military training. But they weren't obvious to him.

Unless Xavier McCarron was lying to her.

That was not a position she could easily discount. But she didn't think he was. Any scion of the Capellan court knew how to say things that weren't true as if they were. It had been the same in Crimson when she'd been a child, and her Aunt Erde had taught her to be a woman at court.

Danai had a nose for such things.

"I will want to do my own research," Danai told Xavier, "but I think you already know my first reaction is similar to yours. If I still feel that way after that research, I will speak to my brother."

Xavier smiled. "I can ask no more, your Grace." He glanced around, as if marshaling his thoughts, or perhaps ticking items off a mental to-do list. Then his smiled turned predatory.

"Now: tell me about these suicide drones on Liberty!"

Danai grinned back. "I need to call for one of my *sang-wei*s for that conversation, *Sang-shao*. She was actually there."

"Then call her. I've read the reports; now I want the details!"

CHANG-AN
LIAO
CAPELLAN CONFEDERATION
30 SEPTEMBER 3149

It had taken Danai two days to arrange a private face-to-face meeting with her father. It had taken most of a day to even get the Chang-an establishment to admit that he was present; finally, she was forced to lean on Xavier McCarron to break the deadlock.

She found him in a small, nondescript conference room, looking at a projected holomap of the Tikonov Commonality and the surrounding space. It reached as far into the former Lyran Commonwealth as Skye, the Wolf Empire to Nestor, and the Federated Suns as far as Barstow. The rest of the lights in the room were dimmed to make it more visible. The worlds recently taken from the Republic burned a gold-rimmed scarlet. Danai found Hall and Liberty with ease.

"You have done well, daughter," Daoshen allowed.

"I know," she said. Her voice was hard, despite her intentions. It was the *daughter* at the end of the sentence; it stripped her control away. It made her want to ask a thousand things, *demand* a thousand things. But she knew those things, every single one, were impossible. So she kept them inside her. She always had.

She always would.

"May I ask," she said, trying consciously to control her voice, "why I was recalled so suddenly from Liberty? There was much work left undone there. Even more than Hall, where it was also cut short."

"The battles were over," her *father* replied.

"The *battles* are not the only need the State has of me," Danai snapped. "The work of reintegrating those worlds was only just beginning. I could have contributed much there." She felt the anger rising, perennial anger at her father mingled with fresh, raw anger over Mina's death. And the crippling sense of helpless responsibility about Mina that she fought in her nightmares every night.

Daoshen made a brushing-off gesture with his hand. "There are others for those tasks."

"Then *why*," Danai demanded, "send me at all? Why send *Mina*, make me duchess, if not to set me on those tasks?" She rounded the table and came to stand beside her father. She doubted more than a half-dozen people had ever been this close to the Chancellor's person, but she didn't care. "I learned the lessons, *Father.* I learned them in pain and love and Mina

Liao, who deserved *none* of it, paid for those lessons with her life. Tell me *why*!"

She wanted to reach out, to touch him, to strike him, to shove him against the wall and shake answers out of him, but she held herself back. That would be too far, even for her.

"The loss of Lady Liao was a loss to the entire realm," Daoshen agreed. "But, if you really learned the lessons she had to teach, perhaps an acceptable cost to pay for the future."

Danai bit her tongue, on purpose, as her hands clenched into fists at her side. "Do not," she ground out, "*ever*. In my presence. Speak of Mina as an acceptable loss." She trembled so fast it felt as though she vibrated. Every fantasy of violence she had ever had about Daoshen flashed through her mind in a montage. Just then, she knew, *knew*, that she could kill him before the Death Commandos outside could get in and stop her. "In fact, never let her name in your mouth again."

Daoshen, to his credit, merely met her stare. He didn't react, not to the challenge and certainly not to the language and tone.

"Tell me of your lessons," he said softly. It was the only sign Danai had ever seen that there was actually a real human person inside that head.

"The people *believe*," she said, softly. "Many of us, people at our level, we understand the forces that shape Capellan culture. We understand how the directorship stays in power, the unseen machinations that keep them there. We understand how a concession given to the commonality can secure the loyalty of an entire world, because otherwise their disloyalty would cripple it. Almost every *Sheng* I've ever met, you can see it in their eyes. The tacit, unspoken agreement that there are understood things we just don't talk about that keep all of this working."

Daoshen nodded. "You illustrate the need for a directorship. We who can see such things must lead; the other path ends in anarchy."

"Yes, but the people, the servitors and the commonality, they believe it. It is real to them in a way that it is not to us." She stepped back and sat down at one of the tables. "That was the main lesson Mina tried to teach me, and I'm ashamed to admit that I didn't understand it while she was alive." She rubbed her thumb against her pant leg. "It's *real* to them, as real as food or dirt or their children."

"Yes," Daoshen said. Incredibly, he sat down next to her.

"Which is why I was so *angry* when you sent Zheng to kick me off Hall," Danai said. "I told myself it was because of Mina, but that wasn't it. I wanted to plant that seed of belief. I had worked so hard to try and plant it. Mina had worked so hard to plant it. I could see it starting to grow inside the capital city mayor—"

"Olatunde," Daoshen said. When Danai looked up, surprised, he shrugged faintly. "We get reports," was all he said.

"Yes. Olatunde. He expected to be imprisoned. Made a janitor, or something. That's how they see us, in the Republic and the Suns and everywhere else, you know. But I appealed to his duty to the people. I helped him see that his duty to the people transcended his duty to a flag. And it was working, until..."

In the silence that followed, Daoshen cleared his throat. "Reports from Zheng in Harney have the integration proceeding far ahead of the ministry's most optimistic projections," he said. "Clearly your efforts bore fruit. It is enough that we have given all the new *diems* permission, if they deem it prudent, to extend caste assignments as you did there."

"This is what you protect," Danai said. "This vision of the people. Because Mina took me to the Great Dam." She blinked back burning eyes. "It was an hour, maybe two. We talked to a couple of foremen, did the tour. She would ask me to think about those people all the time."

"Why?"

"She was trying to help me see this truth: that people live the reality they experience. I should have seen it already, without needing her to set the example. That the life a servitor wants to lead is just as valuable, to them, as the life of a director is to Lord Zheng. That a factory worker on Grand Base values her children just as much as the duke of Capella does his. And that our duty, as Liaos, is to protect all those lives."

Daoshen stood and looked at the map. "You have learned well," he allowed.

"I had the best teacher," she whispered. Then, taking her mindset firmly in mental hands, she adjusted it. She stood. "But now tell me why. Why couldn't I stay on Hall or Liberty and contribute to that work?"

"As we said, the battles were over," Daoshen said. "And you are, first of all, *janshi*."

"Battles are only one part of my duty," Danai argued. "You ensured that, when you named me duchess of Castrovia."

"There are more pressing battles in the future."

"On Terra, you mean?"

Daoshen turned to face her. "You have been talking to *Sang-shao* McCarron."

"He's right. Terra is suicide. You can't lead us there."

Daoshen's face hardened. Danai realized suddenly that the seeming cordiality they had just enjoyed was drying up. Daoshen may have pretended for a moment to be more father than Chancellor, and she may have even let him without knowing it, but the mask was slipping back into place.

"It is our right," he asserted.

"Terra has never been a Capellan world," Danai said.

"It is the birth world of humanity. We cannot profess to seek the unification of Greater Humanity if we do not possess that planet."

Danai laughed. "You weren't listening when I mentioned those unspoken things, were you?"

"Do not presume—"

Danai cut him off. "You have no idea what Stone has gathered on Terra. None. You don't even know if he still control it. For all we know, Malvina Hazen may have taken it by now."

She tried a different tack. "You said you've read the reports: where did Stone's Fury go when they left Liberty? Despite what CBS says, they were not beaten. They *chose* to leave. And we haven't seen them since!"

"Which is why we cannot waste any more time—"

"The liberation of Capellan people is not a waste of time," Danai insisted. "There are plenty of Republic worlds for the taking, still. Every one we retake removes a potential threat from our worlds here in Tikonov. That is work worth doing."

Daoshen's jaw worked, but he said nothing.

"You are Chancellor," Danai went on. "We will go where you lead. But you cannot blindly lead half or more of the Confederation's BattleMech regiments to Terra. You need more information. You need to know what Stone has done with his time behind the Fortress. You need to give the Mask time to learn what our other enemies intend."

"There is a test jump planned for the spring," Daoshen said.

"I know. That is a good first step."

"When it returns, we shall marshal our forces—"

"*If* it returns," Danai interrupted, "we will examine the new evidence and make our plans then."

Daoshen regarded her, then chuckled. "Fine," he allowed. "As you say, there is much work to be done. And when the test jump succeeds—"

"*If*—"

"—*when* the test jump succeeds, you will see our position more clearly."

Danai rolled her eyes. "We shall see," was all she said.

BATTLETECH GLOSSARY

AUTOCANNON

A rapid-fire, auto-loading weapon. Light autocannons range from 30 to 90 millimeter (mm), and heavy autocannons may be from 80 to 120mm or more. They fire high-speed streams of high-explosive, armor-piercing shells.

BATTLEMECH

BattleMechs are the most powerful war machines ever built. First developed by Terran scientists and engineers, these huge vehicles are faster, more mobile, better-armored and more heavily armed than any twentieth-century tank. Ten to twelve meters tall and equipped with particle projection cannons, lasers, rapid-fire autocannon and missiles, they pack enough firepower to flatten anything but another BattleMech. A small fusion reactor provides virtually unlimited power, and BattleMechs can be adapted to fight in environments ranging from sun-baked deserts to subzero arctic icefields.

DROPSHIPS

Because interstellar JumpShips must avoid entering the heart of a solar system, they must "dock" in space at a considerable distance from a system's inhabited worlds. DropShips were developed for interplanetary travel. As the name implies, a DropShip is attached to hardpoints on the JumpShip's drive core, later to be dropped from the parent vessel after in-system entry. Though incapable of FTL travel, DropShips are highly maneuverable, well-armed and sufficiently aerodynamic to take off from and land on a planetary surface. The journey from the jump point to the inhabited worlds of a system usually requires a normal-space journey of several days or weeks, depending on the type of star.

FLAMER

Flamethrowers are a small but time-honored anti-infantry weapon in vehicular arsenals. Whether fusion-based or fuel-based, flamers spew fire in a tight beam that "splashes" against a target, igniting almost anything it touches.

GAUSS RIFLE

This weapon uses magnetic coils to accelerate a solid nickel-ferrous slug about the size of a football at an enemy target, inflicting massive damage through sheer kinetic impact at long range and with little heat. However, the accelerator coils and the slug's supersonic speed mean that while the Gauss rifle is smokeless and lacks the flash of an autocannon, it has a much more potent report that can shatter glass.

INDUSTRIALMECH

Also known as WorkMechs or UtilityMechs, they are large, bipedal or quadrupedal machines used for industrial purposes (hence the name). They are similar in shape to BattleMechs, which they predate, and feature many of the same technologies, but are built for non-combat tasks such as construction, farming, and policing.

JUMPSHIPS

Interstellar travel is accomplished via JumpShips, first developed in the twenty-second century. These somewhat ungainly vessels consist of a long, thin drive core and a sail resembling an enormous parasol, which can extend up to a kilometer in width. The ship is named for its ability to "jump" instantaneously across vast distances of space. After making its jump, the ship cannot travel until it has recharged by gathering up more solar energy.

The JumpShip's enormous sail is constructed from a special metal that absorbs vast quantities of electromagnetic energy from the nearest star. When it has soaked up enough energy, the sail transfers it to the drive core, which converts it into a space-twisting field. An instant later, the ship arrives at the next jump point, a distance of up to thirty light-years. This field is known as hyperspace, and its discovery opened to mankind the gateway to the stars.

JumpShips never land on planets. Interplanetary travel is carried out by DropShips, vessels that are attached to the JumpShip until arrival at the jump point.

LASER

An acronym for "Light Amplification through Stimulated Emission of Radiation." When used as a weapon, the laser damages the target by concentrating extreme heat onto a small area. BattleMech lasers are designated as small, medium or large. Lasers are also available as shoulder-fired weapons operating from a portable backpack power unit. Certain range-finders and targeting equipment also employ low-level lasers.

LRM

Abbreviation for "Long-Range Missile," an indirect-fire missile with a high-explosive warhead.

MACHINE GUN

A small autocannon intended for anti-personnel assaults. Typically non-armor-penetrating, machine guns are often best used against infantry, as they can spray a large area with relatively inexpensive fire.

PARTICLE PROJECTION CANNON (PPC)

One of the most powerful and long-range energy weapons on the battlefield, a PPC fires a stream of charged particles that outwardly functions as a bright blue laser, but also throws off enough static discharge to resemble a bolt of manmade lightning. The kinetic and heat impact of a PPC is enough to cause the vaporization of armor and structure alike, and most PPCs have the power to kill a pilot in his machine through an armor-penetrating headshot.

SRM

The abbreviation for "Short-Range Missile," a direct-trajectory missile with high-explosive or armor-piercing explosive warheads. They have a range of less than one kilometer and are only reliably accurate at ranges of less than 300 meters. They are more powerful, however, than LRMs.

SUCCESSOR LORDS

After the fall of the first Star League, the remaining members of the High Council each asserted his or her right to become First Lord. Their star empires became known as the Successor States and the rulers as Successor Lords. The Clan Invasion temporarily interrupted centuries of warfare known as the Succession Wars, which first began in 2786.

BATTLETECH ERAS

The *BattleTech* universe is a living, vibrant entity that grows each year as more sourcebooks and fiction are published. A dynamic universe, its setting and characters evolve over time within a highly detailed continuity framework, bringing everything to life in a way a static game universe cannot match.

To help quickly and easily convey the timeline of the universe—and to allow a player to easily "plug in" a given novel or sourcebook—we've divided *BattleTech* into six major eras.

STAR LEAGUE
(Present–2780)

Ian Cameron, ruler of the Terran Hegemony, concludes decades of tireless effort with the creation of the Star League, a political and military alliance between all Great Houses and the Hegemony. Star League armed forces immediately launch the Reunification War, forcing the Periphery realms to join. For the next two centuries, humanity experiences a golden age across the thousand light-years of human-occupied space known as the Inner Sphere. It also sees the creation of the most powerful military in human history.

(This era also covers the centuries before the founding of the Star League in 2571, most notably the Age of War.)

SUCCESSION WARS
(2781–3049)

Every last member of First Lord Richard Cameron's family is killed during a coup launched by Stefan Amaris. Following the thirteen-year war to unseat him, the rulers of each of the five Great Houses disband the Star League. General Aleksandr Kerensky departs with eighty percent of the Star League Defense Force beyond known space and the Inner Sphere collapses into centuries of warfare known as the Succession Wars that will eventually result in a massive loss of technology across most worlds.

CLAN INVASION
(3050–3061)

A mysterious invading force strikes the coreward region of the Inner Sphere. The invaders, called the Clans, are descendants of Kerensky's SLDF troops, forged into a society dedicated to becoming the greatest fighting force in history. With vastly superior technology and warriors, the Clans conquer world after world. Eventually this outside threat will forge a new Star League, something hundreds of years of warfare failed to accomplish. In addition, the Clans will act as a catalyst for a technological renaissance.

CIVIL WAR
(3062–3067)

The Clan threat is eventually lessened with the complete destruction of a Clan. With that massive external threat apparently neutralized, internal conflicts explode around the Inner Sphere. House Liao conquers its former Commonality, the St. Ives Compact; a rebellion of military units belonging to House Kurita sparks a war with their powerful border enemy, Clan Ghost Bear; the fabulously powerful Federated Commonwealth of House Steiner and House Davion collapses into five long years of bitter civil war.

JIHAD
(3067–3080)

Following the Federated Commonwealth Civil War, the leaders of the Great Houses meet and disband the new Star League, declaring it a sham. The pseudo-religious Word of Blake—a splinter group of ComStar, the protectors and controllers of interstellar communication—launch the Jihad: an interstellar war that pits every faction against each other and even against themselves, as weapons of mass destruction are used for the first time in centuries while new and frightening technologies are also unleashed.

DARK AGE
(3081-3150)

Under the guidance of Devlin Stone, the Republic of the Sphere is born at the heart of the Inner Sphere following the Jihad. One of the more extensive periods of peace begins to break out as the 32nd century dawns. The factions, to one degree or another, embrace disarmament, and the massive armies of the Succession Wars begin to fade. However, in 3132 eighty percent of interstellar communications collapses, throwing the universe into chaos. Wars erupt almost immediately, and the factions begin rebuilding their armies.

ILCLAN
(3151-present)

The once-invulnerable Republic of the Sphere lies in ruins, torn apart by the Great Houses and the Clans as they wage war against each other on a scale not seen in nearly a century. Mercenaries flourish once more, selling their might to the highest bidder. As Fortress Republic collapses, the Clans race toward Terra to claim their long-denied birthright and create a supreme authority that will fulfill the dream of Aleksandr Kerensky and rule the Inner Sphere by any means necessary: The ilClan.

LOOKING FOR MORE HARD HITTING BATTLETECH FICTION?

WE'LL GET YOU RIGHT BACK INTO THE BATTLE!

Catalyst Game Labs brings you the very best in *BattleTech* fiction, available at most ebook retailers, including Amazon, Apple Books, Kobo, Barnes & Noble, and more!

NOVELS

1. *Decision at Thunder Rift* by William H. Keith Jr.
2. *Mercenary's Star* by William H. Keith Jr.
3. *The Price of Glory* by William H. Keith, Jr.
4. *Warrior: En Garde* by Michael A. Stackpole
5. *Warrior: Riposte* by Michael A. Stackpole
6. *Warrior: Coupé* by Michael A. Stackpole
7. Wolves on the Border by Robert N. Charrette
8. *Heir to the Dragon* by Robert N. Charrette
9. *Lethal Heritage* (The Blood of Kerensky, Volume 1) by Michael A. Stackpole
10. *Blood Legacy* (The Blood of Kerensky, Volume 2) by Michael A. Stackpole
11. *Lost Destiny* (The Blood of Kerensky, Volume 3) by Michael A. Stackpole
12. *Way of the Clans* (Legend of the Jade Phoenix, Volume 1) by Robert Thurston
13. *Bloodname* (Legend of the Jade Phoenix, Volume 2) by Robert Thurston
14. *Falcon Guard* (Legend of the Jade Phoenix, Volume 3) by Robert Thurston
15. *Wolf Pack* by Robert N. Charrette
16. *Main Event* by James D. Long
17. *Natural Selection* by Michael A. Stackpole
18. *Assumption of Risk* by Michael A. Stackpole
19. *Blood of Heroes* by Andrew Keith
20. *Close Quarters* by Victor Milán
21. *Far Country* by Peter L. Rice
22. *D.R.T.* by James D. Long
23. *Tactics of Duty* by William H. Keith
24. *Bred for War* by Michael A. Stackpole
25. *I Am Jade Falcon* by Robert Thurston
26. *Highlander Gambit* by Blaine Lee Pardoe
27. *Hearts of Chaos* by Victor Milán
28. *Operation Excalibur* by William H. Keith
29. *Malicious Intent* by Michael A. Stackpole
30. *Black Dragon* by Victor Milán
31. *Impetus of War* by Blaine Lee Pardoe
32. *Double-Blind* by Loren L. Coleman
33. *Binding Force* by Loren L. Coleman
34. *Exodus Road* (Twilight of the Clans, Volume 1) by Blaine Lee Pardoe
35. *Grave Covenant* ((Twilight of the Clans, Volume 2) by Michael A. Stackpole
36. *The Hunters* (Twilight of the Clans, Volume 3) by Thomas S. Gressman
37. *Freebirth* (Twilight of the Clans, Volume 4) by Robert Thurston

38. *Sword and Fire* (Twilight of the Clans, Volume 5) by Thomas S. Gressman
39. *Shadows of War* (Twilight of the Clans, Volume 6) by Thomas S. Gressman
40. *Prince of Havoc* (Twilight of the Clans, Volume 7) by Michael A. Stackpole
41. *Falcon Rising* (Twilight of the Clans, Volume 8) by Robert Thurston
42. *Threads of Ambition* (The Capellan Solution, Book 1) by Loren L. Coleman
43. *The Killing Fields* (The Capellan Solution, Book 2) by Loren L. Coleman
44. *Dagger Point* by Thomas S. Gressman
45. *Ghost of Winter* by Stephen Kenson
46. *Roar of Honor* by Blaine Lee Pardoe
47. *By Blood Betrayed* by Blaine Lee Pardoe and Mel Odom
48. *Illusions of Victory* by Loren L. Coleman
49. *Flashpoint* by Loren L. Coleman
50. *Measure of a Hero* by Blaine Lee Pardoe
51. *Path of Glory* by Randall N. Bills
52. *Test of Vengeance* by Bryan Nystul
53. *Patriots and Tyrants* by Loren L. Coleman
54. *Call of Duty* by Blaine Lee Pardoe
55. *Initiation to War* by Robert N. Charrette
56. *The Dying Time* by Thomas S. Gressman
57. *Storms of Fate* by Loren L. Coleman
58. *Imminent Crisis* by Randall N. Bills
59. *Operation Audacity* by Blaine Lee Pardoe
60. *Endgame* by Loren L. Coleman
61. *A Bonfire of Worlds* by Steven Mohan, Jr.
62. *Ghost War* by Michael A. Stackpole
63. *A Call to Arms* by Loren L. Coleman
64. *The Ruins of Power* by Robert E. Vardeman
65. *A Silence in the Heavens* by Martin Delrio
66. *A Bonfire of Worlds* by Steven Mohan, Jr.
67. *The Ruins of Power* by Robert E. Vardeman
68. *Isle of the Blessed* by Steven Mohan, Jr.
69. *Embers of War* by Jason Schmetzer
70. *Betrayal of Ideals* by Blaine Lee Pardoe
71. *Forever Faithful* by Blaine Lee Pardoe
72. *Kell Hounds Ascendant* by Michael A. Stackpole
73. *Redemption Rift* by Jason Schmetzer
74. *Grey Watch Protocol* (*The Highlander Covenant, Book One*) by Michael J. Ciaravella
75. *Honor's Gauntlet* by Bryan Young
76. *Icons of War* by Craig A. Reed, Jr.
77. *Children of Kerensky* by Blaine Lee Pardoe
78. *Hour of the Wolf* by Blaine Lee Pardoe
79. *Fall From Glory* (*Founding of the Clans, Book One*) by Randall N. Bills
80. *Paid in Blood* (*The Highlander Covenant, Book Two*) by Michael J. Ciaravella

YOUNG ADULT NOVELS

1. *The Nellus Academy Incident* by Jennifer Brozek
2. *Iron Dawn* (*Rogue Academy, Book 1*) by Jennifer Brozek
3. *Ghost Hour* (*Rogue Academy, Book 2*) by Jennifer Brozek

OMNIBUSES

1. *The Gray Death Legion Trilogy* by William H. Keith, Jr.

NOVELLAS/SHORT STORIES

1. *Lion's Roar* by Steven Mohan, Jr.
2. *Sniper* by Jason Schmetzer
3. *Eclipse* by Jason Schmetzer
4. *Hector* by Jason Schmetzer
5. *The Frost Advances (Operation Ice Storm, Part 1)* by Jason Schmetzer
6. *The Winds of Spring (Operation Ice Storm, Part 2)* by Jason Schmetzer
7. *Instrument of Destruction (Ghost Bear's Lament, Part 1)* by Steven Mohan, Jr.
8. *The Fading Call of Glory (Ghost Bear's Lament, Part 2)* by Steven Mohan, Jr.
9. *Vengeance* by Jason Schmetzer
10. *A Splinter of Hope* by Philip A. Lee
11. *The Anvil* by Blaine Lee Pardoe
12. *A Splinter of Hope/The Anvil* (omnibus)
13. *Not the Way the Smart Money Bets (Kell Hounds Ascendant #1)* by Michael A. Stackpole
14. *A Tiny Spot of Rebellion (Kell Hounds Ascendant #2)* by Michael A. Stackpole
15. *A Clever Bit of Fiction (Kell Hounds Ascendant #3)* by Michael A. Stackpole
16. *Break-Away (Proliferation Cycle #1)* by Ilsa J. Bick
17. *Prometheus Unbound (Proliferation Cycle #2)* by Herbert A. Beas II
18. *Nothing Ventured (Proliferation Cycle #3)* by Christoffer Trossen
19. *Fall Down Seven Times, Get Up Eight (Proliferation Cycle #4)* by Randall N. Bills
20. *A Dish Served Cold (Proliferation Cycle #5)* by Chris Hartford and Jason M. Hardy
21. *The Spider Dances (Proliferation Cycle #6)* by Jason Schmetzer
22. *Shell Games* by Jason Schmetzer
23. *Divided We Fall* by Blaine Lee Pardoe
24. *The Hunt for Jardine (Forgotten Worlds, Part One)* by Herbert A. Beas II
25. *Rock of the Republic* by Blaine Lee Pardoe
26. *Finding Jardine (Forgotten Worlds, Part Two)* by Herbert A. Beas II

ANTHOLOGIES

1. *The Corps (BattleCorps Anthology, Volume 1)* edited by Loren. L. Coleman
2. *First Strike (BattleCorps Anthology, Volume 2)* edited by Loren L. Coleman
3. *Weapons Free (BattleCorps Anthology, Volume 3)* edited by Jason Schmetzer
4. *Onslaught: Tales from the Clan Invasion* edited by Jason Schmetzer
5. *Edge of the Storm* by Jason Schmetzer
6. *Fire for Effect (BattleCorps Anthology, Volume 4)* edited by Jason Schmetzer
7. *Chaos Born (Chaos Irregulars, Book 1)* by Kevin Killiany
8. *Chaos Formed (Chaos Irregulars, Book 2)* by Kevin Killiany
9. *Counterattack (BattleCorps Anthology, Volume 5)* edited by Jason Schmetzer
10. *Front Lines (BattleCorps Anthology Volume 6)* edited by Jason Schmetzer and Philip A. Lee
11. *Legacy* edited by John Helfers and Philip A. Lee
12. *Kill Zone (BattleCorps Anthology Volume 7)* edited by Philip A. Lee
13. *Gray Markets (A BattleCorps Anthology)*, edited by Jason Schmetzer and Philip A. Lee
14. *Slack Tide (A BattleCorps Anthology)*, edited by Jason Schmetzer and Philip A. Lee
15. *The Battle of Tukayyid* edited by John Helfers
16. *The Mercenary Life* by Randall N. Bills
17. *The Proliferation Cycle*, edited by John Helfers and Philip A. Lee

MAGAZINES

1. *Shrapnel Issue #1–4*

Made in the USA
Monee, IL
29 May 2021

69748937R00164